A TREASURE
REBORN

Dedication

To my Lord and Savior, who taught me that sometimes to travel through the wilderness is the only way to know myself and find Him, I dedicate this book.

To many friends I owe thanks—especially to Theo, Therese, Jill, Paige, Ronie, and Mom for being there for me in a pinch and sticking it out with me till the end, as my deadline loomed ever closer. You have my deepest gratitude.

Note from author: Red Cloud's war against the Powder River strongholds, mentioned in chapter 7, actually ended months earlier in November 1868.

SILVER MOUNTAINS

PAMELA GRIFFIN

BARBOUR
PUBLISHING

Cover design: Kirk DouPonce, DogEared Design

Published by Barbour Publishing, Inc., P.O. Box 719, Uhrichsville, Ohio 44683, www.barbourbooks.com

Our mission is to publish and distribute inspirational products offering exceptional value and biblical encouragement to the masses.

 Member of the
Evangelical Christian
Publishers Association

Printed in the United States of America.

Dear Readers,

Treasures come in all shapes, sizes, and forms. Scripture says, "For where your treasure is, there your heart will be also." Some can be seen with the naked eye, like the precious silver the miners desperately sought during the time period these stories take place. Others cannot be seen at all, but only felt. Some treasures can be enjoyed only while living upon this earth. Others will follow us into the heavenly kingdom thereafter.

In these three tales you are about to experience, of an estranged family forced to come together despite a mysterious legacy, all of the Burke siblings' hearts have grown hard and disillusioned by life's grief and troubles. Little do they know that the key to happiness and achieving their dreams will come in the form of some of the most unexpected and bizarre encounters they will ever have.

This is the ongoing story, told through a series of novels, of the reconciliation of a hurting family who is bitter beyond comprehension and appears beyond help. Only through God's loving mercy and divine intervention can the crooked be made straight, and this is my humble attempt to illustrate that. It is my heartfelt wish that the adventurous stories of Derek, Linda, Clay, and their loved ones inspire you and convey the importance of the true treasures to be sought. . .and found. The treasures of lasting reward.

Thank you to the many who have encouraged and supported me through the years. You are all part of God's treasure to me.

Blessings,
Pamela Griffin

Prologue

Silverton, Nevada, 1869

Y ou're insane." Derek glared at his brother. His words seethed with rage, though he kept his voice low so no one could overhear. "Either that or you're as ungrateful a cur as I've ever come across. It's bad enough Pa did this to us, but you're telling me I don't deserve one nugget of his legacy? That's downright cruel after all I've done for you, Clay. Or is that just how your mind works these days?"

"How would you know how my mind works these days or any days? You don't know anything about me. You were never around, not since you turned six-teen and took off running. And you weren't there for Ma either. She got worse, and you didn't come home. Even when she sent a letter asking for you."

Derek grimaced at the painful recollection of arriving home four years earlier to his ma's grave. "I told you then that her letter didn't find its way to me till it was too late. A lot like this letter Pa's go-between wrote for him." He crushed the envelope in one hand and paced to the other side of the dusty room, which tried to pass for a hotel parlor but was little more than the size of a horse's stall with a privacy curtain. "I didn't get that letter till after they put him in the ground, either. You can't blame me for what's happened to our family!"

"You're just like him," Clay insisted. "Full of excuses. Always running off. Never around when you're needed. Where you been for the past four years, Derek? Out gallivanting on another adventure through the West, with nary a care to trouble you?"

Clay's childish taunt threatened to make Derek's anger spill over, but he kept a tight lid on his emotions. "Where I've been ain't none of your business, little brother. I made sure you were well taken care of, or did you forget?" Derek stepped closer until he was almost nose to nose with Clay. "It's high time you grew up. You need to stop your whinin' about the past and start behavin' like a man."

Red rushed to Clay's lean face, which still looked too smooth to shave. He took a wild swing at Derek. Before his fist could make contact with Derek's jaw, Derek caught his brother's arm, spun him around, and twisted Clay's fist to his shoulder blades to thwart further attacks. Clay cursed at Derek to let him go, attempting to squirm out of his hold. Derek responded by shoving his brother's slighter form up against the wall, pressing Clay's cheek to the planks, and imprisoning him there with his body.

"Don't ever try that again," he warned.

Clay swore again. "You're a scoundrel, Derek! A no-good snake—just like Pa. You don't deserve any part of that silver mine!"

"Will you just shut up?" Derek rasped the warning low near Clay's ear, his attention darting to the entryway covered by a threadbare blanket to check for unwanted company. "You want the whole of Nevada to hear about Pa's legacy? We're in a mining town, if you'll recall. And there's not one man outside this room who wouldn't like to get his hands on those maps."

Clay muttered something foul under his breath, but to Derek's relief, he calmed somewhat. A soft clearing of the throat came from the opposite end of the room.

Derek's jaw tensed. He'd forgotten about *her*.

"Maybe if we do as our pa suggested and work together?" the young upstart had the gall to propose.

Derek shot a scathing glance toward the audacious redhead, enough of a warning to keep her quiet. Her cheeks drained of color, and she dropped her focus to her gloves clamped around the drawstrings of her reticule, out of which she'd earlier withdrawn her portion of the treasure map. Everything about the young woman cried indecent, even with the gloves she wore in what he assumed was an attempt to satisfy respectability. Her green silk dress looked like something a lady of the evening might wear and was far out of place in this small mining town, unless she was working in the saloon. After his initial encounter with this supposed sibling he never knew existed and the cantankerous insults he'd hurled her way, Derek had thought Linda would have received the message that she was unwanted and unwelcome, and would have remained mute.

Half sister, my foot!

Derek released Clay with a shove and stomped toward the door.

"Where are you going?" Clay called after him.

"To get to the bottom of this, once and for all."

In less time than it took to saddle his horse, Derek made it to the other end of the small town of Silverton. Passersby on the rutted road took one look at his face and stepped out of his path. For the second time that day, he strode through the door of the claims office.

The squat, elderly clerk behind the desk gave a startled jolt in his chair, his mouth agape when he saw Derek. In three strides, Derek crossed the floor and stood mere inches from the man who withheld the key to his fortune—and only a plank of wood separated them.

Derek noted they were alone and smiled, his jaw tight.

"You again." The clerk made a clear effort to act composed. "I—I told you.

I can't answer your questions if I don't know the answers."

"Right. So instead of telling me what you don't know, just tell me what you do know. How about that?" Derek slammed the well-creased envelope onto the desk, causing the stubborn man to give another jump. Good. He meant business, and the sooner this go-between his pa had bought realized that, the sooner he could get out of this fool excuse for a town and claim what was rightfully his.

He glared down at the missive, its pithy explanation no more satisfying than the scrap from a treasure map that arrived with it. "A silver mine your father discovered not long before he took sick and died," the note said. "To be split among you and your two siblings, each of whom has received a portion of the same map, per your father's instructions."

Two siblings.

Unthinkable. He'd grown up with only Clay and his ma and had no idea that his philandering pa had married a second wife or had a girl by her. That is, if the marriage proved lawful, and with his no-good excuse for a father, one could never tell.

"Listen," he told the white-whiskered man. "You sent us these notes and had us meet up here, so you might as well tell me exactly where our pa filed his claim. What's the point of sending a map in three pieces? We're all in Silverton now. Just tell me what we need to know so we can get what's comin' to us."

"I'm sorry to disappoint you, young fella, but as I said before, even if I did know all the facts, I wouldn't violate your father's wishes. Your father was adamant about the order in which matters were to be executed. He explained his requests after he took sick with the cholera, and I don't intend to dishonor the dead. Even if I did claim to know the entirety of the workings that belonged to the mind of Mr. Burke, I couldn't reveal them to you."

Derek narrowed his eyes, and the man gave an anxious chuckle.

"Not meaning to speak ill of the dearly departed, you understand, but he was an odd one, your father. Yet for all his eccentric ways, he was kind; bought me this watch when I expressed my need for one." He fingered the gold disk suspended from a chain.

No doubt a bribe to buy his silence. Such words of goodwill didn't describe his pa, didn't even come close, and not for the first time, Derek wondered if the situation was an ill-brewed sham. As the letter requested, he and his brother had arrived in this isolated town, within days of each other, to learn that their father's body had been laid in a pine box and dropped in the ground weeks before. Or so he'd been told. He had only this man's word that his pa was dead. That, a rough marker noting the gravesite, and three odd letters, each with a third of one map, were all that remained of Michael Aloysius Burke.

"You must know something more you can tell us," Derek insisted.

"If you and your siblings wish to locate the mine, your best recourse is to do what your pa wanted and use the pieces from the treasure map to work together as he specified in the letters. I refuse to tell you anything else. Though as I said before, even I don't know the entirety of the situation. So you can threaten me all you like, but it won't do you any good."

Derek blew out a disgruntled breath, wanting nothing more than to grab the fancy-talking man by the edge of his starched collar and pull his face nearer for a more forceful inquiry. Weariness and hunger made clear thinking difficult. No matter how he searched for a response that would benefit him, a solution refused to present itself. He'd traveled on horseback from the Utah Territory for the better part of a week, ever since a lone rider had hunted him down and given him the letter, and he'd arrived in Silverton only hours before.

The clerk knew more than he was telling; Derek didn't doubt it. But applying force was useless. He'd met up with men less stubborn and sensed this messenger of his father's would never budge. Nor had he ever struck a man, except in defense, and he didn't aim to start now.

With a parting scowl, Derek reclaimed the missive. He stormed from the office, almost pulling the door off its hinges before slamming it behind him, hard enough to shake the thin walls.

Still the anger roiled inside.

As the eldest, that mine should have been his! Derek had spent most of the past decade sacrificing to provide for his family, unlike his pa. And Clay had a lot of nerve arguing that Derek didn't deserve one bit of the profits.

He took off down the road, past countless miners' tents, and again approached the small hotel where the meeting between himself and his estranged brother had been prearranged—and the so-called half sister who likewise had shown up on the hotel doorstep like a greedy kitten in search of a saucer of warm cream. In this case, the cream proved to be an alleged fortune in silver, and he would be hanged before he would let that little minx get her hands on one nugget. Or let his brother lay sole claim to the treasure, for that matter, which Derek supposed Clay had in mind.

He narrowed his eyes as he stood across the street from the ramshackle hotel—no more than canvas walls and roof and a false front of planks hurriedly hammered together, with filthy hides on which to sleep in common rooms shared with other men. Through the door left ajar, he glimpsed a flash of dark red hair and recognized it as belonging to the sly vixen who aimed to steal his inheritance. On the whole, he held women in high regard, but that one was no better than his brother in terms of avarice.

Derek would find the mine without Clay or Linda. And he knew just how to do it.

Chapter 1

Long before the sun could crown the white-capped mountains beyond Silverton, Derek crept through the room of snoring men with the ease of a wildcat on the prowl. Clay hadn't changed in mannerisms. He still stashed valuables where he slept—in this case beneath the hide he lay on. With stealth, Derek claimed what should have been his.

A twinge of something raw made his heart ache when he glimpsed Clay's face. In the thread of moonlight seeping into the room from beyond closed shutters, his features seemed as smooth and carefree as when he'd been a boy, with no permanent lines of anger or bitterness marring the skin between his brows. Derek pulled himself together and hardened his heart to old memories, shedding all remorse and regrets.

He felt awkward entering the area that concealed the woman who claimed to be his half sister. Hesitant, he pulled back the flap of muslin weighted by stones that sectioned off her room and darted a guilty glance at the sole cot. Of course, she would need a bed and room to herself, being a woman and all. White women in these parts were scarce, but of the few Derek noticed in town, little could be said for their reputations. Linda hadn't flirted with any of the men who'd ogled her from a distance, yet he doubted that greed and deceit were her only shortcomings.

She lay wrapped entirely in a blanket, not a trace of her brazen hair apparent, a lamp turned down low beside her. Not surprised to see her wasteful use of kerosene, Derek still felt grateful for the dim light to aid him in quietly finding his way around the cramped room. So many fussy bows and ruffles covered her discarded clothing, tossed hither and yon without a care. Loops and bows that could catch his boots and trip him. He hoped she was a sound sleeper.

Derek located her drawstring purse next to her hat on the ground. Within seconds, he located the folded paper and slipped from the room, swamped with relief to leave it, and her, forever behind him.

"You're nothin' but a low-down, lyin' cheat!"

At the angry shout, Derek flinched, sure he'd been caught, and swung around to look.

A few buildings down from the hotel, three rough men stood in the street, arguing outside one of many saloons—still lit up and likely never slumbering. One

11

man swung at another, and Derek took advantage of the distraction to saddle his horse. While the drunks scuffled in the street and still others poured out of the saloon, both joining in the brawl and trying to break it up, Derek rode out of town in the opposite direction. All three portions of the map lay tucked inside his saddlebag, and an unrestrained smile of conquest stretched across his face.

"Sorry, little brother. But this is how it has to be."

Day soon broke over the vast, wild land through which Derek rode. An arid land of rough scrub with its patchwork of remote mountain ranges, canyons, and valleys, it challenged a man's fight for survival. He tried to force down any smattering of guilt for what he'd done, but alone, with no one around for miles to talk to, his thoughts made poor companions. His conscience kept niggling at him as fierce as bedbugs in a straw tick.

His father never abided by any law, man-made or otherwise, but in all the courts in the eastern states, the eldest son usually inherited. He doubted things worked any different here in the West. Maybe his pa hadn't known how the court system operated when he wrote his bizarre excuse for a will; small wonder, rogue that he'd been. Yet through a peculiar twist of fate, Derek had met a talkative attorney in a town he'd ridden through after receiving the letter, and the man confirmed his belief.

Derek tried to ease his discomfort and assured himself that, in a sense, he upheld the law by setting things right. Once he claimed his inheritance, he could be generous—more generous than Clay. Four years earlier when Derek had arrived home and found his ma's grave, he realized after one day with his brother that too much time had passed to mend things between them. So he'd arranged for Clay's care and taken off once again, traveling from town to town and finding work where he could.

Had Derek remained in Silverton, he had no doubt his brother would have done the same: taken the maps in secret and gone off to locate the mine. Derek had just gotten the jump on him. Still, he would see to it that Clay never wanted for anything, not if Derek could help it. Clay was now a young man of twenty, four years his junior, but once Derek became wealthy, he saw no reason to quit his role as provider, despite Clay's resentment. After all, he was his only living kin. And he would supply Linda with enough money to return to wherever she came from, too. He could be generous. . . .

The sun reflected off a thread of silver gleaming in the distance, what looked like fresh water. Grateful to find a source of such a coveted requirement in a land that didn't provide much, Derek guided his horse toward a small enclosed valley ringed in by low hills of grass, rock, and scrub. A shanty came into view from behind a fringe of sparse trees at the bottom of a rise. Before he could ride past, a gunshot rang out, and a bullet whizzed past his head.

"What the. . . ?"

"Git, you mangy hooligans!" a woman shouted from near the building. He couldn't see anyone in the vicinity. Another shot pursued her command, this time not aimed at him.

From behind a ramshackle structure, hoofbeats pummeled the earth. Derek swung his horse around in an arc to see a pair of riders gallop away. One of the men aimed over his shoulder and shot at the shanty. Not willing to get caught in the crossfire—with no knowledge of who were the outlaws and who were the innocents—Derek scanned the area for cover while making a grab for his gun.

Something sharp struck his hand; he dropped his weapon as he pulled it from his holster. "Ow!" He shook the offended hand, but before he could tell where the missile had originated from, another flew at him fast and hard, striking him in the arm. He slapped his other hand to his stinging shoulder and glanced at the ground. Rocks. Someone hurled small rocks his way. "Of all the crazy. . .who are you? Come out and show yourself!"

Two more stones flew from another direction, landing far off their mark. Derek tried to control his horse; by the way her eyes rolled, he knew she was getting spooked. But he wasn't about to leave his gun behind. At least the bullets from the lone shooter stopped flying, even if the stones kept coming.

Keeping a firm hold on the reins, he slid off his saddle and bent over, stretching his hand out to grab his weapon. Another rock, larger than before, hit him smack in the seat of his pants. He shouted an oath, falling over onto his hands and knees. Smaller stones peppered his back and sides. He held up his hands as if under arrest. "Enough already! I surrender."

The reins slid through his hands while his horse took off as if a lightning bolt had just struck the dirt nearby. Great.

"You just lost me my horse," he yelled.

"Well, maybe if you'd-a just stayed off my land, you'd still have your beast," a woman countered quietly, a hint of Scottish brogue coating her words. She stepped onto the patch of dirt in front of him and kicked his gun well out of reach with the side of her moccasin-clad foot.

He squinted into the glaring sun to size up his attacker. A young woman with thick, dark hair, unbound and blowing about her waist, grimly surveyed him, a gun aimed at his head.

"Well, maybe if you'd-a had a sign saying to keep away, I'd-a done it," he replied calmly, keeping his hands in the air. He didn't trust a woman with a loaded shotgun, especially one as unpredictable as he sensed her to be.

"Everyone with any sense knows to stay off Crawder land, except for low-down thieves and other despicable varmints. Of course, they've got no sense anyhow." She lifted her chin in a lofty manner. "Have you any sense, Mister?"

"After the pounding I got from them rocks, I'd be surprised if I did."

He thought her mouth twitched as if she might smile, but with the sun behind her, it was difficult to tell. She tilted her head as she studied him. "If you're not aimin' to steal my horses or other goods, then exactly what is your business here?"

"Just riding through." The shotgun remained fixed on him, and he added, "I don't mean you any harm. I saw that stream over yonder from about half a mile back and thought I'd rest a spell. I've been riding all day."

For taut seconds neither of them moved; finally, she lowered her weapon. He heard a scuffle of footsteps over dirt and rocks behind him and looked over his shoulder.

Two small girls with dark braids left their hiding places, one from behind a barrel, and the other from the cover of a midsize scraggly bush. Both approached with caution. A slingshot dangled from the hand of the elder, who looked no more than ten, while the younger by at least five years carried a pail full of small rocks. They regarded him, the expressions on their dirty faces wary as if he were an unfamiliar beast of the wild they'd trapped by mistake.

"Your army, I take it?" He looked at the woman. "You trained them well." With the bearer of the shotgun no longer posing a threat, Derek slowly rose to his feet.

"Sometimes a woman alone needs her own fort."

He studied his captor, whose petite figure barely reached his shoulder. Her eyes, on the other hand, were huge. Thickly lashed, they tilted upward slightly at the outside corners and held hints of gold in the brown. Flames of deep red shimmered in her nearly black hair. Her cheekbones were high, her small nose slightly uptilted. The rest of her features, a shade darker than fair, could be called delicate, much like her form. Except for her pert little chin, which proudly jutted out a mile.

She eyed him just as intently, as if still not sure what to make of him, and then turned to the girls. "Olivia, take Christa to the stream to wash up. While you're there, fetch more water for our guest. Our supply is getting low."

"Yes, Mama." The two girls took off running.

"Guest?" Derek cocked an eyebrow. "You always treat company to an onslaught of bullets and rocks?"

She lifted her chin; he hadn't thought she could raise it any higher. "I can be as cordial to a stranger as any hostess, as long as he doesn't cause me or my girls any grief."

He didn't miss her thinly veiled warning. "So, mind telling me what I rode into the middle of? Just what was that all about?"

"Aye, I suppose I owe you the benefit of an explanation." She sighed, her defenses melting as he watched. "Josiah Cribbs and his sons have been giving me grief for some time—miners trying to run me off my land and steal from my supplies at every opportunity. Some weeks ago, they set fire to my barn in the dead of night, but the girls and I were able to put out the flames and save most of it. I suspect they killed my only milk cow three months ago, though I've no proof. One morning, she was right as a trivet; the next cold and stiff, lying on the ground."

"Is there a town nearby?"

"Only Silverton."

He nodded, not surprised. "Has your husband contacted the sheriff?" He hadn't stayed in Silverton long enough to know if the town had anyone to keep the peace but felt he should ask.

"There's no law in these parts. None whatsoever. My husband's been dead since last spring, a year now, and I've kept things running on the place."

"By yourself?" He lifted his brows in doubtful surprise, eyeing her slight form and hands, not much bigger than a child's.

"I'm a lot hardier than I look. And I have my two girls to help me, Mr. . . ?"

Recalling the shotgun to his head and the ambush of stones that struck his body, he couldn't argue her point. With a slight grin, he held out his hand. "The name's Derek. Derek Burke."

She hesitated, no doubt noticing the bruise on his wrist from her daughter's well-aimed missile, before she slipped her dainty hand into his large one and gave it a brisk shake. "Penny Crawder. Why don't you come in out of this hot sun and rest a spell? I imagine you're famished. I have badger stew, still warm on the fire from our noon meal."

He collected his gun from the ground and slipped it inside his holster. "Being as how I lack a horse at this time, I'd be obliged to accept your offer, ma'am."

Her face flushed like a schoolgirl's. "Aye, well, all right then. Come along, Mr. Burke, and I'll dish you up a bowl of that stew."

He followed her into the shanty, hoping he wasn't walking headlong into an even worse predicament.

⁓

Penny put her idle hands to quick use, glad she had plenty left from their meal two hours before. The entire time she sliced the mesquite bread she'd made that morning and brought hunks of it on a plate to the table, she felt the stranger's eyes watching from where he sat.

A clear, strong blue, they reminded her of her da's eyes, though Derek's had the unnerving ability to appear gentle and piercing at the same time. Brown hair, the color of rich, dark syrup, brushed his neck, just touching the tops of his shoulders, and held a bit of curl. His bottom lip was much fuller than his top one, and she noticed how he often pursed them, as though amused at some secret thing. His lean jaw and the skin above his mouth were dark with a day's worth of whiskers. Taller than both her da and her husband, Oliver, had been, Derek filled the chair, seeming to overpower it, his form both trim and strong.

She imagined her visitor had turned many a young woman's head. He appeared in his midtwenties but seemed much more mature, considering the manner in which he'd dealt with their earlier attack. Penny, though no inexperienced schoolgirl at twenty-seven, found his enigmatic presence distracting. He seemed to fill not only the chair but the room as well. Since Derek was also the first man to sup at her table since her husband died, she told herself that must be why she felt so self-conscious. Perhaps it had been a mistake to invite him inside, but she couldn't help feel some remorse for his predicament, though she'd only been protecting her own. Still, while he no longer posed an immediate threat, she kept her shotgun propped within arm's reach against her side of the table. Just in case.

Not sure what to do with her hands, which suddenly seemed awkward and uncertain, she moved to her black potbellied stove, her last gift from Oliver. She grabbed the coffeepot handle with a dishtowel to refill their cups.

"Please, ma'am," Derek said before she could pour. A tiny shiver ran along her spine at the calm, husky timbre of his voice. "Sit down. I have more than enough to satisfy. If I drink any more of that coffee, good as it is, I'll be awake all night."

She poured herself a tad more, set the coffeepot down with care, and wiped her palms down the front of her apron. Running out of methods to keep her hands busy, she at last did as he asked and perched on a chair across from him. She took a sip of her own coffee and folded her hands around the cup. For a prolonged moment, neither spoke as he filled his stomach and murmured appreciative words about her cooking between hungry bites and hasty swallows.

Penny cleared her throat, determined to break the silence before it smothered her. "So, Mr. Burke. You mentioned you were riding through. Where exactly are you headed?"

Did she imagine it, or did his shoulders tense? "Southwest."

She grew alert. "Anywhere near Carson City?"

He took another heaping bite of stew. "Somewhere thereabouts. I think so at any rate."

"You think so?" she repeated, puzzled. "Doesn't the town you're riding to have a name?"

"Nope."

She gave him an incredulous stare. "You don't even know where you're going, do you?"

"I have a good idea where I'm headed."

"Huh." She gave a little scoffing sound. "You sound as if you live the life of a nomadic drifter."

"Well, ma'am, I don't settle down in one place for long, that's a fact. I don't need nothin' to tie me down." His eyes seemed to pierce through to her soul with his message.

"That seems a sorry state of affairs," she replied, all former awkwardness vanishing like dew in the sun. "Putting down no roots means having no friends, no family. No idea of where you're going from day to day, with no legacy to leave behind to your loved ones."

"I didn't say I don't have family." His tone and expression grew dour. "As a matter of fact, I've got a brother."

"I take it there's no love lost between you?"

He looked up from his meal. "Pardon me for saying so, but are you always this meddlesome?"

She had it coming; still it stung. "I suppose I am." She stood and took his cup to refill it, only just remembering he preferred no more as she again drew near him.

"I didn't mean to hurt your feelings." His voice came quiet. "I'm just not accustomed to talking about mine."

With the slightest smile and nod, Penny replaced his cup. "I should be the one to apologize. I haven't talked with a soul for ages except my girls, and I got carried away."

"I imagine it's difficult, you being out here all alone."

"At times it can be." She reclaimed her chair and looked out the lone window the shanty held, recalling all the troubles that had confronted them this past month alone. "My husband was a good man, but he was no farmer. To my shame, neither am I. The soil is too dry to raise the crop he wanted, despite the stream. And with the constant threat of thieves trying to steal what wee bit I have, 'tis difficult to raise my girls in safety—you're staring again." She turned her head, catching his gaze upon her.

His face tinged red in embarrassment, and he picked up his cup and drained it.

"You're wondering about my origin but are afraid to ask," Penny surmised, accustomed to such curiosity from others during the years she'd lived with her father in a town north of Silverton. "Since I became so personal, 'tis only fair I tell you about myself. My grandmother, my mother's mother, was full-blooded Shoshone. My da said I look like her. She died when I was a wee bairn." She smiled softly, wishing she had known her. "My grandfather was a French-Canadian trapper, my da a Scottish immigrant, his parents both Scots. From him I got what wee bit of accent I have."

"Your parents, they live nearby?"

"No, Mother died when I was a child. Da raised me, teaching me to read and write. He joined her in glory three years ago."

"I'm sorry for your loss, ma'am. But honestly, I was just admiring your bravery at tackling this place on your own."

"I don't know that I'd call it brave. One does what one must to survive." She lifted her brow in smiling doubt. "So, you weren't the least bit curious regarding my heritage?"

He grinned, as if caught. "Well, since you asked, maybe just a mite."

The door flew open, bringing their conversation to an abrupt end. Olivia and Christa, their faces clean and flushed, hurried over the threshold, empty-handed. They came to a quick stop upon seeing Derek, as if suddenly unsure.

"Olivia," Penny said calmly, "Christa. I'm pleased to see my absentminded daughters have found their way home. Did you forget where the shanty was?"

Olivia hung her head in shame.

" 'Tis a good thing I had coffee in the pot and tended our guest. Otherwise, he might have expired from thirst by now."

"I'm sorry, Mama. I forgot." Olivia kneaded her lip with her teeth and turned light brown eyes Derek's way. "I found your horse. In a manner of speaking."

"Where?" He stood to his feet and grabbed his broad-brimmed gray hat from the table.

"Well, um. . ." She fidgeted, sliding the sole of her moccasin along the planks.

"Olivia," Penny prompted. "What have you done?"

"I felt bad that I must've hit his horse with my slingshot and scared it away—I didn't mean to! Honest, I'd never harm any of God's creatures without just cause. I saw it down the valley, drinking at the stream; but I was only trying to make peace with it."

Derek closed his eyes as if fearing the worst, and Penny sighed. "Go on."

"When I got close, it must've gotten scared again. It ran off, north of here. I'm sorry." Her voice trembled with unshed tears.

"Never you mind," Penny said. "Go finish your chores, the both of you. I doubt those miners will be back, not today anyhow."

Once the girls scuttled outside, Penny looked at Derek. "Take one of my horses. If your horse ran north, it couldn't have gone far. The hill that edges that end of the valley rises rather steep, and I wouldn't think a horse would try climbing it."

"Thanks."

"Olivia didn't mean any harm; she was trying to help me."

"I realize that. At any rate, my mare tends to shy easy. She isn't the best tempered beast, but she's all I've got."

"Thank you," she said softly, realizing that was his way of releasing her child from blame.

He settled his hat atop his head. "I best get started so as to get back before the day's gone and leave you in peace."

From the doorway, Penny watched Derek head to the stable, his stride long and sure.

Peace. Strange he should mention such a thing. After her initial suspicions and concerns, he'd put her at ease—more so than she'd felt for some time. His casual and respectful manner invited trust, no matter that he wasn't keen to socialize. Thinking back to their conversation, an idea sprouted to mind. She would dwell on it more, but it just might be the answer for which she'd been praying.

୬

Derek found his bay grazing near the hill the young Widow Crawder had told him about. He approached the animal with slow, careful steps and, with little cajoling, grabbed the reins.

"We've had ourselves quite a day, haven't we, little girl?" The horse gave a slight toss of her head and whinnied as if in agreement. Examining her, he saw no evident damage to her hide from Olivia's stones and no swelling in her legs where one might have struck. He stroked the animal's muzzle before swinging into the saddle and retraced his trek from the Widow Crawder's homestead, leading her mare by its tether.

"You're welcome to share dinner with us," she said once he put her horse back in its stall, unsaddled, and curried it. "Dusk is still hours away, but if you've a mind to consider it, you may as well get a fresh start in the morning. You can bunk down in the barn. There's an empty stall for your horse, too. It's the least I can do after all the trouble we caused."

Derek glanced at the western sky, noting the sun had dropped closer to the horizon. He wouldn't mind sitting down to another of her meals. And he did need a place to bunk for the night. A barn with a roof and hay for a bed would suit much better than the hard ground—at least for one night.

"Thank you, ma'am. I'd be obliged."

After tending to his mare and shucking his bedroll inside the barn, Derek found himself with little else to do and stepped outside. He saw Olivia on the stoop, cutting the tops off a handful of wild onions, and decided to join her. The girl looked up, tilting her head as if uncertain about him, her mannerism much like her mother's.

She opened her mouth to speak, when Christa came running outside.

"Mama wants the onions," she blurted then saw Derek. Suddenly shy, she cast her gaze to her fringed and beaded moccasins. He noticed both the girls and their mother wore them, though the rest of their clothes were the type the women and children wore back East.

"Gotta go!" Olivia scurried up from the ground with the pail, disappearing inside.

"Gotta go!" Christa mimicked her sister and giggled, hurrying after her.

Derek smiled and welcomed the solitude. Gazing out over the endless stretch of shrub-covered hills, he mulled over what the upcoming days might bring: with any luck, a mine brimming with silver. As the land turned a deeper shade of green and gold, he wondered if he should offer his help to the Widow Crawder, then decided it best to stay out of her way. He sensed she still wasn't sure about him, despite her invitation to stay the night in the barn, and reckoned if she needed his help, she would ask. Without anything to keep him occupied, Derek paced the area, restless, and looked out over the valley. A nice stretch of grazing land, like a shallow bowl, with low-sloped hills that ringed the outside lay before him. Cattails grew along the little stream. To the east, the granite peaks of the Ruby Mountains touched the sky.

Olivia returned to tell him dinner was on and, relieved, he followed her into the shanty.

During the meal, the girls chattered to one another; Derek gathered the "seen but not heard" rule didn't apply at the Crawder table. Not that he took offense. Their ma acted distant, with a faraway look in her eyes, as if she had a good deal weighing on her mind. He'd never been much of a talker in any case and felt grateful for the respite after her interrogation during the previous meal. He made quick work of her tasty fixings, consisting of badger meat again, but this time roasted with the onions. Once the meal ended, twilight colored the hills a deep, murky blue, and he figured the time had come to turn in.

"Thank you for the meal, ma'am." He stood and donned his hat, heading for the door.

"Wait!" She seemed nervous as she approached, rubbing her hands down the front of her apron. "I'll get you a blanket. The nights still have quite a chill to them." Before he could mention his bedroll, she disappeared behind a hanging patchwork of hides that divided the room and returned, handing him a bundle of cloth.

"Well. . ." He glanced at his boots and tugged on his ear, then looked back into her eyes. Not quite black and not quite brown, in the lamplight they held a tinge of yellow gold and temporarily made him forget what he aimed to say. "I'd best be getting some shut-eye. I'm beholden to ya for the meal and. . .well, everything." Feeling awkward, he tipped his hat and made haste to the stable, sensing her watching him from her doorway.

Once inside the barn, Derek relaxed on his open bedroll with his back against one of the plank walls, the hay beneath a comfortable cushion, and he propped one arm on his upraised knee. He had no idea how much time passed, but his thoughts prevented him from sleep; to his discomfort, the Widow Crawder filled more than her fair share. He'd never met such a woman: in fortitude, she could match any man, though in appearance she seemed as delicate as one of her girls. Truth be told, Derek had never seen such a beauty in all his born days. She had the most riveting eyes. . . .

And why was he sitting here like a dolt thinking about her?

Disgusted with his drifting mind, he doused the flame in the lamp and settled down to get some rest, pulling the blanket over his shoulder. Reclining didn't help matters any as far as sleep went, and soon he found his thoughts taking him back to Silverton. He imagined the thunderstruck looks that must have been on their faces when his brother and Linda awoke that morning to find Derek and the maps missing. The same uneasy guilt that had followed him during his silent exit from the sparse mining town caught up with Derek now. He stared into the dark, trying to push the blame away. He had every right to all that the mine held.

The brush of footsteps in the grasses, slow and careful, alerted him to an intruder. Recalling the Widow Crawder's account of troublesome miners, with the bitter stench of smoke that lingered in the wood of the barn serving as a further reminder, Derek grabbed his gun. With silent ease, he moved to the door and waited

The footsteps came closer.

The door creaked open, letting in a patch of moonlight and a short figure in a broad-brimmed hat and duster coat.

Derek didn't hesitate. Leaping forward, he grabbed the troublemaker, using his body to slam the thief against the wall and pin him there, while pressing one hand hard against his mouth and bringing the muzzle of his gun to the prowler's head. One sudden revelation startled Derek, barreling through his mind: the body against his wasn't firm or solid but yielded soft curves.

The Widow Crawder stared up at him, her eyes huge.

Chapter 2

Penny's heart thundered against Derek's chest as she gaped up at him; no doubt hard labor produced such solid muscles beneath his shirt. Long strands of hair hung in his face, making him appear wild and dangerous. His riveting eyes, at first murderous, had dulled from shock, though still he didn't budge. With her body pinned against the rough planks, she stood stock-still; even if she'd been free to move, alarm mingled with a strange sense of awareness would have kept her rooted to the ground.

He wrenched his hand from her mouth and retreated. "Woman, what in blazes are you doing here? I could've put a bullet through your fool head!"

Penny worked her sore jaw, rubbing it. "Do you always react with such violence?" She masked her vulnerability with firm words.

"Are you always this foolish?" He shoved his gun back into his holster with unnecessary force. He approached her in the scant patch of moonlight, close, but not as close as before. "I thought you were one of those outlaws who've been robbing you blind! What are you doing skulking about in the dead of night, dressed like a man?"

Affronted, she raised her chin. "You'll recall this is my home, Mr. Burke, and you are my guest. And for your information, these were my husband's things, not that it should matter one whit to you what I wear or why I wear it."

Surprise swept across his face at her quiet attack. She forced herself to calm. Her idiotic pettiness over insignificant matters was of no account; responding with anger defeated the purpose of her visit. In thinking over his action to protect what wasn't his, she couldn't fault him for his rash behavior. Instead, she should thank him.

She cleared her throat, setting her mind on what she would say to steady things between them. "I'm grateful to you for acting in my defense. And you're right—I shouldn't have come. I almost went back to the house, but I heard you moving around and assumed you were awake—and obviously I was right. I must talk with you."

He blew out a long breath, clearly trying to collect himself. "Not to sound disrespectful, ma'am, but couldn't it have waited till morning?" His expression was wary. "It must be nearing midnight."

"Just past eleven. I looked at Oliver's pocket watch before I slipped outside."

She didn't add that she'd been drumming up courage to confront him since dinner. At his incredulous stare, she hurried on. "Aye, 'tis late, but I wasn't sure I'd catch you before you left. My husband was accustomed to waking long before daybreak. And I wanted to wait till the girls lay sleeping before coming to tell you I've arrived at a decision, one with which I hope you'll agree."

He narrowed his eyes. "What sort of decision?"

She straightened her shoulders and took a bracing breath. "When you leave here in the morning, I want you to take us with you as far as Carson City."

⤫

Derek gaped at the woman, sure she had gone daft. "You can't be serious."

"Oh, but I am." Her steady eyes and the strong lift of her chin did not waver. "I've been hoping to break loose from here for nigh unto six months. My daughters deserve better than to be terrorized by lily-livered cowards who bear me the grudge of not only being a landowner who's a female but also the bearer of Shoshone blood."

"So you aim to just up and leave your home behind?" Derek couldn't grasp such a notion. If he'd owned such a valley, depraved miners or not, he wouldn't consider leaving it.

"What good is it to own a parcel of land if one cannot survive on it? We've managed so far, but I won't be diggin' another grave. As I told you, times have been hard. Especially for my girls."

He shook his head. "That's an awful long distance. Why so far, and what makes you think I'm traveling to Carson City, anyhow? There are a few other towns between here and there."

"You said 'thereabouts' when I asked your direction earlier. My guess is you're out looking for that precious metal which every stranger in these parts is searching for—silver."

Keeping his expression a blank, he hid his shock that she'd read him so well.

She stepped closer, her dark eyes intent on his face. This time, he ignored the same muddled swirl of feelings that had clenched his gut once he realized she was the intruder he'd trapped against the wall.

"When I mentioned the miners nearby, you grew alert—your eyes, they give you away, Mr. Burke. If you aren't out searching for treasure in these hills, then I ask myself, why react so strangely?" He didn't answer, and she continued, "It's been my experience that most drifters find themselves drifting over to Virginia City or Carson City or 'thereabouts,' and my guess is that you're one of them."

"Even if I was," he replied, his tone measured, "I don't aim to saddle myself down with a widow and her two young'uns." The woman added up to danger, as unpredictable as they came. He didn't mind helping a lady in need, but he'd be plumb loco to tackle the risky undertaking of traveling alongside a woman in want. And he felt sure she wanted something in addition to what she asked for. What was more, he was certain he wouldn't like it.

She turned up her palms wide in a beseeching manner. "Please, won't you reconsider? All I desire is safe escort. The girls and I won't get in your way. Once we reach Carson City, you need never see us again."

"And what makes you so sure I'm 'safe'?" he taunted, his voice low, hoping he might discourage her idea by giving her a little scare. "I could very well be the worst desperado you've come across. You might do well to rid yourself of my company."

"You didn't yell at Olivia for what she did to your horse, for what all of us did to you. 'Tis a fact, you were magnanimous about the entire misunderstanding."

"Magnani—what?" He wondered if she'd insulted him with her fancy word, but by the gentle manner in which she smiled, he figured she bore him no ill will.

"You were generous with your forgiveness. But if I didn't think you a man of principles before this, you just proved it to me when you defended my home."

Her soft, earnest praise cut into him like a loose ax head, and he turned away from the plea in her brown eyes that tested his resolve. "Lady, you don't know what you're talking about," he muttered, settling his hands on his hips. "You don't know anything about me."

"I've always prided myself on being a good judge of character." She hesitated. "I don't have much in the way of money, but whatever you deem from my provisions as just payment, it's yours."

"I don't want your money or your things."

"Then what. . . ?"

He spun to face her. "Don't you get it? I'm not taking you to Carson City."

"If it were just me, I wouldn't ask. But my little girls. . ." Her voice wavered. With a mounting sense of horror, he thought she might cry. "They're all I have that's truly important. I'm fair enough with a shotgun but not so foolish as to ignore the risks that traveling alone—and for days on end—could entail."

The tears glistening in her eyes didn't fall, but they near defeated him. He rallied what tattered strength of mind he had remaining. "Try more like weeks. I'm sorry, ma'am. I just can't do it. I won't do it."

Where curtness and intimidation had failed, his quiet words convinced her. Her mouth parted as if to answer; then she gave a little, disbelieving shake of her head and turned on her heel, hurrying out the barn door. It swung shut with a muted *thud*.

Derek passed a restless night with the image of the Widow Crawder's pleading, dark eyes branded on his mind. Long before dawn lit the eastern sky, he saddled his bay mare and rode far from her homestead.

∽

Hours passed with no progress.

Derek glanced up from the map sections he'd smoothed out over the ground and scowled at the vista of land spread before him. He squinted against the glaring white sun. The rounded hills that stood closest shimmered pale brown speckled with green scrub. Beyond that, the distant mountain range took on the deep color of violets. No matter how far he rode, the land stayed the same.

There must be thousands of rocks and countless more clumps of sagebrush. But no twisted tree emerged, and he hadn't come across any river, either—what he presumed the long, snakelike squiggle from east to west represented. A shaky hand had drawn the symbols, so he only guessed the sketching of three oblong circles, two leaning atop one, was a butte composed of rock. Or maybe three hills closed in together.

Both Derek and Clay learned to read and write from their ma, but Derek figured his pa either hadn't known how to form letters or didn't care to take the effort. Why else wouldn't he print what each symbol stood for? Unless he just wanted to make matters harder for his offspring. Derek wouldn't put such a scheme past the conniver and imagined him rolling with laughter in his grave. If he really were dead. . .could a man that mean really die?

The morning waned. He rode over low hills of scrub, with endless stops and starts, only to circle back, hoping to spot something familiar. A juniper tree? Or maybe the sketch on the map was a tall cactus, like those he'd seen several days southeast of here. Wherever southeast was. With the sun at its highest point, he no longer knew what direction he rode.

"Thanks a lot, Pa."

Muttering in frustration, Derek dismounted. Lack of sleep clouded his judgment. Worse, the water in his canteen was low, though he'd filled it at the creek before leaving the widow's homestead. Now the heat felt close to roasting him like a side of beef.

He snapped off a reasonably straight stick from some prickly underbrush and stuck it upright in dry, level soil. With a rock, Derek marked where the end of the shadow fell. He waited until he felt enough time had passed and marked the dirt again—a method he'd learned to establish east to west in the arid flat-lands. He imagined it might work in this high desert country, too. He looked in the direction of the second mark. West. Flicking his hat back from his brow, he felt grateful he'd again found his bearings.

The day passed into early evening. Another stretch of time bore no rewards save one. The plant life became denser, and he spotted some sheep and sighted a small flock of large, white birds flying north; water must be close by. Mounting yet another hill, he looked down into a ravine and noted a reflection that flickered and cut through the gradually sloping hills on either side. Water. He'd found the river at last.

As he drew close, he noticed endless parallel ruts embedded deep in the ground from wagon trains of previous emigrants. He hadn't ridden through here for six years, when Nevada was still a territory, but the river had to be the Humboldt. And that was surely part of the California Trail.

That meant—assuming he'd pieced the map together correctly—somewhere between here and Virginia City on this side of the river, he should find the mine. Question was: Where? And how many miles did the map cover? Ten? Fifty? A hundred? Surely his pa wouldn't have them start their journey from a mining town so far distant. On second thought, it sounded just like something a scoundrel with a spiteful sense of humor might do.

A covered wagon stood alone about a half mile upriver. Having seen no sign of humanity the entire day and curious to know what wayfarers would travel without a wagon train, he rode closer, thinking they might need help. Like as not the owners were stragglers left behind. If the wilderness didn't kill them, the ongoing conflict between the Indians and emigrants posed a threat throughout much of their westward journey and persuaded more than a few less hardy souls to turn around and head back East, which was what he presumed had happened. According to the wealthy railroad tycoons Derek once worked for, the completion of the transcontinental railroad would eliminate perilous travel by wagon train, though Derek sometimes wondered if mounted Indians could outrace a locomotive. He wondered, too, if the Indian Wars would really end, as government officials predicted, once all the natives were forced onto reservations. Or might the battles just take a new turn?

Two small girls with dark braids and wearing moccasins skipped out from behind the wagon. Their giggles carried through the warm, heavy air, as if they thrilled in their adventure.

Derek pulled on the reins, bringing his horse to an abrupt stop. His mouth agape, he recognized Olivia and Christa, then watched their mother walk into view toward the shallow river, a kettle in her hands. None of the Crawder clan had sighted him, and he considered turning his horse around and riding away before they could.

Just as the thought surfaced, the youngest girl whirled around and stared. She ran to her mother and tugged at the back of her skirts.

"Mama, look!" she cried out.

The Widow Crawder shifted her attention from filling her kettle to looking where her daughter pointed. Staring at Derek, the woman rose from her crouch, gripping the handles of the kettle as she hoisted it up with her.

A tense moment passed as neither made a gesture of recognition or greeting.

From this distance, maybe she didn't know him. But that didn't make sense; he recognized her.

She turned her back on him and walked away, disappearing to the other side of her wagon. Perplexed, he stared after her a moment, then dismounted and led his horse to the slow-moving water, the width of a creek, first testing it and finding it cold and pure. He knelt at the riverbank and quenched his thirst.

His impulse to turn tail and flee disappeared the moment she walked away, pretending he didn't exist. Now a sense of curious irritation compelled him to make camp. His horse needed rest, and sunset wouldn't be long in coming. That was what he told himself—all truths—but his real reason for choosing to linger was to find out just what that woman was up to.

Last night, she'd fearfully listed the dangers of traveling alone with her small daughters and begged for his help. Now she was out here in the middle of nowhere, with no other escort that he could see. Maybe his first assumption about her had been correct and she really didn't have the sense God gave a mule. To remain on her homestead and fight off attackers had taken daring; he couldn't fault her for her desire to protect what was hers. But maybe a fair share of dim-wittedness also triggered her decisions.

His stomach clenched from hunger, and he pulled from his saddlebag what remained of the dried beef strips. An old fur trader had taught Derek to make the pemmican with dried meat, suet, and berries. But the crimson berries he'd used this time were bitter. He brushed the dust off a brown, leatherlike strip of meat and thought about trying to catch something to roast before day's light faded. The river ran shallow, and through the muddy water, rocks sat along the bed, with no sign of life slithering past, none that he could tell. Nor did he see any small mammals dart through the high grass or brush.

He spread his bedroll on a bare patch of ground. Settling his back and shoulders against a smooth boulder away from any sight of the wagon, he crossed one outstretched leg over the other and stared at the sluggish river. He chomped down into his meal, tearing the tough strip away with his teeth. He supposed he should be grateful for what he had: water and something to put in his stomach, even if the meat had become grainy over the weeks and dull to his taste.

Sensing movement to his left, Derek glanced at the wagon and watched the woman and her girls flutter about their tasks, retrieving items from the back of the wagon. After a few minutes, he shifted onto his side, purposely keeping his back to them. He pulled down the brim of his hat, crossed his arms over his chest, and tucked his hands under his armpits. Forcing his gaze to remain on the horizon, he noted the changes in color as the clouds flamed rose gold, deep blue and yellow, causing the distant mountain range south to appear almost black. The hairs on the back of his neck bristled. Sensing a trespasser into his solitude, he jerked his head around to look over his shoulder.

Olivia and Christa stood several feet away, staring at him. By the dying light, he noticed their round cheeks and chins stained with bright red. Each of them held a huge slab of some sort of berry pie in their hands.

Berry pie?

Christa raised the thick, messy chunk to her mouth and nibbled on more of the sweet.

Derek licked his lips, watching. "What brings you girls over here?" he asked gruffly.

"Mama said it would be okay if we come and 'pologize to you about scaring your horse yesterday," Olivia said.

"Oh, she did, did she?"

"Uh-huh." Christa gave one huge nod and smiled, revealing rose-colored teeth. "We forgot to after it happened and she said it would be polite and the right thing to do and that we didn' have to wait till after supper 'cause the sun was goin' down and she didn' want us to trip over rocks in the dark or nothin'."

He sighed. "Okay, you said your piece. No harm done; horse is fine. You girls better skedaddle on back to the wagon now."

"Okay." They exchanged looks then glanced at him. "G'night, Mr. Burke!"

The girls took off giggling, but Derek wasn't smiling.

Chapter 3

O n the opposite side of the wagon, shielded from Derek's view, Penny added more bait to her trap, or rather an extra pinch of aromatic herbs to the remainder of rabbit stew. Thanks to Olivia's skill with a sling-shot, they wouldn't go hungry; another boon for Penny if she could just do some convincing of that fact to the man bunked inside his bedroll downstream. She had hoped the pie she'd baked the night before when she'd been restless and couldn't sleep would do the trick, but apparently it hadn't. The girls had long ago returned from their undertaking—in the company only of each other.

Penny glanced up. The sky had taken on the color of dry slate, and the air had chilled enough to raise goose pimples on her arms. Knowing she must get some sleep soon if she wanted to be coherent in the morning, she fetched a blanket from the wagon. Dire times called for dire measures, or so her da had taught her.

Olivia and Christa lay inside the wagon, their stomachs filled, both girls exhausted from their first day of travel. The patchwork of hides her da had brought her, which she had stitched together to serve as a privacy curtain for the shanty, now covered her children, keeping them warm. Penny smiled, her heart twisting at the sweet picture of the two girls nestled together, each with an arm around the other, Christa's forehead pressed against Olivia's shoulder.

Her daughters meant everything to her; she would do what she must to ensure they remained safe. Last night she'd packed the necessities important to start a new life, along with a few precious mementos, leaving behind what she couldn't take. And with the girls' aid this morning, she'd loaded the wagon directly after Derek's departure. But as the day passed without sight of the drifter, she'd worried she might never catch up to him. She'd taken the creek to the river that flowed westward, thinking he would do the same. She'd planned to trail him without his knowledge—at least with the hope of his not discover-ing them right away, since she knew at some point he likely would—and hoped the sight of him ahead might aid in their safety should any undesirables catch sight of her lone wagon and consider it easy pickings. But after meeting up with him again and not receiving the brunt of a tongue-lashing—in fact, receiving no greeting, good or bad—another idea brewed in her mind.

She grabbed her quilt that covered her trunk and walked toward the kettle steaming over the fire, taking a stand a short distance from it. With steady motions, she waved the quilt beside it, forcing the white smoke that curled up from the black pot to waft eastward. She kept this up for what seemed an eternity but was doubtless only minutes. The spot between her shoulders began to ache.

"You tryin' to make the fire bigger or tryin' to put it out?"

She jumped at the sudden drawl of Derek's voice coming from behind and whirled to face him. He stood several feet away, his stance casual, hands straddling his denim-clad hips.

"I, um. . .neither." Penny shrugged. As an adult, she'd never told a lie and didn't plan to start. Silence stretched between them while she held the patchwork quilt close and stared back, caught in the act like a barn cat with a fluffy chick dangling from its mouth.

"Okay, here's how it's gonna be," he said at last. "You supply all my meals, starting now, and I'll provide safe escort for you and your girls to Carson City."

Relief made it seem as if a boulder had rolled off her shoulders. "Why, Mr. Burke, that *does* sound like a most practical plan." She directed a hasty smile his way and hurried to fetch a clean tin plate before he could reconsider and withdraw the offer. With the ladle, she dished him up a generous portion of thick stew. "I'm glad you thought of it. 'Tis a grand idea and does work well for the lot of us."

She approached and handed him his dinner. His fingers collided with the tops of hers. Penny gave a short gasp of surprise at the contact. But before she could pull her hands from his warm touch, since he didn't seem in any hurry to move his own, the look in his now dusky blue eyes trapped her, holding her rooted to the ground. Motionless. Her heart, on the other hand, beat out a few swift thumps.

"Truth be told, ma'am," he said, his voice so low it rumbled in his throat, "you had me lassoed with the pie." He moved to take the tin of stew, and his mouth flickered at the corners in a lazy grin. "And I sure hope you have some left. Sending your girls out to me when I had nothing but old, dry pemmican, well now, you sure know how to hurt a man. That was pure torture, through and through."

A bit flustered, she didn't know whether to scold him for his roguish and rather familiar behavior or laugh at his dubious plight and discovery of her plan. The flames weren't all that danced in his eyes.

Finding humor in the situation, she gave him an answering smile. "Well now, Mr. Burke, as a matter of fact, I do have a wee bit of pie I held back in the event I might need it."

"Yeah." He quirked his lips in an amused pucker. "I figured you just might."

Unsure how to respond and still embarrassed that he'd gauged her plan, she moved to the wagon to collect the last two pieces of berry pie.

❧

As Derek led the Crawders along the trail the next day, he shook his head in self-mockery at the proposed arrangement. His mother had once told him a man named Esau gave up his birthright to his brother for a bowl of pottage. He supposed his situation couldn't compare to Esau's story, but the hunger that had gnawed at his belly had led Derek to surrender his privacy and delay his search for the mine, all to provide escort to the scheming Widow Crawder.

The woman was shrewd and as knowledgeable as any man—bold and confident, maybe overly so—in doing what she deemed necessary to steer things her way. His wry disgust with her obvious conniving eased a bit when he recalled her explanation the first night, after he'd caught her skulking near the barn. He couldn't fault the woman for caring for her own and seeing to her girls' welfare. How many years had he done the same for his family, using whatever measure seemed appropriate at the time? Too many to recount. Little good it had done, since Clay didn't understand the meaning of the word gratitude.

Forcing his mind to the more recent past, Derek smirked with the memory of the Widow Crawder's petite form wielding the cumbersome quilt and fanning the fragrant smoke from the stew in the direction of his camp. He'd finally been unable to resist the challenge and silently walked past her wagon, undetected; she'd been so intent on the fire. Moving to stand behind her, he'd watched her actions for some time. Once he spoke to alert her to his presence, he recalled her mortified expression after she'd spun to face him. Odd that his second inclination had been to relieve her mind. His first impulse, and fully what she deserved—to give her a heated earful for her obvious ploy to snare him as her guide as if he were some starving dog in dire need of a bone—he'd pushed aside. One look into those dark eyes swimming with a shamed sort of plea, and he'd decided to put her at ease.

He recalled her joining in his easy laughter and how her eyes sparkled. She really was a handsome woman, her eyes so soft a brown they reminded him of a doe and at times containing flecks of gold that shone in the firelight. Firelight that also brought out the red glowing in her hair. . .

No, he shouldn't—wouldn't—travel down such trails in his mind. The last thing he wanted was to be saddled with a woman, much less entertain even the idea of courting. The Widow Crawder pegged him right: he was a drifter with every intention of remaining unattached and free—"nomadic" she called it— and that suited him just fine. Derek the Nomad. He turned the name over in his mind, liking the sound of it. Once he claimed his fortune, he would become more of a traveling sheik, like they called those princes in Arabia. Or maybe he'd buy him a fancy outfit somewhere in a pretty little valley. Round him up some cattle and start his own ranch. . .

"Mr. Burke?"

Torn from his musings, he looked down to see Olivia, who'd come up to walk beside his horse. She'd tied a rope around her waist as a sash, and sticking out from within the hemp rested the slingshot to which he'd been a victim. Nope. Neither the spitfire known as Widow Crawder nor her two daring girls could be considered helpless by any stretch of the imagination. Reckless and foolish, yes—but not helpless.

"Whatcha need, Olivia?"

"You ever been to Carson City?" Her smile came easy. Both girls had been excited to wake near dawn and learn that Derek would be guiding them on their journey.

He looked toward the distant mesa of a wide plain they now traveled. "Can't say that I have."

"Never?" She seemed shocked.

"I'm not exactly from around these parts," he admitted.

"So what makes you think we're going in the right direction? Do you think the city'll be big with lotsa people there? Mama said cities are suppose-ta be big—that's why they call them cities. So how long do you think it'll take to get there?"

He reckoned the inclination to talk about anything and nothing resided in all those of the female persuasion. "The river runs west. Carson City's west. So we can't go wrong by following this river."

She gave him a doubtful glance.

"I rode through Virginia City years ago, so I do recall some things about this area. And I talked to a retired wagon master a few weeks past, saw a map or two." Reminded of his own map, he ended the topic fast; he didn't need her curiosity roused should he slip and make mention of his father's questionable legacy. "The river empties into a sink—that much I know." He glanced to the right at the ribbon of muddy water they followed. "It twists and turns along the way, and we'll have to make some crossings, even travel a spell without water at some cutoffs, but we shouldn't be dry for long." He didn't want to frighten her with mention of the long stretch of desert they would also need to cross.

She was quiet, seeming to concentrate on her moccasins and the path they took before looking up at him again. "So, you a miner like Mama said?"

"No."

"Then how come you're going to Carson City? Isn't that where miners go? And why'd you go to Virginia City? Miners go there, too. Papa told me."

He looked at her upturned face full of questions and chose to give a single answer. "I told your ma I'd help your family get to where she wanted to go, and that's Carson City."

"But why are you in these parts if you're not a miner? Are you a cowboy? You don't look like a cowboy. You ain't got a lasso or spurs, though you do got guns. But near everyone in Silverton has those. I know, 'cause Papa took me with him to town when he went there."

Snooping into others' affairs must have passed from her ma down to her.

"You got the nosy mannerism, too?" He kept his tone mild. He didn't mind young'uns so much, though he hadn't been around many. But he didn't think they were supposed to be so bold and speak their minds. Not from what he recollected of being a youth.

"Nosy mannerism?"

"You like to pry into matters that don't concern you?"

She grinned wide. "I just like hearing the facts, like Mama does and like my grandda did. I miss him. He came to these parts and became a trapper like my great-grandfather. When there was lots of gold found in the streams, years before I was born, Grandda told me he went to look for it, too, but never found anything 'cept a wee bit of gold dust, and he came back 'cause he missed my grandma and Mama. Sometimes at night, I'd hear my papa talkin' to Mama when they thought Christa and me was sleeping, and he talked about looking for silver like my uncle who lives in Carson City. But Papa said he didn't think he'd make a good miner. He said all he wanted was his family, and he didn't plan to go off anywhere and leave them behind like some miners do." Olivia halted her prattle to pluck up some bright yellow wildflowers in a lone bunch near some rocks before running to catch up to his horse again. "So if you're not mining for silver or gold, what'd you come to Nevada for, Mister?"

Derek had hoped she would cease firing questions once she'd been side-tracked by the flowers, and he felt his defenses rise, almost blocking out the pain her cheerful words had caused.

He scowled, pulling his hat farther down over his brow though the sun shone behind them. "Like I told your ma, I'm just passing through."

"To California?"

"Olivia!" Her mother called from the wagon in back of them, likely needing her to clear the path ahead of small rocks or brush so the wagon wheels wouldn't be impeded. The girl whipped around without another word and ran her way.

Derek blew out a thankful breath that the childish interrogation had ended. Between Olivia and her ma, he wasn't sure how much longer he could keep his private matters private. He was determined the Widow Crawder not ferret out the truth of his affairs in trying to stake sole claim to his pa's silver mine. From what he'd experienced of the dogged woman, she entertained no remorse in speaking her mind; nor, apparently, did her girls. He sensed the young widow would soundly condemn his methods, though she obviously possessed a blind eye when it came to her own. And he had no desire to hear her harp her disapproval clear to Carson City.

Chapter 4

Near sunset, Penny looked across their campfire and watched her silent escort wolf down his stew as if food hadn't passed his lips in days. Thanks to the roots and plants she'd collected through the past year, drying and storing them in her herb box, she prided herself that her aromatic stew was better than palatable, and those herbs that she found fresh made her meals even better.

Derek received a fair portion for his troubles, and she would continue to provide his meals as arranged. Certainly what she offered was better than the pemmican he'd been eating. So the guilt that pricked her conscience made no sense. He'd entered the trade with his eyes open, letting her know she hadn't tricked him one bit. She disapproved of deceit in any form. But lately, her motives were jumbled with confusion about what was truly right or wrong when it came to the safety of her girls.

Derek looked up, catching her gaze on him. Embarrassed, she turned her attention west toward the range of hills and the play of light and shadow as the sun dipped ever lower. It shed deep violet and rose over irregular-shaped rocks, turning them even more intense shades of the earth colors they bore.

"What do you aim on doing once you get to Carson City?" Derek asked, pulling her away from her appreciation of their surroundings. "I reckon a woman as clever as you must have some plan in mind." He handed her his empty tin.

Without asking, Penny took it, ladling him a second helping of stew. She had learned in the short time they'd supped together that when he set his tin on the ground, he'd had his fill, and when he handed it to her, he required seconds. By the manner in which he regarded her, he clearly read her surprise that he should be the one to ask her a personal question—to be sure, that he should start a conversation at all.

He pursed his lips, and they flickered at the edges in a slow smile. "I imagine it's none of my business," he went on, "and I'm not one to go barging in where I'm unwanted. But since I took on this job as your guide, I can't help but feel a mite responsible for you and your girls. I've never lived in Carson City, but I heard about its workings from others, and it's no decent place for a lady and her two small daughters."

He thought her a lady? She marveled, wondering how long it had been since someone had addressed her as such.

"Living in Carson City is nothing like living in the valley and dealin' with a few ornery miners," he added.

"I'm not going into this blind, Mr. Burke. I'm well aware of the evils involved, perhaps more so than most." Her mother had lived with the stigma "half breed" and the prejudice that came with the name. Her da often told Penny her mother was proud and strong, a convert to Christianity, not allowing the narrow-mindedness of others to sully the person she'd known she was: beloved by God. Like her mother, Penny was determined to face head-on whatever conflicts came her way. Unlike her mother, she felt uncertain she could ever forgive those who brought them and realized she'd failed miserably.

Not all miners were ornery, but she couldn't summon even a morsel of forgiveness toward those men who'd tried to drive her and her children off her land and, in a sense, had succeeded. That only intensified her guilt since her da taught her that God commanded everyone to forgive and that He'd forgiven all crimes men had wrongfully done to His Son. He, too, had been taunted and mocked, looked upon with revulsion. . .then beaten and hung upon a cross to die.

"Olivia mentioned you've got kin there?" Derek broke into her muddled thoughts, which had taken a turn she didn't like.

"My husband's brother. Last I heard, he planned to mine in Carson City. I haven't seen him for more than ten years, and he doesn't know about Oliver. I hope to try to find Ben, though I don't intend seeking his aid."

"Then you do have a plan?"

"Aye." She smoothed the creases of her skirt over her leg in an attempt to remain unruffled. "A good plan. Before my mother died, she taught me to make beaded pouches; I'm certain they would still be in demand and fetch a fine price. I thought to make an arrangement with whoever runs the trading post, to sell them there. In a mining city right off the California Trail, I should bring in good business."

"And just where do you plan on living, if you don't mind my asking? Finding room in a boardinghouse for three new lodgers, two of them children, is bound to be difficult. And a hotel is costly."

She appraised him. "Mr. Burke, for someone who allegedly prefers private matters to stay private and accuses others of bearing a—'nosy mannerism' I believe you called it?—you certainly seem to be living up to the name."

He grinned, one side of his mouth curling up in its usual lazy fashion. "I see your point. But I'm not the least bit comfortable with the idea of dumping you and yours off in Carson City like three lost lambs to fend for yourselves in a den of rabid wolves."

"What are you suggesting?" Her breath caught, and she let it out slowly.

Surely he couldn't be proposing an affiliation of ill repute; he didn't seem the sort of man to take advantage of a lone woman's desire to protect her daughters at all cost. Nor did he seem the type to offer protection through the sanctity of marriage, and she almost laughed at that track off which her mind derailed her. He looked at her a curious moment, his brow puzzling, clearly noting how she'd choked off a nervous laugh. "I'm suggesting you reconsider and head back home. I'll even provide escort back. We're only a couple days out."

"No."

"I'll admit," he said as though he hadn't heard her low, adamant reply, "you're right handy with a gun and as iron-willed as they come—able to outsmart most any man, I reckon. But not everyone—man or woman—is gonna respect that or take them facts into account. And I'd hate to see any man try to take advantage of a woman. As steadfast and brave as you are, you've no idea what's in store for you in a place like Carson City."

Penny bowed her head, thinking over a reply. She hadn't been mistaken to entrust him with their safety. With each word he spoke, he proved himself an honorable man.

"I appreciate your concern, Mr. Burke, but it isn't your place to decide what's best for my girls. It's mine. And to remain on my husband's homestead would have been unwise. I've struggled with attacks, with near starvation—and with this decision. Why, just the night before we met, I told myself if ever an opportunity arose, I wouldn't ignore the chance. Then you showed up out of the clear blue sky like an answer from the good Lord above. And even though you refused my request at first, my mind was made up that I would leave. Given my life and what's come of it so far, I expect I will face hardship in Carson City, but I'm willing to take that risk. I'm hoping to find at least a few like-minded, godly people and possibly a church or, if not that, a parson to preach God's Word and a better environment for my girls." She thought about the buildings of communal worship her da had told her stood in every town and city in the East and hoped to find such a place in a city of the West.

"A church tucked in among the saloons?" He chuckled at that. "Likely all you'll be finding in the way of preaching is a circuit rider who comes through town every once in a great while," he muttered.

"Then I shall be content with that. A circuit rider is better than nothing at all, and for years, nothing is all we had."

Ill at ease, she looked toward the sputtering flames. She desired to raise her girls to be godly women, but her absence from such women, and men, had caused her own fire to dwindle to embers, the fire for God her da had instilled in her since she'd been old enough to ask questions. Much to her shame, she couldn't remember the last time she'd knelt by her bedside and prayed.

At her sudden twinge of conscience, Penny rose from the ground and whisked the soil from her skirts. "I think all that needed to be said between us has been said. I hope we're agreed that this journey will continue as planned?"

He considered her with steady measure. "I'm not the sort to go back on my word, ma'am."

She couldn't pinpoint the reason, but something about his relaxed manner and the steady way his eyes regarded her made her senses come alert. For an irrational moment, she recalled him pressed flush against her when he'd thought her an intruder, and her face burned with heat. When she'd realized he only meant to protect, she felt both safe and alive, more alive than she had been since Oliver's death. She hadn't been in close proximity to a man for almost a year; surely the unfamiliarity of that startling moment in the barn with Derek explained why she now relived it while standing across the fire from him.

"Fine," she answered, "that's settled then. I'm turning in. There's more stew if you want to scrape the bottom. I'll clean out the kettle in the morning. You'll tend the fire?"

He nodded, and she strode to her wagon before he could respond. If he chose to do so. She wasn't sticking around to find out.

As she reclined on the wagon boards and pulled the blanket of hides over her, snuggling beside the sleeping Christa in the tight space left, Penny couldn't keep her gaze from wandering to the slit in the canvas, and the view of the lone drifter sitting beside a dying fire.

᠆ᢒ᠆

Derek stared into the low flames long after she'd gone. Why should he care so much about the fate of one woman and her two girls? He'd hardly demonstrated the same kindness or concern toward Linda. Even if she was a conniving snake out to steal his inheritance, she was still a woman, the "fairer and more genteel sex," as he'd overheard a sheriff a few days' ride from Silverton put it. He'd had no right to speak to her in the belittling way he'd done. Derek could still remember his sharp, bitter words, along with the cruel names he'd used, and how Linda's face had gone from glowing rosy to chalk white.

Shame gnawed at his gut; he'd never treated a woman, any woman, in the spiteful manner he'd used against Linda. He'd been exhausted, shocked, and angry, but that was no excuse. His ma would have been horrified to hear such vile words spewing from his mouth. He'd reacted like a mad dog at Linda's declaration of kinship. If his ma had been alive, she might have pulled him by the ear to endure a good mouth-swabbing with her lye soap, no matter that he was no longer a boy in knee britches. Now that he'd had a few days to mull over his encounter with Linda—and truth be acknowledged, she did have his pa's piercing gray eyes—he had calmed some. While sharing the company of a young widow who thought him a man of honor, he acknowledged that he'd been nothing more than an uncouth scoundrel.

Once he found the mine and staked his claim, Derek would not only send Linda off on a stagecoach back home, wherever home was, he would also make sure she had enough to care for her needs until she found a husband. She had mentioned she was alone in the world, and Derek supposed he owed her that much—half sister or not. With her attractive face and figure in a land where men far outnumbered women, he didn't imagine her finding a groom would take long. If Derek really was her older brother, as the letter from his pa and her portion of the map seemed to establish, then it was the least he could do for the girl. He sure wouldn't feel right if some calamity befell her on his account.

Recalling his reason for being in this part of Nevada, Derek retrieved his saddlebag and the map. He wanted to look at it by what firelight remained, away from curious eyes, to see if he could recall any of its poorly drawn symbols as resembling anything he'd seen today.

With careful measure, he unfolded all three portions and laid them on the ground before the fire, connecting them into a whole. He smoothed out creases, poring over the faint squiggly line that covered all the pieces, what he assumed to be the river they traveled alongside, and paid particular attention to the symbols on both top and bottom. He recognized nothing, though he'd kept a close eye on the area as they'd traveled—what probably amounted to no more than three miles today, or so it seemed. The widow didn't exactly delay the journey, but she often requested they stop so she could gather cuttings of some plant she'd spotted. In fact, she didn't seem in any real hurry to reach Carson City, though at her homestead she'd implied a need for haste.

A man could never tell what a woman was thinking, Derek reckoned. They still had time before the season shifted full into summer and the heat became unbearable farther west. With that in mind, he hadn't hurried her along when she'd strayed from their purpose. The woman was a fine cook with the few ingredients she had, making her stews come alive, which was what he assumed all the plant cuttings were for. Far be it from him to detract from the makings of a good meal.

He corralled his wandering attention back to the map, again speculating if this was nothing more than his pa's cruel joke, a final slap in the face to the offspring he'd left behind. What if Derek really was wasting his time and efforts on a mine that didn't exist?

A stir at the back of the wagon and the appearance of a small foot stretching out of the wagon's tarpaulin caused him to grab up the pieces of map, clumsily fold them, and stuff them inside his shirt.

The second foot followed, the bearer's white nightdress riding up to her knees before Christa's slight form appeared. Clutching a corn-husk doll in one hand, she slipped to the ground, the hem of her gown falling around her ankles. She turned, caught sight of Derek watching her, and halted in her tracks.

"What are you up to so late at night?" he asked.

"I need to tend to nature's call," she mimicked the words she'd evidently heard spoken by her elders and shifted from foot to foot in clear discomfort.

"Go on then, but not far." He didn't like the idea of having to look for her in the dark if she should trip and fall on the rocks or prickly shrubs; likewise, the threat of night predators always presented a risk outside the safe ring of the campfire. When he saw she headed in a direction opposite to the one he'd thought she would take, toward a cluster of thick undergrowth and rocks, he quietly called out, "Not that way. Go to the other side of the wagon and come right back." He hoped she didn't plan on making this a nighttime ritual.

Christa scurried out of view, as swift as a little white ghost, and Derek let a long-contained breath of relief escape. Had he had his back turned to her, she could have come up behind him and spied the map. Then she might have told her ma.

He would need to be more careful.

The chill air seeped into his bones, and he laid his bedroll close to the fire and slipped inside. But Derek didn't close his eyes until he saw the young'un crawl back inside the wagon and felt sure everyone remained where they were supposed to be.

Even then, he couldn't shake the disquiet that unfurled in his gut at the prospect that hit him: leading the feisty widow and her two carefree girls across this wilderness and keeping them safe would be a much more difficult task than he'd first supposed.

And by no stretch of the imagination had he assumed it would be easy.

Chapter 5

The following day went much like the first. Endless clumps of sagebrush hindered travel, and at times, Olivia needed to clear the path of small rocks so the wagon could roll forward. Whenever Penny spotted a familiar plant or flower she needed, she sent Christa ahead to Derek to make a request that they stop.

Not all the vegetation Penny used was for food. Some made good healing teas and poultices, while she used the seeds of other plants as colorful beadwork for her pouches. Of all her tasks, she enjoyed the beadwork most. Images of graceful birds within patterned circles she had stitched with cobalt and yellow seeds onto her own deerskin moccasins, and the girls' footwear she'd also ornamented with similar colors in geometric patterns. Only half a pouch of the precious glass beads for which her father had traded his pelts remained, and she reserved those for a special occasion.

Besides the beadwork, Penny's mother had instructed her in what she herself had been taught—that the natives saw the land as one of promise, with each plant and rock significant to daily life. Penny's grandmother, a convert to Christianity, had taught Penny's mother, "Our Father who lives above the clouds created all things for us to survive what my people call tomes, the 'sky motions'; what the Taibonii, the white man, call years. Importance and beauty lies in each cactus; from some we find water for our thirst. . .from each plant, every one with its own purpose. . .from each hill and rock, many which provide cover from our enemies. Even the bones of the creatures of this land serve as tools to aid us. . . ."

Almost able to hear her mother's soft instruction like a faint echo in her head, Penny looked toward a group of high, rocky hills in the distance, an ample area behind which a war party could lie in wait. The sagebrush-covered slopes seemed to radiate the sheen of heat, and at times she thought she saw a flash of light near the top. An arrow? A gun? Or just sunlight hitting the ore in the rocks? She shivered despite the heat and hoped no enemy lurked nearby. . . .

"Mama, please tell me a story," Christa pleaded from the wagon seat beside her. Since she'd woken up that day, Christa had been wan and listless, and Penny had insisted she ride instead of walk.

She thought a moment, putting aside her own discomfort. "What would you like to hear?"

"Tell me about where we come from. I like to hear that."

"First you must have another sip of water."

This time Christa didn't balk at the taste but took from Penny her da's ancient water container made from a buffalo bladder and obeyed without comment.

"My mother's father—your great-grandfather—was a French Canadian trapper who proved himself trustworthy to the Shoshone, my grandmother's people."

"Kimama?"

"Aye, her name was Kimama. My grandfather traded furs with her people for many years before I was born. During the time he lived with the tribe, he and Kimama married."

"He was a peacemaker? That's what Livvie said."

"Olivia is right. He wished only for peace. When the troubles came, he listened to both sides—the white men and the Shoshone. Once settlers began to move west, many of my grandmother's people feared what would happen to them and their ability to live as they always had. Your grandfather tried to act as a peacemaker, and my da was no different. They met long ago while both were trapping and became friends. Both men understood the concerns of each side and tried to help as long as they lived. Your great-grandfather died in his sleep, six years after my mother, Haiwee."

Penny recalled how, feeling helpless to do more than lend an ear or a nugget of advice when asked, both her da and grandfather had lamented the situation to her mother. Both men had been gifted with the ability to listen and understand. Her mother had also been able to reason and knew peace throughout her life no matter the hardship. But Penny had difficulty seeing the bigger picture, much less understanding the motives of men.

She wiped beads of sweat from her brow with her sleeve and lifted the container to her own lips. Taking a short draft of the warm and brackish river water, she nonetheless felt grateful for the liquid that wet her tongue, then handed the container to her daughter, again ordering her to do the same.

"Ma'am?"

Startled out of hazy reflection, Penny looked away from a distant boulder resembling a skull to the opposite side of the wagon. Their escort had ridden back without her being aware. He studied her from beneath his hat, as though he couldn't quite figure her out. "You feeling all right?"

"Aye, Mr. Burke. You wished to speak with me?" She managed the question with as much dignity as her dust-caked lips could muster. A dry, hot wind had blown most of the afternoon, and she imagined a goodly portion of the high desert's earth stuck to her face as it did to Christa's. Always a stickler for cleanliness, she could scarcely tolerate the thought.

He studied Penny a moment as though doubting her well-being. Despite the ache in her back from the constant pull of the reins for hours on end, she managed to jut her chin up a little higher and square her shoulders, not wanting him to think her weak and in need of special treatment.

"I'm fine," she stated with quiet emphasis.

He offered a short, distant nod, and she wondered if he felt as light in the head as she did. The day had been hotter than others before it.

"All the same, we'll make camp here," he said. "Not that much light left in the sky."

Penny looked west, noting the sun had dipped lower. She figured they had little more than an hour of daylight remaining to cook the sage hen their guide had shot earlier, the feathers of which Olivia now plucked as she sat in the back of the wagon. Between Olivia's ability with the slingshot and Derek's skill with a gun, along with what flour and cornmeal and other staples she'd brought, Penny should keep them all well fed. As for water, if the need arose, they could find that from a barrel cactus, when and if they came upon them. She'd heard tales of how her da and grandfather once traveled southwest, and to quench their thirst, they'd needed to hack the top off one of the spiny plants with a hatchet—a skill learned while her grandfather lived among the Shoshone. She'd never attempted the feat but could direct Derek in doing so.

He'd proven himself strong and quite smart, like her da and grandfather had been. He made an excellent hunter and showed patience with her girls, who could be trying in the best of times. Still, she knew so little about him.

Her mouth flickered at the corners with the recollection of their first meeting, when she and her small pair had gotten the better of Derek Burke and he'd surrendered on his knees with his hands in the air. Given what she now knew of his intellect paired with his skills, she imagined few had been awarded such a sight. Much less been allowed the opportunity to best him.

He watched her, his horse keeping deliberate pace with her wagon. "Something peculiar with what I said?"

"What? Oh no. I agree; this is as fine a place as any. To make camp," she added when he continued to study her.

"You have a queer sort of look on your face. As if you were a mite touched in the head. You sure you're feeling all right?"

Touched in the head? Really! Before he could inquire further and make the situation worse, Penny reined to a stop and called out to the back of the wagon, "Olivia, bring the bird to me so I can get dinner started, then gather some greasewood so Mr. Burke can start a fire. We're making camp here. Mr. Burke?" she challenged lightly as she again turned to him.

He squinted, still indisputably curious, small lines fanning from the corners of his eyes. He tipped his hat. "Ma'am."

Penny tied off the reins and watched their guide dismount from his horse with nimble ease. He wasn't the only one brimming with curiosity.

On hindsight, she'd been foolish to entrust their lives to a near stranger, though she felt her instincts correct and he wasn't a man to be feared. Still, Penny wished to know more about this man who led them, and she no longer felt she could dam the questions from gushing forth.

She took another swig of gritty water from her container, wishing for the sweet, fresh liquid of the stream by her old homestead. Despite the fact she boiled what they drank to prevent sickness, it didn't help the taste. Leaving had been the sensible thing to do, she assured herself as she'd done every day when faced with yet another hardship. Perhaps she felt woozy because she'd allotted herself only small sips all day, giving the greater part to Christa. And Olivia had their other container to drink from. At least she still perspired; her da had warned her that when a man ceased doing that, he could take it as a sign he neared death. They'd passed so many scattered graves of emigrants and bleached bones of livestock along this trail. . . .

"Enough of yer frettin', Penelope MacPhearson! No daughter of mine nor yer dear mither's be a weakling. And you're stronger than most: ye have the blood of warriors— Scots and Shoshone—coursing through yer veins. Be of a mind to remember that and remember it well!"

She heard her beloved da's stern reprimand wing through her mind as though many years had not elapsed since childhood, when she'd faced a challenge she'd been fearful to tackle. Her da only called her by her given name, not the cherished nickname he'd coined for her, when angered by her hesitancy to confront something she must, and she'd made certain he didn't often have cause to call her Penelope.

With disgust, she shook herself from gloomy thoughts of the grave and stepped down from the wagon, careful to move slowly so as not to fall. Both she and her daughters would be fine. And tonight, while the cool of the evening settled around them and she felt more lucid, she would put her plan into action and find out what she could about their taciturn guide.

❧

"Mr. Burke, have you an idea of how long it should take us to reach Carson City?"

Puzzled, Derek eyed the young Widow Crawder. At least her skin had taken on a healthier hue and didn't look as faded as before; he'd been half afraid she would keel over once they'd stopped to make camp.

Hadn't they had this conversation before? Or maybe one of her daughters had asked. The three Crawder females did like to talk. Still, he had the oddest feeling by the remote manner in which she posed her question that their timing for reaching Carson City wasn't all that lay in the front of her mind.

"My guess, it should take at least two weeks, maybe more. Assuming we don't come up against any quandaries to set us back." As often as they stopped for plant cuttings, it could take them more like a month!

"Hmm." She gave a vague nod. "Have you ever been out this far west, Mr. Burke? Or farther? Past the Sierra Nevada range and on into California, perhaps?"

Bent over the kettle, she seemed intent on preparing their meal, but he doubted the conversation was as casual as she made it appear. "As a matter of fact, I've been to California."

"Really? Out panning for gold or looking for silver?"

At her mention of the prized metal, he narrowed his eyes, wondering if she'd somehow figured out his secret. "Neither. Most of that's been found, I reckon."

Propping his knee up, he leaned against the tall wagon wheel, the iron rim digging into his shoulder, and nudged the brim of his hat back as he watched her. She continued her task as if she hadn't noticed his unease, and he came to the conclusion that she didn't mean any harm. He supposed she couldn't help it if she was the sort to pry and decided to satisfy a portion of her curiosity. Anything to get her mind off the subject of silver.

"Before coming here, I worked for the railroad. They're laying tracks for expansion through the West. The Union Pacific and Central Pacific are in Utah Territory now, after working from opposite ends of the country to join together. I expect it'll happen any day. I overheard word that each of the leaders plan to take turns driving a golden spike into the final tie." He withheld a chuckle as he recalled the effort it took to lift and swing the sledgehammer to hit the small head of the spike dead center, and wondered if the pampered, well-to-do gentlemen had the strength in them.

"Well, now, that's a pure waste of gold if ever I heard it." She frowned and tasted the stew with a wooden spoon, then threw more of some plant she'd crushed with her hand into the kettle.

"You don't approve of progress?" he guessed.

"My husband wasn't in favor of people losing their homes for progress's sake, and neither am I. We learned from strangers traveling through that settlers were duty bound to leave their homesteads or suffer the consequences—since the surveyors claimed the railroad's best course was to lay track through their land. Supposedly, the railroad tycoons paid them well for their losses, but I don't condone the idea of forcing people off their land. The same thing happened to my grandmother's people, you'll recall, and in a sense to me. Stealing is stealing, plain and simple, and it's just wrong, no matter what government official says otherwise."

He stared, not offering a response to her impassioned words. Her face washed to a bright shade of rose.

"I imagine you're not accustomed to a woman speaking her mind or being knowledgeable about the politics of the day? My husband and father often conversed on civil matters around the dinner table, encouraging me to join in their conversations."

"Truth be told, ma'am, I'm not accustomed to consorting with womenfolk at all. Except, of course, for those women—matrons most of them—who ran boardinghouses or bathhouses in the towns I rode through. And those who fed me. I haven't had a sociable connection with a female in a long time."

"What about your mother? You don't communicate with her?"

Her words, gentle and curious, didn't seem to probe but did hope for an answer. Again he chose to ease her curiosity.

"She died several years back."

"And your father?"

"He's long been gone from my life." His words came out terser than he meant them.

"I see. I didn't mean to intrude."

He doubted her claim, but she didn't see his skepticism. She dished out stew and handed it to him, then ladled out three more servings for her and her girls. "So, tell me, what's it really like being a drifter?"

Olivia and Christa quit sketching pictures in the dirt with rocks and collected their dinner, claiming places on the ground on either side of Derek. He was a bit surprised at how often the two sought a spot near him, sometimes saying nothing at all, other times chock full of chatter, and he felt a mite uneasy for the same reasons. He wasn't accustomed to young'uns or their conversation and often didn't know how to respond. Much like now with their ma.

"What's it like?" he repeated her question. He had no idea where this was heading and wasn't sure he wanted to know.

"Yes, I mean, I've never known a drifter. My da was one for a time, I suppose, till he put down roots and married my mother. But of course, I never knew him in his drifting days, and I've often wondered. My grandmother's people were nomadic, drifting from place to place before they went to settle on the land the U.S. government gave them. But of course, they did so with their families. Never alone."

"Well. . ." Derek pondered a moment on how best to describe his life. "I have the stars for company and soft grass for a bed when I'm not bunked in a hotel in some town, if I'm lucky. I guess you could say the world is my threshold."

"That's really quite poetic," she said with some surprise, as if assuming he'd never held a book in his hands. He may not often have a pretty way with words, but his ma had drilled him in his studies and read to him from her esteemed collection of books during his boyhood days. He figured part of that must have stuck.

"I imagine the days are lonely with no one to share them with," she continued. "I can't imagine living such a life of solitude."

The days had been lonely, but he wouldn't admit it to her. "I never thought much about it. I'm not all that sociable if you'll recall." He ate a good helping of stew.

"So you've said, but I find that hard to believe. You carry on a conversation well when you've the inclination to do so." She paused for a spoonful of her own stew. "Was there no special woman in your past, one who could've changed your mind?"

He managed to swallow what slid down his throat without choking at her forthright question. Lowering the bowl, he squinted at her, wondering what track her mind had taken this time. "None that appealed enough to make me want to change my course and put down roots—no."

"*Tsk*. That's too bad. I suppose, living the life of a lone drifter, you never reach a stopping point, do you? You just drift about aimlessly throughout the countryside with no true destination in mind."

"I suppose." He took no offense at her soft, probing remark, since to a degree it did ring true.

"And I imagine that, being a drifter, you've had plenty a job besides working for the railroad?"

He pursed his lips and nodded thoughtfully. "I imagine I have."

She gave a soft little grunt, as if frustrated when he offered no further comment. "Aye, well, do you care to be enlightenin' me as to what they were?"

He studied her flushed face, not answering, and she set her empty tin on the ground with a slight bang. He was surprised she'd found time to eat what had been inside.

"Or I suppose we could just sit here and pass the rest of the evening in silence, staring at the wee cactus," she suggested with a wry twist of her lips.

"Yep, we could do that, too."

Derek pursed his lips in a half smile at her stiff remark and decided to play along to see just how far she would take this. Oddly enough, he no longer felt threatened by her endless supply of questions. He had associated with a few women years ago, nothing serious and too long ago to recount well; he'd been a wild young colt visiting the saloon in each town before he'd wised up and quit spending what money he didn't send home on shots of whiskey and cards. But he'd never met a woman like this one, a lady not the least bit intimidated to speak her mind. She captivated him, and he didn't mind looking into those flashing, golden brown eyes of hers as long as she aimed to keep talking—though he wondered if she planned to carry on with this bizarre exchange through nightfall.

The little girls rose to their feet and wandered away, clearly bored with listening to their elders' stilted discussion and in need of other amusement.

"I, for one, prefer conversation, Mr. Burke," Penny said. "I haven't had a good fireside talk with either man or woman in too long to remember."

"Given such circumstances, I'd say that's understandable."

"Is it now? It's understandable. Well then, let's have a go at it, shall we?"

"I figured that's what we were doing."

At his calm, measured words, she lifted her hands in the air. "Och! This is your idea of holding pleasant conversation? I call it more of a cat-and-mouse game you're playing with me, and I'd like this twaddle to cease and to gain solid answers to my questions."

"Why?"

"Why?" She appeared as surprised as he'd felt by her quiet outburst. "You're our guide. I should know more about you."

"Your lack of knowledge regarding my history didn't seem to bother you before when you begged for my help in your barn." The memory of her softness pressed against him when he thought he'd caught a wrongdoer made him lower his gaze to her slight form without thought. He looked up into her eyes again. By the manner in which her lips slightly parted, he wondered if she recalled that moment, too.

"'Pleasant conversation' aside, why don't you tell me the real reason for your curiosity, Mrs. Crawder. Why all the questions?"

"I. . ."

For once, the lady seemed tongue-tied.

"Real reason, indeed! I was desperate that night." She glanced at her lap, smoothing her skirt with her hands. "I've had time to think matters through since then."

"If you're uneasy with my company, I'll go."

"No!"

At her emphatic response, he lifted his eyebrows in surprise.

"I mean. . .that's not what I intended when I said what I did. That you should leave us."

"Then mind tellin' me exactly what you did intend?"

She cleared her throat and fidgeted, plucking at a fold of her skirt. "Only that since we're taking this journey through this wilderness—together—I think it wise if we know more about one another. Don't you?"

Derek held off answering, uncertain what she wanted him to say. He'd told her about his job at the railroad, about his ma, and even answered her question about his pa. That was personal, wasn't it? More than he'd told the men he'd worked side by side with every day. He sensed something other than curiosity settled beneath the exterior of her words, and he wasn't sure he would like it.

"In my travels, I've learned there's an unwritten code pertaining to the West." He kept his eyes and voice steady. "A man doesn't ask questions about his neighbor's past or nose into his affairs or goods—and the two are bound to get along just fine."

"Well then," she said, her chin lifting a notch, her uneasy twiddling coming to a stop. " 'Tis a good thing I'm a woman and not a man, so I don't have to abide by such a silly code."

His lips flickered into a smile, and he pursed them to quell it, deciding it best not to air his agreement. For the first time since they'd started this journey, he could admit appreciation for having Penny as his travel companion—and for more than just meals. She could be maddening at times, but her quick wit entertained while her intelligence made for good company. And the pleasurable sight of her womanliness didn't disappoint, either.

Before Derek could form a reply that she just might find tolerable, a terrified scream from one of her girls cut through the descending twilight.

Chapter 6

Thunderstruck, Penny stared at Derek a split second before knowledge fully hit that one of her girls needed help. She shot up from the ground at the same time he did. His hand went to one of the guns in his holster as they both ran around the wagon and toward the scream, Derek taking the lead.

"Livvie!" Near a piling of small rocks and prickly brush, Penny caught a glimpse of her daughter moving backward. She appeared free of blood and in one piece. "Whatever is the matter?"

"Mama!" Olivia's weak cry offered nothing more as she kept a clumsy and fast pace in retreat. Her gaze never left the ground. Christa stared at Olivia from several feet away, eyes big with fear. Before Penny could grasp the problem, Olivia's heel caught against a rock. She stumbled and fell, then screamed a second time, her apprehensive stare never leaving the pale dirt. For the first time, Penny saw something on the ground dart toward her daughter, who screamed a second time.

"Roll to the side, Olivia!" Derek yelled, bending to grab a fist-size rock. She did, and to Penny's alarm, he threw the rock inches from Olivia, who scuttled backward on her hands and feet. Puffs of dry soil wafted up at the impact.

Olivia scrambled up and ran to Penny, throwing her arms around her and burying her face against her bosom. Instinctively, Penny wrapped her arms around her trembling child. She watched Derek hurry to the spot where the rock landed and kick it aside, then stomp on something with the sole of his boot, grinding it with his heel.

"Did you get stung?" he asked, looking over his shoulder at Olivia.

She shook her head no, tightening her hold around Penny's waist.

"A scorpion," Derek explained to Penny.

Horrified, she broke away from Olivia with a hushed reassurance and moved closer to make certain the creature no longer posed a threat to her children. In the fading light, she noted the brown peril was about the size of her little finger, with its segmented tail now separated from its body, thanks to Derek's boot. The same lightheadedness she'd earlier felt seeped over her at the thought of one of her precious girls sprawled within inches of the vicious dirt dweller. She'd heard a scorpion's sting could be lethal to one so small, or at the very least the victim would be in such excruciating pain they'd wish they were dead. . . .

"Whoa now." Derek's voice came low. His hand went to the other side of her waist and he pulled her close to his side. "Easy there."

He spoke to her as if to an unbroken filly, but she didn't take offense. Penny placed her hand on his chest near his shoulder and worked to regain steadiness in her mind and limbs.

"Olivia's fine," he reassured. "Nothing happened."

She glanced toward Olivia, whom Christa now hugged fiercely.

"I was trying to get some rocks to practice with for my slingshot," Olivia explained as if knowing she'd be asked, her eyes on Penny. "When I turned over that big one, that thing came running from under it toward me. It ran so fast."

"Scorpions can be fast." The words rumbled in Derek's chest, the vibrations they made soothing against Penny, though his message evoked caution. "Best to be more careful from now on. Try not to pick up any rocks larger than a pebble."

"I will," Olivia promised. "Thank you, Mr. Burke."

"Glad to help."

"Aye, thank you." Penny stepped away from Derek, confused by her heart's strange reaction, skipping beats, and the way her breath caught in her throat. She felt even more perplexed that she missed his warm strength and wanted to retrace that step back into his arms to be held by him a moment longer. There she'd felt safe, an emotion she hadn't felt in a long while. To cover her confusion, she took charge.

"Girls, get on back to the wagon and ready yourselves for bed," she ordered, thankful to find her voice again. "The scare is over."

"Yes, Mama." Both girls ran for the wagon.

"You all right?" Derek asked when Penny remained fixed. She sensed his gaze intent on her face; however, she couldn't look at him, not with her emotions still in a whirl.

" 'Twas a momentary spell. Rather inane when I think of the many hardships we've faced. I've encountered scorpions before. And to react so strongly at such an occurrence when all worked out well in the end—well, that was foolish. I've never come so close to swooning in my life."

"Don't take on so," he soothed. "I expect every man or woman has that staggering moment when they come up against the unexpected and it knocks their feet right out from under them. I imagine the heat today didn't help matters, either. It takes time to get accustomed to traveling in it. Have you been drinking water?"

"Aye." She wondered if he'd forgotten this was her home. True, four days away and not as barren as the land through which they now traveled, and she'd possessed a roof to give her shelter from the unforgiving sun, though it had seldom been as hot. Nonetheless, it was a land with which she was familiar.

The rest of the evening passed without occasion. After she'd cleaned up from supper and stored the utensils, she returned the small crate to the wagon. Her gaze went past her sleeping children to the trunk that took up a third of the wagon bed; it had taken all three of them to load it, and they'd had to empty it beforehand. Penny thought a moment, then grabbed the lantern hanging outside the wagon, climbed within the shielding canvas, and pulled up the heavy lid.

With care, she lifted a fold of her mother's wedding dress from the trunk, admiring the intricate beadwork that both her grandmother and mother had sewn at the neck and hem. Symbols that told her mother's story and of meeting Penny's father, symbols of happiness for their future. She pulled the dress all the way out, and a fall of the soft, tanned deerskin poured down in light brown folds to her lap. Her fingertips rested over one rectangle of many in the cobalt, green, and white seed and stone beads, and her mind wandered as it had often done of late.

A long time had elapsed since she'd felt or behaved like a woman with a woman's soft qualities; she wondered if any such traits still existed inside her. For what seemed endless months, she had needed to assume the fierce, protective, and fighting characteristics of a man and taken on a man's job to protect what was hers. In the process, she felt her womanliness had dissolved. Had her da or husband been alive, she doubted they would even recognize her. She'd been astounded when Derek referred to her as a lady on their first day of traveling together.

Penny thought about their quiet guide and the odd desire she experienced to be near him. She had long hoped for a God-fearing, faithful companion, a hard worker, someone to become a good father to her girls, and had made the request for months in prayer. She'd loved her husband, but time dulled the pain of losing him and helped her to let go. She felt prepared not only to accept the notion of marrying again but also to picture her future with another man. The more she learned of Derek Burke—however difficult the task to piece together such information—the less she believed any man other than Derek could take the place of Oliver.

She'd heard tales from her father of God-fearing men and women who married for convenience's sake, some barely knowing the other. Some men sent for brides from the East, sight unseen. With that knowledge, she didn't discount the possibility of a union despite their scant time together. But Derek made it clear he planned to remain a drifter, more or less stating flat out that he didn't have it in his mind to settle down with any woman. Could she change his heart to reconsider the idea? Did she truly wish to? Or were such ideas nonsense and too soon in their acquaintance to broach or even ponder?

"What's that you're holding, Mama?" Olivia questioned.

Surprised, Penny looked her daughter's way. "I thought you were asleep."

Olivia's tousled, dark braids swept her nightdress, one falling over her shoulder to the small of her back as she rose to sit in the cramped wagon. "The light got in my eyes when they was shut, but I couldn't sleep anyhow."

"Were shut." Recalling her daughter's earlier scare, Penny wasn't surprised. She noticed Christa's face bore a slight smile as she slumbered like an angel curled up beside Olivia and felt grateful that one of her children invited sweet dreams. Her gaze returned to the velvety cloth in her lap. "This was your grandmother's dress. She wore it for her wedding and other special occasions."

"Did you wear it when you married Papa?"

"No, I made another." Penny's remark came distant, her mind still wrapped up in Derek.

"Why didn't you wear this one? It's so pretty."

"Aye." She couldn't explain to her daughter that Oliver's parents had never accepted her because of her heritage. Out of respect to Oliver, she'd foregone wearing to the ceremony anything native that might provoke disapproval from them, but often since then, she'd regretted her decision.

"You going to wear it tomorrow?"

"What?" Penny looked at her eldest daughter in surprise.

"You should wear it, Mama. It would look nice on you."

"This isn't a dress one would wear to travel through the wilds."

"Why not?"

Why not, indeed!

"Mr. Burke might think it's pretty, too."

Christa giggled, and Penny sent a sharp glance her way. Her youngest child had one eye opened and quickly shut it.

"So, Christabel Louise, are you playing possum, too?" Penny asked, deciding to ignore Olivia's last comment.

"Playing possum?" Christa pushed herself up to sit beside her sister.

"What your grandda said to me when I was your age. It means pretending to sleep."

"I did try—honest." She covered her mouth with her hand to smother another giggle.

"Of course you did," Penny agreed with mock sternness, doubting it. She imagined both girls had been whispering together as they often did at night. Yet this night, she would not scold. This night felt oddly different, as if a strange weight of import had come to rest on her shoulders. Catching sight of the sacred book in her trunk, she thought she understood in part and resolved to resume a lost tradition in full.

She folded the dress, setting it back in its sheltered place, and pulled out the book. "Do you girls know what this is?"

Christa shook her head no, and Olivia drew closer to peer at the leather-bound cover.

"You don't recall when your papa would read to you from the Holy Bible?"

"I remember," Olivia answered quietly.

"Aye, you did love to sit at his knee." Penny sighed with bittersweet fondness at the mental image her words evoked. "This belonged to my mother. My da sent for it from back East during a trip to town. He taught my mother to read from these pages just as a parson's wife taught him from one similar when he was newly come from Edinburgh to Boston as a youth. He stayed with the parson and his wife for a time. Not many people then or now receive the privilege of such instruction—to read and write. And sadly others, though they can read, never learn the words from this book. My parents were two of the fortunate ones, and what they taught me, I now teach you."

The girls' eyes widened as Penny spoke, and they each gave a solemn nod.

She opened the cover and caressed the thin, onionskin-like page with tender remembrance. A dried flower stem stuck out from between the bottom of some pages, and she turned to that section of the New Testament. She couldn't recall having seen the stem before or how it got there, and wondered if it had been her mother's. "I want to renew the tradition of reading from this book each night. I think it would be pleasing to God, and we should strive to please Him in all that we do. We want to start out our new life as it should be." *And should have been all along.*

Penny had attempted to carry on with the readings after Oliver died, and for a while she had succeeded. But the cares of the world weighed upon her, until one evening she forgot to retrieve the Bible from its place in her trunk. With the difficulties that continued to beset her daily, forgetting had become easier with the passage of time.

Forgive me, Father, for disobeying Your Word and not keeping up the custom of sharing with my girls what lies within Your Holy Book.

After issuing her silent prayer, she drew the kerosene lamp close. It would probably be wisest to conserve oil and use the dawn's light to read the tiny print, and after this night, she planned to do just that. But now that she'd retrieved the family Bible from her trunk and the pages lay open, she didn't wish to put it off any longer. A long-fermented seed of eagerness sprouted within her heart to again turn its pages and look upon the stirring words. She instructed her girls to lie down but to keep their eyes open.

"This isn't a bedtime tale," she explained while they did as they were told. "Not one like your grandda told you, before he went to live in glory. There are accounts of adventure within, 'tis true, much like your grandda's stories were—but this is the Almighty God's Word and His message. It's important you not only hear these words but that you act on them so your life will be blessed."

"Yes, Mama," her daughters said one after the other. Their brown eyes big and full of curious anticipation, they again pulled the quilt of hides over them as they prepared to listen.

In a low, soothing voice, Penny read the page on which the dried flower marker rested, figuring it as good a place as any to start. She read to them parables that Jesus Christ told. But when she reached the Lord's instruction to forgive a man seventy times seven, she grew troubled and ended the reading.

The girls' eyes were heavy-lidded as she smoothed their hair and kissed them good night, each of them soon falling into trouble-free slumber.

However, her burden did not ease.

❧

Derek watched the back of the wagon where Penny had disappeared, no longer interested in his map. It told him nothing he needed from the day's travel, and again he speculated on whether he'd been fooled into some wild goose chase for a nonexistent fortune in silver.

He recalled Penny's words, muted but understandable, as she'd read to her girls just like his ma had done with him when he was a boy. He'd recognized the stories and felt a sweet nostalgia upon hearing them again, remembering how his ma chided him when she'd caught him in some mischief and often compared his misdeeds to one of the parables Jesus taught. At one point, Derek had begun to think of himself as the prodigal son, though he wasn't the one who'd left home—his pa had done that. But as often as his ma recounted that story, he'd figured she was trying to get some sort of message across.

A stir at the canvas brought his attention from the fire where it had wandered, back to the wagon. Hurriedly, he folded the map sections and tucked them inside his buckskin jacket under one of his suspenders as the Widow Crawder climbed down from the wagon bed. She looked his way, as if uncertain, before approaching him.

"I want to express my thanks once more for what you did for Olivia," she explained.

"Well, ma'am." He rose to stand, a bit embarrassed by all the fuss she made out of the incident. "Isn't that what you hired me for? As an extra gun for protection?"

"Aye. Be that as it may, when I asked you to join us and thought of the girls needing protection, I had in mind the two-legged variety of predator, not the. . .

however many-legged thing that vile creature was. I never stopped to consider that the dangers are unending no matter how careful we are." She looked off to the side in the direction of a black mass of hills that blocked out part of the nighttime sky as if trying to search out the answers to her problems there.

After a moment, she cleared her throat, returning her attention to him. "Also, I want to say. . .that is, I wish to tell you. . ." She took a deep breath and rolled her glance up to the stars, clearly ill at ease. "I wish to apologize for prying into your affairs yet again. Three times I've done so, and I haven't the right. 'Tis a fact, one shouldn't judge a man by his past, as my da used to say. . .whatever your past may be. So it is irrelevant. You've proven to me twice over that you're a man who can be trusted."

He studied her, mystified as to what she had in mind now. "I appreciate the apology, but there's no need. I wouldn't have told you anything if I hadn't wanted to."

She blinked. "Oh. All right then. Well, I'll be wishing you a pleasant evening, Mr. Burke." She nodded a hasty farewell and turned to go, then turned around, her motion as swift. "One last matter, then I'll be leavin' you to your. . . whatever you may have been doing. Not that I'm asking." She paused to allow a response, but when he offered none, she cleared her throat and continued. "Aye, well, I plan to read to the girls from the Bible of a morning before we break the fast, and I'd like to issue an invitation for you to join us. Only if you'd care to attend; I'm not forcing the matter."

"Thank you, ma'am. I'll consider it."

Derek watched her retrace her steps to her wagon and wondered if she considered him a soul in need of reforming and if that had been the driving force behind her sudden invitation. He feared God but didn't trust Him, nor did he believe God cared anything about him. And he doubted if the Widow Crawder could change his mind in that regard. Even so, he supposed it would be impolite to decline her charitable, if awkward, offer. Besides, likely nothing existed in the Good Book that he hadn't heard his mother tell him before.

Chapter 7

The miles of tedium progressed, and their sightings of game diminished. With no meat, Penny made do with johnnycakes cooked in her three-legged, cast-iron spider. What stores remained of flour, coffee, and other staples had been acquired during Oliver's trip into Silverton last year, and she hoped to replenish her supplies once she arrived in Carson City—or perhaps at a trading post if they came across a town. At least the blisters on her fingers from holding the reins had toughened, and she felt thankful for small blessings.

Each morning, Penny read a chapter aloud from the Bible. She'd decided against doing so before breakfast, with the hope that everyone could then concentrate on the readings and not the rumblings in their stomachs. Nevertheless, Derek still seemed jittery when she read, and she wondered if he didn't often get a chance to hear the Good Book's wisdom. Or perhaps he felt uncomfortable standing for so long in respect for the occasion. No matter, Penny couldn't place blame. She should have furthered her girls' spiritual instruction instead of distancing herself from God. On this journey through nowhere, she felt as if she was once more beginning to find Him.

On the seventh morning, they reached a bluff and had to leave the river behind to take a cutoff. For what seemed like endless miles, they traveled up and down some of the steepest and most stony terrain Penny had ever encountered. At times, she wasn't sure the horses could manage the hills, and Derek needed to lead her team on foot, his horse tied to the wagon.

Through her da's tales, she'd learned of the cutoff and also that an additional day's journey would bring them to a canyon with a treasure. Not silver or even gold. But instead, hidden at the edge of a hill, a sheltered pool of heated water bubbled up from beneath the earth, protected from the sun's rays.

At this point, any water would be welcome water, even hot.

Finally, they came to a spring that, although fresh, turned out to be muddy. Seeing no feed for the horses, they rested only long enough for Penny to collect and boil water for their containers and for the horses to take their fill from the watering place. They traveled another few miles and returned to the river where, exhausted, they stayed the night.

∽

Long before the rising sun glazed the rocks with vibrant rose, Penny awoke, weary but determined, and set to work making breakfast. Grateful to note the cloud banks to the west, thicker than the wispy trails of the past week, she hoped they would act as a shield against the sun since she doubted they would produce rain. The land seldom received it.

While the wagon rolled forward along the plain, her mind revisited former years. She replayed memorable events: the happy ones when she'd married Oliver and given birth to each of her children, and the most tragic moments when she'd buried her stillborn son and two years later her husband, after bites from a rattlesnake had killed him. Even if she'd reached Oliver in time, she doubted she could have saved him with her plant cures.

Her father's lilting words came back to her in the midst of her sorrowful daydream: *"Ye need t' get a grip on the reins o' your life, lassie, no matter which way the trail takes you. Yer the only one who can."*

That was what she was trying to do, wasn't she? Guide their destiny rather than sit on the outskirts and let the future be wrested from her hands? At times, she could convince herself of that, but at night as she tried to sleep while the distant, wavering howls of coyotes sounded far beyond their camp, her heart accused her of giving up and letting *them* win. And when that happened, the old fears and bitterness she kept buried deep inside festered like a poison, the pain so intense she thought her heart might stop.

What made her think life would be any different in Carson City? Had she been rash to sweep her girls away from what had been home for more than ten years?

"No matter; what's done is done," she assured herself under her breath, using her da's words. Some semblance of law must abide in such a large city, contrary to what Derek led her to believe. Surely a widow with two small children wouldn't be preyed upon, robbed, or harmed in an attempt to run them out of house and home. Her recent troubles of the hatred and bias they'd endured from a select few heathens settled like a thick, noxious brew in her throat, as if to strangle her.

"Mama, did you say something?" Christa asked from the wagon seat beside her.

"Hand me the water container, please."

Her daughter took the buffalo skin from her lap and offered it to her ma.

Taking in slow, deep breaths to try to ease the lump in her throat, then a sip of water when that didn't reduce it, Penny resolved to forget the pile of ruins that cluttered the life she'd left. Instead, she would concentrate on the flicker of hope that beckoned her forward to a future in Carson City. It was the only right thing to do: leave her troubles behind. Why, then, didn't that knowledge alleviate her every qualm?

Morning passed into afternoon, and afternoon into early evening, until finally they reached the canyon as the sun began its gradual drop to the western horizon.

"Christa, do you see how the rocks and sagebrush form at the top of those hills to look like horns and eyes? It brings to mind a buffalo head." Another landmark about which her da had told her.

"Do you think I'll see a buffalo some day? Maybe in Carson City?"

Penny glanced at her youngest. "Maybe." The buffalo had long disappeared from this part of the land, killed off in droves; Penny hadn't seen one since she was Christa's age.

Engrossed in thought, she almost missed the huge gray boulders of cliff that rose from the ground, one almost rectangular like a door, the other two cut out of the hill to angle on either side and atop it. "Three Leaning Rocks" her da had called it. A thread of sentimentality to know her father once camped here wove around Penny, making her feel close to him.

She looked at her daughter, noting her flushed cheeks. "Are you feeling any better?"

Christa nodded. "My stomach doesn't hurt no more."

"Anymore." Penny smiled. "Please tell Mr. Burke I'd like to stop here for the night." She hoped Derek would agree. From the sun's position in the sky, they still had an hour or so before they usually made camp.

Christa slipped off the slow-moving wagon to the ground and scampered to where Derek rode about fifteen feet ahead. He also looked to the right, to the outcropping of rocks. As Christa delivered Penny's message, he turned to her girl for the brief moment it took to answer, then looked back at the three rocks.

Penny wondered what about them he found so fascinating. They were rocks like any other; only she guessed what lay beyond that hill.

Christa scampered back to the wagon. "He said that would be fine."

"Good. Now go check if Olivia's caught anything." Christa ran to the back of the wagon, and Penny drew her team to a halt. She kept quiet as they made camp and noticed Derek's frequent glances of puzzlement turned her way mixed with what appeared to be a measure of concern. Her frequent ponderings had triggered a personal melancholy she couldn't seem to shake.

"Mama." Olivia cradled her arm, walking up to Penny as she unpacked utensils from the box. "I'm sorry I didn't catch the rabbit I saw. And now I can't catch anything. It hurts to hold my slingshot."

"What did you do to yourself, Livvie?" Penny held her daughter's arm up for observation, noting the reddish bruise on her forearm and wrist.

"I was running after a rabbit, and I fell." Olivia's face was downcast as if she'd committed some grievous blunder.

"That's all right, love." She pressed her palm against Olivia's cheek. " 'Tis a wee bit swollen, but only bruised, not broken. I'll make a salve for the pain. And it certainly won't hurt us to have another evening without meat."

Olivia didn't look convinced. "Maybe Mr. Burke will go and hunt us up something?" she suggested hopefully. Penny knew her daughter wasn't fond of the johnnycakes prepared with flour and water. They didn't hold together well and tasted bland, even with salt.

"I'm sure he would if we ask, but we shouldn't trouble him. He's done enough."

"What shouldn't you trouble me about?" Derek came up behind them, almost startling Penny out of her skin. She looked at him, and he gave an awkward smile. "I imagine you were talking about me, being as I'm the only male for miles around."

"Actually we were, but—"

"I was hoping you might go hunting so we don't have to eat johnnycakes again," Olivia interrupted with her usual forthrightness, earning a stern glance from Penny. "I saw a rabbit, so I know there's animals around here somewhere, but I hurt myself—see?" She held her arm up for his observation. "But Ma said I shouldn't ask 'cause you helped us so much already."

"Well now," he started, and Penny couldn't mistake the amusement glimmering in his eyes. "Your ma's johnnycakes aren't so bad, not like some of the doughy lumps I've had in my lifetime. But I don't mind going out to look for dinner."

"Or perhaps I should look for an anthill and gather up the ants there to brown in a skillet for a change of course to please my finicky daughter?" Penny said in quiet reprimand. "That's what my grandmother and her tribe ate when food was scarce."

"Eww," Christa intoned, joining them as Penny spoke. Her youngest wrinkled her nose in distaste.

Olivia dropped her gaze, shamefaced. "I'm sorry, Mama. I try to be thankful for the food the good Lord's given us. Honest, I do. I'm not trying to be ill-mannered or greedy. But is it so awful to wish for something that tastes good and don't have dirt in it?"

Olivia did have a point. Dust granules found their way into everything, even the food supplies.

"I don't mind," Derek inserted. "As a matter of fact, I'd like to scout around, see what's behind them hills. Animals use the rocks for shade. Snakes, too."

"Eww." Christa again made her idea plain on the subject of dinner.

He grinned. "Aw, rattlesnake meat isn't so bad. Tastes like tough chicken." Penny inwardly shuddered. She'd eaten snake before, but with the recent memory of her husband's demise, the thought of rattlesnake for a meal didn't sit well. "I'm not sure it's wise to leave the trail and go scouting through the canyon. Other forms of life use the hills for places to hide, too." She thought of the warring renegades but kept her words vague so as not to frighten her girls. "Christa, go with Olivia and bring me my box of plant cuttings. I'll make that salve for you."

The girls hurried off, and she made quick use of her words, taking little care how she delivered them. "How do you know you might not come face to face with a renegade in war paint or, God forbid, a war party? I dinnae think you should hunt in such concealed areas where you could wind up cornered and scalped. If you went and got yourself killed, what good would that do any of us, I ask you?"

He regarded her with amused disbelief; that same hint of merriment lit his eyes and flickered at the corners of his mouth. "Ma'am, I assure you I can take care of myself. Been doing it for years and plan to for many more. Maybe you hadn't heard, cut off like you were, but since the Paiute War ended a number of years ago, there hasn't been much trouble reported in this part of the West. Many of the natives hereabouts have gone to live on reservations."

"Believe me, Mr. Burke, if anyone knows that, I do." She hadn't heard news in well over a year regarding the conflict between the natives and the settlers, but his words brought slim reassurance. Peace treaties with many tribes had formed at other times in the past, and some misunderstanding had erupted, leading to yet another war. Pocatello, a chief of the Northwestern Shoshone where her grandmother Kimama had come from, once engaged in massacres against the emigrants before taking his people to Fort Hall Reservation for fear of starvation. "It is not the supporters of peace of whom I speak."

"Who then? Red Cloud? I doubt the warrior chief of the Sioux abandoned his lands to ride south to Nevada and hide behind this particular group of hills."

She bristled, recognizing enjoyment in his voice. He seemed in quite the cheerful mood—more so than she'd ever seen him. His eyes fairly radiated with energy, odd after such a long day's travel.

"Mr. Burke, are you ridiculing me for my ignorance of the situation?"

His smile faded. "No, ma'am. Sorry you took it that way." He looked toward the nearest hill, rife with boulders, his expression pensive. "As a matter of fact, I found myself in a skirmish with Red Cloud and his band of warriors a few years back when I rode with a group of men who took the Bozeman Trail."

"What happened?" Penny was almost afraid to ask.

"I was one of the lucky ones. Most were killed in the attack; the U.S. Cavalry arrived just in time to save me my scalp. Last I heard, Red Cloud is still waging war in his demand that the military remove their forts from the Powder River territory."

"Aye," she said distantly. "'Tis a difficult state of affairs to be sure. My husband believed that both sides have been in error throughout this entire conflict of wars, ever since the settlers first came to the West."

"I reckon that's so."

"You do?" Penny hadn't expected that. The rare times she'd ridden into Silverton with Oliver, some of the miners' hateful looks made it clear exactly which nation they blamed. And her grandmother's people had been one of the peaceful tribes, negating war.

"I've heard talk in my travels. Neither side has been without its share of blame," he said. This time she couldn't mask her surprise, and he lifted his brows in question. "You think just because my skin is white I can't reason out the facts that my own eyes and ears tell me?"

"No, it's not that. It's just. . .my husband thought the same way, as did my father. Not many people do."

"You never talk much about your husband." His words came soft, a prod she chose to acknowledge.

"Oliver was a quiet man who believed in the Bible, in the Almighty God, and in all He said about men being equal through Christ." She smiled, remembering his gentle nature but fervent heart. "He met my da at the trading post, and I was with him at the time. They bonded at once, finding like-minded kinship and speaking of what was then and still is the talk in these parts—the ongoing wars with the natives and expansion of the West. Oliver came by wagon train with his family and planned to travel farther, but he ended up finding a home here. It may seem odd, to claim a dwelling in such a barren land, but my father had ties here, and I formed them, too. Oliver respected that."

"Your grandmother's people." His words were a statement, almost gentle.

"Aye, though I've seldom seen them since my da died. They have gone to a reservation north of here."

"And Oliver?"

"He came to respect the land, though it never yielded much harvest to him."

"But you stayed."

"Aye." She looked toward the hill of rocks. "This land can be brutal, even dangerous, but it contains a fierce beauty I respect. When the sagebrush blooms along the hills and wildflowers of all colors flood the valleys, it near takes my breath away. This land can even seem gentle, such as when the tamarisk blooms a soft rose in cloudy plumes like fans of feathers. I wouldn't wish to live elsewhere." Conscious of her faraway, rambling manner, she made mockery of her words. "Och, don't be mindin' me blather. Waxing poetic, that's the Scots in me.

With the native ways I learned from my mother and my grandfather, even my da, we survived. And I will go on surviving," she added as an afterthought.

"I don't doubt it. You have the tenacity of a mule."

The words hardly flattered, but she couldn't mistake the admiration in his eyes and voice. His lips twitched as he sought to restrain a smile. "You're like this land of yours. Fierce, strong, dangerous but admirable. . ." His words trailed off as if he would add more. With the manner in which his eyes gentled, intent on her face, she thought he might say *beautiful*. But he didn't.

Before she could manage a reply that wouldn't cue him in to her strange and sudden discomfiture, the girls returned from the back of the wagon with the box of cuttings, and Derek stepped away. "I'll be going now."

"Don't feel you must," Penny hurried to say.

"I wouldn't mind a nice rabbit roasted in your spices myself." He gave a parting nod and strode away.

"You ought not to have said anything, Olivia," Penny chastised once he was out of hearing range.

"Please don't be mad, Mama. I didn't mean any harm." Olivia held her injured wrist, her soft brown eyes pleading for forgiveness. "But won't it be nice to have meat again? I think it'll help Christa, too. She's been acting all tuckered out lately."

Penny glanced at Christa, concerned, as she had been ever since Christa had chosen to ride rather than walk. Perhaps Olivia was right.

She tried hard to act grown-up but was still so much the little girl, and Penny didn't have the heart to scold her elder daughter further. Olivia and Christa had been through so much, more than any children should have to suffer. Losing their pa and the following year reaping the hatred of men without fully understanding why had left a brand of injury on their own hearts.

She gave Olivia a slight smile. "I suppose it will help Christa to feel better. Aye."

Penny lifted the hinged lid of her box and noted the dirt caked into her hands and forearms. She wished to clean off the ever-present dust and grime that had blown against her and buried deep inside the crevices of her skin, sullying her skirts and smudging the gray cloth with brown. Morning, noon, and night, she could taste the dust in her mouth, her teeth gritty from the exposure. Derek assured her no dangers from warring tribes or renegades existed in this area, and likely he'd heard more recent news and been better informed than she, since he was a drifter who traveled from town to town. Given that he showed no qualms to go off exploring, she decided her anxiety must reside only within her mind and determined such fears would end here and now.

Penny mashed roots of the yellow dock she'd gathered days ago and applied the paste to Olivia's swollen wrist. As she bound a strip of cloth around it, Penny issued strict orders for Olivia and Christa to remain inside the wagon, even giving permission for Olivia to retrieve whichever of two books from the trunk she chose to read to her little sister—a McGuffey's reader that had belonged to her husband, or a book of poetry her da had given her mother. Her da traded with a wagonload of pioneers for it and other books, as well as for a few bolts of pretty sprigged material and a fancy silver hand mirror with engraved swirls and flowers etched into the heavy metal. All the possessions had become a burden to the California-bound travelers who'd needed to shed weight in order to complete their journey, but they proved a delight to Penny's mother. Penny could still remember her exclamations of joy with each parcel opened—as if Christmas had come early—and how once her da saw Penny in her new blue calico dress, he'd lifted her high in his brawny arms, near to the ceiling. With her giggling the entire time, he'd swung her around the room, singing to her that she was the "finest wee bonnie lass in all the Nevada Territory."

"Mama?" Judging from Olivia's wide-eyed expression, she was astounded by the unexpected privilege of reading the treasured books. At least her tears had dried, brave though she'd been in not uttering a sound the entire time Penny had treated her injured wrist.

"Aye, you heard correctly." Penny knotted the ends of the cloth. "Go off with you then."

"Thank you, Mama!" With a smile, Olivia scampered away.

Unable to shake the longing, Penny glanced toward the tall canyon wall of shielding rock and sagebrush, in the opposite direction Derek had taken. Surely it would take time to hunt game, since sightings had been so scarce. What she wouldn't give for that feeling of contentment, to be safe and loved again, and for a cleansing bath as well. Perhaps she could not have the one. . .but she could very well do something about the other.

Chapter 8

Derek found their dinner a lot faster than he would have imagined after not having seen hide nor hair of one wild critter all day. The rabbit raced across his path when he'd ridden a bare mile from camp, and he wondered if it was the same one Olivia had spotted. Now he hoped for an early dinner and could imagine the meat rubbed with Penny's herbs and baked over a slow fire. His mouth watered just thinking about it. He peered at the stands of rocky, scrub-covered hills that stood at least two stories tall on either side.

Unless he missed his guess, those three odd rocks in the hill nearest the wagon were exactly like the shape of the ones on his pa's map, near what looked like a sketch of the cutoff they'd taken; and if that was the case, he was headed in the right direction. The X marked on the map went westward from the pile of rocks nearly the length of his little finger, then hooked up to the north. Whether that distance meant a few miles or days, he had no way of telling, and he also wondered why he, Clay, and Linda had been instructed to meet in Silverton rather than at a more local mining camp or town, since Nevada teemed with them from what he'd seen in his travels. Surely, as far as they'd gone, there must be one nearby. But then, there was no way of telling what scheme his pa had cooked up at the time he'd sketched the map, or why.

From this angle, Derek noticed Olivia and Christa, their skirts and moccasin-clad feet dangling out the back of the wagon where they sat, but he saw no sign of their mother. As he rode closer, Olivia looked up and spotted him. A smile spread across her face when she shifted her gaze to the rabbit slung across his saddle. She jumped down from the wagon and closed the distance, Christa following her lead and running at a slower pace.

"Will this do?" Derek lifted the rabbit by its back paws when both girls stopped near his horse.

Christa let out a squeal of delight and jumped up and down, clapping her hands. Derek was relieved to see a more rose color to her face than the unhealthy pallor it had taken on at the noon break. He guessed the sagebrush leaves her ma'd had her chew helped to correct whatever had ailed her.

"I reckon it will, then," he chuckled, holding his find out to them.

Olivia took the carcass with her unbandaged hand, her eyes gleaming with appreciation. "Aye," she said, sounding like her ma. "That'll do right well, Mr.

Burke! No more of them awful johnnycakes tonight."

Derek looked past her, expecting to see Penny walk from around the wagon. When she didn't appear, he drew his brows downward in a puzzled frown and, calling out her name, guided his horse to the other side of the wagon. The area was empty except for more sagebrush and rocks.

"Where's your ma?"

"She took her shotgun and went behind that hill." Olivia nodded in the opposite direction from where Derek had gone.

"She told us we weren't to move a hair from the wagon," Christa added shyly, smiling at Derek. "And that she'd be back soon."

"Behind that hill there?" Bewilderment made Derek lean forward in his saddle. "Why would she do that?" He wondered if she had decided to try her hand at hunting game, but that didn't sound like Penny.

"Don't know," Olivia said with a shrug.

"Don't know," Christa mimicked her big sister.

Derek frowned, his attention wheeling back to the hill with the three odd rocks. What business could Penny have wandering off like she did? He couldn't see any plants from this point, nothing different from what grew nearby, so she sure couldn't have seen anything to add to her box of cuttings.

He dismounted and tied his horse to the back of the wagon. "You girls stay out of trouble while I skin this rabbit. Olivia, you might lend a hand by doing whatever it is your ma has you do to get a meal ready."

"I can help! I can make the meal, too. Mama showed me how." With an eager light in her eyes, Olivia scrambled to the back of the wagon and began to pull out utensils with one hand.

"Me, too!" Christa called and ran after her sister, dropping her doll and stopping to pick it up again before joining Olivia.

Derek wondered if Olivia was as gifted a cook as her ma; it would be a shame to let such a coveted find burn to a cinder. He glanced toward the hill again before he withdrew his knife and made quick work of preparing the rabbit for cooking. Afterward, he collected greasewood to start a fire. When Penny still hadn't returned once the flames flickered low beneath the gathered brush, worry began to gnaw at his gut.

"How long ago did your ma leave?"

"Not long before you got back." Olivia's attention remained on the meat she placed inside the black pot. She wrinkled her brow, as if indecisive, then grabbed the long fork and stuck it into the meat.

He studied the rocks again. "I'm going to look for her. You girls stay by the wagon, like she said. Don't wander off."

"Oh, I won't. I have plenty to keep me busy." With her uninjured hand,

Olivia proudly held up the long fork with which she'd impaled the skinned rabbit. The carcass fell off the two tines and at her feet. "Oops. Guess I didn't poke it through hard enough." She picked it up, brushing off the dirt that had caked onto the flesh.

This didn't bode well.

"I'll hurry."

Derek took off in the direction Olivia had shown him and stepped through the narrow gap between hills, with room for only one person to walk. He had to climb over rocks before again meeting level ground. Why on God's green earth would the woman take it into her head to go off exploring, especially when she'd been opposed to the idea? He stepped sideways along the rough ground, squeezing past a narrow crevice. Beyond that, more rocks stood close together. From somewhere distant, he heard something out of place. Coming to a halt, he waited, silent, straining to hear. A woman's faint groan reached him.

Realizing Penny was in trouble, Derek quickened his pace, his hand going to the handle of his gun.

⌘

Penny awoke from partial slumber, letting out a sigh of sheer contentment as she delighted in the silky water of the small, shallow pool. Hot, but not uncomfortably so, the springs bore the smell of rust and eggs, but she didn't mind. She'd found the hidden oasis with little trouble and submersed herself wearing only her chemise, figuring it the best washing it would receive at this point. She should get back, she reasoned. On the heels of that thought, she again heard the lilting trill of the girls' faraway laughter echo off the canyon walls, assuring her all was well at camp.

Perhaps just one minute more. . .

Again she swept up the thick fall of her hair and held it atop her head with one hand, rescuing the bottom tendrils that had fallen and gotten wet when she'd nodded off. Letting her neck rest against the smooth rock, she smiled and issued another sigh of pleasure, closing her eyes.

"Ah, Da, you were right. This is pure bliss."

Her grandmother's people used hot springs like this one for cleansing of body and spirit, and she could certainly use a dousing for both. She recalled a verse Oliver often quoted from Psalms and whispered it now, "Create in me a clean heart, O God; and renew a right spirit within me." Up until that moment, she hadn't realized how much she needed renewal and how like this land—parched and arid—her spirit had become.

Her da had mentioned the location of the springs through accounts of his travels. He'd found it purely by accident, and she wondered if anyone else knew of its existence. Before this, Penny had never visited a spring and wished now that she might live near one in the future. Every taut muscle in her body relaxed, soothed by the hot water that made her feel as light as the very air. Had the day been as miserable as the previous, she wouldn't have been able to bear it, but she'd been fortunate that the thick clouds had stolen some of the heat from the afternoon.

The crunch of hurried footsteps brought her upright in the water with a jump. Her neck and bare shoulders broke the surface, the dripping sleeves of her chemise pulled down by the weight of the water. Sure that her adventuresome girls had disobeyed and followed, she primed herself to deliver a scolding, when suddenly her intruder appeared from beyond the shielding rock, a gun aimed in her direction.

Her brown eyes met the startled blue ones of their guide.

They stared at one another for a few shocked seconds before Derek spun around at the same time Penny immersed her body completely beneath the surface until her mouth skimmed water. The action to dunk came without thought, and she strangled on the water she'd inhaled. As she groped to sit up, her hair fell in.

"Sorry, ma'am," he mumbled, replacing his gun in his holster. Clearly awkward and undecided, he raised his hand and swept it along his nape, knocking his hat awry, then settled both hands at his hips.

"What are you doing here?" she managed once she could stop coughing.

"I heard you moan. I. . .uh. . .thought you were in danger or hurt," he stammered without turning around. "I figure you're not, though."

"No, I'm fine." Embarrassed that he'd heard her enjoyment of what she'd thought to be a private moment, she slid down against the smooth rock until her chin skimmed water. Something he said didn't ring quite true. "You heard me from the campsite and came to investigate?" She didn't think her expressions of delight could have carried that far, but then again, she'd heard the girls' laughter from here.

"Not exactly. I was looking for you."

"Looking for me?" Dread pricked her conscience. "The girls, they're okay?" She never should have left them alone, not after the scorpion scare almost a week before. What had she been thinking? Yet neither did she want to smother them or allow her maternal fears to resurface and control her. She hadn't thought they could get into trouble reading a book inside the wagon, though.

"The girls are fine. They didn't seem to know much about where you'd gone or why, and it made me wonder." Hands still straddling his hips, he looked up at the sky, craning his neck as if to get rid of a crick. "Look, this was a big blunder on my part. I. . .uh. . .should go now. Yeah, I should go." Before she could respond, he hurriedly moved out of sight. "You might want to return soon," he called from behind the hill. "Olivia has it in mind that she's going to cook dinner."

"I've taught her some, so she should be able to take over," she called back, then remembered her daughter's injured wrist. "Aye, I'll be there soon."

Penny remained as motionless as the rocks around her, wanting to make sure he was well and truly gone. Her mind replayed the incident until she could begin to see the humor, enough so that she smiled. The poor man seemed far more embarrassed than she. It could have been worse; Derek could have caught her in a mortifying state of complete undress rather than covered in her chemise and immersed in water up to her shoulders. Such musings made her feel a bit more poised and able to face him again.

Penny wondered if he'd found game; he hadn't mentioned it, and in the embarrassment of the moment, she hadn't thought to ask. She certainly hadn't thought he would return so soon from his hunt or she would have never allowed herself the luxury of a bath.

She stepped out of the pool, her eyes keeping wary watch on the shielding slab of sandstone around which he'd disappeared. She didn't really think he would come back; he seemed too honorable to do something of that sort. She ducked behind another large slab of rock, nonetheless, to pull off the dripping chemise that no longer ballooned around her but stuck to her like a second skin. With no toweling with which to dry off, she made do with the cleaner inside of her skirt, then snatched her mother's dress from atop a boulder nearby and struggled into it. The supple doeskin hugged her form, and she appreciated its velvet-soft texture. She smoothed the material over her hips, then sat down to pull on and lace her moccasins.

In the dress, Penny wondered if she favored her mother. The desire to feel more like a woman coupled with her girls' eager suggestion she wear it helped to ease her mind as to whether she was being foolish. They'd both smiled when she took it from the trunk earlier, along with the two books she'd promised them. Now, as she combed her fingers through her wet hair, working out the tangles from her crown to below her waist, she wished she had a looking glass or some other method to see her reflection. Her mother's silver mirror had cracked years before when Olivia, a little whirlwind even at age three, accidentally dropped it.

Not keen to waste further time with braiding her hair or pinning it up, Penny bundled the dirty clothes and wet chemise under her arm, grabbed her shotgun, and headed back, deciding she would return and wash her clothes before they left in the morning. And the girls should have a good bath, too.

As Penny approached camp, Derek looked up from where he cooked something over a fire. The surprised appreciation in his eyes encouraged her that she'd made a worthwhile choice.

Olivia's mouth dropped open. "Mama, you look so pretty."

"Pretty Mama!" Christa's smile was wide.

Derek continued to stare.

Flustered by all the attention, Penny looked to the fire. "I see you found dinner, but you shouldn't be doing that. That's what I'm here for." She tried to take the fork with the hunk of whatever meat he'd found away from him, but he shook his head.

"I don't mind. I figured you could use the rest." Their eyes met; behind his intent gaze, she could tell he also recalled their recent encounter and her "rest" there. Her face grew hotter, and his went a tinge darker as he glanced away, back to the meat baking over the flames. "So you might as well claim a patch of dirt, sit, and rest your heels for a spell while I'm in this frame of mind," he added.

Silence settled between them, thick and uneasy, while Penny's thoughts thrummed like a ceremonial drum inside her head. Relaxation was the last thing she needed with her mind all aflutter. She preferred to keep her hands just as busy and strode to the wagon to collect the eating utensils. Out of sight of the others, she pressed her fingers to her warm cheeks, chiding herself for her wayward recollections, which seemed intent on taking her back to the awkward moment they shared.

They needed a diversion. But what, in the middle of this wilderness, could be used for diversionary purposes? She looked at the trunk a moment, then opened it. Her eyes fell upon her da's mouth organ. He hadn't been the best of musicians by his own confession, but music, even poorly played, had always served to fill lengthy gaps of quiet.

Ignoring the box of plates, Penny reached for the harmonica partially twined within a necklace of miniature blue and red glass beads that once belonged to her mother. She pulled them out as well and stared at them. Perhaps because they went with the dress or perhaps because she felt caught up in memories of the past, she slid them over her head and pulled her thick hair from beneath the strand. She then polished the silver instrument, rubbing it against the soft leather of her skirt, as fond memories of her da caused her lips to turn up in a bittersweet smile. Olivia had been learning to play years ago but had lost interest shortly after Penny's father died. Perhaps she could talk her daughter into treating them to a tune or two.

She returned to Derek and the girls, who both talked around the fire.

"What have you got there, Mama?" Christa asked, her gaze dropping to Penny's hand.

"This belonged to your grandda," Penny said with a smile.

"I haven't seen one of those in years," Derek mused. "Not since the one I had."

"You play?" Penny asked in some surprise.

"It's been awhile." His eyes remained on the harmonica. "I was a boy, not that much older than Olivia. I haven't touched one since then."

"My da didn't play much in the years before his heart gave out; just a tune now and then. He wasn't that accomplished, either, though I did love to hear him play when I was a child."

"Who said I wasn't accomplished?" Derek's smirk boded mischief.

"You said you only played when you were a boy."

"Responsibility comes with a hard price; I didn't have time to play after my pa left." After his curious explanation, he turned to Olivia. "Think you can handle a turn at holding this?"

"Oh, sure. My wrist feels a wee bit better." She moved closer to Derek, taking the long fork with the browning meat on it.

He held out his hand to Penny. "Mind if I give it a try?"

She offered him the instrument. He took it, turned it over in his hands a few times, then put it to his lips and blew. The resulting discordant notes brought a giggle from Christa.

"All right there, little moppet," he teased. "Just give me a minute. I didn't say I wasn't rusty."

Penny's heart tugged at the pet name he called her daughter, and she wondered if he'd begun to regard them from a viewpoint other than that of a guide. The more she got to know him, the more she approved of what she saw. The girls were fond of him; he seemed to get along and connect with them in some manner that she hadn't seen since their pa died. Still, she and the girls had lived cut off from everyone and shared little contact with any man other than the pitiless miners whose sole connection had been mutual hatred. It wasn't so difficult to understand why her girls would be drawn to Derek's kindness. But the fact remained: the girls needed a pa, and Penny needed a husband. She further dwelled on the idea of Derek filling that gap in their lives.

After a few more awkward wails, a sudden string of lyrical notes trembled through the air, resounding off the canyon walls, and he went into a rollicking tune that had Christa jump up from the ground and spin around in a loose form of a Scottish reel. "Dance with me, Mama!" she laughed, grabbing Penny's arm. "Show me how again!"

Infused with Christa's contagious enthusiasm and delighted to see her feeling well, Penny laughed and linked elbows with her daughter, twirling her round and then in the direction opposite in a dance her da had taught her from his homeland. Olivia, too, became caught up in the excitement, her feet moving in rhythm, so much so that she dropped the meat in the fire.

"Oh, my!" she cried.

Derek ceased entertaining them and saved their supper from becoming charred ruins.

"I'm sorry," Olivia rushed to say, her face twisted as though she might cry.

"I didn't mean to drop it."

"Nothing to worry your head over," Derek responded with a smile her way. "I like my meat well done."

Olivia grinned. "Will you play some more?"

Penny gave a slight, disbelieving shake of her head, again amazed at how well Derek related to her girls for being such a self-declared loner. But in the best interest of their meal, she suggested they save further music until after dinner.

The rest of the evening unfolded in a relaxed atmosphere missing on previous days, and Penny could almost imagine them as a family. Derek teased the girls and told them stories of his travels, much like her da had done when she was a child. Once their stomachs were filled, with everyone content, she washed the dishes with sand and water, tapping her foot in rhythm while Derek played the harmonica and her girls danced with one another to the lilting melodies. Every time Penny glanced his way, she noticed him watching her, though she couldn't place the look in his eyes. Curiosity? Interest? Confusion?

She wished she could read him, but he remained a mystery.

A mystery much like the length of folded paper she'd glimpsed him pull from his saddlebag late the previous evening as she'd studied him from inside the back of her wagon. He'd sat near the fire and stared at it a long time without opening it, his features somber, before stuffing the paper back into the casing, unread. Somehow she didn't think he carried a packet of poems. She hoped he wasn't pining over a love letter, though he'd told her no special woman had appealed enough to make him want to change his course.

But what if his course contained a case of unrequited love? He had seemed rather curt with his answers on the evening she'd sought them.

Penny transferred her feelings to the kettle as she scrubbed it out hard and hoped that a woman from his past had not already laid claim to Derek's heart.

Chapter 9

Once twilight settled its blanket of dusky purple over the land, and Olivia and Christa said their good nights and headed for the wagon, Penny sat down near the fire to rest.

"It's so pretty out tonight, so peaceful," she mused, staring up at the scattering of stars that glittered above the hills. She turned her head to look at Derek, who sat on the ground nearby. "I must admit, Mr. Burke, you're good with my girls. I'm surprised; you don't seem the type to be a loner. . .sorry." She recalled her promise not to interfere. "Forget I spoke."

He continued staring into the fire, his lips pursed in that amused, resigned manner with which she was fast becoming familiar. Her apology seemed destined to fade into darkness along with the smoke before he gave a brief, decisive nod and looked at her. His lips quirked again and squeezed into a smile. What was it about that small mannerism of his that made her heart give a couple of quick thuds? Preposterous! She, a widow and the mother of two small children, was not a besotted young girl.

"I was born in a small lean-to in the Ozarks, the eldest son of an Irish immigrant and an English schoolteacher," Derek said in a slow drawl. "One day, Pa heard news of the Comstock Lode and got it into his head he no longer needed a family. He headed west to mine for silver. I was fourteen at the time."

"Excuse me?" Penny asked in bewilderment, her mind stalling at his swift change of topic.

"You wanted to know my past."

"Aye, but it isn't any of my business, as I said before." Flustered by his blunt comment, she focused on smoothing the wrinkles from her dress. "Please don't feel obliged to tell me."

"You no longer interested?"

"Well, no, I didn't say that."

He barely lifted his brow, giving her an intent look as if his mind worked hard to get her preferences straight. "Which I take to mean that you'd like to know more?"

She hesitated, loath to utter the smallest fib. "Well now, if you're of a mind to tell me your story, Mr. Burke, I wouldna be ignoring you."

He grinned at that. "You're a peculiar woman, Penny Crawder."

They both seemed a bit startled by his slip of familiarity in using her Christian name. Before he could apologize, she raised her hand to stop him.

"Out in this wilderness and taking into account all we've been through together, it seems strange to stand on formalities. You may call me Penny." She smiled at his assenting nod. "And before I'll be forgetting, I would be most interested to hear what you mean by calling me 'peculiar.'"

He let out a laugh, rich and deep but low enough to not wake the girls. The masculine sound of it lit something sweet and warm within her belly, making her smile.

"Oh, I doubt there'd be any likelihood of you forgetting anything when you latch your mind onto it. And I mean that in the nicest way possible." The glint in his eye was roguish, and she did what came naturally. She leaned over and swatted his arm in mock annoyance as though they'd known each other for years. A bit stunned by her spontaneous act, she waited to see how he would respond, but he only dipped his head with another flicker of his lips, as if trying to mask his amusement.

"Well, bein' as how you've introduced the subject a second time, and not I, would you be holdin' any resentment toward me if I were to ask a wee bit more concerning your family?"

His smile grew as he looked at her.

"What?" she asked, wondering what she'd said that made him smile so.

"Did you know when you get anxious or excited, the Scot in you comes out?"

"Does it now? Well, I suppose I have my da to thank for that, bein' as he was the one to raise me."

"I like it," he stunned her by saying. "That, mixed with your Indian heritage, is all a part of what makes you special. What makes you. . .you."

Oh, my. Heat flamed her face. Maybe he did live as a drifter, but she wondered if he'd ever turned a young lady's head with such an uncomplicated remark, one that made a woman feel so special. Not that he'd need to do a lot of turning! Looking into his eyes, shining as blue as an evening sky in the first bloom of springtime, she sensed that Derek Burke spoke just as he felt.

She cleared her throat, trying to regain the thread to their prior conversation. "The day we met, you mentioned you have a brother. Does he live in Nevada?"

"He's in Nevada at present."

The words didn't sound happy. "Any other kin?"

"None that I plan to claim."

Now, what did that mean? Curious, she stared, noting his pensive scowl. Rather than ask, she waited, not wanting to push him so that he withdrew again.

"As a matter of fact, I saw my brother last week," he said after a moment. "The day before I ran into you."

"He lives near here?"

"Not exactly."

When he offered no further explanation, Penny took in a deep breath for patience. Oh, he could be the most infuriating man sometimes! Recalling her resolve to keep silent, Penny waited with the hope he would continue. Her desire for information had gone beyond curiosity due to caution; now she wanted to know, simply to learn all she could about this man.

"My pa. . .passed away recently. My brother and I met up not long after in a small mining town about a day's ride from the valley where you lived."

"Silverton?"

He nodded.

Now she felt bad for her earlier irritation. "I'm sorry for your loss."

"Not necessary. I barely knew him. Last time we spent any time together, I was just a young'un, and the time we spent was scarce."

"Your brother or your pa?"

"Both. And now it's too late. I wouldn't have even come here if not for the letters we three got informing us to meet up at Pa's request."

"Three? So there's more than just you and your brother?"

Another uneasy stretch of silence passed.

"No one, really. Someone trying to pass themselves off as family," he muttered.

"Why should they do that?" She posed the question under her breath, trying to sort out the puzzle of the history his life presented.

"Why else? She wants to interfere where she has no place."

Sensing him withdraw, she thought it wise to change the subject. "You once spoke of your mother. Tell me about her."

A slight, wistful smile tilted his lips. "She was a wise woman with faith as big as a mountain, though she was stern enough when it came to any of my shenanigans."

"You loved her."

He nodded. "I did. She'd been a schoolteacher before she married my pa, and she took to the words of the Bible just like you do."

"But you don't?"

He shrugged. "I believe there's a God, all right, was raised that way by my ma. I just don't see that He ever did all that much good for me."

A lode of pain was buried beneath his solemn words. Any rebuttal Penny might have given lodged in her throat when he turned her way and she saw the sorrow mirrored in his telling eyes.

She cleared her throat to speak. "Well now, Derek, with that I would have to disagree." At her easy use of his Christian name, his eyes flickered in surprise, followed by a faded grin and approving nod. "After all," she continued, "I have in my possession a sacred and revered book with what must amount to thousands of pages to prove the very opposite."

"That sounds like something Ma would have said."

"You did mention she was a wise woman."

He chuckled, then grew quiet, studying her face. "She would have liked you."

So many compliments in one night after a year without any put her off balance, and she rose to her feet. "I should get busy with putting things away." She didn't miss his disappointed expression and knew a moment's surprise. Perhaps now that she'd finally gotten him to converse with her, he found he liked it. She didn't want this pleasant evening to end between them, either. Several tasks, however, awaited before she could bed down for the night.

"You knew that hidden spring was there all along, didn't you?"

His low words coming so suddenly after a lapse of quiet caused her to start. She looked his way before gathering the tins and stacking them in the empty kettle. "Aye."

"How come you didn't tell me about it?"

She hesitated before speaking. "I suppose I should have. But I figured if I mentioned it, you might think me foolish to go off searching for the springs when we have the river near."

"I wouldn't have thought that of you."

"No?" His assurance made her smile. "You called me foolish once before."

He fidgeted with his hat, which he'd pulled off. "That was before I knew you."

His sincere words hit Penny with the force of a strong wind; oddly shy, she looked away. "My da told me about finding the spring in his travels. From the manner in which he described the area, I assumed this must be the place. Have you ever bathed in a heated spring?"

"Can't say that I have."

" 'Tis a delightful experience. One of the best that I've encountered."

"So I've heard."

She shot him a quick look at his choice of words, sensing a thread of humor woven through them. His attention had moved to the harmonica he now held in his hand.

Penny thought of her sleeping girls in the wagon but wanted to prolong her time with Derek. "Do you know any quiet tunes on that mouth organ?"

He raised his brow and looked at her. "Quiet?"

"Slow. Fit for the night."

"I might recall a couple. Ma liked that type of tune, too. Especially after a hard day's work was done. She'd often sit on the porch of an evening and watch the sunset. Said it was a shame not to enjoy the colors in the clouds that God painted to close each day."

Penny nodded, recognizing where he'd received his ability to simplify pictures into appealing words.

"Once the day ended, she had a rule that all the cares went with it. Then she got sick and needed medicine." He propped his knee up, laying his forearm across it. "That's when I left to find work and earn money to send home. I never went back, and Clay never forgave me."

"There's still time."

At her soft words, he swung his brooding gaze her way.

"Your brother isn't dead. And neither are you."

"I might as well be for all the good it'll do me. He isn't willing to forget or forgive. And now he likely never will." His jaw hardened.

She wondered at his peculiar words and what ran through his mind but decided this time she wouldn't ask. Regretting that she'd stirred up a nest of bitterness, Penny changed the subject, hoping to recapture the easy peace they'd shared. "I remember when life seemed free of all cares. As a child, the world didn't seem so harsh, and it was easy to get caught up in one's imaginings and just dream the bad away. My da was a hardworking man, but he knew how to find pleasure when life offered it, much like your ma, I expect. He taught me the reels from his homeland and an appreciation for music, though he could scarce carry a tune." She chuckled. "I miss the manner in which he would sweep me 'round the room with my small hands in his big ones."

Derek smiled in acknowledgment, seeming to relax by degrees, and she turned to resume her task of sorting and packing up the tins. Behind her, the mournful, soft notes of a familiar tune trembled in the air. She recognized it as a song her da used to play, though not as well as Derek. Busy at her task, without paying much attention to anything but her work and the sweet music, she began to hum the melody and continued for a few notes, even after the harmonica's notes abruptly ceased.

She heard Derek approach from behind. To her surprise, he laid a gentle hand atop her shoulder. She glanced at his fingers, lean and strong, then looked over her shoulder into his eyes, turning slowly as she did.

"Don't stop," he said, "you have a beautiful voice."

"Sure, and you wouldna be wantin' me to—"

"Please," he insisted, his tone soft, quelling her hoarse refusal.

She looked up into his steady blue eyes. Confidence gradually crested inside her, and she began to hum again. His question and her response suddenly seemed so natural, so fitting into this entire evening. The night belonged to a fantastic tale much like the ones that stemmed from her da's homeland.

Wrapped up in the dream, Penny felt little shock when Derek reached for her hand that hung by her side and took it in his large one. Her voice died in her throat at Derek's first warm touch. He wrapped his long fingers around hers with care, lifting their clasped hands to the level of her shoulder. "Don't stop," he whispered again. He then cupped his other strong hand with the slightest pressure at her waist, and slowly began to circle with her, his steps agile and sure. When he began to dance with her beneath the star-tossed quilt of the black velvet night, she found a thread of the song again and resumed humming. Uncertain what to do with her free hand, she laid it against his sleeve, her fingertips pressed against his strong muscle for balance.

She'd never learned the steps to this dance and felt awkward. But Derek exercised patience, and she soon attuned to his lead, as if she'd danced with him for years. They both smiled as he swirled her over the sand and past the sagebrush in the pale ring of security cast by the light from their campfire. Feeling giddy, not remembering the last time she'd known such freedom, Penny tilted her head back and laughed low in delight.

Derek stopped so suddenly she caught her breath. His expression grew earnest, his gaze intent, as he stared at her mouth then back to her startled eyes.

"You can dance," she managed the only words that came to mind, no matter how banal or obvious. "I wouldn't have thought a drifter would know how."

His lips quirked into the slightest grin. "Ma showed me, thought I should learn." His voice seemed to come from afar, and again his gaze drifted to her mouth. "When she was young, a wealthy friend taught her. Said someday it might benefit me, knowing a waltz or two."

Penny didn't retreat as he unclasped his hand from hers and moved his finger beneath her chin, tilting it up. "And she gave you her love for music," she whispered, glancing at his mouth as he lowered his head.

"Yeah. . .I'm beholden to her for that."

When his lips touched hers, the caress came as soft as a breath. Warm and gentle, yet so powerful she felt she might be knocked off her feet. Her pounding heart rivaled the quiet, tender moment, and she tightened her fingers against his arm to remain upright and steady.

When he pulled away, no apology for his unexpected act entered his eyes. Nor did she want one. They stared at each other breathless seconds before she lifted her face to receive his second kiss.

The sound of the girls' soft laughter reached Penny's ears. Stunned, she broke away from Derek as though he'd scalded her. She took a step back, her hand covering her bosom, though nothing would calm her racing heart. She glanced toward the wagon, as did he. Both Olivia and Christa peeked at them from around the canvas, giggling behind their hands.

◈

"I—I should go and tend to them," Penny stammered, her dark eyes huge in her flushed face.

Derek nodded. "It's getting late. I'll finish up here."

"You?"

"I learned how to pack a dish or two, being a drifter and all."

With the way she winced before she nodded her thanks and gave a weak smile, he wished he could retrieve his ill-thought-out words. They sounded like a reminder of his preference to remain a loner. And that was what he did want, wasn't it? Not to get involved with a woman? Not to put down roots or saddle himself with further responsibilities?

As he watched Penny hurry to the wagon, Derek tried to forget the feel of her in his arms. He realized he'd been foolish to follow through with his desire to kiss her. Her inborn strength amazed him, solid and rare like a precious metal; something most men sought after. While at other times her self-determination and stubbornness provoked him. Yet she was all a woman should be, too. Soft and warm. Gentle and caring. All those traits wrapped into one bundle were reason enough to not kiss her. She was getting under his skin in a way no other woman ever had.

When he'd heard her quiet words concerning her da and seen the sweet sadness in her eyes at the memories, that had been bad enough, striking in him a chord of similar regret. But once she began humming along with Derek's tune, her pleasing voice, both lyrical and wistful, touched him in a way that made him want to help her forget the pain and recall all the joy.

And that was dangerous.

He'd spent more than half his life trying to be the man of the family and fill the empty shoes his pa left behind—both in action and in fact. They'd struggled a great deal after his father left to seek his fortune, and Derek had needed to wear his pa's huge castoff boots since they'd had no money to buy new ones. He'd despised each step he took in the hard, roughened leather, not wanting to be anything like their former owner. Realizing his pa had taken his life journey in the ill-fitting boots made the fourteen-year-old Derek hate him all the more.

The first thing he'd done when he left home and earned enough money was buy himself a new pair of boots. Other than necessities, the rest of the money went to his ma and Clay. He'd done more than his share in taking care of family and had received little gratitude for his sacrifice; was it so wrong that he now wished to take care of himself and realize his own dreams?

With the profits from the mine, he'd thought about claiming a parcel of land and starting a ranch. He'd had some experience as a cowboy a few years back, one of many jobs he'd taken on. Since then, the idea of ranch life had found a comfortable home in his head. When he got the itch to travel and felt too settled in, a roundup always loomed on the horizon. Yet a successful rancher needed a wife, or so he'd been led to believe by the man who'd hired him—a gracious, well-mannered woman to entertain his guests, with the inborn strength to handle the difficulties that came with life on a ranch. A woman with the fortitude to give him sons. But Derek wouldn't mind a few strong daughters, either.

His gaze went to the wagon, where he could see Penny's silhouette through the canvas. He watched the shadow of her arms move as she braided her hair.

A woman like Penny. . .he couldn't go wrong there.

Derek shook his head at the crazy rabbit trail his mind had taken. One brief kiss, and he planned a future with her as his wife?

"What's the matter with me?" he muttered as he finished the few tasks she'd left undone. He couldn't afford such thoughts, not now. Not when he was so close to finding his fortune. The claim must come first; nothing could take priority over that.

Derek passed a night of fitful sleep. Dreams of himself and Clay as youngsters troubled his mind, with Penny suddenly standing off to the side, beckoning to Derek, her brown eyes beseeching—and he awoke with a start. The sky was still dark, the moon hidden behind a hill. After failing to get comfortable, Derek sat up to feed the burning embers of the fire. He grabbed the coffeepot from the hot, white ashes, finding it near empty. If the coffee beans weren't kept in the wagon, he would start a pot to brew. He sure could use more than one cup right now; he felt so tense.

A black-blue haze soon filmed the land with the approach of sunup, and a dark shape materialized by the wagon, detaching itself from the back. Derek recognized Christa, but before he could call to her, she scampered for the same hill her ma had visited the previous day.

"Christa! Come back here!" His quiet but firm shout didn't do a bit of good. She either ignored him or didn't hear, and Derek set down the coffeepot with a muttered oath.

Grabbing his gun belt, he took off after her. Too many dangers lurked beyond those rocks, and he wasn't about to wait for her safe return.

Chapter 10

Penny woke at the same time she always did, just before sunup, as the forerunner to daybreak painted the hills and land in a mist of dusky blue. To her alarm, she noticed both girls' spots empty in the wagon bed and hurried to climb down. During this journey, she had slept in her moccasins and dress, considering the discomfort necessary in the event she might have to rush from the wagon for whatever reason.

Like now.

"Morning, Mama!" Christa's cheerful voice greeted her. She hopped up from where she sat with her cornhusk doll and ran to Penny, throwing her arms around her, doll and all.

"Good morning." Still disconcerted by the scare but at the same time relieved all was well, Penny noticed Olivia feeding bits of sagebrush to the fire. Their guide was nowhere in sight. "Where's Mr. Burke?"

Christa craned her head to look up at Penny. "He went behind that hill. Can we have a breakfast like dinner was?"

Surprised, Penny glanced at the shadowed hill in curiosity before returning her gaze to her daughter. "Did he say when he'd be back?"

Christa shook her head. "I wanted to see the spring, but he made me come back here."

"Made you come back. . ." Penny assumed a stern countenance as she pieced the meaning of her daughter's explanation together. "Christabel Louise! Did you go look for the hidden pool without me?"

A guilty expression filled the girl's dark eyes, and she bowed her head. "You said it wasn't far. I thought it might make my stomach feel better. And I *had* to go."

Penny shook her head. Christa's late-night ventures to tend to nature's callings often led her down trails that sparked her childish curiosity.

"You know you're not supposed to wander off from the wagon. I said you should wait till dawn when I would take both you and Olivia to the spring."

"Can we go now?"

"No!" She blurted her answer, recalling the previous day's incident when Derek sought her out. Seeing Christa's confusion, she collected herself. "Not till after Mr. Burke returns. If he is taking advantage of the hot springs, I have no wish to disturb him."

Penny collected the items needed to make breakfast. First, she boiled water to start coffee, then ground a handful of beans and dumped them into the pot. "What are you so glum about?" She shifted her attention to her eldest, who'd said nary a word nor showed the slightest amount of cheer.

Olivia continued to stare into the fire. "I don't see why we always have to bathe in the river or anywhere else besides. Why not just stay dirty?"

"Olivia! What a question!"

"Being clean didn't make nobody else like us. And I'll bet Mr. Burke doesn't care." She looked up at Penny. "What if the new people don't like us, either?"

"What new people?" Penny wrinkled her brow at her daughter's solemn question.

"In Carson City. What if they don't want nothin' to do with us, either? I'll bet most of 'em are miners, just like back home."

Cutting words, hopelessly aired; words that Penny had avoided even in thought from the moment she'd devised this plan to go farther west. They twisted like brambles around her heart, piercing her with pain surely only a mother could feel; the thorns, her child's sorrow.

"Maybe we should've just stayed there," Olivia added quietly.

Penny refused to succumb. From experience she knew the best solution was to snap her daughter from her doldrums. "Now then, Olivia Meredith, do you mind telling me what put such a fool notion into your head?"

Her eldest let out a dismal sigh and flicked the band of her slingshot a few times. "I was just thinking about that story we read in the Bible yesterday, about them lepers and how nobody wanted them around."

"Those lepers. And the lepers were people who had a disease others could catch. It makes sense that people in the city wouldn't want them around so as to protect their own. Just like I protect you and Christa, and Mr. Burke protects all of us."

"But Jesus healed them and made them whole again, didn't He? That's what you read. But we'll always be the same, won't we, Mama? What happened to those lepers isn't much different than the way them—those miners treated us. But Jesus made it so people could like them. Do you think He'd do the same for us if I asked Him to in my prayers?"

Oh, if she could take all her girls' heartache so they'd never again have to suffer the ignorance of men! Penny counted to three under her breath and composed a calm response.

"Well now, Olivia, there's not a blessed thing wrong with either of my girls. Och, and it's a good thing to pray and ask God for those things that you know would please Him as well. Asking Him to make you more likeable isn't a bad thing. But you and Christa are perfect just as God made you. As for those fool miners, not everyone is so crude or so cruel. Your dear papa was a kind man who had not an ounce of prejudice in him. Your grandda was the same. And your great-grandfather, and Mr. Burke. . ." That she should feel her cheeks flush at the mere mention of his name made her flounder. "Well now. He's proven to be a man of admirable qualities. Most trustworthy." Again she busied herself, briskly stirring flour and water in a bowl and pouring the mixture into her iron spider, which she set over the low flames.

"You like Mr. Burke, don't you, Mama?"

How to answer that! "Aye. I would imagine everyone who meets him recognizes the good in him. It's easy to appreciate a man like that."

"You plan on marryin' him?"

Penny froze. Eyes going wide, she swung her head around to stare at her daughter.

"You kissed him." Olivia shot a sly grin her mother's way and Christa giggled. "I was just wondering." With the prongs of her slingshot, Olivia began to trace lines through the sandy topsoil. "'Cause I wouldn't mind if you did. He's not Papa, but I like him. And he plays the harmonica real good. He said he'd teach me what he knows."

"I like him, too!" Christa added with enthusiasm.

Penny felt her face warm again. A better question to ask, whatever had gotten into her head? She could scarce believe she'd allowed him the liberty. But last evening she hadn't thought much at all. The sweet music gently rolling through the canyon had reminded her of happier days, while the cool night refreshed her and the canopy of twinkling stars, with the moon winking at them from beyond the clouds, had set her imagination soaring. When he'd taken her in his arms in what he called a waltz, it had seemed quite right, and she hadn't thought to deny him. Nor had she wanted to deny him the kiss. Two kisses. . .

He's a drifter who wants nothing to do with marriage, her pesky thoughts reminded. *Nor does he seem to really serve God.*

"Mama?"

Snapped out of her musings, Penny returned her attention to her eldest daughter.

"You really think we'll have a better life in Carson City?"

"Ye canna spend a lifetime runnin' from your problems, Penelope MacPhearson." Penny inhaled a swift breath as her da's old admonition ran through her head, gentle words of firm counsel he'd given when as a small girl she'd fled from the mocking, hurtful words of children at the trading post to find a place to hide. *"Ye'll spend a lifetime runnin' in circles, never t' find the end of the road ye think will take ye t' happiness—and that be the gospel truth, lass. True happiness can only be found in here."* He'd patted his chest. *"With the good Laird dwellin' within.*

And dinnae be forgettin' I spoke so."

"I think," she started and cleared her throat from the catch that made her words waver, "we Crawders are strong enough to bloom and survive wherever we're planted."

Olivia looked confused. "Then why did we leave the valley? I liked it there. Well, except for those evil miners. But we had good times, too, especially when Papa was alive and the miners left us alone."

"Change can be a good thing. We'll have good times again." Penny smiled, trying to make light of her words though the heaviness inside refused to budge. "We have that grand thirst for adventure in our blood that came from your grandda and your great-grandmother Kimama. Her tribe was nomadic, and many, many days ago, they wandered over this great land."

Olivia's eyes shone, wistful. "Will you tell us their stories again? And about their lives among the Shoshone?"

"Later perhaps. First we must have our daily reading." Derek had taken to joining them when she read from the Holy Book, and she didn't want him to miss the opportunity.

"It might help me feel more keen on the idea of living in Carson City," Olivia said simply, her impish grin somehow managing to appear guileless.

Penny recognized a bit of innocent manipulation on her daughter's part and debated whether she should give her a gentle scolding or fulfill her hopeful request. She loved passing down the stories her da and mother had told her and decided that this morning, she would overlook the bit of skillful artifice on Olivia's part. She thought back to a story her daughter always enjoyed, that of her da's first encounter with the Shoshone, when he'd returned to a trap he'd laid to find the woman who would become his wife, her ankle caught in his noose.

"Mama." Christa came up beside her, her voice wavering in fear, and clutched Penny's shoulder tight. Her wide eyes focused on the trail from which they'd come.

Penny looked over her shoulder to see two men on horseback, not fifty feet distant and headed their way.

"Olivia," she said calmly as she rose from her crouch and slipped a protective arm around Christa's shoulders. "Get the shotgun from the wagon and bring it to me."

Olivia threw a look in the direction of the men, and her face lost color. She shot up from the ground in a flurry, running to the wagon while Penny turned around with Christa. She took a step forward, keeping her child well behind her.

As the men drew near, she noticed one held a rifle across his saddle. Both wore guns at their hips. Their clothes were shabby, and dark, days-old beards whiskered their faces. Their hair hung long and straggly about their shoulders.

These men didn't appear to be simple miners, and the word *outlaws* flashed across her mind.

She heard Olivia's running steps behind her, but before Penny could turn to retrieve her shotgun, the man minus the rifle hunched over, one hand going to the saddle horn, the other to his handgun.

"I wouldn't do that if I was you," he growled in a mock pleasant manner as he withdrew his gun from his holster in a flash of silver. His sorrel picked up pace until scant distance separated them. "Put the gun down, Injun gal, 'less you want a bullet through your head."

The other rider brought his gray to the other side, closing them in.

"Put the gun down, Livvie." Penny kept her voice firm, masking her fear. She wouldn't let these scoundrels frighten her into submission, but at the same time, she would do anything to protect her children. *God help us.*

The leader flicked his hat up from his brow with the hand holding the gun, taking time to eye Penny from the top of her braided hair to her moccasin-clad feet. "Well, now, what've we got here, Jonesy," he said in an aside to his partner. "An Injun squaw, I reckon. A right pretty one, too, and ripe for the picking."

"Yeah." The second man also leered her way. "Maybe we should rest here a spell, Amos."

Penny kept her silence, ready to fight them, biting and clawing if she must. She glanced at the iron spider in front of her, hot from the fire, and wondered if she could move quick enough to do damage with it.

As though he read her mind, the leader dismounted, swaggering toward Penny. "First, we'll take some of that coffee I smell brewin'. And whatever breakfast you can cook up. Once we fill our bellies, we can get to know one another better." He stroked the muzzle of his cold gun from the corner of her mouth to her cheek, then followed it with the back of his coarse hand. She flinched at his touch, knocking his arm away.

He guffawed, seeming both surprised and amused. "So, you got fire in you! But too fair a skin and light-colored eyes for a full-blooded Injun; and your hair's got red in it, too." As he spoke the last, he fondled one of her long braids, taking it in his meaty paw. "I reckon you must have some white man's blood in there. . . but you're still nothing but a squaw."

She recoiled at his vicious words. He gripped the plait hard, yanking it toward him so that her scalp burned and she fought for balance. Behind her, Christa began to cry softly.

A shot rang out of nowhere, echoing through the canyon. The lecher's hat flew to the dirt. Startled, he released her braid.

"Keep your hands off her, or the next bullet will go through your head," Derek called out. Relief made Penny dizzy, and she struggled to remain standing.

The two outlaws frantically looked around—at the wagon, at the hills on both sides. Derek was nowhere in sight. The second man still on horseback swiftly moved to train his rifle on Penny. Before he could complete the act, another shot had his hat flying.

"If you pull a stunt like that again, next time my aim centers on your middle," Derek shouted. "Though I doubt you have a heart to put a bullet through. Throw down your guns—both of you. Then get back on your horse, nice and slow, and head back the way you came. If either of you comes near them again, two busted hats will be the least of your worries."

The man called Jonesy threw down his guns. The leader delivered a hateful glare to the hill in the opposite direction that Penny thought Derek's voice came from. Letting his gun drop, he glanced at her in disgust and turned toward his horse.

"That goes for the other one, too."

At Derek's order, the man grimaced and pulled the second pistol from his holster, letting it drop next to the other. The leader took a few steps, scooped up his hat from the dirt, and strode to his horse. He faced his saddle as though he would mount up. Instead, his hands went to the butt of the rifle she now noticed sticking out from the side.

Before Penny could call out a warning, Derek emerged from a waist-high grouping of rocks near the wagon, both his pistols aimed at the men who swung their focus his way.

The leader snapped his rifle from its leather scabbard and brought it up fast. Two more shots rang out, and Christa screamed.

Chapter 11

The leader swore and grabbed his arm. Bright red spread across his blue sleeve.

"I said drop your guns," Derek reminded, his voice calm but cold as flint. "That means all of them."

Derek continued his easy stride toward camp; in a lightning swift arc, he spun both his guns by the trigger loops with his index fingers. As they completed their rotation, he again grabbed them by their handles and aimed one at each man. "You don't want to try me."

The desperado he'd nicked in the arm spewed a string of vulgar words at Derek that contained mention of him being a "no-good Injun lover." Out of the corner of his eye, he noticed Penny clap her hands over Christa's ears at the first onslaught.

"That's no way to talk in the presence of a lady or her girls," Derek said, keeping his voice still though his blood boiled. "I recommend you just do as I say; then the both of you ride on out of here before I really get upset and teach you a lesson."

With a final glare, the leader dropped his rifle to the ground and mounted his horse with some difficulty. Both outlaws turned their horses east and galloped away.

Derek waited a moment before holstering his guns. Despite his legs feeling shaky, as though sand filtered through his knees, he walked toward Penny, gratified to see her safe. She held both her girls close. The muscles of her slender jaw stretched taut, and he reconsidered laying his hand upon her shoulder, though what he would have really liked to do was pull her into his arms and hold her close to his heart. It had near stopped beating when he'd returned from his visit to the springs and seen that despicable snake fondle her.

"Are you—" he began.

"I'm all right," she said before he could finish his concerned query. "I should have known better than to leave my shotgun in the wagon. I usually have it within reach at all times. What was I thinking?"

Both girls turned their faces up to look at their mother. By the frowns etched in their foreheads, he saw that they also worried about their ma and the high pitch in her usually quiet voice.

"You ought not blame yourself," Derek insisted.

Before he could say more, she speared him with a glance that silenced him. "I need to finish breakfast." She retreated from all of them toward the three-legged skillet sitting over the fire. The three watched as her hands gripped her folded arms and she hugged herself, staring down at the spider. The girls swung their confused gazes to Derek as if seeking direction.

"Livvie, why don't you take Christa to the wagon and show her that harmonica of yours. Or maybe there's something else you can do before we break camp, some chores your ma has you do of a morning?"

"Okay." She glanced at her ma, then at Derek, and took her sister's hand. "Come along, Christa."

Christa looked up at Derek. "You gonna take care of our ma, Mr. Burke?"

The gentle smile he gave at her soft, plaintive words didn't release the fear from her eyes. "Your ma will be fine. I'll talk to her."

"I'm glad you'll be with us in Carson City so no bad men can hurt us anymore."

Before he could correct Christa's somber words that he would remain with their family, she turned and walked to the wagon with Olivia. Someone needed to set things straight; he had no idea how the girls had gotten it into their heads that he would stay with them. But there was time to sort that out later.

Again he watched Penny, who stood with her rigid back toward him. First, he supposed he should try and talk to her. He wished he had better experience with such a thing but felt out of his depth, like the time years ago when a riverbank he'd crossed had suddenly given way and swirling water had closed over his head.

Derek moved to stand at her elbow, but she paid him no mind. She dumped out the charred mess of a johnnycake and poured more of the runny mix from the bowl into the spider. Her actions came jerky, as if her bones weren't fused right.

He cleared his throat. "About what just happened—"

"I'll try to hurry breakfast. I know you're hungry." Still she didn't look at him. Her tone sounded unnatural, forced. "And I promised the girls I'd take them to the spring before we leave. But I don't have to do that if you'd rather get a quick start."

"You don't have to hurry. Take your time."

"Nonsense." She snatched a tin mug from the crate of utensils. "Can I pour you some coffee while you wait? I know a man likes his coffee of a morning. My husband and da did, and I imagine you're no different."

Before she could grab the coffeepot from the fire, he gently grasped her forearms and turned her toward him. "Did he hurt you?"

"No." She evaded his gaze. "I don't want to talk about it."

"I understand that, Penny. But you're scaring your girls." He watched her dart a glance to the wagon. Both Olivia and Christa had withdrawn behind the canvas and now peeked around it. "You can't blame yourself for what happened, if that's what you're doing," he said again.

"I can." She pierced him with her gaze, keeping her voice low. "And I do. I'm their mother. Things could have ended far worse had you not come along. I should have known better, to have my gun nearby at all times—"

"And now you have eight, including mine," he joked, hoping to draw her from her foul mood and get her at least to crack a smile. "You really are a woman with her own fort."

She looked at the piles of discarded weapons. "It seems wrong to take them, somehow."

"Would you rather I had let those men remain armed and given them good reason to sneak up on us to seek their idea of a reckoning?"

"No, of course not. I just. . ." She bit the edge of her lower lip. "Do you suppose it's all right? They don't belong to us."

"The snakes and lizards don't have use for them. Only other choice would be to let them bake in the heat, which would lead to their ruin. If they can be used to protect you and your girls instead of for a crime, which I'm sure those scoundrels used them for, then I don't see the problem. I've had the misfortune of meeting up with that sort before; likely those men stole the guns off their victims."

"I see your point." She continued staring at the guns. "I suppose it would be all right then, if we give them over to the sheriff in Carson City once we arrive. Or come to a town before that with a lawman. That way it wouldn't really seem like we're taking what isn't ours, only doing our civic duty by delivering the guns into safekeeping."

"Fair enough."

She smoothed her hands down the front of her skirt, casting him a rueful glance. "Thank you for. . .everything. I should have said that first."

"Only doing what you hired me to do."

"No, you've done so much more." For the first time, she smiled, and though it came strained, she seemed to have again found that inner strength he so admired.

❦

After supper, with the canyon behind them and what she hoped were many more miles between them and their attackers, Penny sat near the fire. The breeze felt almost pleasant, not the hot wind of the afternoon. Enough daylight remained, and the focused work of sewing seed beads onto buckskin helped soothe her nerves.

With slow care, she stitched a design onto one of the flaps of five pouches she'd brought to sell at the trading post. She'd been jumpy ever since the morning's encounter. The events had rattled her composure, and she'd waited to read their daily chapter at the noon break when she felt calm again, with no further thought that she might break down and cry if she tried.

Now, with the day well behind them, she finally began to relax.

Olivia perched at the edge of the wagon, swinging her legs and repeatedly blowing the notes to a short tune Derek had taught her, as she'd done since she finished her meal. Grateful that the warbling from the harmonica had grown steadier, Penny glanced up and across the fire at Derek, appreciating the manner in which his hair blew back from his face. He'd shed his hat and sat near Christa, who peppered him with questions concerning the noon reading as she'd been doing since he poured his first cup of coffee.

"You think King Solomon was wise?" Christa asked, and Penny again glanced up from her work. Her daughter's eyes glowed with curiosity as she regarded Derek.

"I imagine so." He took the last swig of his second cup of coffee, tipping the tin back to drain it.

"But why would he tell the women he was going to cut the baby in half? Isn't it bad to kill, no matter what? And that was just a wee baby."

"Well now, he didn't use his sword, did he?"

"No. . . ," Christa trailed off. "But he might have."

"I think he just wanted to get those ladies thinking. He knew the woman who really loved the child would never let it die. And that would be the real mama."

"But she almost gave her baby away." Christa wrinkled her brow, hard at thought. "So she must not have loved it much if she'd give it away to the other woman. Isn't that so?"

Derek seemed stymied for an answer, and Penny hid a smile, sensing he was flummoxed by her girl's insistent questions.

"Christa," she said under her breath, her attention never straying from the needle as she carefully stitched the cobalt beadwork in a triangle pattern. "Moses's mother did much the same. Remember when I read his story? And she loved her son very much. Fact is, sometimes a mother must make hard choices for the best interest of her child. And sometimes mothers—anyone really—must give up those things they want most in the world to help their family or keep them together. I expect God blessed both women for their sacrifice and their willingness to let go, all for the sake of their children. Family is all that any of us have, really; all that God gave us. Family will stand beside us and love us till our dying breaths. The good Lord intended it that way, that no one should be alone."

She looked up to catch Derek's gaze on her and wondered what put such a somber look in his eyes, then recalled his words about his own family. She hadn't intended to go on so but got carried away in the opportunity to teach her daughter a worthy lesson.

"But, Mama, King Solomon might have killed that baby if its mama hadn't given it up." Christa's brow clouded. "Do you think he would've killed it, Mr. Burke?"

"I think Solomon was a fair man. I don't think he would have done wrong, since everyone had such a high opinion of him."

"Have you ever killed anyone?"

Derek jerked his head in surprise, and Penny sensed his unease as he looked into the fire.

"Christa, that's enough." She looked over the pouch at her daughter.

Christa let out a sigh. "Sorry, Mama. Sorry, Mr. Burke." She stood to her feet. "Can I go lie down now?"

Surprised that she didn't have to instruct her child to go to bed, Penny peered at her face, noticing it seemed a little more drawn than before. "Aren't you feeling well? Did those sagebrush leaves that I gave you help?"

Christa pulled a face. "They taste icky."

"That's no reason not to chew them. Not everything that's good for you goes down sweet."

"Okay." Christa sighed, hugging her doll close.

"Tell Olivia it's her bedtime, too."

Christa took a few steps, then looked back at Derek. "I think you're a fair man, Mr. Burke. Mama said so. So I'm sure if you killed someone, or almost did, God'll understand."

"It's never okay to kill, Christa," Derek said quietly. "But sometimes, in defense, a man isn't given much choice." He looked up at Christa. "I came close when I met up with some cattle rustlers once, but no, I've never killed a man. Not to my knowledge."

"You were a cowboy?" Interest lit Christa's eyes. "On a ranch? Is that where you learned to shoot so good? And to spin your guns like you did?"

"Christa. . . ," Penny cautioned her errant child.

Derek chuckled, though it sounded tight. "You'd be surprised what a man does to pass the time when he's alone, like learning fancy tricks with his guns. I had a friend teach me a few things, too, before he became a sheriff. I reckon I've been a number of things, and yeah, a cowboy was one of them. I'll tell you about it sometime. But you should obey your ma now."

Christa nodded without another word and left for the wagon.

"So you do have friends somewhere?" Penny inquired with a smile.

"A few." His tone didn't share her amusement at her less than subtle prod, and she noticed that he watched Christa's retreat with sober eyes. "Has she always been sickly? Ever since I joined up with you, she seems to lose more strength each day."

Uneasy, Penny returned her attention to her beadwork. "I nearly lost her two years after she was born. She got sick with a fever that winter and has never been the same since." When he remained silent, she glanced up. His brows had pulled together in a worried frown. "Something else troubling you, Derek?"

He took in a deep breath and let it out slowly. "I didn't know that when I agreed to be your guide." Penny felt as if a fist grabbed her heart at the gravity in his eyes. "I can't take you any farther without you knowing what we're up against."

"Up against?" Dread made it difficult to breathe.

"The river ends in a sink. Beyond that lies nothing but forty miles of desert. No water. No shade. No feed for the livestock. Alkali flats as far as the eye can see and loose sand that buries wagon wheels and makes travel near impossible. The sun reflects off the land and hills so hot you feel as if your eyes are burned and you're being baked alive. Men much stronger than Christa haven't made it across."

Horrified, Penny stared, putting into words what he didn't say. "You're telling me that you don't think my little girl can survive the journey."

She could see how difficult it was to answer by the way he averted his eyes and shifted his hat a bit where it sat propped on his knee. "Frankly, yes. That's what I'm saying."

"What about Virginia City?" She would have preferred Carson City, to try to find her brother-in-law, but now grabbed at any alternative. "Is that safer? We could go there instead."

He looked at her. "We would need to cross the same desert."

His quiet words, his grave expression sent her mind into a spin, and she rose to her feet. "I—I have to go. To think things through. I'll speak with you further about this in the morning."

He nodded and again stared into the fire.

Barely able to contain the whirlwind of her emotions, Penny headed for the wagon.

How. . .how could a few words spoken cause everything to go so wrong? Cause her long-held dreams to vanish so abruptly? All her bright hopes crashed around her like fallen sparrows struck by a hunter's merciless bullets. Why had her da never told her about that particular stretch of desert and the alkali flats? She knew he'd been as far as Virginia City; if he knew, why hadn't he said anything? Had he been anxious he might frighten his little girl with distressing accounts unlike the inspiring tales he'd told? The emigrants she'd met must not have known what they would come up against to speak of it, but Penny should have. She should have asked Derek what the entire journey was like in advance. She'd been so sure she could do this, that it was the right thing to do! To leave her homestead and follow Derek to Carson City.

There had to be some way.

She climbed into the back of the wagon and looked upon the wan face of her youngest, now fast asleep. Her heart whispered the truth, echoing his cautions. Christa was too weak to survive days in a situation such as Derek had described, one that would test the mettle of the strongest men.

"Mama?" Olivia whispered. "Is everything okay? Why are you crying?"

Penny hadn't realized she was and lifted her hand to swipe at her cheek, only just realizing she still carried the pouch with thread and needle attached. She'd left the pouch of seed beads open near the fire.

"Everything is fine. Go back to sleep." She failed to keep the tremor from her voice and left the wagon, not wanting Olivia to see her distress.

As she again quietly approached the fire, she watched Derek pull some papers apart to spread on the ground, what looked like the same papers she'd seen him stare at on a previous night. He weighted one corner of the first with a rock, but before he could do the same with the second, he caught notice of her and jerked his head around. The breeze caught the other two slips of paper. He scrambled to catch one. The third flew toward her, plastering itself against her fringed hem and moccasins.

"Wait!" he called out at the same time she bent to grasp the paper and lift it to her eyes. Her finger ran along the edge as she did, and she felt the sting of a cut.

A map. The papers were a map—all one map since the symbols ran off the edge and one of the sketches was half there. But not a map torn in parts from being worn. . .the sharp edge that cut her finger had been sheared. All the sides were straight, not ragged. Three parts. One map. . .with a black, bold X in the upper left corner. A treasure map. *Three* parts. . .three. . .

Penny blinked as awareness dawned, slow and bright and painful. She gaped at Derek. The wary manner in which he regarded her, the guilt in his expression told the truth.

"You took these from your siblings?" she whispered in disbelief, making a guess while hoping it wasn't true.

His eyes grew hard. "I took what belonged to me."

"Belonged to you?" She glanced at the paper in her hands, memory of other conversations clicking inside her mind. "This was your pa's, wasn't it? This map. He did this. You said he went out looking for silver and recently died. . . ."

"Penny, give me the map." Derek rose from his place by the fire, reaching for it, but she took a step back, still thinking, remembering all past conversations when she'd finally gotten him to open up. She had kept all he shared about himself locked inside her heart, yearning to know everything about him, to know him. Now those words brought only torment.

"You met up with your brother in Silverton after years of being apart. You said you two didn't get along. You said you doubted he'd ever forgive you now. And the woman. . ." She lifted eyes unfocused with tears to him and blinked them away. "Your own flesh and blood that you will not claim. You dinnae want her to have a thing, so you took the law into your own hands and took the maps for selfish gain."

"I only have her word she's kin!" Derek shot back, his voice just as low. "Pa was wrong to do what he did—in all he did. He was an ornery cuss who enjoyed twisting the knife and gave no regard to his family. Or what happened to them."

"And you do?" She regarded him with disbelief, her heart feeling as if it, too, had been stabbed. "I trusted you. Trusted you with my girls. But you're no better than those miners who stole from me. You're a thief, just like them. Only worse. You stole from your own kin."

He winced, as if feeling the slash of her words. "You don't understand, Penny. I'm the one who took care of my family for years, toiling at jobs when I was barely old enough to grow whiskers. Sending money home so Ma would have medicine, so they'd both have food and clothes. I'm the eldest and should inherit all of the mine Pa left—if he left anything and it's not all some cruel joke."

"It would serve you right if it was!" She struggled to keep a tight rein on her anger; regardless, it burst forth. "You have a wicked idea of what's right and wrong! Who are you, Derek Burke, to decide what should belong to any man if another man gave of his own possessions in his dying wish? It's not your place. The good Lord above left His throne to save sinful men, and once He died and rose and reclaimed it, He aimed to give all His good things to all His children, not just one. How would you feel if someone stole your blessings, the blessings God intended for you?"

"You don't know what you're talking about," he muttered.

"No. For the first time, everything is clear. I've had men steal from me my entire life. My goods. My pride. My safety. And I won't let it happen again, not if I can do something to stop it." She squared her shoulders, which felt weighted down by sorrow. "This is where we part ways."

Surprise lit his eyes. "I would never harm you or your girls. You should know that by now. I'm not a thief!"

"You took from your own kind, your family." Penny shook her head slowly in pained disbelief. "And you can't even see the wrong in what you've done. If you would steal from blood kin, then how can I be trustin' you with what's mine?" Each thought spoken yielded such pain she found it difficult to breathe, to continue. She knew she had to leave him before she gave in to more tears. "I'll expect you gone in the morning when there's light enough to find your way."

Before he could reply, she crumpled the paper in her hands and threw it at him. "And here be the remainder of your fine legacy!" It bounced off his shoulder, landing at the edge of the fire. "A loner's life is all you deserve, Derek Burke."

He scrambled to save the paper, beating out the flame that curled one blackened edge.

His final act twisted the knife she felt as though he'd plunged into her back. Unable to look at him further, Penny made a fast pace back to the wagon.

✍

Derck didn't wait until morning.

His temper just as fierce as Penny's, he made quick work of saddling his bay and rode out of camp without a backward glance. The moon hadn't yet reached its fullness, but it shed enough light to continue west.

He rode half the night, muttering harsh remarks under his breath about the nerve of that woman. She'd had no right to say all she did without having lived his life. She couldn't know how callous his father had been, how resentful Clay had become. How angry and hurt Derek was to face even more proof of his father's betrayal to his wife and sons—a half sister. But that wasn't what bothered him so. That Penny's scornful words had taken seed in the soft soil of the growing ache inside him, cultivated by the guilt he daily battled—that was what angered him now.

"She had no right," he muttered. "She doesn't know."

At last, his weariness overtook his irritation, and Derek stopped for the night. Without bothering to gather branches from a nearby bush to light a fire, he slipped into his bedroll. His last image before sleep claimed him was the remembrance of the anger in Penny's wounded, dark eyes.

Chapter 12

Penny slapped the blanket of hides over herself, tucking the edges in with unnecessarily harsh pats, struggling to understand how Derek could hoodwink his own kin. The revelation coming so soon after her plans for Carson City fell apart had made her furious, unable to restrain the words she'd hurled at him.

She was still furious.

She closed her eyes, but her thoughts remained active. Weary but unable to sleep, she rolled over as best she could in the tight space, wondering how she might have felt had her da done the same—left her mother and her and sired a child by another woman. She'd been blessed to know a family's unreserved love, but not everyone had that honor. Even raised within the circle of such love, she still possessed shortcomings she tried hard to overcome.

Her thoughts added to her sorrow, taking her into her dreams. Dreams of home. Of her girls. Of Derek.

Penny awoke with a start and a sense of dread. Darkness still colored the canvas surrounding her; she figured she'd been asleep for little more than an hour. A quick check showed that her girls lay deep in slumber, their breathing slow and steady. Knowledge that Christa was too weak to finish the journey stirred up the lingering ache inside Penny's heart. No trek to whatever better life beckoned was worth the possible sacrifice of her child.

She sat up, knowing what she must do.

Derek had proven himself as nothing but trustworthy. He'd given in to her insistence and manipulations to be their guide and had saved their lives—twice. If he'd wanted to steal from her, he'd had plenty of opportunity to do so and ride away as they slept. Instead, he'd remained with them and done all he could to guarantee their comfort and safety.

He'd been wrong to take the maps; nothing could convince her otherwise. But didn't everyone struggle with flaws of one type or another? She wished now she'd been more patient once she'd discovered his secret. She'd seen the shame spread across his features when she'd looked at the map and the hopeful appeal in his eyes when he first regarded her, as if her opinion really mattered. It was absurd, really. She had forever been urging him to talk; when he'd done so, she wouldn't listen to what he had to say.

The sun had yet to rise; she could still stop him. Apologize. Offer to listen if he would again open up and trust her. And this time, if she did offer advice to his quandaries, she would do so with gentleness and a quiet voice as her ma had done for her. Having decided, Penny scrambled down from the wagon, her hand clutching the cover for balance.

The moon's glow revealed the campsite, the shadowed clumps of sagebrush against the pale hills, the nearby river glowing nearly white, reflecting the moon. She stopped and blinked in disbelief. Derek's horse and bedroll were gone. He hadn't waited for daybreak to leave camp.

Despairing of ever seeing him again, Penny dropped her forehead to the stiff canvas. How much more pain could a heart withstand? For the first time, she realized how empty everything seemed without him there and how much she would miss his presence. For the first time, it occurred to her: she loved him.

Turning the blame on herself, she grimaced, bunching the canvas tighter in her fist. What right did she have to judge him for his treatment of his family? She, who could not grant the God-commanded absolution to strangers for stealing her goods throughout the past several months, condemned a man who blamed his kin for injustices that stretched out over the years.

The hypocrisy of her actions rankled, making her sick.

"Why is it so difficult for me? Why can't I let things go like Mother did? And Da? I don't want to feel this way. I despise feeling this way." It gave her no comfort to hold on to the old pain and bitterness, but Penny had no idea how to let go.

❧

Derek groaned at the pricks of something sharp along his face and neck. He opened burning eyes to the rising sun, realizing that at some point during the night his hat had fallen away from shielding his face. Swatting at the swarm of black, biting flies, he rolled over. Within several feet of his bedroll, partially covered by greasewood, lay what little remained of the carcass of a small animal. Dead more than a day, judging by the look of the bones. Likely a coyote's kill.

The memory of what had brought him to this place made him scowl. She'd had no right, but he was also angry with himself. He should have never left, even if Penny had demanded it, but he hadn't thought clearly at the time. He supposed he'd given those outlaws a good idea of what would befall them if they returned, but that didn't ease his fears of what could happen to her.

Sitting up, he noticed his horse was missing.

"What the. . . ?"

He shot out of his bedroll so fast he got his legs twined in the cloth and stumbled to a stand. Miles of sagebrush, greasewood, river, and hills—as far as the eye could see.

But no bay mare.

He clenched his teeth and grabbed his hat from the ground, then craned his neck to look far into the sky. "Why, God? Why are You doing this to me? You got something against me?"

He slapped on his hat, rolled up his bed, strapped on his guns, and picked up his saddle. Taking off on foot, he went in search of his missing horse. He noticed among the boot prints the hoof marks were unclear—like those of a horse running—but the tracks headed east, back the way he'd come. And none marred the way west. It figured.

As he covered the rough ground, Penny's words returned to haunt him. No one had ever given him any "good thing," least of all God. Derek had fought for every morsel of a good thing he'd owned. Why should Penny think the Almighty God would actually do something nice for him, when his own father hadn't cared enough to show a kindness in the past twenty-four years while he'd been alive? And for a lot of that time, he hadn't been visible to Derek, either. Why should he trust God at all?

He died so that you could live.

The words from her reading and the following discussion with her girls whispered through his mind.

"Why would He do that, Mama?" he remembered Olivia asking, tears in her eyes. *"His death sounds so painful. Worse even than being tarred and feathered. Like Grandda talked about in his story of what happened to that man in Boston."*

"Jesus' death was far more painful. He went through it because He loves us. He wanted us with Him. Like family."

Family.

Brooding, Derek looked at the rose-colored sun. He'd been given the opportunity to reunite with his family on more than one occasion but had lost the chance then. Had lost it now. His ma was never coming back, and he'd ruined any possibility of reconciling with Clay. As for Linda. . . Now that the shock of his pa's indiscretion had passed, he acknowledged the truth of their kinship, despite what he'd said. He wondered about the woman, who looked younger than the nineteen years she'd claimed. Her bravado was as ill fitted as her gown, and he wondered for the first time if it were all a ruse. Now that he recalled, she had seemed a mite too anxious, jumping at every sudden noise. But any chance of trying to get to know his half sister he'd likely shot full of holes with his harsh treatment of her.

Derek's thoughts traveled to his legacy and the outlaws from the previous morning. His jaw hardened, and he tried to recall if he'd seen them in Silverton. Was it just happenstance that they traveled along this river and the path to the mine at this time, or was his pa's secret map not so secret after all? His pa had always been a braggart. Maybe those outlaws had heard about the silver that Michael Burke had uncovered and aimed to try to steal the claim right out from under Derek's nose. Just as they'd stolen his horse.

They had to have stolen his horse.

And they would live to regret it.

☙

With grim resolution, Penny fed her girls breakfast, fielding their questions about Derek's absence with carefully chosen words. "He had something he needed to take care of. He won't be coming back."

"You mean he just left us?" Christa hugged her doll tighter, tears glistening in her eyes.

"He wouldn't do that," Olivia assured her sister, then turned to Penny. "Would he, Mama?"

"Sometimes a man is given little choice. Olivia, would you like to pick the reading today?" Penny said, changing the subject, her words overbright. "I'll even let you read."

The coveted honor didn't make her daughter's eyes sparkle as Penny had hoped.

While Olivia stumbled over an account they'd previously read—of a man who'd received mercy for an enormous debt, who then refused to forgive another man who owed him a pittance in comparison and was delivered to his tormenters—Penny felt a measure of the same discomfort that had struck her the night before. The girls were silent once Olivia closed the book.

Christa's expression grew even more solemn. "Does that mean we gotta forgive them evil miners, Mama?"

Penny sought for an answer concerning the other subject she would have preferred to avoid.

"I did." Olivia's quiet admission stunned Penny. "I was mad when they took our laying hen and we didn't have any more eggs. But I knew I had to do it."

"You did?" Penny asked.

Olivia nodded. "The words didn't come easy, but I remembered Pa telling me that the hard things never are. We talked about forgiveness the week before he got bit. I was mad at somethin' Christa done, and he said I had to forgive her or I'd never rest easy. So I told God I forgave them miners during my prayers before bed. Did you feel any different when you forgave 'em, Mama?"

Choked, Penny turned away. "We have to get these things packed up. Olivia, I need your help to hitch the team to the wagon."

"We're going west without Mr. Burke?" Christa asked.

"Not west. East."

Both girls stopped gathering the utensils and stared at Penny.

"We're going home."

"Yippee!" Christa's smile lit up the glum morning, and she clapped her hands as best she could with the spoons in them, clinking them together.

"Really, Mama?" The sparkle that had been absent now shone in Olivia's eyes. "Back to our valley?"

Penny regarded them in confusion. "You want to go back there? Those miners are still somewhere around, and I can't see them leaving any time soon. They can still make trouble for us."

"Yeah, but there we have the stream to fish in!"

"And our valley with all the pretty wildflowers," Christa added.

"And the wee butterflies to chase!"

"Aye, that we do." Penny shook her head in amazement that her girls had never wanted to leave. "I suppose your mother has even learned a lesson from all this."

"What's that, Mama?" Christa cocked her head, as though surprised to hear that her elders never stopped learning.

"Troubles find us no matter where we go. Running doesn't solve a thing, and I'm thinkin' if we are again forced to fight, it might be easier to do so when we're in home territory and secure in our surroundings."

Christa smiled. "You miss our valley, too, Mama?"

Penny came to terms with what she'd been denying ever since she left. "Aye, I miss it. But never you mind now. We need to stop this foolish bit of reminiscing and start this day. I want to cover as many miles as we can travel."

"I'll tend to the horses!"

"I'll help Livvie!"

Penny watched her girls, secure again in their happiness, scurry to the area where the black mare and stallion were tethered.

She, too, had something that must be tended and didn't wish to put it off another moment now that she'd made the difficult decision. Facing the birth of the sunrise over the hills, she stared at the misty veils of rose, blue, and violet. Veils that opened the day and announced the glorious approach of the sun.

The words to forgive didn't come easy, as Olivia had warned. But the desire to release the wearisome burden pushed them to the surface. Once her prayer was complete, Penny smiled, at last sensing her Father's approval.

∽

Derek continued his trek eastward, his anger at the outlaws mounting with each stumble he took. To steal his horse, they would have had to come across Penny's camp before they had reached Derek. Worry dueled with rage, each trying to find a target in his mind.

He'd been a fool to leave.

They'd been fools to try him.

"If they hurt her or those sweet girls, so help me. . ."

His muttered threat went unfinished. Up ahead, partially shielded by a tall patch of greasewood, his bay stood, calm as could be, as though Derek hadn't spent the past mile or more walking.

"I don't believe it." Derek gaped at the sight before approaching his mare, slow and easy. A quick appraisal assured him she was all right, and a second one showed him the tether he'd tied to the branches last night was frayed at the bottom.

His jittery mare must have shied at something while he slept, and the worn leather had broken loose. He'd been so weary he could have slept through an earthquake. But instead of being a horse that was faithful to its master by returning or at least remaining in the near vicinity, his mare had decided to lead him on a merry chase.

"Why do I put up with you, horse?"

His beast whinnied, giving a little toss of her head.

He'd never named his horse like some men did their animals. He hadn't planned to keep her after he'd first bought her three years ago and discovered her quirk of shying at every blessed thing. Her reputation foiled every attempt to sell her.

"Maybe you have more courage than I gave you credit for," he mused. "You knew we shouldn't leave Penny on her own. So you headed back, even if I didn't have the sense God gave a mule to do the same."

The horse whickered, her muzzle finding rest in Derek's palm.

"Sorry. A horse." Relief to find his bay made him calm some. "Maybe you do deserve a name."

In no time, he saddled his runaway mare and continued east.

The memory of how it felt to think someone stole his goods while he'd been sleeping brought back the guilt that had dogged him ever since he crept past his slumbering brother and half sister to take their maps. If he hadn't known deep in his gut that it was wrong, he wouldn't have been so secretive about the whole thing. And he didn't wish on anyone the horrible, gut-wrenching feeling of waking up to find his valuables missing.

Valuable. First time he'd ever considered his horse valuable. He supposed he could even consider her a blessing—that is, when she didn't shy and run away. He had bought her at a fair price, and they'd shared numerous days together, traveling the countryside. But she didn't talk back, and he found he missed hearing another human voice. Penny's voice wishing him good morning. The girls' smiles and laughter. Even their never-ending chatter he'd eventually grown accustomed to, though they'd stymied him at times with their unexpected questions.

Now the silence of the plains felt deafening and not the least bit comfortable. Penny and her girls were a "good thing"; he would even go so far as to call them blessings. Most of the time. But what if. . .what if God did have a hand in Derek's life? What if He aimed to give Derek a family and would rather he no longer remained a lone drifter? And what if Penny and her girls were that family? They'd been thrown together by chance—or had it been more? No matter that Derek had gotten away—twice—he always found himself drawn back to her. Desired to be with her. Even now. Especially now.

He loved her.

"What have I gone and gotten myself into this time?" he muttered, but his heart confirmed his thoughts. He couldn't imagine living the rest of his life without Penny Crawder by his side. Could he convince her to take another chance on him? Would she be willing to listen if he tried to talk to her again?

As he rode on, her teachings to her girls about God, about His desire for His children's happiness, about so many things revolved inside Derek's mind until he couldn't take any more and he bowed his head, yielding to the strong tug at his heart. Despite the blazing sun, he took off his hat and held it over his chest.

"I was wrong to steal from my kin. I admit it. I think I was wrong about You, too, Lord. Ma said You forgive men, and I sure could use a dose. I've messed things up pretty badly. But if You're willing to take a chance on me, I'd be grateful."

The curious ease that filled him, like floating atop saltwater, dissolved when in the early evening he reached the last place they had camped. Only the remains of a dead fire and the ruts from wagon wheels marked that they'd ever been there. He peered over the land to the east, hoping to catch sight of her wagon in the distance. But that was too much to hope for, he supposed, since she likely left after dawn. He had assumed he would meet Penny on the journey back, but she must have turned around, now that she realized the trail was too dangerous for Christa. That meant she was headed back to the canyon and might come across those outlaws a second time.

Six guns or not, Derek didn't rest easy at the idea of her meeting up with them again. And he had the troubling sensation that something wasn't right.

He prodded his mare to a faster pace. "Sorry, horse, I know you're tired." And for the second time, he uttered a prayer. "Please, God, keep Penny and the girls safe."

By the time he neared the canyon, nighttime had wrapped the land in a shroud of darkness. He was grateful for the moon, though he still didn't see the wagon. Penny had covered more miles than usual, clearly eager to get home. He urged his horse forward, between hills.

At the glow of a campfire, his heart beat a little faster, and when he made out the pale canvas of the wagon's tarpaulin, he drew a breath in relief.

A breath that died when he entered camp and saw no one there.

"Penny?" He rode closer to the back of the wagon. "You in there?"

When no answer came, he edged back the cover to peek inside.

Empty.

Alarmed, he scanned the area. Something pale and out of place caught his eye near a clump of sagebrush by the river. He rode closer and dismounted to pick up what looked like twined husks covered by a strip of calico. He turned it over.

His heart lunged as he stared down at Christa's doll.

Chapter 13

"Mama, I'm scared."

Her arms around a woolly gray coyote pup, Christa retreated a step, almost losing balance as another pup frisked at her heels. In front and around her a coyote pack moved in, slow and dangerous. Teeth bared. Growling low in their throats. Their long bushy tails stuck out behind them in clear threat.

"Don't move, Christa. Don't be scared. And don't put down that pup."

Penny had scarcely known such terror as she did standing several yards behind the pack and watching the three ferocious beasts bear down on her tiny daughter. She sighted her shotgun on the lead dog's head, targeting the scruffy white area behind its pointed ears. Two shots. She had two shots in the dark against three angry coyotes.

"Livvie," she said in a hushed tone to her eldest, who stood quiet and trembling beside her, slingshot poised. "Don't use that. Not yet. If you miss, you'll make them angrier, and they could turn on you. As long as Christa keeps holding that pup, I think she's safe. No mama is going to attack and risk her pups getting hurt."

At least she hoped not. Again a fervent prayer for divine protection rose to her lips. She silently issued the brief plea and kept the shotgun ready in her hands now slick with sweat.

"Livvie, hurry back to camp and fetch a branch from the fire!"

Penny jerked her head around, shocked to hear Derek's whisper behind her. She'd been so focused on her daughter and the growling beasts she hadn't heard his approach.

Sitting on horseback, his eyes on Christa, he raised his pistol into the air and shot. At the explosions that echoed off the canyon walls, the coyotes jumped in their looming semicircle, clearly startled, but didn't scatter. The two biggest dogs turned halfway around and snarled at Derek.

Penny watched as Olivia came running back with a torch and handed it up to him. He rode closer to Christa, thrusting the fire at the nearest coyote. Penny's heart nearly stopped to see how close his hand came to the beast's sharp teeth. Growling and barking, the pack backed away from both Derek and Christa. One of the dogs suddenly jerked and yipped as a rock hit its long snout. Penny swung her gaze to Olivia, who stood poised with her slingshot. The coyote ran off.

"Christa, put the pup down, slowly," Penny called. While her tiny daughter did as instructed, Penny followed Derek's lead and fired a shot into the air. The female coyote grabbed her pup by the scruff and raced away. The second pup scampered after her at a slower pace and disappeared from sight. The remaining coyote, which Penny assumed was the male lead dog, glared at Penny and growled. Its eyes glowed a menacing yellow in the fire from Derek's torch. Penny backed up and stumbled. The huge, lean beast moved her way.

Olivia let loose with a volley of rocks and another shot exploded from Derek's gun. The lead dog yipped and Penny saw dark blotch its gray coat as it turned, racing after its pack.

∾

The coyotes gone, Derek threw his torch to the ground and grabbed Christa, swinging her atop his horse. He had struggled to control his mare and was shocked his beast hadn't shied as he fought off the coyote pack. Penny ran and met him halfway, holding her arms up for her daughter. Derek gently lowered Christa into her embrace and watched Penny hug her child close.

"How many times have I told you not to wander off?" she chided, kissing the top of her head.

"I'm sorry, Mama." Christa's voice trembled. "I had to go tend nature's call, and I saw the pups and followed them. They wanted to play. Then them big ole mean dogs came."

"Promise me you'll never do something so foolish again, Christa."

She nodded, solemn. "I promise."

"Thank you," Penny mouthed to Derek, and he gave a short nod.

"We should head back to camp and put more distance between us and them," he said quietly, his heart tugging at the picture they made. "Their den must be near. Them pups are too young to go far from it, and where you camped is too close for my peace of mind."

Penny nodded, asking no questions. In the shock of all that had happened, she seemed to take his return to them for granted.

Once back at the campsite, she gave quiet orders for Christa to get inside the wagon and stay there and for Olivia to help hitch up the team. Instead of joining her, however, Penny only stared into the fire, hugging herself as if in a stupor.

"I told the girls, just this morning, that we can't escape from troubles," she said, "that they always have a way of finding us. But I had no idea I'd be fightin' a pack of angry coyotes to top off the day." Her shoulders trembled as she took a deep breath. "I bedded down early and awoke to find Christa gone. I was terrified to find her with that pup and the pack closing in."

Derek moved to stand beside her and laid his hand on her shoulder. He understood. His own heart had chilled at the sight. And later, his fear had soared when he'd seen the lead dog stalk Penny.

"I'm all right," she assured, but her smile faltered, her eyes still holding a hint of the terrible panic she must have suffered.

"No. You're not pulling away this time," he whispered and drew her to him before she could resist. "Lean on me, Penny. I'm here. And I'm not going anywhere."

Once his arms closed around her trembling body, she melted against him, soft and warm. He held her for some time, his hand smoothing her silken hair, while around them, insects buzzed, and nearby, the fire crackled low. The night again grew still and at peace.

Her shaking subsided, and she pulled away to look into his eyes. "I never thought I'd see you again. Why did you return, Derek? Did you read your pa's map wrong and lose your way?"

He deserved that. Her gentle words held no bite; still they stung. "I came to tell you I was wrong. And to ask that you come back with me to Silverton."

"Come back with you?"

He nodded, unsure now how she would respond to his next request. "While I was heading back here, I made my peace with God. And I want to try and set things right with my family if it's not too late."

"Family?" Her eyes had begun to sparkle, her smile growing throughout his explanation. She raised her brow, urging him to speak the words.

"Yeah, family. My brother. And my sister."

"I can't tell you how pleased I am with your decision," she said, her words cautious. "And I feel so wretched for the shameful way I acted earlier. I was wrong, too, to lash out the way I did."

"Don't give it another thought. Fact is, your words helped set me on this course."

"Then I'm glad, though I still wish I would have dealt with the matter differently. It's the right thing to do, Derek, no matter how difficult. I'm not sure how I can help, being nothing but a stranger to them, but aye, I'll come with you. After all you've done for me and mine, how can I refuse?"

A bit nervous, he pulled his lips into a pucker and rolled his tongue along the inside of his cheek. "Well, it's more than that really. Fact is, my heart hasn't been quite right since I met you."

She paused. "Maybe I can find a cure for you among my cuttings."

"Well, no. That's not exactly what I meant, either."

"Then tell me, Derek. What is on your mind?" She thought she knew but wanted him to say it.

"I love you," he said simply. "I'm tired of being a loner, and I want you to spend the rest of your days with me."

Even though she'd hoped for it, his straightforward answer nearly took her breath away.

"Marry me, Penny." His hands gently clasped her arms. "Come back with me to Silverton. There must be someone there who can tell us where to find a man of the cloth to perform the ceremony."

"Aye, Derek."

His brow shot up at her swift answer. "You'll marry me?"

"Of course."

"You don't need time to think it over?" From what little he'd heard from an old acquaintance, women always asked for time to reach that decision.

"I've thought of little else. I've hoped for this almost since the day I met you. Could you not be tellin'? 'Tis not any drifter I allow the favor of a kiss."

Baffled, he shook his head at her teasing words and returned her smile. "You've known that long?"

"Aye."

"So you're telling me I never had a chance?"

She laughed. "Of course you had a chance. We must make our own choices, Derek. I just hoped you would come to see that marrying me was the right one for you."

He chuckled at her logic. How he longed to pull her into his arms and kiss her! But he held back as Olivia walked into view, and he recalled their need to break camp. He doubted the coyote pack would return to their den soon, if they returned at all, but he didn't want to take that chance.

Unable to resist Penny's appeal, he did kiss her smooth brow. "We won't go far, just enough to put some distance between us and them coyotes." He glanced at Olivia, who brought the horses around. "Should we tell the girls about us?"

"Maybe it's best to wait till morning. I don't want them whooping and hollerin' and alerting every wild beast in the area to our presence."

"Coyotes tend to shy from loud noises. I've had a run-in with their kind before."

She grinned. "Well then, maybe we should tell the girls now, so as to keep the coyotes away."

He laughed; she had the gift for bringing that out in him. "Are you sure Olivia or Christa won't mind having me for a pa?"

"Judgin' by how miserable they behaved after you left, I think they'll be so excited they won't sleep for days."

He drew her to his side. "Thank God you're safe, Penny, and that I got here in time."

"Aye. I have a great deal for which I need to be thankin' Him." She looked up at Derek, a light in her eyes he'd never before seen. "I had thought that to take my girls and find a better life in Carson City was God's will, as well as my own, even though I faltered with misgivings. Now I realize what must have been His true intent—that I find and become acquainted with you. And I feel peace in that knowledge, that this has been His will from the start. Where we live doesn't matter as long as I'm with you, Derek. I love you, too. I think I must have for some time."

This time, he didn't resist as he leaned down and touched his lips to her soft ones in a slow, tender kiss, one she returned in full.

Afterward, they both noticed Olivia had broken from her task of hitching the harness to the team and stared at them, her mouth agape. Her lips turned up until they stretched into a jubilant smile. Christa also peeked from behind the canvas at the back of the wagon, grinning wide, then covered her mouth and giggled when Derek caught sight of her.

"Well, if they didn't know before, they know now," he whispered, and Penny laughed.

"Olivia, Christa," she said, "before we leave here, we have something to tell you. . . ."

Derek and Penny shared a glance and a smile, before he took her hand in his and they walked closer to share their news with her girls. . .soon to be his girls, too.

Penny had been right. Their whoops and hollers filled the canyon, enough to scare any coyote away.

Chapter 14

Both eager and anxious, Penny once more donned her mother's native wedding dress and necklace of glass beads. She had been given the room Derek's half sister, Linda, once used, and which she and her girls now shared. Upon their arrival to Silverton more than a week before, they had learned that Linda vanished the morning after Derek left, without a word to anyone. Only the man at the livery remembered her hitching a ride on a miner's wagon leaving town, and Penny had seen both regret and concern in Derek's eyes when he heard the news.

"We'll find her, if that's what you're wantin'," she'd assured him softly.

"I'm not sure I have the right or even that she'll welcome my concern. Clay sure hasn't forgiven me."

Regardless, Derek searched but found no trace of his half sister.

Penny mused over her initial meeting with her soon-to-be brother-in-law, Clayton, who favored Derek and possessed the same lean strength and quiet, often brooding manner. He'd treated news of their engagement with shock, and addressed Penny with a shy, almost boyish respect. To her surprise, others in the small town had been polite to her as well, though she received suspicious, even bitter looks from some. With Derek near and her own experience using a gun, Penny felt assured she and her girls would be safe.

Yet while Clay had been kind to her and her girls, he barely spoke to his brother. That first day he'd accepted his portion of the map from Derek, but not the apology, leaving the small parlor area before Derek could finish.

Penny sighed. So much hurt. So many wounds to heal.

All week, she had played mediator between brothers, trying to exhibit both patience and understanding as her da and grandfather had done when they acted as go-betweens for the settlers and natives. This war between brothers was far different, and she hoped less brutal. At least she witnessed Derek make the effort to offer peace on more than one occasion. Gently she'd advised him not to stir up more strife and to let God work with Clay, and Derek agreed.

She ran her fingertips over the yellow and blue border she'd stitched in the deerskin over her heart, using the last of her precious glass beads to symbolize the sun and the Son, who'd led Penny and Derek through the wilderness. God had played such an important part in their tattered lives, and she knew that He would always be at the core of their marriage. He had brought them together and ordered their steps. When their foolishness had torn them apart, His Spirit whispered to both their hearts, mending each with bright love and mercy and bringing them together once more, soon to be as one.

They had talked over their future and decided to live in her beautiful valley but not in the shanty Oliver had built. Instead, Derek would build them a home on the other side, at the end of the stream. He planned to start a ranch with his share of the profits from the silver, and when he'd told her what their future would involve, she felt eager to begin life as a cattle rancher's wife. "But first," he'd told her gently, "we have to find the mine."

She didn't mind. As long as she was with him, anywhere was home.

"Penny, are you in there?"

Clay's voice coming from beyond the muslin that covered the entrance jarred her thoughts to the present. She moved forward to pull the weighted cloth back.

He'd shaven off his thick growth of whiskers, and his shoulder-length curls still hung damp. "You look nice," he said, seeming uncomfortable. "You sure you want to go through with this?"

"Completely."

"You could do better." With the way she stared in shock, his face flushed. "No, I don't mean me. Like as not, I'll never marry. But any man would be better than my brother."

"You don't really mean that," she chided softly, and he lowered his eyes. "Clay, I know there's been a lot of hurtful things said and done between you both, but trust me when I say Derek has come to a full understanding of his mistakes. He wants to be makin' amends and doin' right by his family."

Clay scoffed. "Tell that to Linda, if you can find her." He shuffled his boots as though ashamed of his outburst. "I know you mean well, Penny. If it weren't for you and that you asked me to come, I wouldn't even be here today."

"Thank you for that." She laid a hand on his sleeve, already feeling a strong sisterly kinship for this young man, seven years her junior. She hoped he would one day find the happiness that she and Derek had found. Like Derek had once done, Clay, too, was running from God.

"I came to tell you the preacher's arrived," he said. "Derek had to ride outside town to some miner's camp to find him. He was delivering last rites. Kind of a fitting mood for the day."

"Clayton," she quietly chided. "Please don't do this."

At her steady look, he sighed with a sort of weary resignation. "Sorry."

"I love him. I want to be his wife. I'm happy to marry him."

He shook his head as if he couldn't understand her. Nothing Clay said caused her to hesitate or regret her decision. Throughout these past weeks, she'd seen the bitter conflict silently rage inside Derek—but a burning sincerity in his eyes had replaced it, along with his fervent desire to do right. Given time, Clay would see that his brother had changed.

"Mama, Mama!" Christa burst into the small room, her face aglow with excitement. She looked a good deal improved, and it was no secret she'd ferreted a soft spot in a couple of the gruff men's hearts—men who'd lost family, like the hotel manager, who'd become protective of Penny's small girls. She'd warned both never to go near the saloons, but she knew her girls had their own watchmen to ensure they stayed safe, as well as Derek and their soon-to-be uncle Clay.

"Lookit what I found!" Thrusting a bunch of blue and white posies upward, Christa almost hit Penny in the nose with them. "Livvie says brides are s'pposed to have bouquets, and I made one for you."

"Thank you, Christa." Penny took them in delight and inhaled the sweet fragrance mingled with earth and sun. "They're beautiful."

"Just like you, Mama." Christa grinned from ear to ear.

Olivia trailed in, blowing out a few high notes on her grandda's harmonica. Derek had spent hours instructing her, and Olivia rarely went anywhere without it. She stopped and grinned, lowering the instrument at the sight of Penny. "Mr. Burke is gonna flat keel over when he gets sight of you."

"I hope that's not the case." She smiled at her two daughters, their own hair shining and freshly braided, their faces rosy. "I declare, it isn't often I see my two girls looking so clean. And Olivia, don't you think after today you should call him something other than Mr. Burke?"

She cocked her head, seeming to consider. "You think he'd mind if I call him Pa?"

"I'll see you in the parlor," Clay murmured and left the crowded room before Penny could acknowledge him.

"Aye, I think he'll like that," Penny answered her daughter.

Olivia regarded her with uncertainty. "You think our real papa would mind?"

Christa's expression also grew anxious.

"No." Penny drew her small daughters close and held them. She thought she understood; they had come to love Derek and wanted him for a pa, but they didn't want to betray their real father by accepting a new one. "I think he'd agree 'tis a fine thing. And it's perfectly all right for you always to keep that special place in your heart meant just for him. There's room enough in those big hearts of yours for two papas, don't you think?"

Olivia smiled and nodded.

"Do you think he's watching us from heaven?" Christa whispered, peering up at the wooden beams.

"Well now, I don't know about that. But if he can and is, I'm sure he's looking down on his two girls with a great deal of approval. He'd be pleased to know we're content and going on with our lives. That was the kind of man he was; he wanted everyone happy." And that was the one reason why Penny finally had been able to release her pain of losing him; she knew Oliver would prefer that she not mourn his absence but would want instead that she open her heart to find love again.

She took a deep breath, preparing for the next step, and smiled. "And are you both ready to be joinin' me in this bonnie new adventuresome life that will be ours?"

"Aye!" Olivia said without hesitation, and Christa giggled, clapping her hands.

Minutes later, with one of her daughters on each side of her escorting her, Penny made her way into the cramped parlor area where Derek, Clay, and the minister waited.

"Hello, Mr. Matthis," Christa said in a loud voice to the man standing across the room near Clay. "I didn't know you were coming." Penny shushed her daughter, and the elderly hotel manager winked at Christa in greeting.

Then Penny saw Derek.

Her breath stalled as he turned from speaking with the preacher to face her, and she paused a moment to take in the change.

Clean-shaven, with his long, wavy hair trimmed and slicked back, he made a striking figure. A clean shirt of deep blue accented his eyes, and the black string tie he wore at his collar made him look like the gentleman she knew him to be. She'd rarely seen him minus his hat or without his hair hanging in his face and appreciated his fine, strong features, amazed at how handsome he really was.

As she walked forward, holding Christa's bouquet, and took her place beside him, his admiring gaze showed her he also approved of her choice. Derek touched the few wildflowers Penny had woven into one of her braids at her temple and smiled.

"My Penny." His words came quiet so only she could hear, but they echoed to the very core of her heart, creating a warm glow.

Behind them, Olivia began to play the harmonica. Stunned, Penny glanced her way, recognizing the tune as an old Scottish love song her da had once played, one of her favorites. She looked back at Derek in question.

He shook his head. "I taught her other songs and gave advice. She picked out the notes to that one from what she remembered your da teaching her. She thought it would make you happy and asked if she could play it today. I hope you approve."

"Aye." Tears misted Penny's eyes, and she felt, while listening to the sweet, lilting music, as if a part of her da were there with them. In his granddaughters, his legacy and her mother's legacy would never die. She would see to that.

She laid her hand in Derek's, hoping that with her eyes she expressed all the love she felt for him. With Derek, she would start a similar but new legacy.

A legacy of love and hope and faith that would carry on throughout the generations.

A TREASURE REGAINED

Dedication

A bundle of thanks goes to the special ladies who were there for me in a pinch—my faithful critiquers, without whose help I would surely be lost. Namely: Paige Winship Dooly, Theo Igrisan, Jill Stengl, and Therese Travis, and last but in no ways least, my mom. As always I dedicate this book to the Almighty Father, my Lord and my God, who was my steadfast anchor as I wrote through some of the most difficult times in my life and who has always been there for me.

Chapter 1

1869

Linda had learned three things in life: Never trust a stranger. Never tell a family secret. And if a stranger proved to be a scoundrel, always have a derringer close by.

Before the filthy miner with whom she'd hitched a ride could again clamp his meaty paws on her, she withdrew the small pistol strapped to her calf from beneath her ruffled petticoats—and pointed the weapon inches from his face.

"I may have only one shot," she said, her voice steady though her heart thundered in her ears, "but at this range, there's no way I can miss, even if I weren't good. And I am."

He lifted his hands in the air, his leer of desire altering to a mask of doubt.

She could jump off his wagon and travel on foot, but he might come after her. Even if she took his gun poking from the gun belt beneath his big belly, he could easily overtake her in his wagon.

"Get out," she commanded.

He stared at her as if she was loco then swung his head to look at the miles of sagebrush-covered plain and distant range of hills surrounding them. "You're joshing me."

"Either you get out, or I waste a perfectly good ball by shooting it betwixt your eyes."

He awkwardly scrambled over the edge of the wagon seat and stumbled to his feet. Linda kept her gun trained on him. She considered leaving him with nothing but felt the slightest twinge of conscience. Silverton was almost a day's journey west. Traveling on foot in the dark, he could lose his way or even die. No telling what would happen to him once night fell. Not that she cared one whit about his welfare, but she wouldn't be responsible for any man's demise, though there were those in Crater Springs who might argue that point. If they caught up with her.

Streaks of rose had begun to paint the underside of the clouds in tufts; sunset was fast closing in. She imagined the situation could become far worse for this lecherous miner.

On the evening before, from the room that her father's go-between had arranged at the hotel, Linda had heard the coyotes' not-so-distant howls, mournful and chilling, and had pulled the threadbare blanket high over her head. Then Derek, cunning beast himself, slipped inside her room and raided her belongings to take the one thing she'd hoped could give her a new start—the precious piece from a map he claimed should be his. Her mouth had gone dry when she'd first heard the slow, steady footsteps creaking over planks, and she peeked out from beneath the worn blanket to see who invaded her privacy in the dead of night. She'd met her relation only once, but in the glow from the lamp she'd left turned down, she recognized Derek from the back as he pawed through her reticule. Fear of what he might do to her if he knew she discovered his thievery kept her mute, barely daring to breathe. He'd withheld no disparaging remark upon their first encounter, and recalling his quarrel with their brother Clay, she wondered if Derek was capable of violence toward a woman.

Once he'd crept from her room and out of town, like the loathsome desperado he was, she hadn't delayed to make her own escape. Desperate to put distance between herself and Silverton, she'd left without a word to anyone and hitched a ride with the miner she now wondered what to do with.

The lecher's hand inched up his side, and Linda imagined a bullet lodged between her shoulders the moment she turned her back to him.

"Hand over your gun."

"Over my dead—"

She cocked the trigger.

"All right—all right." He fished the gun from the leather sleeve with a scowl. She held one hand out for it, keeping her derringer steady. "You can't leave me here with no means of survivin'!" he argued.

His weapon secured in her lap, she nodded to the back of the wagon. "Take your canteen, then. And be quick about it." She certainly wouldn't drink from anything he'd touched. He pulled the container from the wagon bed while she kept her gun fixed on him. "Leave the rifle," she warned when she noted him falter as though he might reach beyond the canteen.

"You're a crazy woman," he muttered, glaring at her.

"And you're the most despicable sort of snake alive."

"I was just tryin' to be friendly."

Glaring at him, she took up the reins and flicked them as she'd seen him do. She gave a curt "hyahhh!" To her relief, the mule obeyed her command. Ignoring the miner's curses that followed as she drove away, Linda recalled his last words to her. His punishing grip on her arm had been anything but friendly. And his wet lips aimed for hers had found only her cheek as she'd twisted from him, but their contact sickened her. She had ordered him to leave her alone, but he'd laughed and pulled away to unhook his gun belt. That's when she'd made her move and grabbed her own gun.

She'd robbed him of his snide laughter, and her virtue remained intact. Once again, she'd narrowly escaped a dark fate. But how many more times would fortune grant her such uncommon favor?

Linda drew a shaky breath. His intentions had been all too clear, and never would a man despoil her as her excuse of a father had done to her mother. The name Michael Aloysius Burke had spread into a condemning stain she wished to scrub from her life. And his two sons, her half brothers, had proven to be just as spiteful and stubborn and ornery. And downright hateful—especially the eldest, Derek. Clay hadn't been so bad, but neither had he defended her womanly honor, nor said more than a few obligatory sentences to her.

Impatient, she brushed away her tears with the back of her hand still holding the derringer. The memory of Derek's cutting words about her character sliced into her heart; she was none of those things he claimed. Let the Burke brothers keep their vile mine! She no longer wanted any part of it. Or them.

She would find a way to survive, as she had done since her ma died. She would find a new town, start over, change her name. Linda only hoped she could find a way back to civilization, some town with a stagecoach station where she could buy a ticket to anywhere with what little money remained. A horse-drawn carriage with six swift horses could take her someplace far, far away, never again to meet up with the despicable Burke brothers. . .or with Grady O'Callahan and his men.

The previous week's nightmare dashed up behind her with the unwanted thought, overtaking her and threatening her resolve, pushing her to find a cave in which to hide. Shivering, she flicked the reins with the vain hope that the placid mule might do more than walk; she knew little of how to control such a beast.

Linda studied the hills distant, to the east. No matter what community she found to begin anew, she wondered if she would truly be safe while those cutthroats were yet alive.

⋘

Kurt Michaels slipped his guns inside their holsters and grabbed his broad-brimmed hat from the table, hoping to make a quick exit.

"Kurt, is that you?" Doreen called from the back room.

No such luck. He withheld a frustrated groan as she hurried out to the main room, still tying her wrapper around her thick waist. Her face was flushed, her brown eyes anxious. "You're not leaving? Not without breakfast?"

"I didn't mean to wake you. My intent was to slip out real quiet-like. Guess I'll have to work on that strategy."

"And cause me no end of worry?"

"It all comes with the job."

"Which I wish you didn't have."

He didn't bother with a reply; he'd heard it all before but was power-less when it came to his ability to manage the circumstances. "Hobbs spotted two strangers near the hills west of here who fit the description of those men involved in the stagecoach robbery of the gold shipment. I need to go."

"Before breakfast?"

"I'll stop by for dinner. I appreciate you letting me use a room."

"You're always welcome, Kurt. You know that. I just wish you didn't practi-cally live down at that musty, depressing excuse for a lodging. But I suppose you must. Especially during those times you have a guest." She fumbled over the last word and sighed, pulling the edges of her woolen wrapper tight. "Do be careful. Don't do anything dangerous. You hear?"

He smiled with affection but gave no guarantees. His choice of a job put him dead center to every threat known to the West, and she knew it. But he realized her vain warnings stemmed from concern and her vow to his parents, both of whom had died on the California Trail eleven years before. Sometimes he wondered if Doreen still thought him the orphaned boy of twelve who needed to be looked after. She wasn't any relation, though she was like blood kin. She'd been his ma's best friend for years before they'd taken the wagon train together on that fateful journey; Doreen also lost family at the time.

Kurt gave her a comforting kiss on her plump cheek before heading outside to saddle his horse. Truth was—and they both knew the facts—each time he rode out, he never knew if he'd see her or Jasperville again.

The morning meandered into noon, the ever-rising sun unloading its full arsenal of heat. After hours traveling west, with no humanity in sight, he heard a mule bray in protest beyond the crook of a hill. To his shock, a woman's hoarse order of angry desperation followed.

"Get yourself up, you hear me? You fool beast! What's the matter with you?"

Kurt quietly rode farther and encountered a bewildering sight.

A young woman with hair as red as the deepest sunset and skin almost as pale as the snow-topped Ruby Mountains pushed on the hind end of a mule, attempting to get it to stand. Kurt wasn't sure what shocked him most: the sight of her bright green gown, as fancy, shiny, and unfitting as any saloon girl's, all torn and dusty with a rip along one sleeve, or the slim bearer's wild, thick ringlets of hair—half of them coming out of the pins, half still anchored inside them. Never had he seen hair of such a color.

He sized up the situation before she could spot him. The mule bore dark stripes on its sorrel coat, testament of its abuse. But this girl hadn't bothered grabbing the whip he noted in the back of the crude wagon filled with mining equipment. And she sure didn't look as if she owned part or parcel of the wagon or the mule. Instead, she grunted as she planted her heeled black boots in uneven ground and tried to push the animal that would not be budged.

"Maybe she's letting you know she's had enough," Kurt said so low that at first he wasn't aware he'd spoken his thoughts aloud.

The woman startled and jumped from her crouch to a stand, whirling to face him. Her eyes were wild—and as pale a silver as the sky on a cloudy day. Unusual eyes that glowed and seemed to burn from betwixt coal-dark lashes. Her gaze rushed over his face and seated form, then back up again. "Who are you?" she croaked. "What do you want? And why'd you come sneaking up behind me?"

Sneaking had been a worthwhile trait Kurt learned in his ten years of living in the West.

"I figure I'm the one who should ask the questions." He remained calm, though he felt suspicious of the situation and the way she eyed him with a guilty sort of misgiving. "This your wagon?"

She cleared her throat, edging her chin up a mite. "And who else's would it be?"

He nudged his horse into a walk around the small, rickety mode of transport, taking it all in at a glance. From the corner of his eye, he noted her anxious gaze never left his face.

"Had any luck in these hills?"

His change of topic seemed to rattle her. "Luck?"

"Mining for ores. Must be a difficult chore in that dress." He glanced down past the ruffled hem of her petticoats. "And those shoes."

"My. . .my escort left. For a short time."

"Really." He lifted an eyebrow. "Out here in the middle of no-man's-land, 'your escort' just took it upon himself to leave you out here all alone and take a stroll through the sagebrush?" He grew serious. "So, tell me. Where's your escort now?"

"He. . .I. . ." She floundered for words, sliding her palms down the sides of her dusty satin skirts. "He should be back soon. So you better get going. Before he comes back."

Kurt shook his head in slow refusal, a wry grin twisting his lips. "I highly doubt this mule and wagon are yours, little lady." He dismounted and wrapped the reins over the wagon rim. "So the one question I have for you"—keeping a watchful eye on her, he moved closer—"is where'd they come from?"

Swift as a rattler's strike, she bent down and grabbed something from beneath her skirts. Before he could react at the glint of silver, Kurt faced the short muzzle of a derringer pointed his way.

"Stay right there!" She held both her arms outstretched before her, hands clamped around the pistol's handle while she took a step back. "Don't come any closer."

Slowly he raised his hands, though he doubted at this range the lead ball could do much harm. Over the distance of a card table, the slow shot fired from the small gun could kill, but with him standing some ten feet away, he wasn't so sure. He'd never taken the risk and decided not to tempt fate now. He moved his arms higher, until his hands were level with his shoulders. His vest pulled away, and the sunlight glinted off his badge. He hadn't thought her eyes could go much wider.

"You're a. . .a. . ."

"Deputy Kurt Michaels." He took another step. "And you are?"

Rather than answer, she hurriedly backed up another few steps, reminding him of a cornered, wounded wildcat. Her eyes glazed over with fear.

"I'm not going to hurt you," he soothed while trying to remain unaffected by her seeming vulnerability.

She glared at his attempt to put her at ease. Slight as a girl, appearing young enough in features to be one, but bodily endowed enough to show she was a woman, his fiery adversary mystified him. With the manner in which her arms went from trembling to outright shaking, he didn't think she would remain armed for long. He'd never tangled with a female outlaw, had been raised by Doreen to treat the few women in Jasperville with respect, and had no clue of how to handle this situation.

"But, lady, if you don't tell me who you are and where you got those goods, I just might have to take you back with me. Put you in a jail cell and let you cool your heels off for a while."

His mild warning provoked a curious reaction. She seemed to fold, as if her knees achieved the texture of lard. Thinking to catch her should she fall, Kurt leapt forward but halted within a few feet of the vexing female when she recovered and lifted her aim the short distance it had fallen. This close, she definitely could do damage with her derringer.

"Leave me be." Her words rushed out in a whisper. "Just please, go away and pretend you never saw me. I haven't done anything wrong. *Honest. . .*"

Her last words came out like a child's mournful plea, the hint of tears honing a high edge to them. She backed up until she reached the edge of the hill, then whirled around and raced behind it. Kurt gave chase. She stumbled on some brush, losing her hold on the small pistol. As she bent to scoop it up, he caught her before she could make another escape. An explosion rocked his ears as the gun went off in their struggle and the lead ball slammed into the dirt near his boot. A steady amount of pressure to her slim wrist, and she released the weapon with a little cry. He bent and swiftly tucked it in his waistband behind his suspender while keeping his hold on her upper arm.

"No, don't—please!" She pulled away and beat at him with her fists, her arms flailing as he attempted to get a firm hold on them. "Don't touch me!"

"Calm down, I'm not going to hurt you," he said between clenched teeth. Her elbow connected painfully with his jaw.

In two moves, he bent and gripped her tight over his shoulder. With his other arm clamped around her kicking legs, he walked with her back to the wagon. Her head hanging down behind him, she squirmed and pummeled his back with her fists. One swift slap to her derriere stopped her, likely from shock at his authoritarian act. But Kurt had reached the end of his patience with this childlike female bandit or whatever she turned out to be. He deposited her in a heap next to the wagon wheel. Blinking like an owl, her mouth agape, she looked up at him.

"Let's you and I get one thing straight." He kept his voice quiet, with a warning edge to it to show he wouldn't tolerate any more of her nonsense. "I'm the law in these parts. And something mighty peculiar is going on here. That's reason enough for me to investigate. Until I get some answers, you won't be getting rid of me."

Where earlier he'd thought she might cry or swoon, now the glint of defiance shone bright in her strange, pale silver eyes. She crossed her arms over her chest and clamped her lips shut in a compressed line, making her seem even more of an errant child.

"That the way you want it? Fine." He scooped some rope out from the back of the wagon and grabbed both her wrists.

"What are you doing?" she gasped as he tied her hands together in front of her.

"I would have thought that obvious." He looked into her eyes, and she averted her gaze to her skirt and upraised knees. "I'm taking you back with me. As my prisoner."

If he'd thought his pronouncement of her fate would stir up a little surrender on her part, he was sadly mistaken. Determination swept over her features, fast and furious, carving a hard set to her angular jaw and prominent chin. She remained mute as he lifted her up under one arm, helping her stand, and walked with her to his horse. She stumbled, and he increased the pressure of his hold to keep her balanced.

The mule hadn't budged, and Kurt let it be for now. He had no desire to get into a skirmish twice in one day with a stubborn female.

Chapter 2

If Linda had her way about it, she would never talk to the insufferable lawman again. But when he hoisted her up like a sack of flour onto his wide saddle, then swung up behind her, she protested the arrangement profusely.

"Betsy there isn't going to move, and I'm not about to let you walk all the way on foot."

The image of her staggering behind his horse into town, the deputy leading her bound with rope like a notorious desperado of the worst sort, made her wince. "Betsy?"

"I call all mules Betsy."

She grimaced at the ornery beast that didn't deserve a name so sweet and cupped her hands around the saddle's pommel, dropping her gaze to it. "*You* could walk."

He chuckled low as if her remark oddly amused him. "It's hours back to the town I'm from, and I don't aim on arriving footsore and weary. And I sure don't intend chasing you all over these hills should you take it into your mind to break free and steal my horse, too."

"I didn't steal that mule."

"No? Then where'd it come from? You can't tell me those mining tools belong to you, either. Not with those smooth, lily-white palms you have. I'd be interested in knowing the location of the true owner. I don't believe he took off on any short trek in the middle of nowhere without a beast to ride, and I wonder if maybe a man's blood doesn't soil those pretty hands of yours, as well."

She didn't answer but stared at her hands, her knuckles made even whiter from clutching the pommel. She should have kept her gloves on, though likely he would have found that even more suspect.

"That's what I thought."

"Wait!" She hesitated, not desiring to ask any favor from the uncouth deputy but seeing no way around it. "My reticule. It's on the wagon seat. I don't want to leave it behind."

He brought his horse around and bent to scoop her purse from the high plank seat. Instead of offering it to her, however, he stretched the black cloth open and looked inside.

"What are you doing?" she objected. "You haven't any right to look in my bag! That's my property, you—you—"

He didn't close the drawstrings until he'd made a thorough search—the second stranger to rifle through her belongings. Obviously, he was no better a man than her half brother Derek.

Her captor slid both drawstrings over her bound wrists. "I had to make sure you weren't carrying any more weapons," he explained dryly. "I don't want to have to dodge another bullet or a knife and go west before my time." He scooped the miner's gun from the seat where she'd left it and tucked it at the back of his waistband.

Linda compressed her lips into a thin line. She'd had a lot of practice with her derringer; regardless, she didn't think she could ever kill a man, even in defense. Maim, yes; kill, no. Faced with the opportunity twice in two days, she'd failed on both occasions. That this lawman thought otherwise didn't astonish her; it seemed her curse to carry around the black mark of a wanted criminal wherever she went, regardless that she'd done no wrong and he didn't even know her name or history. Neither of which she planned to tell him. True, the alternative was a jail cell, but surely she could convince the sheriff of whatever town they were headed to that she wasn't guilty of any crime, without having to wade knee-deep into explanations this deputy wouldn't likely accept. She scarcely believed them, and she had lived through the painful realities of each one.

She needed to think out her words, produce a sincere argument that would be believed without question. Everything had happened too fast with the deputy; he'd come upon her with an element of surprise that disallowed time for rational thought. But now she had more time to plan a careful rebuttal to the sheriff. One that would ensure both her innocence and swift release.

As the lawman's horse made its way over uneven ground, Linda's shoulder blades knocked against her captor's hard, unyielding chest more than once. Each time it happened, she sat as far forward as she could without sliding off or toppling over the side. His arms closed her in as he held the reins, though his sleeves only brushed against her upper arms now and then. He also appeared to make every effort not to touch her more than required.

After what seemed like hours of such torture, but likely was closer to one, they stopped at a river that appeared at the bend of a hill. He dismounted. Before she understood his intent, he again manhandled her, his big hands circling her waist. He pulled her down from his saddle, setting her upright on her feet.

"You could have left me up there," she said, her low words petulant.

"Let's just say I'm a cautious man."

His quiet admonition rang all too clear. She had no experience with either horse or mule, save for the fiasco of the past day when "Betsy" took it into her head to ignore all orders. And Linda certainly wouldn't try to escape on his beast with her hands tied. But she refrained from admitting that, sure he wouldn't believe a word she said in any case. She licked her lips as she stared at the shimmering water.

While he held his canteen under the stream and his horse stood nearby drinking its fill, she took the opportunity to study her guard. Lean and strong, he stood almost a head above her though he crouched at the riverbank now. His mode of dress was much like any other man's in the West: tan shirt, brown leather vest and trousers, with a pale brown kerchief around his throat. From this angle, she could see his face beneath his gray felt hat, the dark cord from the broad brim dangling below his strong chin. Curiosity mounting, she lifted her appraisal higher.

His thick dark brows, straight and demanding, winged the slightest bit at the corners. Beneath them, his clear green eyes shone so pale and bright they had appeared to see right through her. Swiftly, she lowered her gaze before he could look her way and again subject her to their power. A straight nose lent further strength to his character, and a dusting of whiskers darkened his jaw and upper lip. But it was his mouth that gave her pause. Firm and set and every bit as determined as the rest of his features, his full lips appeared oddly soft and gentle as well, curving up a tad at the corners, even when he didn't smile, which he'd done only in mockery. The deep crescents that had creased his cheeks made him seem more boy than man, but only then. She wondered if any morsel of gentleness or kindness existed inside this law-man and recalled how he'd spoken when he first came upon her. Calm and peaceful, as though assuring a startled doe. . .

With a start, she realized he now stared at her, and she shifted her attention to a distant range of blue hills. When she looked back at him, he still watched her, his eyes narrowed in a squint though the sun hovered behind him.

She mustn't let him unnerve her, couldn't afford to lose her resistance, even for a moment. She firmed her jaw and stared right back.

Still watching her, he lifted the canteen to his lips. Before he took a drink, however, he hesitated, then lowered it. Linda watched as he stood, slow and wary as though sizing up an unknown foe, and strode toward her.

"You must be thirsty." He surprised her by holding the canteen her way.

Her fingers prickled and stung, almost numb from the hemp binding her wrists, but she lifted her hands pressed palm to palm to try to get a good hold of the container. As if aware of her predicament, he lifted the canteen to her lips and tilted it so she could drink.

Having had no such refreshment since the previous day, Linda tipped her head back and gulped the water in relief, not caring that it dribbled down her chin and neck and dampened the ruined dress that had been her mother's. She lifted her bound hands to the container to tilt it back farther.

"Easy," he cautioned. "You don't want to drink too fast."

A small involuntary whine of protest escaped her throat when the metal rim left her lips. He stared at her a moment longer before taking his own pull from the canteen, then stared again as he swiped the back of his hand along his mouth.

"You know, you can make this a lot easier on yourself if you'll just give me the answers I'm looking for." His voice came as easy and warm as a stream of thick, slow syrup. "Who owns the wagon and mule? The Greer brothers? Have you been working with them, maybe even had a part in robbing the gold shipment last month?"

The brothers' name sparked a flicker of recognition in her mind, but too dim to realize fully. From his frown, he'd seen her blunder. She pressed her lips together, loath to make the mistake of trusting a man who might betray her.

He sighed and shook his head. Taking hold of her arm, he turned her around. "Time to go." Again, he lifted her onto his saddle and swung up behind her. This time, she was prepared for the contact but no less annoyed by it. Annoyed and uneasy.

When his horse made a swift dip as it took a slope downhill, she braced her arms, holding onto the pommel for dear life. Regardless, she felt her skirt slide against the smooth leather and threaten her balance. Without a word, her guard switched the reins to one hand, and his arm wrapped around her middle to anchor her securely against him.

Linda gasped at the feel of his lean strength along her back. A tumult of emotions shivered through her, emotions that sent her heart into an erratic thrumming pattern. She wondered if he felt it beat against his arm. No man had ever held her in such a familiar manner, though some had tried. It made no sense, but she knew no fear. Odd, considering he'd made himself her enemy. Whatever triggered such strange reactions inside she failed to recognize. Nor did she care to speculate, now wishing only to arrive at their destination and put distance between them.

With relief, she soon noticed two rows of buildings in the distance. His town. As they approached, he dropped his hold from around her waist, and she felt a morsel of gratitude that he would not add to her indignity if anyone should see them. To arrive in her bound state, practically sitting in his lap, was humiliation enough.

A replica of other nondescript mining towns, the deputy's boasted one main street, two saloons, a hotel, and a telegraph office from what she could see. Aside from its large size, the town's one difference was that most of the crude buildings appeared entirely made up of wood or stone, though she spotted tents with false fronts, too. Many structures that lined the smaller town of Silverton were nothing more than mean canvas walls and roofs with wooden false fronts. Here as there, men swaggered along the boardwalks or busied themselves in the tasks of their trades. Up ahead, a team of grays pulled a ramshackle wagon loaded down with supplies. Linda's heart surged a beat when she recognized a wooden sign for the Wells Fargo stagecoach station. She averted her gaze before her captor could note her interest.

Those men who caught sight of the deputy with his female prisoner stopped what they were doing and stared, all a-gawk. Noting the lack of women in the township, Linda surmised that her bound condition wasn't the sole reason for their keen interest, though she was sure it sweetened the yawning pot of their curiosity. She was accustomed to being ogled, but never in such a mortifying state of disrepair. Her face burned with embarrassment, but she kept her head held high.

They stopped before a small structure of wood and stone. Iron bars in the high, square-cut window made their destination apparent. Her guard dismounted, then lifted her down. At his nod that she was to go inside first, she preceded him into the cramped, one-room building, feeling much like a lamb soon led to the slaughter. She hoped the sheriff proved more sympathetic than his stoic deputy.

As they entered the dim jailhouse she darted a look around, hoping for sight of his superior. A small desk and empty chair sat against the wall facing a long row of bars. Three posters with drawings of sullen outlaws wanted dead or alive, along with the price on their heads, hung from the walls. One of the surly faces looked strangely familiar, and she looked away from the penned sketch, uneasy. A tall wooden case held a set of rifles on the wall behind the desk. A ring of keys hung on a hook near that. Other than a short stool where a stack of books sat, the cramped room held little else, save for the dismal row of metal bars enclosing what looked like a huge cage, with another row of bars inside, halving the cage into two separate cells. No one else occupied the building.

Her captor untied her hands, then took the ring of iron keys and opened the door, his silent order clear in his grave eyes. Tenderly rubbing her chafed wrists, she brushed past him and into the cell.

"So, where's the sheriff?" she asked, turning to face him.

The deputy's smile was tight, scornful. "U.S. Marshal Wilson is still doing poorly from a gunshot wound he suffered during the gold shipment robbery, not quite two weeks ago. All courtesy of your associates, the Greer brothers. But then, you probably already knew that. Didn't you?"

She gaped at him in shock as the cell door swung shut with a condemning clang.

Chapter 3

With one ankle crossed over the other, the heel of his boot propped on the edge of his desk, Kurt leaned back in his chair until it touched the wall. He stared at the open page of the book he held until his eyes burned in an attempt to get his mind off the woman in the cellblock before him. Usually the Psalms gave him a sense of peace; today, he felt more aware of his prisoner, who sat silent on her cot, than of King David's exalted poetry and prayer.

"Deputy?"

He lifted his attention off the page. How could the woman give off such an air of innocence? With her big eyes hopeful in her slim face, she looked little more than a child. But he'd seen by her expression, which she wasn't quick enough to shield when he'd brought up the name, that she did indeed know Amos and Jonas Greer. So she couldn't be as innocent as she pretended.

"Could I please have some water?"

Every trace of the spitting and clawing she-devil he'd first confronted had retreated in the hour since he locked her up. In her stead, a meek stranger watched him, as docile and polite as a prim schoolmarm, eyes gentle, cupped hands held palms up in her lap. Kurt suspected her entire manner had to be a ploy.

Heaving a sigh, he righted the chair back to its four legs and set the book on the desk. From a pail of water on the floor, he brought a full dipper to her cell, holding it to her between the bars. She reached with both hands and took it, emptying the tin cup of the dipper in a few hasty swallows.

"Thank you." Her eyes downcast, she handed the dipper back.

He remained fixed until she again looked up at him. Vulnerability shimmered in her dove gray eyes; she did seem as out of place behind iron bars as a bird trapped inside a dark cave.

"At least tell me your name and where you come from."

At his gentle urging, her eyes flickered in surprise. She looked at the floor again.

"You're only making this harder on yourself," he grumbled.

The door creaked open from behind, a ray of light cutting a path to where they stood.

129

"Deputy?" Lance Campbell strode inside, his twelve-year-old twin sister behind him. "Mrs. Doreen wants to know if you'll be comin' to dinner." The boy halted, his mouth agape as he caught sight of the prisoner. "Glory be. . ."

"Lance," Kurt cut in before the boy could ask questions he didn't want to answer. "Does your ma know you two are here?"

The boy nodded.

"All right, then. I need to step out and send a telegram. Think you can keep an eye on things for a few minutes?"

"Sure!" Lance's eyes shone with excitement at the long coveted task. He wore a kerchief around his neck, just like Kurt, and had made no secret that he hoped to become a deputy someday.

"I can help, too," Lindy was quick to assure. "Just tell me what to do."

"Help your brother." Kurt replaced the dipper in the pail. "If she needs more water, give it to her." He changed his mind about hanging the keys on the hook, instead taking them with him. The unknown woman, despite her innocent appearance, seemed cunning; he didn't put it past her to trick the children into setting her free.

"Is she an outlaw?" Lance's stage whisper sounded both thrilled and puzzled as he stared at the quiet captive, who'd again taken a seat on her cot. "I never seen a woman one before."

"Time will tell, I suppose." Kurt grabbed his hat and slipped it on before heading to the telegraph office. He ignored the curious looks of several men who'd seen him bring in his prisoner and felt somewhat surprised that no one stopped him to ask questions about her presence.

He passed by the abode that belonged to the washerwoman, stopped, then turned around and went inside. Tillie Riverdale looked up from a pile of men's shirts and smiled, revealing spaces of a few missing teeth. Her cheeks were forever rosy due to the constant steam from the kettles of lye, and her eyes sparkled with life.

"He doing any better today?" Kurt asked with a smile of greeting.

"Same as usual and ornery as ever. Go on back. He's waiting for you."

That surprised Kurt; he hadn't told the marshal he was coming. The moment Kurt walked into the bedroom, the patient abandoned any greeting. "I hear tell you have a new prisoner."

Kurt stared in surprise, part of his mind noting that his friend's face still looked a shade gray. But he seemed more energetic, and the fresh bandage across his ribs bore no blood. With no practicing doctor in town, Kurt had been the one to cut out the bullet the Greer brothers had lodged in the marshal's side. He'd used a knife held over a flame and whiskey from one of the saloons to douse the wound. At least the marshal's widowed sister had a passel of homemade cures, and obviously they'd done their job. Marshal Wilson still appeared weak, but Kurt noted the feisty sparkle in his eye and imagined Tillie had a hard time keeping her normally active brother in bed and out of the jailhouse.

"Don't look so surprised, Kurt. You must realize that in a town this size, news of a pretty little lady with her hands tied and riding in front of the deputy spreads faster than lard in a hot kettle."

Kurt nodded and took a seat in the chair by the cot. "I suppose I should have figured you'd be the first one informed. Truth is I know nothing about her or where she comes from, so I can't tell you much."

In the next few minutes, Kurt spoke of their meeting and everything that elapsed since he'd left the jailhouse to search for the two strangers. "I haven't the foggiest notion of what to do."

The marshal puckered his lips in thought. "I'd send a telegram to the lawmen who preside over the closest towns, ask about her. Send a description. Sounds like she's one to stand out in a crowd and not easily forgotten."

Kurt couldn't deny that. "And meanwhile?"

"Matters being what they are, I'd keep her right where she is. You acted wisely. If she's in trouble or runnin' from a dangerous situation, that cell is probably the safest place for her, under your guard. And if she's wanted, then that goes without saying. I have faith in you, boy." He slapped Kurt on the knee. His senior by at least ten years, the marshal often acted like a father to Kurt, ever since they'd first met ten years ago. He'd seen something in Kurt that no one, except Doreen, ever had. "You have more brains than the townsfolk give you credit for. I made you my deputy for a reason, and now you're in charge till I get out of this godforsaken bed and again take up my duties."

"Just don't push things before you're ready," Kurt said in concern. "Last thing we need is for you to go busting up my patchwork." He winced, recalling the gruesome task of cauterizing the wound and the repulsive smell of burning flesh.

"You did a pretty good job with that, too, though I wouldn't recommend you to the blacksmith. But you saved my life. I owe you, son."

Uneasy with the praise and sudden emotional turn of the conversation, Kurt fidgeted. "I reckon I should send those telegrams and head back. The Campbell twins are keeping a watch on her till I get there."

"Lance and Lindy? Well now. I reckon that boy'll make a fine deputy one day. He sure has the desire to learn."

"Not if his ma has anything to say about it."

The marshal's ears perked up. "You been by her place lately?"

"No." A wash of heat crept up Kurt's face. "Not after that supper we shared.

We just don't think alike, don't have the same ideas. She's a loyal, hardworking woman who would make any man proud. But she isn't the one for me."

"Not too many females to pick from here in the West. Not much room for bein' so picky." Staring down at the sheet that covered his legs, the marshal chuckled, as if some idle thought amused. He lifted his hand to his side in pain and winced.

"What?" Kurt prodded.

"I was just thinking of your lady prisoner gettin' the jump on you, and you facing down that little ole derringer and tryin' to get it away from her. That must have been a sight! One doesn't see that kind of thing happen, not with you."

"Glad to hear I'm a good source of amusement," Kurt said dryly, hiding a smile as he realized the marshal must indeed be faring better since he sounded more like himself. He stood. "Guess on that note, I'll take my leave."

"Come by if you need my help with anything else. And on your way out, if you wouldn't mind, tell my sister I'll take some of that gruel she offered. A man could do worse, I suppose."

Kurt nodded in acknowledgment as he moved through the doorway. Tillie stood nearby and rolled her eyes to look at the ceiling. "I heard."

With a lazy grin, Kurt inclined his head in farewell, his finger and thumb touching the brim of his hat, and left for the telegraph office. He hoped the mystery of the gun-toting female who occupied his jailhouse would soon be explained and someone would take her off his hands. Kurt didn't want to admit it, but she was getting under his skin in more ways than one.

⌑

Linda sat on the lone cot of her cell.

Her cell. . .

She laughed in self-derision. The destiny she didn't deserve and had tried so hard to evade had caught up to her, trapping her in its punishing bonds. Why did she seem fated to suffer for another man's crime? The short string of good fortune she'd been surprised to receive earlier in the week had evidently frayed. All she'd ever wanted was a chance to start over in a life free of troubles and gunmen and smooth-talking snakes who lied through their teeth, roping everyone into believing their every word and never seeing past their disguises. Only she had not been fooled.

The jailhouse door swung open, and the deputy strode inside. The children, having grown bored with questioning her and getting no response, had resorted to amusing themselves with the few items on Kurt's desk. Now they jumped to attention like small soldiers waiting for their captain's next command.

Linda assumed he would scold them for touching his belongings as his gaze swept over the short stack of books now strewn across the desk and laid open, and she was astonished when he did no more than give a slight shake of his head and smile as if their behavior didn't surprise him. "You two go on home now. Did she give you any trouble?"

"She don't say much," the boy complained.

"No, she doesn't do much of that," Kurt agreed.

Linda frowned at the manner in which he spoke, as if she was absent from the room. No doubt he did it to rile her and compel her to speak up. She clamped her lips and shifted her focus to the blank wall.

"You comin' to supper again soon?" the girl asked hopefully.

"Don't know. Maybe someday." Kurt seemed uneasy.

She heard the children's steps hurry to the door, the creak of hinges, and wood scuffing wood as it swung open. The early evening sun again warmed her shoulder as a ray of it slanted through the bars.

"Lindy—"

Shocked, Linda turned in question as Kurt spoke the name so like her own, the same endearment her mother had called her as a child. Too late, she saw Kurt addressed the girl but hadn't failed to notice Linda swing her head in his direction.

His eyes squinted as with revelation, and he stared at Linda while he spoke to the child. "Please tell Mrs. Doreen I won't be able to make it for supper after all, but I sure would appreciate a meal. And one for my prisoner, too."

"Sure thing, Deputy!" the girl sang out with a smile.

Linda looked back at the wall, wishing she hadn't been so foolish. Her telling gesture had presented him with what she'd never meant to offer. The door closed and he moved toward the cell. Warily she observed him.

"So, your name is Lindy. Who would have figured you'd share a name with Lance's sister. Guess the Almighty gave me a hand there."

She remained quiet.

He shrugged and quirked his mouth as if unconcerned. "Doesn't matter if you don't talk. I sent telegrams out and should receive the answers I need soon. But just so you know, things might go better for you if you don't put me through all that waiting."

She considered his words. He had shown himself to be clever and determined. Likely he would find out about her soon enough, and with this deputy in charge and the marshal wounded. . .

"With that bright red hair of yours and those eyes, I don't imagine it'll take much for someone to remember a young woman like you."

"Linda," she said abruptly. "My name. It's Linda."

She sensed him grow alert. "You have a last name?" His voice was low, gentle, as if inviting a confidence.

She paused only a moment. "Burke."

"And where are you from, Miss Burke?"

She supposed he would ferret out that information soon enough, but she just couldn't be the one to disclose it. Too much depended on her ability to convince him of her innocence before her enemies assured him of her guilt. Like it or not, the deputy who'd captured her was the sole person on whom she could rely. That fact rankled her, and she hoped she wasn't inviting another mistake with her decision.

"Instead of telling you my history, Deputy, how about if I satisfy another of your curiosities and tell you how I came to be in possession of that mule and cart? It's somewhat of a long story, but I imagine you've got the time."

His eyes brightened, and he nodded. "I do at that." He moved to grab his chair and set it backward in front of her cell, then took a seat, straddling it. He laid his arms across the backrest. "I'm listening."

She took in a deep breath and told him everything since the moment she'd left Silverton, though she left out the part about her half brothers, saying only she'd been searching for kin. Deputy Michaels listened with keen interest, and his eyes flashed with grim purpose at her mention of her hasty parting with the miner whose cart and mule she'd taken.

"I. . ." She hesitated. "I know I shouldn't have left him out in the middle of nowhere and robbed him of his things, but I was desperate to get away. I didn't mean to break the law. I didn't even want his things. But it was the only way I could see of protecting myself at the time."

"No man has any right to force himself on a woman." His voice came low, dangerous. "Under the circumstances, I don't blame you for what you did. But under the law, as a deputy, I'm sworn to uphold the letter of it and keep the peace." Clearly frustrated, he inhaled deep and let his breath out in a gust. "Anything else you want to tell me?"

She barely shook her head. His unexpected reaction in her favor produced a slender thread of hope that he might listen, might believe the rest of her story. Yet no one else had trusted her words.

"I understand your position, Deputy," she whispered, her gaze falling to her lap. "You have to do what's expected of you."

"Yeah, I do." His words came clipped.

Moments later, he shot up from his chair and paced to his desk, restless, as if he were the one caged. Astonished at his abrupt reaction, Linda looked up. With his lips pulled tight, he tidied the books in a neat stack, though she sensed his mind didn't order his actions and he struggled with another matter.

Wondering what she'd said to make him upset, she noticed the door again swing open. A plump woman of indeterminate age, with skin as pale and smooth as ivory, whisked inside, a covered tray in her hands. Linda's stomach lurched at the delicious aromas that wafted into the room with the new arrival. The woman stopped short at the sight of Linda, her mouth dropping open as she took her in from head to toe before glaring at the deputy.

"I got Lindy's message. I brought dinner."

"Thanks, Doreen. Just set it on the desk."

"A word with you, Kurt?" the woman ordered crisply when he failed to look her way.

He sighed. "Can it wait?"

"No, it most certainly can not." She set down the tray with a slight bang and swept out the door.

With an exasperated sigh, Kurt took his keys from his belt, and one of two plates on the tray. He unlocked the cell door, handing supper to Linda, who rose from the cot to take it. He held her gaze a moment, his eyes serious, as if he wished to say something that weighed heavy on his mind. Instead, he stepped out and closed the cell door, locking it behind him.

Linda watched him leave the jailhouse, curious about the conversation going on outside.

Chapter 4

Doreen didn't leave Kurt wondering for long.

"Kurt Michaels, you can't keep that woman here." Disbelief mingled with the edge in her voice.

"Well, the trough's too wet, and I haven't got anywhere else to put her." His flippant remark was a mistake; her eyes burned with grim severity, and he felt twelve years old again.

"It just isn't proper for you to be in that room alone with her, all that time and on through the evening. . ."

A flush of heat burned his ears. "Doreen, what kind of jailhouse do you think I'm running here? This isn't a saloon. She's my *prisoner*."

"I still say it isn't right. Tell me, what did a little thing like her do anyhow? Steal a chicken?"

"As a matter of fact, she did break the law and rob a man of his belongings." Though he didn't blame the girl, and if it had been him, he probably would have conked the filthy varmint over the head with his gun for good measure. He despised men who exerted their greater strength to subdue or injure the gentler sex. Women were to be treasured and protected, as the Good Book said. That was God's plan for men, not to bring women to harm. Which made him despise all the more that he'd been forced into this position because of his sworn oath always to put justice first. Her panicked behavior and evasion of him when he'd first ridden across her path made sense now, too.

Doreen crossed her arms, clearly dissatisfied with his answer, and Kurt sighed. "I don't know the full story yet, but there's a lot more she's not saying. She hasn't been forthcoming with much. Fact is I don't know much about her at all. Jail could be the best place for her right now. Other than keeping others safe from her, it might be keeping her safe from others. That's what Marshal Wilson said anyhow."

His mention of the marshal's name caused her expression to soften, though she gave a grunt of disapproval at Kurt's explanation. "Doesn't surprise me. Being a bachelor, he isn't seeing things clearly, either. You could ruin that girl's reputation by leaving matters as they are."

Now she was taking things too far. "You don't think I would do anything to—"

"Of course not. You're every bit the courteous gentleman when it comes to the ladies. But outward appearances can be just as damaging. People will talk."

Incredulous, he shook his head, wondering how his exercise in duty had ended up on a serving platter of parlor gossip. At least in Doreen's mind. But then, she was smart and usually correct when it came to judging character, whereas Kurt often felt inexperienced.

"I don't suppose you'd want to play chaperone for the evening?" he asked.

"That's a marvelous idea."

He hadn't thought she'd take his flippant remark seriously and got an image in his mind of her with her knitting needles, rocking back and forth on the creaky rocker she would likely bring along. Before he could object, she spoke.

"But I can't. I have too much that needs doing at the hotel." Her eyes lit up. "Why, that's the perfect solution! She can stay there. I have a room available." When he passed away, her husband had left Doreen with the reins to run the hotel that once had been a saloon—the first all-wood building to go up in town.

"Doreen, she's a prisoner, maybe even an outlaw."

"Posh! She's no more outlaw than I am."

How she could come to such a conclusion just by one swift appraisal, Kurt had no idea.

"If you're that concerned," she went on, "you can sit outside her door and guard it, if you really think there's a need. But she can't cut through wooden walls like she could canvas ones, and I doubt she'd try if given the chance."

"You have no idea what that woman is capable of." He shook his head at the memory of their meeting. "It's not that I don't appreciate the gesture, I just have never heard anything like it. Putting a prisoner in a nice hotel?" He scoffed. "She's not an honest traveler looking for a place to stay. And there's not a remote possibility that she might be innocent. She admitted she broke the law—"

"I thought you said you didn't know all that much about her."

"She's a thief, and thieves belong in jail." He finished his statement as though she hadn't again interrupted. But his words sounded as hollow as the unsettled feeling in his chest each time he declared Linda Burke's guilt. He needed to get out of there, and with nothing more to say on the subject, which as far as he was concerned was now closed, he ended their conversation. "I'm not all that partial to cold food, so if you don't mind. . ."

With a little huff that showed she minded a great deal, she curtly nodded. "I've said what needed to be said. I'll come by for the dishes in the morning."

The parting glance she gave made Kurt feel like the worst kind of rogue.

Uneasy, he strode back inside the jailhouse and to his now docile and gentle prisoner, who didn't act anything like one. At least when she'd clawed and spat and called him names, he'd felt vindicated by his actions. Now, after having heard her story, they felt unjustified.

⁘

Linda looked up as the door opened, noting the scowl on Kurt's face. Evidently his discussion with Doreen hadn't gone well.

Remembering his earlier words, Linda asked, "Is everything all right with the marshal? He hasn't taken a turn for the worse?"

"What?" His mind obviously elsewhere, he looked at her.

"The marshal. You mentioned earlier he'd been shot."

Kurt's eyes squinted in studied concentration as if he didn't know what to make of her. "He's on the mend."

"Glad to hear it." And she was. The Greer brothers were pure evil. Now that she remembered where she'd seen them, it didn't surprise her to hear they'd been the villains behind robbing a stage of its gold. She wondered if they'd acted under orders or if they'd committed the crime on their own.

The deputy continued to stare at her, then seemed to make an effort to do the exact opposite. Snatching off the napkin that covered his plate, he sat down, bowed his head in brief prayer, then tackled cutting his meat with a vengeance.

The minutes ticked by in a silent march leading to who knew what? Her execution by a hangman's rope? She looked at her own plate, the food barely touched but not from lack of flavor. She poked her fork into another hunk of what tasted like badger meat, forcing herself to chew and swallow. After sitting still in the quiet for so many hours and no longer brimming with irritation at the deputy, she felt the culmination of all the weeks leading to the past two days crash together inside her mind.

She was going to die. He would soon learn of the crime, believe all their lies, and step into the obligation expected of his office—ordering her execution. And she would die.

Linda trembled, imagining the thick, coarse rope tightening around the tender flesh of her throat. The tines of her fork repeatedly clinked against the stoneware, and she set it and the plate on the cot. She folded her hands and closed her eyes, trying to control her hitched breathing, loath to give in to the roaring fear that threatened to rip her insides asunder if she didn't give the tears release. Regardless, she felt moisture slide past her lashes and roll to her chin. She squeezed her eyelids tighter, her fingers curling into fists, nails digging into her palms. Desperate to regain calm, she thought of her gentle mother, who'd never done anyone harm and had passed mercifully, quietly, into death. Her mother may have been no saint because of her chosen profession, but at least she'd been spared all knowledge of O'Callahan's treachery before the disease took her life. Linda thought about her mother's soft arms enfolding her as a child, of her sweet Celtic songs from her family's homeland that calmed Linda when she couldn't sleep because of the carousing and coarse laughter in the great room below.

Thoughts of her dear mother quieted the roiling thunder inside Linda until she could again breathe evenly; the hot tears in her eyes cooled and she opened them. Realizing that all had gone very quiet, she looked toward the deputy and caught him watching her. He stared transfixed as though stunned, his mouth parted.

Feeling somewhat vulnerable knowing he had just witnessed her near hysteria, she looked away, brushing the backs of her fingers against her cheeks to whisk the telltale moisture from them. As she eyed the sparse contents of the cell where she was doomed to stay the night, something she'd never before noticed became awkwardly apparent.

"Deputy?" Her forehead and cheeks warmed with fiery heat, and she dared not look at him as she spoke. "When I need to, um. . .that is, when I should need privacy—not that I do now—but when I should. . ."

His chair legs suddenly scraped the planks. The thuds from his rapid foot-steps preceded the clank of metal as the key turned in the lock and the iron door swung open. She looked up in surprise, expecting him to hand her something. Instead, he took hold of her upper arm in a gentle but firm manner and escorted her from her prison.

"Where are you taking me?" she asked, bewildered as they left the jailhouse.

"To the hotel."

"Hotel?"

At the dour set of his mouth and hard edge to his jaw, she didn't dare question him further.

⤚

Keeping a firm hold on her arm, Kurt frowned. He walked with Linda along the boardwalk lit with dusky gold from the occasional lanterns that hung in open doorways and from posts. All of a sudden, he stopped and turned, pulling her to face him. "Just so you know, I'm doing this against my better judgment. Before we go one step farther, I need your word that you won't try to escape."

"Escape?" Clearly confused, she blinked. "From where?"

"I'm putting you in a room at Doreen's hotel."

Her jaw dropped.

"Your word?"

At his grim reminder, she stared at him bewildered but gave the slightest nod. "Yes. Of course."

He stared hard at her, wondering if he could really trust her. A shaft of moonlight lit her face and eyes, which looked up at him with earnestness. He grunted, hoping her cooperative reaction wasn't all a ploy, and turned back around with her, resuming their rapid gait. A few troublemakers congregated outside the swinging doors of the saloon, men who Kurt had frequently needed to throw in jail. That further strengthened his resolve. Even with separate cages, Kurt didn't like the idea of another likely candidate for imprisonment gawking at Linda or speaking foul to her. As he passed the men, who stared with blunt curiosity and more, his hold on her arm tightened.

"Deputy," one man Kurt recognized as Bart drawled in greeting. His lackey, Stan, tipped his hat to Linda, his manner in no way polite. Two other men leaned against the building, eyeing her as if she were prey.

"Boys." Kurt kept walking.

"Taking some time out with your prisoner, Deputy?" Bart called after him, his tone lewd. "Mighty fine night for a stroll." The other men guffawed.

"Ignore them," Kurt told Linda, never breaking his pace. He had Linda almost running to keep up with him.

"But—I don't understand," she said. "Why are you doing this?"

Good question. He didn't understand, either. Whether it had been the moving sight of her silent tears followed by her clear struggle not to break down but remain strong, or his sudden understanding of matters relating to her need for privacy, or even the gut knowledge that his whole treatment of her didn't feel justified—that she wasn't a true criminal and didn't deserve to be treated like one—Kurt couldn't say. Maybe his decision came from a mix of all three. But Doreen was right: jail was no place for Linda.

"Instead of questioning, just thank the Almighty for your change in circumstances." He glanced at her and stopped, turning her around to face him again. "But just so you know: I don't trust you, and I'll be keeping post outside your door."

He wasn't sure what he expected, but it hadn't been her grateful smile. Her eyes glimmered a soft silver in the moonlight. "Thank you, Deputy. You have my word that I won't try to escape."

Bemused, he stared a moment longer, then gave a swift nod and resumed walking with her to the hotel. Already, he questioned his decision and hoped it wasn't a mistake. Doreen greeted them, a shrewd light in her eye as if she realized all along Kurt would surrender.

"You mentioned a room?" he reminded before she could speak.

"Of course." She chuckled, then smiled at Linda and greeted her as if she was a guest. Taking hold of her other arm, she gradually pulled her from Kurt's captive hold. "I have a nice warm bed for you. The nights can be so cold. Are you new to these parts?"

"Yes, somewhat. Not really though." No longer to Kurt's surprise, Linda's answer revealed little.

Kurt shook his head, watching them, then followed the two women upstairs and to a room already prepared. A patchwork quilt had been pulled down from the mattress in invitation, and a kerosene lamp burned low. He shot a glance at Doreen. Her brows lifted in smug question, as if all the rooms were prepared in advance in case a guest might walk into one at any moment. Having spent a number of nights in just such a room, he knew that was not the case.

He sighed. "I'll need a chair. A blanket would be nice, too."

"I'll get them straight away. Right after I finish seeing to. . .what was your name, dear?"

"Linda," she answered quietly, her eyes huge, dazed, as she perched on the foot of the bed and stared back and forth between them as though uncertain of what would happen to her and waiting for the next scene to play out.

Kurt cleared his throat. "I'll just wait outside then."

"You do that," Doreen answered, not looking his way as she fluffed the feather pillow.

Feeling abruptly dismissed, Kurt strode into the dim corridor to wait. Soon, but not as soon as he would have liked, Doreen quit the room, closed the door, and fetched him a chair and blanket. She hadn't said a word since.

"Okay, what have I done now?" he asked in weary acceptance that he'd again upset her.

Doreen's eyes glittered. "That little gal in there needs your help something fierce. I can sense it, even if you can't. Poor thing. I have a feeling she has no one else to turn to."

He spread his hands out in confusion. "And me bringing her here isn't helpful? Allowing her to sleep in a comfortable bed rather than a cold cell isn't to her benefit?"

"Oh, don't give me that, Kurt. You've already condemned her in your heart, and that's a crying shame."

"If I had condemned her, she wouldn't be enjoying your hospitality right now."

"I hope you mean that." She looked intently at him. "God gave you wisdom, Kurt, I'll grant you that. And though I'm curious to know what made you relent in bringing her here, I won't ask. But I sense you struggling with the situation. And I'm sorry to say, I think you'd prefer seeing her guilty rather than searching out anything that might prove her innocence."

Her accusation stung. "I don't *prefer* anything, and right now I sure don't prefer wearing a badge. But I have to be impartial," he replied, irritated that she should reproach him for doing his job. "She's *not* innocent. I have to take that into account. She *did* take a man's things. A miner's mule and his wagon. And you know as well as I that here in the West, if the law isn't around to stop an angry mob, a man is hung for stealing another man's horse. From what I've witnessed here in town, I doubt many men would make allowances for her being a woman."

"She must have had good reason to take them." Doreen waved aside her guilt as if Linda had done no more than tell a small fib. "A girl like that doesn't have any need for picks and other sundry tools of the mining trade."

From what Linda had shared, she did have good reason, and her response had been a result of her fear. But Doreen didn't know that. Kurt stared at the usually principled woman, not sure if he'd understood correctly. "Tell me you're not condoning thievery?"

"Of course not. I'm merely suggesting that instead of looking only at the wrongs she committed—and I'm not saying she hasn't erred in judgment—try looking beyond all that. To her soul. She seems so lost and alone, and there may well be good reason she came here, having nothing to do with matters pertaining to the law."

He shook his head in bewilderment. "You've lost me."

"I don't think so." She smiled mysteriously and patted his shoulder. "If you ponder the matter, Kurt, you'll come to understand. I could tell you, but this is something I think you have to figure out for yourself. You're an intelligent man. Deep down in that golden heart of yours, I believe you already know what should be done." With that inscrutable answer, she left him to his guard duty.

Shaking his head, he sank to the chair and mulled over her words. Ever since he'd been a lad, Doreen had a habit of urging him to dwell on the problem to discover the proper solution, which she always claimed to know and said he must find. More irking than her enigmatic puzzles was the fact that she was often right. He appreciated that she taught him to think things through, but at times, he wished she would just give him a straight answer.

If only he had taken a different route that morning, far from those hills. Then none of this would have happened. Ever since he'd met his frustrating prisoner, he'd almost gotten shot, had endured a goodly portion of unease in her company and from others—all due to her company—and had struggled with his law-abiding decisions he once never questioned, unsatisfied with any he'd made. Leaving her at the jail rankled, but bringing her here didn't ease his conscience, either. He wondered what the marshal would say if he found out. Shouldn't be long now. Linda's presence was news to a town crowded with men.

Unleashing a weary breath, he pulled his hat over his eyes and leaned his head back against the wall. Always a light sleeper, Kurt had no doubts that should Linda try and escape he would awaken at the first creak of the door. But it wasn't a creak or her step that shook him from his light slumber.

A shrill scream pierced his mind, chilling him to the bone. He bolted from his chair, grabbed the latch, and threw open the door while withdrawing his gun from his holster. With one foot across the threshold, he came to a sudden halt and stared in shock.

The room lay in semidarkness. The lamp turned low gave him a clear view of the bed. In the throes of a nightmare, Linda lay tangled in a blanket that had twisted around her nightdress. Her eyes were squeezed shut, her face pale and glistening with beads of sweat, her flame-dark hair wild all around her. She cried out again. "You did this! *You!* No, don't come any closer. I won't let you harm me, too. . ."

His heart dropped, weighing as heavy as the rest of his body. His feet seemed to have turned to stone because he couldn't move them forward.

"Sweet Lord above, have mercy!" Doreen raised the plea heavenward as she hurried down the hall, her wrapper undone. "Kurt, what's happened?" Seeing him poised with his gun still raised, she added, "What did you do to her?"

Unable to find his voice, he shook his head in denial at her assumption that he'd had anything to do with Linda's terrified state. Doreen swept toward him; he managed to step aside so she could enter the room. He watched as she hurried to the bed and sat on its edge, gently shaking Linda's shoulder.

"My dear, you need to wake up. You're having a bad dream."

Linda awoke with a choked gasp, as if reality muddled into her nightmare and the person she'd been dreaming about had grabbed her as Doreen had. Linda's eyes were huge, her eyebrows bunched in fear. She blinked, clearly trying to sort fact from fantasy. Her breathing came ragged, as if she'd run the entire length of the main street.

"It's all right, dear." Doreen gathered her up in her arms. "It was only a dream. Nothing more. And dreams can't hurt you." As she murmured the soothing words, Linda stared over Doreen's shoulder at Kurt. Her expression was filled with confusion, shock, dread. He felt the impact of her terror straight to his bones.

He turned from the door, but rather than reclaim his chair, he faced the wall, head bowed, and closed his eyes. Doreen was right; Linda needed help. Yet without the full knowledge of what she was up against, or why, he struggled with how and where to draw the line between duty and compassion.

How, Lord? How am I supposed to do this?

What sounded like a minor stampede hit the stairs as a pair of boots clomped up them at a run. "Deputy! Come quick. Big fight going on over at the saloon."

Kurt wasn't surprised by the news, not after the way the rest of his day had gone. He nodded in acknowledgment at the young man, one of the miners' sons. "Thanks, Harlem." Weighing the balances between remaining with his prisoner and needing to break up yet another fight in a roomful of drunk and surly miners, Kurt grunted in disgust. Of course, he had no choice.

"We'll be fine here," Doreen called from the room. "You go on and do what you need to do."

Kurt pulled down his hat firmly and followed Harlem outdoors. He doubted Doreen would be privy to a jailbreak—or in this case, a hotel break—by allowing his prisoner to flee while his back was turned, though with Doreen's strange behavior tonight and her clear partiality toward the young woman, the likelihood wasn't entirely implausible. Still, he reasoned her strong ethics would kick in and she wouldn't break the law, even for Linda. What really troubled him about leaving his prisoner was the recollection of the words she had cried out in her sleep and the mounting certainty that she was in grave danger.

Chapter 5

Linda awoke to the sweet lilting of a lark's song. Feeling warm and snug, she opened her eyes, confused. At first, she couldn't place her location, until the memory of the previous day swooped through her mind like a hawk intent on the prey of her contentment.

Heart racing, she shot up to a sitting position and found herself the sole occupant of the room she'd been given. A padded and warm prison, thankfully, but a prison nonetheless. A pale gray sliver from the chink in the drawn curtains gave light to the room, testament that morning had dawned. Someone had extinguished the flame in her lamp, and she shivered at the realization that she'd passed the night in the pitch dark. At least she had slept, oblivious to the knowledge.

Memory of Kurt at her open door, his eyes burning into hers across the room while Doreen comforted her from the nightmare spurred Linda to jump out of bed and locate her dress. The green satin lay in a heap where she'd dropped it, and she frowned, wrinkling her brow as she bent to lift the soft dusty folds in her hands. Her fingers moved along the tear in the sleeve as she straightened.

When she'd chosen her mother's best dress to wear to her appointment with Mr. Townsend, she had yielded to a maudlin impulse in a desire to feel closer to her mother and give herself a measure of comfort. Little had she known she would be running for her life that day and fleeing to Silverton, with no opportunity to change into her everyday skirt and shirtwaist. Even so, she'd thought the gown would gain her admiration as it had for her mother. How wrong she'd been! On her mother, the material had shaped her slim curves well and had not pressed so tight around the bosom, nor had her mother had as much cleavage to reveal, and with shame, Linda recalled the manner in which the men leered at her as if she were a fallen woman. Or a dance hall girl meant to satisfy their lustful desires. Derek had regarded her with contempt, while Clay had averted his gaze, clearly uneasy.

Tears welling in her eyes, she let the dress fall back in a heap, both despising its sleek lines and feeling a strong sentiment toward the gown. She had so very little left of her mother, who'd sacrificed to ensure that Linda never went without. Regardless of how she felt about the dress, she could never wear it

145

in such a condition and grimaced when she remembered catching her sleeve against a protruding nail in the miner's wagon bed.

Her attention drifted to a dressing screen tucked in a corner of the room, and she drew a breath in shock, walking toward it. Across the top rim hung a skirt of soft gray wool, along with a fresh shirtwaist. She wondered if the clothes had materialized for her purpose alone because she wished it, then shook her head at such a foolish idea. She pulled the articles down, figuring them to be her size or very close to it.

A washbasin, toweling, and pitcher filled with water sat on a stand nearby, and gratefully she made use of them, sponging away the dirt. Minutes later, she discovered her hunch had been correct. The waist of the skirt fit a little loose, but not so much that it would slip down and cause embarrassment; stuffing the voluminous folds of the shirtwaist inside helped, and she felt grateful for the change into modest, clean clothing. She then pondered what to do with her hair. Half the pins had been lost the previous morning in her tussle with the deputy. Pulling the thick tangled mass over her shoulder, she did her best to braid it while stepping over to the one window the room held.

She peered between calico curtains. Directly below, a narrow veranda stretched across the entire front of the second level. She had noticed it upon their arrival last night, but her mind had been too muddled to give close scrutiny. She wondered how far of a drop it would be from her window. The distance didn't look so great. She switched her focus past the white balustrade to the street. Men walked along the packed dirt, and a man led a mule by a rope, making her think of the stubborn Betsy. Her heart seemed to leap to her throat when she recognized the building directly across from her window bearing the sign of the stagecoach station, the only sure means to her escape.

Catty-cornered to that, a saloon rose up, its white and red facade much like the hotel's, with its own veranda along the front. A girl, scantily clad, with dark hair falling in ringlets past her bared shoulders, leaned on one of the balustrades and addressed a man in the street. A surge of pity for the woman made Linda pucker her brow. She felt as if she stared into a looking glass of what could have been and saw an image of herself had she yielded and chosen not to fight back. How easily that woman's fate might have been her own.

Now she not only struggled to guard her virtue, but she also fought to cheat death. She had promised the deputy she wouldn't run; already she questioned her weakness at that moment. His burning eyes had compelled her to give her vow, one she felt powerless not to grant; she'd felt safe with him so close, the irony being he was responsible for her current distress. She shook her head, trying to jar the memory of him being near from her mind. She must flee this place, this town, and run if she wanted to live; she could see no other choice.

Behind her, the door creaked open. Shocked that he'd entered without knocking first, Linda swung around, guilty, sure her jailer had heard her desperate thought. But it wasn't the deputy who strode inside. Doreen entered, bearing a platter with something fragrant and steaming.

"I brought you something to eat," she explained. "I felt you'd prefer to take your meals here, away from the other guests who breakfast at my table." Her eyes took in Linda's change of wardrobe. "I see the clothes will do. You're a mite small in the waist, but the skirt can be taken in. At least the moths didn't get to it, tucked away like it was."

"I. . ." Linda looked down, somewhat ashamed and awkward for her earlier thoughts of fleeing in light of this woman's generosity. "You've been so kind to me."

"I'm happy to help, dear. Those were my sister's." She set the platter down on the bed. "I kept her trunk of things after she passed away on the trail years ago. I'm glad to see they can finally be put to good use." She smiled in a reassuring manner.

Linda stood still, uncertain what to do, not knowing what was expected of her. Curiosity almost made her ask about the deputy and why he'd not yet made an appearance to haul her back to jail. As vigorous as he was, she figured he was the type to awaken before dawn and would expect that of his prisoners as well. Doreen smiled as if she'd read Linda's mind.

"Kurt had his hands full last night, breaking up a brawl at the saloon. Beastly place." She fluffed the pillow and drew the covers up over the bed, somehow without jarring the breakfast tray. "Wish they'd just blast all such sites of ill repute from the area with that black powder they use in the mines, but of course they'd never do that. Too much of a boon to pad their pocketbooks, more's the pity. Saloons are the sole excuse, next to mining, that keeps most of the men in town by providing them with their so-called amusements. My dear husband knew the former owner of this hotel—did I mention it was once a saloon?" She looked over her shoulder, and Linda shook her head. "The two came west together and helped found this town; had conflicting ideas on issues, but maintained a strange sort of friendship. Poor Hal died in an accident his first year here; had no family to pass his things along to, and bequeathed the place to my husband. Charlie made it into a hotel, but wouldn't you know it, another saloon sprung up a month later. Across the road. Wish it wasn't so close. Wish Charlie and I would have had more time together." She sighed as she straightened to a stand. "But that's the way of things. A time to be born, a time to die."

Her voice sounded almost cheery, and Linda looked at her puzzled. "You don't fear the prospect of dying?"

"Fear it?" Doreen snorted. "Well, I'm not looking forward to the idea any time soon, but what's to fear? Death means I'll join my Lord in a place that promises supreme happiness, and I'll be reunited with my loved ones, too. Though I wouldn't want any sort of slow, lingering death. Still, if that is to be my lot, the Lord'll see me through it. He's always proven Himself faithful."

Amazed to hear such strong faith, to see the conviction in Doreen's eyes, Linda thought back to her mother. She, too, had seemed so certain, as she lay dying, that she would meet God. Nor did she dread that final moment. Instead, she'd embraced the idea, her eyes taking on a contented glow. . . .

"Well, I have plenty to do yet. Kurt had quite the time of it last night from what I heard a few guests say. Poor boy must have gotten no more than a wink of sleep. But I imagine he'll be by to visit you shortly."

She spoke as if Linda and Kurt were courting, though surely she must know their situation was anything but amenable. Quite the opposite, since they weren't even friends and closer to being enemies. Still, Linda couldn't prevent the flush that warmed her face, and she rued its appearance.

Doreen smiled wisely. "I'll just leave you to your meal then, shall I?"

Linda waited until her hostess swept out of the room, leaving the door open, before she sank to the edge of the bed. She pulled the snowy white napkin off the platter. Eggs, light and fluffy, whetted her burgeoning appetite. Despite the uncertainty of her bleak situation, for the first time in days, she felt capable of doing justice to the delicious food. She was halfway finished with her meal when she heard a step at the door followed by a light knock at the doorpost.

Startled, she looked up to see Kurt standing on the threshold. She dropped her hand with the fork in it to her plate and waited.

Evidently as ill at ease as she, he paused before grabbing the chair near the door outside, taking no more than a couple of steps into the room before setting it down. His actions seeming awkward for what she recalled of his agility, and she watched as he swung the chair around and straddled it, then nudged the brim of his hat up a notch in a gesture that she now knew was habitual.

Noticing his eye for the first time, she let out an involuntary gasp.

He fingered the shiner, grinning wryly, his dimples flashing. "I seem to bear the misfortune of always being in the wrong place at the wrong time. I get punched by accident with more flailing fists than by anyone bent on doing me real harm."

Remembering her own flailing elbow hitting him in the jaw, she lowered her lashes. She didn't know what insanity came over her, but all of a sudden she had the most absurd inclination to giggle, and she bit the inside corner of her lip hard to quell the need. "I imagine they got what was coming to them?" she inquired sweetly, lifting her eyes to his.

His eyelid, the one that wasn't almost swollen shut, lowered in a squint, as if trying to figure her out, but his lips pulled into a smile. "Let's just say that the jailhouse's two cells are near to bursting with those I arrested, and it isn't the first time." He shifted in his chair, wincing. "Which brings me to here and now and what I've come to tell you."

Horrified at the thought of sharing a cell with even one of the men who'd ogled her, she waited for him to decide her fate.

"Don't look so nervous." The timbre of his voice took on a gentle quality. "I'm not about to put you in there with those filthy scoundrels."

She exhaled in relief, not realizing she'd been holding her breath. "Thank you. I mean, considering that you think me just as—that you think about me the way you do." She stopped short of saying that he thought her as wicked as his recent prisoners. No use reminding him of the fact when he was being so nice to her.

"I'm not an ogre, Miss Burke." He shifted in his chair as though uncomfortable and again winced. "I spoke with Doreen, and the best choice appears to allow you to remain here. I can't watch you day and night, but being the generous woman God made her, Doreen's willing to take you in. It was her idea. So again I ask for your word that you won't try to take advantage of her goodhearted nature and skip town."

She hesitated, uncertain and a little worried. "You look tired," she surprised them both by saying. His eyebrows rose a fraction, and he shifted in his chair again, straightening. Ever since he'd come into the room, he'd seemed jittery.

"It isn't the first night I've been without sleep," he replied. "But I assure you, I can still be swift on my feet should the need arise." His eyes bored into hers in silent warning. She again felt uneasy and lowered her gaze to her lap.

"I won't run."

He exhaled a long breath. "Good. At least we have that little matter cleared up." She heard the chair skid along the planking as he rose, and that brought her to life.

"Deputy?" Swiftly she stood, fearing he would leave before she had the chance to question him. "Have you heard anything? I mean has anyone contacted you? About me?" Desperate to know her fate, she clasped her fingers tightly with one hand. The immediate sense that she shouldn't have spoken came over her. Without a doubt he would have introduced the subject had he learned the truth. And ogre or not, once he knew, he most certainly would have put her behind bars, which made it apparent that he hadn't heard a thing.

He made a slow survey of her face, picking up on every nuance of her expression, though his own was difficult to read, his face a blank. "You sound worried. Care to tell me anything I might not already know?"

She almost pressed her hand to her wildly beating heart, wishing to slow it, but such a telltale gesture would doubtless make her look even more guilty. "I've told you everything. Everything you should know." Or more accurately, everything she wanted him to know. "I'm innocent of any crime."

When she released her hand, his gaze dropped to her wrist and the pink stripe of raw skin there. He flinched before looking back into her eyes. "Then you have nothing to worry about." With a parting nod, he left the room.

But her fit of nerves remained to taunt her.

He would discover the truth; it was inevitable. The question she struggled with was if she should be the one to tell him, to trust him. Could she rely on his help? He had proven to be tough, a man who would uphold the law no matter the situation, but he'd also shown that he possessed a gentle heart by bringing her to Doreen's hotel. The thought of being jailed back in that miserable cell wasn't half as bad as the reality of what would happen should O'Callahan's men find her. Kurt had put her in danger when he'd sent out telegrams with her description. But once he learned the truth—or the truth as those in Crater Springs would tell it—she pictured herself dangling from a rope. Last she'd heard, killing a man was still just cause for a hanging. And if the law didn't exert its justice first, O'Callahan's men would.

She shut her eyes at the fearful prospect. No matter how she looked at it, her outlook remained grim. Whether by death from her enemies or execution according to the law, her demise loomed ever nearer.

≪

The day wore on, the hours seeming to trail away. Kurt labored at his duties, ignoring the raised brows from passersby at the shiner he sported, which had darkened to blue-black. But it wasn't the bruise on his eye that bothered him so much.

The previous day had taken more of a toll on Kurt than he'd let on, and a night without sleep hadn't helped matters. Besides the wild punch in the eye he'd received when he tried to break up the fight, as peaceably as he could under the circumstances, he'd also gotten a good slam in the stomach from a drunken miner crazed with whiskey, who'd blindly struck out at anyone within reach with his chair. That had been enough for Kurt to pull his gun and fire a couple of warning shots at the ceiling to shock the brawlers into silence.

Tagged in his youth as a shy, quiet boy, it had taken time for Kurt to earn the townsmen's respect. The badge helped, but the older men, the founders, still treated him as if he were too young to know better and ignorant on how affairs ought to be run. Toting his guns had made his voice heard, though he'd never used them to kill and hoped he'd never have to. But if the day came that he was required to take a life in order to protect another, like the prisoner under his charge, he would do what he must, no matter how much he detested the thought of it.

The more he watched Linda and kept her company, the more he couldn't see her as an associate of the Greer brothers. Her risqué, ill-fitting gown didn't match the polite, quiet creature he'd come to know since he'd taken her into custody. He no longer presumed her behavior an act designed to trick him. Doreen was good at ferreting out troublemakers and deceivers within minutes of meeting them and had championed the unknown Linda after having done no more than sweep a perfunctory glance over her.

That's what bothered Kurt. The woman was still an unknown, though she'd finally broken down and told him her name. He didn't understand why she should refuse to answer his personal questions if she was innocent. And after all this time, he still didn't know the truth. He'd received two telegrams back, both of them negative replies to the knowledge of any woman who fit Linda's description—and he still awaited a reply from the sheriff in Crater Springs. Maybe that town would hold the key needed to open the locked door of his silent captive's identity.

His duties done, the afternoon waning toward evening, he ambled into the hotel to check on his charge. Doreen met him at the door to the parlor.

"Where's my prisoner?" he asked. "Still upstairs?"

She harrumphed at his choice of a greeting. "Upstairs and stripping the beds, putting on clean linens." At his raised brows that Doreen should put his charge to work, she added, "Said she didn't want to stand around being useless and asked me to give her a task. I've done all I can to keep up this place, but I'm not getting any younger, and I could use her help. She really is a treasure."

This time he snorted. "Or she's hiding one."

She shook her head. "Now what would make you go and say a thing like that?"

"Just a hunch. She's hiding something. I can feel it."

Her mouth turned down in disapproval at what he could tell she thought of as his pigheadedness. "That eye doesn't look so good."

"It's as good as a black eye can look, I suppose." The sofa in the empty parlor invited him to move that way. "Since she's so busy, don't disturb her. I don't need to talk with her just yet." With careful, measured movements, he settled his tall frame onto the stiff cushion, unable to keep the wince from his face as a sharp pain stabbed him in the ribs. A gasp escaped though he tried to muffle it. He had barely allowed himself to sit all day and now wished he hadn't.

"Kurt, what's the matter?" Doreen remained standing in the doorway.

He should have known nothing would escape her notice. "Nothing. I'm fine."

Skirts swishing, she swept toward him in determination. "Right. And I have a fortune in gold sitting beneath these floorboards."

"If I were you, I wouldn't make such frivolous statements, however untrue. You never know when a greedy miner is lurking close by, and you might find your hotel floor dug up come morning."

"Well, if I did have any such fortune, I certainly wouldn't put it to waste beneath the flooring."

"Knowing you," he said fondly, "you'd build a church and contract a blacksmith to craft a bell, so people could hear it for miles around, and maybe even start another hotel or add onto this one. Taking in charity cases and making it some sort of mission, like the ones back East?"

She smiled as if caught. "Never you mind, and stop your stalling. Since such a day will never likely arrive, there's no use wasting time in discussing what will never be when there are more important matters to attend to. Now, let me see what *you're* hiding." Her words brooked no further hedging on his part. Knowing she would never relent, he pulled the hem of his shirt from his trousers and undid a few of the buttons of his union suit in the area that pained him most.

She gasped. "How did that happen?" Her fingers gently pressed against his ribs, and he sucked in a gasp at the pain.

"Brawl last night. Chair attacked me. But it met its end against my side."

"Kurt Michaels! You mean to tell me that you've been hiding your condition the entire day?" She shook her head, her mouth pulled into a thin line. "Well, I never!"

"It's nothing," he said, uncomfortable with the way she carried on. "I'll feel right as a trivet tomorrow."

"Yes, you will. After I tend to you." When he opened his mouth to protest, she raised her finger as if scolding him. "I won't hear any argument. It's bad enough we don't have a doctor. Worse still that poor Marshal Wilson lies abed, injured, with a patched-up hole in his side. This town sure doesn't need its only other lawman as one of the walking wounded. Those ribs are bruised. I can see that as plain as the nose on your face. I doubt they're broken, or you wouldn't be breathing as well as you appear to be, but that doesn't mean you don't need tending, especially after seeing the pained way you just sat down. Good thing I did, too."

"Yeah, good thing," he retorted wryly.

"Now then, I won't tolerate any more nonsense. Is that understood?"

Amused at her motherly persistence, he quirked his mouth, pursing his lips. "Yes, ma'am. I wouldn't dare." He may not like being fussed over, but he appreciated her concern.

"Well, you'd better see to it that you don't." Her eyes twinkled in mirth. "It's a good thing your badge hasn't let you forget who you're dealing with."

"Only the sweetest hotel keeper in all of Nevada, I reckon."

"Kurt." She laughed as though embarrassed and shook her head. "Go on with you! The room you took when you last slept here is empty. I'll be up soon to get a closer look at those ribs."

Kurt did as told, too weary to argue. Maybe a little fussing wouldn't be so bad. At the top of the landing, he entered his room and closed the door. With care, he pulled down his suspenders and unbuttoned his shirt, wincing as he slipped the material off his shoulders and let it fall to the floor. He thought about bending over to pick it up and toss it on the bed but decided against such needless exertion. Every movement of his torso felt as if someone had branded him from the inside. He sank to the edge of the mattress and unbuttoned his union suit to the waist of his trousers. Carefully he shrugged his arms from the wool flannel sleeves, each movement searing his ribs with fire.

As Kurt waited, his mind went over what he knew about his prisoner. Which didn't amount to much. Surely she must know he would find out the truth about her soon. Like Doreen, Kurt was beginning to think his first judgment of Linda's character wasn't accurate. She didn't seem the type to be an outlaw, or even to aid one. . .but why was she being so evasive?

The door swiftly opened, and Kurt twisted his head around to greet Doreen.

Linda stepped into the room, then halted, her mouth falling open. She dropped the bundle of sheets she carried, her gaze flicking to his bare chest. Her face flooded with bright rose.

"For-forgive me." She backed up a step, then swooped down to collect the bed linens. "I thought these rooms were empty. Doreen said they were. I. . .I didn't know you were in here."

"It's okay." Heat warming his own face, Kurt grabbed the sleeves in a hurry to try to push his hands through the holes. The pain that came with his action was immediate and swift, and he let out a loud groan, abandoning his task. He wondered if he'd made things worse by not tending to his injured ribs first thing. The soreness hadn't been half this bad when he'd visited the jailhouse that morning.

With the sheets clutched to her chest, Linda darted a glance upward then down at the floor again as she rose from it. "Are you hurt?"

"I'll be okay." He ground out the words through teeth clenched against the pain.

"Is. . .is there anything I can get you?"

"No. Thanks."

She backed up another step, avoiding looking at him, and bumped right into Doreen coming into the room. Linda whipped around, almost slamming into the wall and knocking a bottle from Doreen's hands. "Careful," the older woman said calmly as if trying to soothe a panicky mare. "I wouldn't want to have to tend two patients if you should take a fall."

"I'm sorry." Linda's face flamed red. "I didn't mean. . ." She let her words trail off, giving a slight shake of her head.

"There now, all's well. Actually, I could use your help, dear. If you wouldn't mind tearing up one of those clean sheets, I could use some linen strips to bind Kurt's ribs. You'll find some shears in the kitchen."

"Bind his ribs?"

"It's nothing," Kurt insisted, but Doreen spoke over him.

"Fool man doesn't know to seek aid as soon as it's needed," she said, as though Kurt were still a naive lad in britches. "But yes, his ribs do need binding, and that's what I aim to do now."

Kurt wondered how she'd come to such a conclusion since she had yet to really examine his ribs and had only seen a fraction of them through his clothes. He doubted they were cracked or broken, or he wouldn't have been able to move at all. But if binding them helped to make the pain more tolerable, he wouldn't protest.

"I'll just go and make those strips." Linda fled the corridor, and for an uneasy moment, Kurt wondered if she would flee the hotel as well.

"Take that look off your face," Doreen chided as she soaked a rag with the potent liniment, guaranteed to clear up any man's head with just one whiff. She began sponging it on his bruised skin.

"Ow! Not so rough," he muttered. "What look are you talking about?"

"She isn't going to run like you think. Her response to that little exchange you two just shared should prove what I've been trying to get you to see all along."

"And just what is that?" he asked wearily when instead of elaborating, she wordlessly rubbed in the smelly liquid.

"That girl is as innocent as the days are long. She isn't any of the things you thought about her; no saloon girl, that one. And certainly not a lady of the evening, despite her inclination to dress like one."

"I tend to agree with you."

She stopped rubbing the liquid into his skin and stared at him. "Well, will wonders never cease? Miracles still happen."

He ignored her wry retort. "Even so, my thoughts and feelings aren't going to matter one whit to a judge who comes to town and hears the case. It's only the evidence that he'll take into account, as well as her confession. The confession she made to me."

Kurt frowned. There was still so much about Linda that he didn't know.

❧

Linda cut the sheet into strips, taking the much-needed time to let her cheeks cool and her mind settle. When she returned, she was careful to avert her eyes from any sight of Kurt while handing the linens to Doreen. Task accomplished, she quickly left and entered the next room, noting from the open door that no one was inside.

As a child living with her mother above the saloon, Linda had on occasion glimpsed things she shouldn't. She'd always averted her gaze and hastened away, but to come upon the deputy so unexpectedly had thoroughly rattled her composure.

Reminded of his build, both slim and muscular, she knew he would prove a worthy defender should trouble occur; but her reaction to his defenselessness of that moment is what surprised her most. Her first womanly thought when she realized he'd been hurt—to tend his wounds—had led to another more shocking urge. She had wanted to trace the bruised skin with gentle fingers of sympathy and. . .what? Kiss him? The heat of the day must have addled her mind for it to entertain such bizarre notions. There could be no other reason to think about the deputy in such a way, or to think about him at all.

Once she finished with the bedding, Linda pondered her next move. Should she return to the room she'd been given? Go downstairs and wait for Doreen? Not wanting to be trapped in close quarters after her recent internment in the cell, she opted for the latter choice. She found Doreen already downstairs in the main room talking with two well-dressed gentlemen who Linda assumed were new guests from the carpetbag each of them carried. Catching sight of Linda, the men tipped their hats to her. Made uneasy by their continued interest as they stared, Linda retreated into the shadows near the bottom of the stairwell. The men advanced, likely to their rooms, and Linda was grateful when Doreen also strode her way.

"I have a stew on the fire. I imagine you're hungry."

The kindly woman smiled at Linda, as if Linda's mortifying encounter with Kurt hadn't occurred, and Linda smiled in relief.

"Most of the patrons have eaten, so the room I use for dining is empty."

"Yes, thank you. I'm famished." Linda wanted to ask about Kurt's condition but couldn't bring herself to say anything that might introduce that uncomfortable moment between them.

She followed the woman into a dim room with one long, roughhewn table and noticed another guest sitting on the opposite side. A kerosene lantern stood in the center of the table, the glow from it flickering across his lean jaw as he chewed. As Linda came around the table to take a seat, he looked up. Her heart stopped. Her face warmed, and she felt unprepared as an idle thought flitted through her mind. With his hat off, and in the lamplight, his hair gleamed a smooth, dark golden brown.

"Kurt," Doreen said, "Linda's decided to join us." Her hand on Linda's shoulder, she practically pushed Linda to sit down. Knees weak, she took the bench. "I just remembered," Doreen added, "I need to check on something, so let me just dish you up a bowl, and then I'll leave you two be. I'm sure you have plenty of important things to discuss."

Linda hazarded a glance toward Kurt and stifled the urge to chuckle when she noted his parted mouth as he stared at Doreen, who made quick work of fetching Linda's dinner and even quicker work of excusing herself from their company. He shook his head a fraction, as if trying to dislodge his shock. Only then did he glance Linda's way.

"What just happened here?" Kurt's voice came dazed. "No, never mind." He gave a wry chuckle. "I think I can figure it out."

Linda stared into her bowl brimming with steaming vegetables and meat in a thick brown liquid. She also thought she understood but dared not say. For whatever reason, Doreen seemed intent on bringing them together in a sociable manner. Odd, considering the circumstances. Surely, due to those same circumstances, she couldn't be playing matchmaker, though it sure did seem that way.

Kurt finished his stew then set his spoon in his bowl. She realized she had yet to take a bite and quickly picked up her own spoon.

"I've been thinking on the matter all day," Kurt said at last. "And I want to help you."

"Help me?"

"I think you're running from something or someone. And my guess is you're in a heap of trouble because of it."

The impact of his words screamed through her mind, but she could only blink. He offered to be her savior; no man had ever done that.

When she neither admitted to his claim nor denied it, he studied her face. "I'm not going to break any laws or twist them around in helping you, just so you know it. But I think you could use someone on your side, Miss Burke, and any time you care to share, I'd like to hear your story."

"Deputy?"

Both Linda and Kurt looked toward the doorway. The boy Lance stood there.

"What are you doing here so late?" Kurt asked.

"You best get down to the jailhouse, Deputy, sir. Bart and Stan are putting up quite a ruckus. You can hear it clear down the street."

Kurt sighed. "I reckon now that they've slept off the whiskey I haven't got any choice but to let them go. Too bad. Another night in jail might have improved their dispositions some." He stood up with difficulty, wincing, and directed his gaze at Linda. "I may not be tearing through town any time soon, but I'm a quick draw with a gun and know how to handle one. I won't let anything happen to you while you're in my care." His last words came lower, so the boy couldn't hear, and he grabbed his hat, offering Linda a brief parting nod. "We'll continue this conversation later."

She watched his tall figure depart with the boy. Could she trust him? Or was this all a trick to goad her into letting down her guard and confessing the truth that had become rooted in her nightmares? With her arms crossed on the table, she bowed her head, earnestly wishing she could confide in Kurt, but she'd known the man a total of twenty-four hours. In that time, he had chased her, seized her, and thrown her into a cell. All part of his job: she understood that even if she didn't like the position he had put her into. But complete reliance on the deputy, or on any man for that matter, loomed beyond her reach at present. Maybe she might never learn how to trust again.

Chapter 6

Clutching the telegram in his fist, Kurt stalked out of the small office. Bent on his course, he headed straight for the hotel, barely acknowledging those he passed in the street with a warning look or curt nod. He found Doreen sweeping out one of the lower rooms from the ever-present dust and grime trekked inside. He had no idea why she even bothered with the useless chore.

"Where is she?" He came straight to the point.

"And a fine day to you, too," she came back at him.

"Not now, Doreen." His voice hadn't lost the hard edge, and a knowing look came over her face as it creased with worry.

"You've found out something, haven't you?"

He compressed his lips. "Miss Burke?" he reminded.

"I sent her across to Tillie's with a basket of bread."

"You did *what?*" His eyes fairly bulged out of his head. It was no secret that Doreen was sweet on the marshal, except maybe to the marshal, and she connected with him from a distance, through others, by indirectly sending little things to his sister, meant for him. Since the marshal had been shot, her little kindnesses had increased, but she usually asked Kurt to make her deliveries. That she should let his prisoner out from under her watch. . .no. Not let her leave—*ask* her to go. She might as well have given Linda a ticket for the stagecoach while she was at it. He hadn't failed to note his prisoner's interest in that establishment when he'd first brought her to town.

Upset, he ran his hand along the nape of his neck and paced a few steps away.

"I was swamped with things needing to be done," Doreen went on to explain, "and since it is just right across the street, and she'd earlier said something about a need for fresh air. . ."

He turned on his heel before she could finish and headed for the door.

"Kurt—"

Rushing outside, he ignored her, hoping he wasn't too late. Doreen's compassion for charity cases and giving of herself to those less fortunate was commendable, though sometimes her common sense took a wrong turn. He should have gone with his gut instinct that had lately warned him something wasn't right. Linda had been so edgy, nervous, and distant; now he understood why.

He scanned the area as he quickly strode to Tillie's. In front of the stage-coach office, he caught a flash of red hair in the sun and clenched his teeth, just barely keeping his pace to a fast walk. The object of his frustrated ire carried a large basket of linens under one arm and balanced on her hip as she stepped out into the dusty street to cross it.

The sudden loud rattle of harness stopped him. A team of horses stampeded at a crashing run, bringing every head around, including Linda's. She stood as though turned to stone and stared at the wagon that barreled straight for her.

Just as she dropped the basket, Kurt flew at her, tackling her out of the path. Pain sliced through his already wounded ribs, but he ignored the discomfort as he rolled with her out of harm's way. Mere seconds later, the wagon raced past, the gust from the flying spokes of the wheels so close he could feel the warm air hit his face. His arms still around her middle, he rolled Linda from her stomach onto her side.

"You okay?"

She gave the barest nod, her face pale, her eyes wide with stunned fright.

"Stay here," he ordered, keeping his voice quiet in an attempt to reassure before scrambling up from the ground and running as fast as he could manage in the direction of the wagon. As he ran, he held his bandaged side, his breaths rasping short in pain. He would never catch up to the wagon on foot, and there was no time to fetch and saddle his mare.

"I need your horse, Jake," he called out to the barber, who had just dismounted.

Taken aback, Jake gave a little nod. "Sure thing, Deputy." He handed Kurt the reins.

With his boot in one stirrup, Kurt swung his leg over the saddle and took a seat, turning the horse around in a fluid move. He groaned as fire again lanced his ribs, hoping the fall hadn't made them worse, but gritted his teeth against the pain and clamped the reins in his fists, determined to catch the culprit responsible.

A short distance out of town, he closed upon the wagon. No driver sat on the bench, and the reins dangled over the box, between the horses, and dragged on the ground. A cloud of dust rose from their hooves as he prodded his horse faster to run abreast of the team. "Whoa!" he yelled, reaching over to grab at the bridle of the lead, but the horses wouldn't heed his command. Whatever had spooked them had done a good job, and his ribs were in too bad a shape to attempt jumping across to try and stop the panicky beasts. He didn't know how else to calm the team.

The horses continued running wild. The wagon swayed and the front wheel hit a boulder, splintering the rim as wood flew in all directions. The corner of the wagon bed slammed to the ground and dragged, plowing the dirt and slowing the team. Within seconds, the horses were at a trot, and he was able to maneuver them to a stop.

"Easy there," he quieted the lead horse. Agitated, it tossed its head. The other horse was restless, but not as uneasy as the sorrel. Kurt dismounted, keeping a hold on his reins, and slowly moved to the panicked horse, murmuring reassuring words, while smoothing his hand over its gleaming coat. When he stroked along the horse's back, it sidestepped, as if again about to bolt. He never ceased his words of comfort as he investigated and found a thorn deeply embedded in its hide beneath the harness.

"What the. . ." Kurt scowled to see such abuse of one of God's beautiful creatures. Again, he consoled the beast. "Easy now. We'll need the blacksmith's tools to get that out, so I'm afraid you'll just have to endure a little longer. No way can I dig for that with these short nails of mine. Sorry."

A quick inspection of the wagon unearthed nothing about its owner, and a scan over the countryside showed no one nearby. Everything had happened so fast Kurt hadn't gotten much of a chance to see if there even had been a driver. Now he realized the rogue who planted the thorn must have slapped the horse on the back, embedding the thorn deep, and had set the scene up to make it appear as if the wagon had been a runaway. A runaway aimed directly for Miss Burke. A dire warning? Or attempted murder?

Kurt frowned. He didn't like the way his thoughts traveled but could think of no other reason for what happened. After what he'd learned minutes ago, he wouldn't be surprised if either explanation proved true.

The horses quieted, and he removed their harnesses and tied their reins to one rope he held, leading the team back to town. No one came forward to admit ownership, and he tied the horses to a post across the street from the hotel, alerting one of the boys gawking nearby to hurry and get the blacksmith to remove the thorn. He noticed then that his prisoner wasn't where he'd left her. A quick scan of the street yielded no trace of her bright red hair. The basket of clothes was missing, too.

Grimacing with dread, he hurried into the hotel and checked the lower rooms. Neither of the women occupied them. Glancing up the stairs, he took them at a run, meeting Doreen coming out of Linda's room.

"She's a mite shaken up," Doreen warned upon seeing the scowl on his face, as if worried he would hurl a verbal attack Linda's way.

"Then she's still here?"

"Of course she's still here." Doreen laid a hand on his arm, lowering her voice to a whisper. "Think before you say anything. I need to see to the bread before it burns."

She hastened downstairs, and Kurt squared his shoulders as he stepped through the open door of Linda's room. She stood at the foot of her bed, her back to him. At the sound of his step, she spun around. The sight of fresh tears tracking her face robbed him of his words and his breath. Her expression yielded terror, and she looked much as she had on the night she'd had the terrible dream. She stared a moment, then lowered her gaze and walked straight toward him, wrapping her arms around his middle. Tentatively, she laid her cheek against his shoulder, her face turned away, and loosely held onto him.

Taken aback, Kurt stood as still as a post. He felt her body's tremors as she fought back tears, and his anger with her and the entire situation began to melt. Without conscious thought, he raised his palms and pressed them to the middle of her back in reassurance. His ribs burned from tackling her to safety followed by his mad chase, but he gave them little consideration as he held her close to the strong beating of his heart.

After a moment elapsed, he felt her quick intake of breath and watched her face as she drew a quick step backward, away from him, swiping at her cheeks with her fingertips. Another moment passed before she glanced up at him, then away again.

"Thank you, Deputy." Her words came low, humble. She smoothed her hands down the front of her skirts. "That was somewhat of a fright."

Memory returned and with it his irritation. "I stopped by the telegraph office and was on my way to talk with you." He stared hard into her eyes. "I heard from Crater Springs."

He hadn't thought it possible for her face to become any whiter.

~

"Oh?" Linda feigned ignorance, as though curious to hear his news. But her madly beating heart disproved her calm deportment.

"The sheriff wasn't there—but the person who answered said my description fit that of a Miss Linda Grayson. . ."

She swallowed, feeling as if bonds had been looped around her wrists.

"And this Miss Linda Grayson is wanted. For murder."

She remained silent, the invisible bonds squeezing the life from her veins. Her blood ran cold.

"I think you'd better start talking. This time I won't take silence for an answer."

His words came low, ominous. Any hope she'd nurtured for his aid died a quick death. She let the silence stretch.

"You're not going to confess, even though you've been caught in a lie?"

"I didn't do anything wrong. I told you that once before, and my plea still stands: I'm innocent of any crime."

"Maybe our ideas of what's right and wrong differ."

At his scornful words, she lifted her chin. "I do know it's wrong to kill."

When she offered nothing more, he blew out his breath in amused disgust. "So—what? You're telling me that this Linda Grayson—also appearing a couple of years shy of twenty, with hair as red and bright as fire and eyes like molten silver—is another Linda?"

His description of her attributes left her stunned and floundering for a response. "I. . ." She took in a deep breath. "My father's name was Burke." When he waited, still not satisfied, she frowned. "That's the God's honest truth, Deputy. I'll swear to it on the Bible if you want."

"Do you even know the meaning of truth? Would you recognize it if it walked up and struck you in the face?" His curt words came soft but startled her as the weight of them hit her; his eyes seemed to burn clear down into her soul. "Do you even know God, since you're so quick to speak His name in your defense?"

She blinked, realizing she'd never seen him so angry. Even on the day he'd captured her, he'd kept some restraint on his words, but now she noted what looked like hurt glimmering in his eyes. She shook her head, uncertain of what to say. Doreen had tried to comfort her with how the Lord would intervene in her troubles and care for Linda, should she ask Him to, but she had given the older woman's words little heed. God never had involved Himself in her affairs before. Why should He suddenly care now? Despite her bitter confusion, in the short time she'd known Doreen, Linda had come to wish it were possible. Kurt's questions sparked the memory of the last time she'd held her mother's hand, at her deathbed, and the peace she'd never seen before taking every weary line from her mother's face.

"What if I were to tell you that I believe you might be in danger?" The deputy's query jolted her from her thoughts, and she looked into his eyes, seeking answers and wondering how he'd finally arrived at that conclusion.

"That runaway wagon was staged," he continued. "And I believe whoever arranged it was intent on one thing: making your stay here in Jasperville a lot shorter by removing you from the area. Permanently."

She clutched her throat, his declaration acting as a sieve that seemed to drain the blood from her body until she felt dizzy. "Not an accident?"

"No. And I believe you know why." He took a step closer. "Now you're going to tell me, and I'm not leaving this room till you do."

"I—I can't." Retreating, she shook her head, but he grabbed her arm.

"I want to help, can't you understand that? But if you don't let me in on all the facts, I might not be able to."

"To do what?" She tried to wrench away, but his hold firmed. "Give you an even better reason to lock me in that horrid cell again?"

"I told you I'm not comfortable with putting you back there."

She shook her head, her emotions in tatters. "Doesn't really matter now, does it? You've become my judge and jury in assuming I killed a man. And we both know what the sentence for unlawful death is."

"I never said it was a man who was killed." His grave eyes never left hers. "But you're right. It was."

Her laugh came short. "Well, congratulations, Deputy. So now I reckon you have the proof you need? How will you justify your sentence—call it guilt by partial declaration? And do you now escort me to a gallows or use one of those guns to carry out my sentence with a bullet aimed at my head?"

"Stop it," he softly ordered, giving her arm a little shake. "That's not the way things work. No one's going to hang you or shoot you without a fair trial, not if I can help it."

She hardly felt relieved. A jury was composed of twelve men, who likely would all side against her—that is if her enemy didn't first pay off a judge to dispense with a trial and declare her guilty. She didn't know much about how the court system worked, but she didn't have much faith that it would be to her benefit. "Why should you even care?" she challenged. "Don't tell me this isn't what you've wanted since the day you brought me here. I know better."

"All I want is the truth, Miss Burke. And I won't take anything less. Are you Linda Grayson?"

She glared at him. By the set of his jaw and the fixed look in his eyes—just as hard and just as bright as clear green, glittering peridot gemstones—she knew he'd never relent. No matter what she said to the contrary, those unsettling eyes of his would see straight through any fabrications, and she was tired of fighting to survive. Tired of fighting him. They both knew the truth, and by his own admission, he would stand here all day until she confessed it aloud.

"Yes," she bit out. "Grayson was my mother's name."

He released a soft sigh, sounding nothing like the victor in their ongoing struggle. "Now that we have that cleared up, I want you to tell me all of what happened."

She gaped at him. "You're still interested? After knowing I'm the one they're after and hearing what I'm accused of?"

"I'm the type who likes to hear both sides before making up my mind."

"And what then?"

"I'm still a deputy, Miss Burke. I'm sworn to uphold the law, whatever that entails. My feelings have no say in this." His lips quirked in silent contemplation as he studied her. "But that doesn't mean I won't make good my promise on my offer to help you in whatever way possible. Without breaking the law, of course."

"I still don't understand why you'd want to do that." Her words tumbled out, close to a whisper as she struggled to understand. "Why would you want to help me? I haven't exactly given you an easy time of things. You hardly even know me."

His eyes flickered before he looked away. "Doreen has taken a special interest in you. She asked the favor of me."

"Oh, Doreen. Of course." Confused by why she should feel a twinge of disappointment that his motive didn't stem from his own desires, she pondered what to tell him.

The truth.

He accused her of not recognizing it, and under the circumstances she couldn't blame him. Part of the reason she'd given her father's name had been her desire to start anew. But she had to admit, if just to herself, she hadn't wanted the deputy or any other lawman linking her to the name she'd carried all her life. Now she had no choice but to tell him the truth. If she dared tell him everything, would he believe her?

"After almost being trampled underfoot, I need a strong cup of coffee," she hedged, hoping for time to compose herself. "I'll tell you what you want to know. But. . .not here." Their quarrel ended, the intimacy of their surroundings brought the reminder of how good it had felt to be held in his strong arms. And she dared not tempt her own feelings of weakness that had threatened her control ever since the wagon almost ran her down.

Kurt studied her a moment, as if trying to decide if she were evading the issue, then nodded and held out his arm to escort her downstairs.

Chapter 7

The kitchen was empty, Doreen nowhere in sight, as Kurt escorted Linda to the table, not removing his hold from her arm until she sat down on the bench. He took the tin pitcher from the stove. Finding enough coffee still inside, he poured them each a cup, going through the motions to give his anger time to cool. A kerosene lamp hung on a hook nearby. He grabbed the handle and set the lantern on the table to get a clearer view of her face. Usually he could get a good idea of when someone deceived him from the look in their eyes and the involuntary twitches in their features. He wouldn't give her opportunity to tell another falsehood.

She cradled the cup between her hands and stared into the steaming liquid before bringing it to her mouth and taking a gulp that must have scalded. Tears brimmed her eyes from the pain, but he sensed the ache lay much deeper than from her tongue being burned by coffee.

He sank to the bench across from her and waited.

"That telegram is right," she said at last, staring at her cup. "I am wanted for killing a man. But I didn't do it. Not that you'd believe me."

"Never mind what I would or wouldn't believe. Just tell me."

Still, she wouldn't look at him. "I think I know who killed him. And he knows I know. I've been running ever since. An errand boy saw me. In his office. The banker's."

Kurt tried to make sense of her tense words. "It would be a whole lot simpler if you'd just start from the beginning. Tell me what happened."

"The man killed was the banker. It was. . .horrible." With a little shiver, she shut her eyes as if she again witnessed the image and tried to block it out. "He'd been shot in the head. Blood was everywhere—on him, over the papers on his desk, on his ledger. . . The boy saw me standing over him. I–I'd picked the gun up off the floor. I don't know why. It had just been fired. I could smell the burnt gunpowder."

"Why would they suspect you of shooting the banker?" Kurt studied her hunched shoulders. That the man had taken his own life seemed plausible.

She snorted, a humorless laugh. "*He* needed someone to pin the blame on and to get rid of a pesky problem at the same time. Me. Calling me a killer only aided his cause. But it wouldn't surprise me in the least if he pulled the trigger himself. I know he was behind the killing somehow, I just know it."

"And just who is 'he'?"

She took another slug of the steaming coffee as if taking a stiff shot of whiskey, then shivered again as though the liquid had chilled to ice. "Grady O'Callahan. He's wealthy, owns a lot of land as well as just about all the men in town. The Greer brothers work for him."

Kurt sat back, absorbing the information. At his intent stare, she brusquely shook her head. "No, I told you I wasn't in on any part of that gold shipment robbery, though O'Callahan tried to force me to do things for him. Like he did with my—" She cut off her thought and blinked, as if catching herself. "He tried blackmailing me into doing certain. . .favors for him. I refused, but the angrier I'd get, the more he enjoyed the challenge. He gained a morbid sort of satisfaction from our arguments; I could tell by the cunning way he smiled. I felt like small prey the wild beast amuses himself with just before it goes in for the kill. But I knew the games he played with me couldn't last forever; he isn't the patient sort. After I got the letter, I thought it the miracle needed to make a clean start."

"What letter are you talking about?"

"From my pa's attorney. Pa died, and the letter said I was to meet up with some people in Silverton." She grimaced. "That didn't work out as planned, and you found me after I left there."

Kurt sensed the anger and pain tight in her words, making him curious, but he needed to know more about the murder. "Once the boy saw you, what happened?"

"He yelled that a man had been shot. I got scared and ran off before anyone else could find me there. I didn't know where else to go, so I went home to get my money." Agitated, she crossed her arms on the table, holding her elbows. "O'Callahan found me. He promised if I agreed to do what he wanted, he'd make sure nothing happened to me. But I refused. I didn't want any part of his shady dealings." She looked back down in her cup. "I took a man's horse but left it at the stagecoach station in the next town. I assured myself that I wasn't really stealing, only borrowing, so as to escape a precarious situation."

Kurt decided not to correct her erroneous idea of thievery as a form of a loan. He remained silent, nodding for her to continue.

"Only problem, I think his men have been following me. I sensed someone watching me. At the station, I saw someone who seemed familiar. He was far enough away that I couldn't tell who he was, but I didn't stick around to find out. Even then, I barely escaped his notice. O'Callahan wants me dead, and he'll do anything he can to make sure it happens."

Kurt only had her word on all of what happened, but looking into her eyes, he reckoned a woman would have to be a mighty fine actress to brandish such an expression of contained terror. Her eyes glowed even brighter in her fear.

"Please, Deputy. . ." She moved her hand a little, as if unsure, then reached across the table to lay her hand over his, the one that still held his cup. "You offered your help, and I've told you everything. Please, don't let O'Callahan find me."

He stared at her slim fingers touching the back of his hand. Warm. Featherlight. Earlier, when she'd embraced him, the strongest urge to protect her replaced the shock of her unexpected act. Since they'd met, he'd done his duty in guarding her safety; later, his actions regarding Linda's care were, in part, due to Doreen's wishes. This new desire to protect had come from within and grown personal. Her warm hand touching his in entreaty only intensified his resolve.

"Miss Burke. . ." He lifted his eyes to hers, his gaze steady. "I promise you, no matter what it takes, I'll do everything humanly possible to help you. But you have to promise you'll be straight with me from now on. No more lies."

She gave a small nod of agreement.

A few of the pieces still didn't fit. "Why should this O'Callahan fellow be pursuing you, even take the time to have you followed? Once you left town, that should have been enough to satisfy him. Does he have some type of claim on you?"

"No! And I have no idea what he's after." She shrugged, nervous, and removed her hand from his.

"See, that doesn't make sense. There has to be a reason for his tracking you. Maybe you took something that belonged to him, something he wants back?"

"I didn't take anything." Her eyes were earnest. "You've looked through my reticule, Deputy. That's all I own. What money I used to take the stagecoach to Silverton was money my mother put aside for years. She told me to use it if ever I needed to escape. And I did. . ." Emotion warbled her abrupt words, and he saw moisture glint in her eyes before she ducked her head. "I didn't take anything of his. I wouldn't be that foolish. I've seen what Grady O'Callahan does to the men and women who swindle him, and it's not pretty."

"All right then. Maybe O'Callahan had some kind of hold over your mother?"

His inquiry was soft, but she snapped her head up as if he'd slapped her.

"She's dead and has been for months. What can the details of those last years of her life possibly matter?"

"They can matter a great deal to make sense of the current situation."

She fidgeted in her chair. "They had an. . .understanding." Her face warmed to a shade of rose.

"Just how close were you to O'Callahan, Miss Burke?"

Her eyes flashed molten silver. "If you're asking if we also shared the same kind of understanding—or any kind of understanding whatsoever—I assure you, Deputy, we most certainly did not."

He hadn't meant to rile her so. "Then with everything else ruled out, my next guess is that he must consider you dangerous to him."

Her mouth dropped open in disbelief. "Dangerous? To *him*?"

"Maybe he thinks you know something. Or saw something. Something that could make a lot of trouble for him."

She shook her head as if dazed, furrowing her brow in concentration. "I can't think of what it could be. I kept my distance from him or anything concerning him."

"What were you doing at the banker's office?"

"What?"

"The day he was shot."

Her gaze lowered to the table, and she seemed cautious. "I had thought to get a loan."

"I thought your mother had money put away."

"She did. But it wasn't a great sum. And well, Mr. Townsend was considerate to me. He didn't look at me the way so many other men did. He used to smile and greet me in the street in passing, inquiring after me and my mother when she was ill. His wife also regarded me kindly when I saw her at the dry goods store one day. I'd recently received my pa's letter and thought. . .that is, I'd decided to travel to Silverton."

She seemed evasive, and Kurt peered intently at her until she looked up.

"That seems a risky venture with him thinking you might not return to pay him back."

"I wanted his advice, too, about the letter, but I wouldn't know what he thought, regardless. I never got the chance to talk it over with him, except once briefly in passing. To tell him I wished to visit with him for advice. He was dead before I got there." She lifted her hand in a pledge. "I swear it's the God's-honest truth."

As many times as she referred to God, Kurt wondered about her personal knowledge of the Almighty and recalled Doreen's desire to share the gospel with Linda.

She clasped her hands on the table when he didn't respond. "So what now, Deputy? What happens to me?"

He considered the matter. "The sheriff in Crater Springs is out of town. Someone else sent the telegram. Until I receive word on what's to be done, you're still under my authority."

"And once you receive word?" Her low query sounded stuck in her throat, and she rubbed her thumbs together, hard.

"When the time comes, we'll deal with it. Right now, the most important thing is to keep you safe. That means you're not to leave this hotel."

She didn't look at all happy with his order. "We both now know someone out there wants me dead. But what if he's not out there? What if he's here? In the hotel. And he's been a guest here the entire time?"

Sensing her rise into hysterics as her tone rose in pitch, he spoke low and calm. "I talked to Doreen earlier. She complained how she hasn't had any new business with the last stage arrival except for two men working for the railroad. I highly doubt either of them is after you. Only a few other guests are staying here, but I'll check them out."

She avoided his gaze, and he guessed that she was hatching an alternate plan.

Leaning forward, he covered her clasped hands with one of his own. She gave a little jump at the contact, her eyes stunned as they met his grave stare.

"You're not to leave the hotel," he stressed.

"For my safety? Or because I'm still your prisoner?"

"Either reason will do."

She looked down again, and Kurt wished he knew what was going through her head.

⤕

Kurt's warning spun inside Linda's mind until she thought she might scream with the never-ending rote of it. With each firm revolution of the damp wash-cloth over a plate she held, his words spun round and round inside her head. He wanted to be her protector—she was his prisoner. He would help her, but if ordered, he would hand her over to those men controlled by her greatest enemy, who would then destroy her. She sensed O'Callahan had the power to issue orders to their sheriff, if he didn't already own him. An honorable man, Kurt would act in whatever manner the law required. And that frightened her. She both admired his integrity and resented it, knowing full well it might mean her demise.

She forced her mind onto the looming danger and not the distant one. Someone in town had tried to kill her. Likely, one of O'Callahan's men. Even more likely, he was still in town, waiting for a second opportunity. And if that also failed, a third. O'Callahan's men didn't quit until the job was done.

Shivering, she froze over the dishpan of steaming water. She had to skip town, had to take that chance. She couldn't just do nothing like a lamb waiting to be picked off by a coyote. She had to act. Now. Kurt would be livid when he learned she had run, and a twinge of regret made Linda pause. Doreen had shown her nothing but kindness, and she hated to betray her trust or break her vow to Kurt. Linda valued people who kept their promises, no matter the odds, and wanted to be like them, wanted to be a woman Kurt could admire. But her life was at stake, and she wasn't willing to up the ante or bluff her way out of another risky gamble for fear that Death might hold the winning hand. She had no choice but to run.

Kurt was at the jailhouse, Doreen upstairs. Linda set the plate on the draining board and wiped her wet hands down the front of her apron. Swiftly she untied it and laid it over a chair, hoping that she could slip out the back door before anyone became the wiser. She had brought her reticule downstairs, never went anywhere without it, and grabbed it now.

The long drape that covered the door to the kitchen swept back with a quick rustle. She whirled around and inhaled a startled gasp. A man stood in the entrance wearing clothes covered with a layer of grime. His dark eyes were hard in his leathery face carved in lines by many years outdoors. She didn't recognize him, but he stared at her as if he knew her. A puckered scar ran down his jaw, slid across his neck, and disappeared past his shirt collar.

When he didn't move, Linda gulped down a breath and clutched the edge of the table. "Can I. . .can I help you?"

His cold, menacing smile sent shivers down her spine.

Chapter 8

"What were you thinking, Doreen?" Kurt straddled his hands on his hips. This was the first time he'd had a chance to speak with her since the fiasco of the afternoon. "You can't just let a prisoner run loose, out of your sight."

"Posh. The girl didn't run, did she?" She knotted and bit off the thread she'd used to sew a new button on Kurt's shirt that he'd lost when he tackled Linda away from the runaway team. Doreen saw to it that his clothing was always mended, as well as his body. She mothered him, but she could be as irksome as a sibling, since in age they were closer to being sister and brother.

"She didn't get the chance." Kurt stressed the words, attempting to get her to see logic. "But that's not to say she might not have tried had she been given the opportunity."

"She knows a good thing when she sees it. I'm convinced of that. And she's not fool enough to turn down your help. She won't run."

Kurt shook his head, giving up. A desperate man would do almost anything to survive, and he had seen that same desperation flicker in Linda's eyes. "I don't suppose you know where she is now?"

"In the kitchen. She offered to wash the dishes. Having another woman here is such a godsend to me. I'm beholden to you for bringing her, Kurt."

"Mm-hm," he mumbled and headed for the back of the hotel, by this time accustomed to Doreen's insistence to treat his wanted prisoner as her bosom friend.

He pulled the drape back and stopped short. With her head lowered, Linda stood near the stove, her back to him. At his step, she twisted around, and for the first time he noticed the knife clutched in her hand, blade outward.

"Easy," he soothed, as he moved closer. She looked at him, her eyes wild as if she didn't know him. "I'm not going to hurt you, Linda. Give me the knife."

She blinked, then looked down at the carving knife she gripped in her hand. Shaking her head as if she couldn't remember why she'd picked it up in the first place, she laid it on the table. Whatever had happened had shaken her up a good deal. The desire to comfort stronger than the duty to apprehend, Kurt stepped close and drew her to him. For the second time that day, he smoothed his hands along her back, his fingertips tangling in her hair that hung loose past her shoulder blades.

171

The feel of her in his arms, soft and warm and all woman, felt right, and he knew he could easily get used to this. Stunned at the random thought, he pulled away and grasped her forearms, forcing his mind to the matter at hand.

"Tell me what happened to put that look in your eyes."

"I. . ." She paused, as if struggling to remember. "There was a man. He came in here a little while ago. The way he acted, the way he smiled at me. . .it just gave me a bit of a fright."

Kurt frowned. He reasoned it must have been more than "a bit" if it had compelled her to brandish a knife. "Did he say something to alarm you?"

"No, he didn't say a word. At first." She shook her head as if trying to clear it. "When I asked a second time what he wanted, he asked for Doreen and wanted to know where she was. But. . .I got the sense that he didn't really care to know. That he was only saying whatever came to mind because I asked why he was there."

"You think he's one of O'Callahan's men?"

"I've never seen him before, but that doesn't mean much. O'Callahan's wealthy and powerful. He has plenty of people working for him." She shuddered. "I don't know all of them."

"What did this man look like?"

"Average height and build. He had. . .a scar running down his neck."

Her description didn't sound like anyone Kurt knew. "I want you to go up to your room. Don't let anyone inside."

"Where are you going?" She grabbed his arm when he would have gone.

"I plan to do some scouting around, see if I can find him."

"Don't leave me, not without any means of defending myself." Her plea came soft, but her eyes were demanding. "You don't know these men. If it *was* one of O'Callahan's cronies, no barred door is going to keep him from doing what he was sent here to do."

Kurt considered her words. She had a point, but not under any circumstances would he lend her one of his guns. "Take the knife then. But don't betray me."

She winced, as if his caution prodded her guilt, but her expression was sincere. "I won't."

"Come along then." Grasping her arm, he hurried with her upstairs to the room she'd been given. He pushed her through the entrance but held back from stepping foot inside. "Bar the door with the chair and stay here till I tell you otherwise." He began to move away.

"Wait!"

Kurt turned, curious. She held to the edge of the door, seeming to hunt for words. "Be careful."

He paused, a little startled by her concern for his welfare, but nodded. "Don't open the door till I return. And don't worry. Nothing bad is going to happen to you."

✺

Fear locked Linda in a choke hold. She paced inside the room, trying to shake it off, feeling much like a trapped animal soon to be picked off by a predator. She drifted to the window and stood catty-corner to it, moving the drape a fraction to peer out at the dark town disguised in shades of night. She wondered if any of the men outside were killers hired to remove her. In the shadows of the building directly across the street, she picked out the form of a man leaning against the wall. A kerosene lamp hung near him and cast his shoulder and arm in yellow light. His face remained obscured by shadows, but the tilt of his pale hat suggested that he looked up. At her.

With a startled gasp, she let the curtain fall back in place, then paced some more. Perhaps hers was nothing more than a hysterical reaction to an inconsequential occurrence and the man in the kitchen really had been looking for Doreen. The recollection of his eyes, cold as black ice, roaming her, and his slow, menacing smile again made her feel cold all over. After Linda had summoned up a morsel of bravado and told him that Doreen and the deputy should be joining her at any minute, the stranger had left without another word. His intentions hadn't seemed pure, but maybe his presence had no connection whatsoever with O'Callahan. Maybe he was just another lewd miner looking to find a fleeting thrill with a woman he assumed to be free with her favors.

Her mind traveled over the past year. Her mother, bless her soul, had done everything possible so that Linda wasn't forced to endure such a fate, the fate that had been her mother's. Linda managed to survive without sullying her body and giving it in return for money and trinkets. Her mother's wishes for her aided Linda's desire to remain pure, but O'Callahan had done his utmost to force her hand and make her dependent on him. Odd how, years ago, an association with Linda's father had brought her mother's fall into disgrace, whereas Linda had escaped a similar misfortune because of her father's recent letter.

A swift knock at the door made her jump. She pressed a hand to her wildly beating heart, grabbed the knife from the sideboard, and approached the thin planking of wood. Only inches of pine separated her from who knew what. . .

"Who's there?" she whispered, loud enough to be heard.

"It's Doreen. Open up, dear, and let me inside." When Linda hesitated, remembering Kurt's order to let no one in until he returned, Doreen added, "It's all right. Before he left the hotel, Kurt asked me to come up and check on you."

Did he not trust her and so had sent a guard in his place? Why that thought should rankle, even cause pain, Linda didn't know. She certainly had given him little reason to trust her. She pulled the chair from the door and opened it. Bearing a cup of something steaming and a platter, Doreen entered with her smile that always consoled.

"I figured you could use a good meal," she explained.

Linda hadn't eaten since breakfast and wasn't sure she could force anything past the blockage that terror had formed in her throat, but she thanked the woman and closed the door, lodging the chair back in place.

"I don't suppose you'd know a man with a scar on his neck that a knife fight might have put there?" Linda asked as she took a seat at the edge of the bed.

"I'm sorry, dear. I wish I could tell you otherwise, but I don't. Kurt asked me the same question. Once in a while, a few of the miners refer newcomers to my establishment. But more often than not, they set up their own tents around town. Not many of those men have the means to take a room here at close to a dollar a night."

Doreen set a plate of meat and cooked turnips on the sideboard. In her duties, Linda had earlier removed the basin of dirty water and forgotten to replace it with fresh. She thought back, hoping she'd remembered to do so with the other rooms. Strange what insignificant trifles her mind played over in the midst of her terrors.

Doreen took a seat beside Linda and patted her hand. "Kurt is proficient in his job. He double-checked every inch of this place before he left. You're in safe hands. And don't be forgetting God is always faithful to provide what we need when we need it."

Linda attempted a smile. "You have such strong faith. I don't believe I've ever met anyone like you before."

"It took a lifetime of experience to get where I am. When I was little more than a girl traveling westward all those years ago, I had a great deal to fear." Her voice took on a faraway quality, as if she lived within her memories. "The threat of raids was constant when we crossed Indian Territory, as well as the fear of disease or starvation throughout the entire journey. People died every week. My own pa was killed in an attack by Indians, and shortly after that, my mother and sister passed away from diphtheria, the same illness that took Kurt's parents. I was left alone in the world and clung that much more to God."

Doreen paused, as if thinking. "The wagon master was a harsh and difficult man. He didn't want to take me any farther, since I was a young woman, not quite six years older than Kurt. Kurt suffered the same fate. He was too young and scrawny to be of any use in aiding the men on the wagon train—hard to believe to look at him now—but in our grief, we came to rely on each other. I begged the wagon master to let Kurt and me team up. I've thought of him as my younger brother ever since, and with the way we sometimes squabble, I imagine that's not hard to tell." She chuckled fondly. "But I do love him, impossible though he can be at times. When I married my late husband and settled here, it just seemed natural to bring Kurt with me."

Linda smiled with a taste of the bittersweet, beginning better to understand their relationship. She wished she'd had a sibling. In a manner of thinking, she supposed she did, not that it did any good to claim Derek and Clay as her brothers. They wanted nothing to do with her, and every day, she told herself she wanted nothing to do with them, either.

"I'm convinced that God never forsakes us," Doreen continued as if hearing Linda's train of thought. "He brings us what we need, when we need it. You can rely on Him, Linda. His gift of salvation is free to all who ask. Doesn't matter what you've done or haven't done, He'll not turn you away."

Linda glanced down at her lap. Doreen sounded a lot like her mother in those last few weeks before consumption had robbed her of her final breath. She had stood on the outskirts of a revival that a visiting missionary held outdoors. On that first day, Linda had been with her, and they'd stumbled across the meeting on the way to the shack that had become their home. After that one afternoon, her mother visited as often as she could, when the weakness wasn't so bad, her limbs didn't tremble, and she wasn't coughing up too much blood, while Linda stayed home and tended to their meals.

"Do you believe what I said?" Doreen asked gently.

Linda sighed. She wanted to; oh, how she wanted to! It would make her hardships easier to bear, to believe that an Almighty God cared about her welfare and watched over her. "My mother came to believe the way you do before she died." Faced with the prospect again, something in her yearned for what Doreen had. What her mother had found. Last year she had shied away from it, but now she was willing to listen.

"You've had a hard life, haven't you, dear?" Doreen's voice was both gentle and sad. "You've felt as if you were all alone at times, as if no one cared about what happened to you."

The soft words unearthed her insecurities, and tears blurred her vision. "How do you know?"

"Because I've suffered similar hardships, though our situations may be different. Loneliness and fear visit every man or woman at one time or another. It's terrifying to think you're all alone in the world, especially when so many dangers are involved. But, Linda. . ." Doreen wrapped her arm around Linda's shoulders. "You're not alone. Not only does God care what happens to you, I care. And Kurt will do whatever he must to keep you safe. It's in his nature to protect. He's always done so, especially with those he has a personal interest in."

Her words suggested a deeper reason for his actions, as if Kurt truly cared about her welfare, but Linda knew better. She was his prisoner. Any protection he offered, he gave out of necessity in his duty as a lawman, to keep her safe until he could turn her over to the sheriff in Crater Springs. And after that. . .

"Now come," Doreen urged, squeezing Linda's hand. "You must eat before your food grows cold. You'll want to keep up your strength, and I noticed you barely touched breakfast."

With her stomach twisted in knots, Linda didn't see how she could manage but nodded like an obedient child, grateful to have someone care about her again. She had been alone for so long; it felt nice to be coddled and petted.

"Before you go, can you tell me more about your faith?" Linda fidgeted, ashamed to ask Doreen to postpone her duties to cater to her request, but the woman's bright smile allayed any doubts.

"Why, I would be most happy to."

Long after Doreen spoke the last quiet word and excused herself, Linda sat lost in thought. She believed there was a God. After witnessing her mother's peaceful expression as she died and hearing her joyfully speak to Jesus in those last few minutes that she breathed, stating that He'd come for her as she smiled and looked toward the wall as if He approached, Linda didn't doubt it. But this was the first time she'd thought about Him with regard to herself.

She pushed the cold food around the plate. No matter its flavor or temperature, she doubted she would have noticed or been able to taste anything. Nonetheless, she went through the motions of eating, forcing herself to chew and swallow from routine. But she never looked away from the closed curtains. The certainty that someone who meant her harm stood outside watching her left her chilled to the core.

Chapter 9

Five days had passed since Kurt had sent the telegrams. He'd found nothing with regard to the mysterious stranger who'd given Linda a fright or any leads on who was behind the runaway wagon. No further attempts had been made on Linda's life, and he wondered now if the entire situation had been a strange coincidence, though that didn't explain the thorn beneath the horse's harness. Maybe whoever had set it up had intended the malicious deed as a cruel prank aimed at another person, having nothing to do with Linda, who'd just been in the wrong place at the wrong time. With matters as peaceful as they'd been in the past few days, Kurt reasoned that must be the case, though as a precaution he ordered Linda to remain indoors. The time she didn't spend behind the barred-up door in her room, she shared in either his or Doreen's company, never alone.

When Kurt wasn't at the jailhouse or trying to keep the peace elsewhere, he sought Linda out. At first his reason came solely from the need to provide her with protection, but at some point, his feelings had changed. He *wanted* to be with her. Her beauty mesmerized him, while her inner fire held him spellbound. She had shared little else about her history, urging him instead to talk about his. Whether he was a fool for doing so or not, he believed her account of the murder and had from the start. And now that he'd quit looking at her as no more than his prisoner, his mind opened to possibilities that his logic just as quickly blew full of holes. The longer he knew her and kept her company, the deeper his feelings became involved. And he didn't need a sage to tell him that was unwise.

He thought it odd that he still hadn't heard from the sheriff of her town, but he had little choice other than to wait until he received orders on what to do with her. And he'd vowed to be with her when he could, to see to her safety. Marshal Wilson had felt recovered enough to return to the jailhouse that afternoon. Full of his old energy, he was raring to get back into the thick of his job, and once Kurt updated him on the situation regarding Linda, he'd ordered Kurt to spend all of his time guarding her.

Now he stood, unnoticed, outside the parlor where Linda and Doreen sat in two chairs facing one another. Doreen's Bible lay open in her lap. From the look of things, Doreen had just read a chapter, her usual custom of a night, and the women were discussing it.

Linda's face shone in the lamplight, her eyes aglow with a hungry earnestness Kurt had never seen.

"We never had a Bible," she explained to Doreen. "Even if we'd had one, I just knew what little reading Ma taught me from what she'd learned when she lived in the East. There never was much time for such things, but I wasn't a good reader with the one book she owned. She never talked of God till the end, so if I seem ignorant in all of this, I apologize. But I am."

"No need for apologies, my dear." Doreen reached across to pat her hand. "My husband once told me it's more foolish never to ask questions than it is to admit a lack of knowledge and seek the answers. The Bible instructs us to ask and we shall receive. God only waits for our knock at His door. He'll always open it and welcome us inside."

"I haven't led a life I'm all that proud of," Linda admitted. "I've been selfish too many times to count and done some things I knew weren't lawful but thought I needed to in order to survive."

"God judges a person's heart, child. He doesn't judge them for their faults, not when they're willing to change. It's for the sinners He came into the world to spread His message and He died on the cross as He did. He wrote the book on forgiveness." She motioned to the Bible. "And while you're on this earth, it's never too late to seek it."

Ill at ease with his unintentional eavesdropping, Kurt moved away from the door, but the creak of the planking under his boot gave away his presence. He grimaced, knowing they must have heard it. Before he could make it to the outside door, he heard footsteps and the rustling of skirts behind him.

"Deputy?"

He inhaled a long breath and turned around.

"You're leaving?" Linda took a few steps closer, then stopped a short distance away. "But why? Without first saying hello?"

Kurt noted the sudden flush on her cheeks and the manner in which her gaze dropped to the floor, then lifted again. Puzzled by her sudden awkwardness, he masked his own unease at being caught. "I didn't want to disturb you women."

"You could have joined us." Once she spoke the words, an uncomfortable expression crossed her face, and she shook her head a little, as if wishing she could take them back. "Did you find out anything? Has the telegram you've been waiting for arrived?"

He peered at her closely. "If I had, I wouldn't have tried to leave just now. I told you I'd share any news with you the moment I found out. "

The clomping of footsteps alerted them that they weren't alone, and they cast furtive glances toward the heavyset man who moved past them and toward the stairs. The guest stared at them in curiosity. Once his loud tread faded, Kurt took hold of her elbow, steering her toward the kitchen.

"This isn't the place to hold a conversation of this nature," he warned.

She held back. "Please. I've hardly taken a breath of fresh air for days, cooped up within these walls like I've been. I'm grateful for the safeguard, but can't we go outside to talk? Just for a few minutes? I'm not accustomed to living a life solely indoors."

Kurt took a minute to think the matter over and consented, changing direction and leading the way to the boardwalk outside. "You say you're not accustomed to a life indoors, but your hands tell a different story." Darkness had fallen, and the nearest lantern flickered far enough away that the two of them remained in shadows. Still, Kurt scanned their surroundings, keeping a watch for any danger. The street was as quiet as a tomb, but through its swinging doors, the saloon across the road was as noisy as ever.

"Is that a roundabout way of asking my profession?" Her tone carried with it a hint of irritation.

"If you want to put it that way. You're a mystery, and it's my job to solve them. When a crime is involved, that is. Like now."

She sighed. "All right, Deputy. Fine. You win. For a time, I did work in a saloon. But not as a prostitute or even as a dance hall girl or singer. I have the grace of an ox when moving to music, and I sing like a frog. That's what you really wanted to know, isn't it? If I'm a fallen woman."

He didn't deny her claim, though his reason for asking wasn't to cast judgment. He had witnessed plenty of squalor in his lifetime, because of bad choices made, as well as the pain and desperation that often lay behind making such decisions. "There's nothing involved here about winning or losing—this is about saving your life. But I am curious; in a saloon, what else is there for a woman to do?"

"I cooked for the men and women who worked there, even served drinks. But I never—never took a man to my bed," she stammered.

Kurt found her claim suspect. Her pale skin was flawless, the bold color of her hair and strange eyes fascinating, her slender form well endowed. He found it hard to believe a woman so stunning could retain her virtue while living in a den of immorality among men who wouldn't care to safeguard an innocent.

"You don't believe me," she accused.

He shifted his position, uncomfortable. "Did I say I didn't?"

"No, it's all in your manner." She sighed. "Not to say it wasn't difficult. O'Callahan barely gave me a moment's peace, and that's when I finally knew I couldn't stay there any longer and that, if I ever had the opportunity, I would leave."

"O'Callahan?"

"He owned the saloon."

"A man like that, I'm surprised he didn't force himself on you."

She gave a humorless laugh. "He enjoyed the game too much, toying with me, frightening me. It was his way. But his games soon took on a sinister twist, and I realized he was done playing."

He shook his head, voicing his thoughts. "Being the woman you say you are, why would you go there in the first place?"

"I grew up there."

Her admission took him by surprise, and he peered at her face, what he could see of it in the shadows. He got the distinct impression that she might be close to getting teary-eyed from the way her words wavered. The last thing he wanted to do was make her cry. "Forget I asked. You don't have to tell me anything that won't aid your cause in proving your innocence."

"Then you do believe I'm innocent?" she asked, her voice soft with hope.

The day he'd found her and put her in the cell, he'd been assured of her guilt; five days with her, and he had the gut feeling that she was being framed. He couldn't confirm his hunch to satisfy the law, but maybe it wasn't beyond his ability to find out what he needed to prove her not guilty. "Yeah. I do."

She let out a little breath of relief. "I don't know what to say."

"Anything that can help me get to the truth of the matter will help." He noted movement across the street and turned his head. Two men walked close by, silent except for their boots shuffling on the boardwalk and an occasional murmur of conversation. From their appearance, they had just exited the saloon. "We should go inside."

"Please. . .just a little longer. I can't tell you how good it is to breathe in fresh air, even if it is cold."

He gave a grudging nod of assent. "Just a few more minutes then."

She cleared her throat as if she had something on her mind and was itching to say it. "I imagine the twins found you earlier, and that's why you're here later than usual tonight?"

"What?"

"The twins. Lance and Lindy dropped by hours ago looking for you."

"Did they?"

"Said their ma sent them and to tell you they were here."

He nodded thoughtfully, pondering the reason for the Widow Campbell to send her children to find him.

"So you didn't see them?"

Kurt peered at Linda, wishing it weren't so dark. He wondered if he imagined the edge of relief rimming her words. "Nope, didn't see them."

"Then you haven't been to see the Widow Campbell this evening?"

"Couldn't very well drop in if I never got the message." He leaned his shoulder against the post and crossed his arms casually over his chest.

"That's true enough I suppose," she muttered, half to herself as she stared out at the street. "I saw her the other day." She raised her voice a notch. "When I delivered that bread to Doreen's friend and brought home the laundered shirts. We passed each other on the boardwalk. She's a handsome woman."

"Yeah, she is," Kurt replied, sensing that she expected a response and not knowing what else to say.

Her head turned swiftly to his. "Yes, well, I can see why you'd be interested. She's a good deal refined, too, isn't she? As if she attended one of those fancy boarding schools back East. Though it makes me wonder why she'd come all the way out here. She sure doesn't look as if she's cut out for the rigors of the West."

Kurt smiled to himself, noting the unmistakable ring of jealousy. It tickled him to realize Linda cared, more than he should admit or allow. It would be wisest to let her go on thinking that he had designs on the Widow Campbell, to help prevent anything between the two of them before it could happen, not that he had any designs on Linda, either. She was his prisoner, for crying out loud. And he a deputy, sworn to office.

"While the Widow Campbell does make a fine pot roast, I've found she's a mite too refined for my tastes," he admitted, tossing caution aside.

"Too refined. Really?" She sounded skeptical. "So then, Deputy, just what are your tastes?"

At her bold question, he hesitated. She didn't back down. He wished it weren't too dark to see the expression in her eyes. At the same time, he felt grateful for the night, which cloaked the color of his face that must have gone a shade red by now. For reasons he couldn't identify, he told her what he'd told no other. "Like any man would, I like a woman both warm and soft in body and heart, but with grit and spirit firing her actions. Parlor-room deportment and manners don't matter so much to me. Beauty isn't all that important either, though it doesn't hurt." Before he could add that he would want her to share his faith, she spoke, again hushed under her breath, as if to herself.

"I can see how she wouldn't measure up."

He wondered to which of the attributes she referred.

"Me, I just want a man who'll love me for who I am, regardless of my past, which I can never go back and change. Would that I could. I want a man I can respect and love back with equal measure."

At her wistful words, he studied her, doubting it would be difficult for her to find a man to love her. He imagined a number of them had been smitten with her, but it might be harder for her to find one to admire, judging from the pickings in this town alone. He reckoned most mining towns and miners were the same, obsessed with finding ores and little else. "You never talk much about yourself or where you come from."

She pivoted sideways, again staring out on the street. "My past is like a pile of dirty linens. And who wants a good view of that!"

"I would."

At his quiet admission, she looked at him in surprise. "Why? To give you reason to build up a case against me?"

He winced to know that she still thought him the enemy. "Because I'd like to know more about you."

"Why?" When he didn't answer, she looked away again. "It isn't pretty, Deputy."

Before either of them could speak, Doreen came through the doorway. "There you two are." She pressed her hand to her heart. "With all the ruckus going on lately about someone being after you, I near panicked when you didn't return. Why didn't you tell me it was Kurt you saw, dear? As for you, Kurt— just what have you been up to, to arrive so late when it's nigh getting on to bedtime?"

He grinned. "To hear you talk, I'm breaking curfew."

"Humph, such sass. You were no better at the age of ten." The lamplight coming from behind the door made her grin easy to see. "Did you get Lance's message?"

"As a matter of fact, we were just discussing that." He looked at Linda, who stared at Doreen. "Marshal Wilson came back to work late this afternoon. I spent the evening keeping him company and updating him." He didn't miss how Linda darted a look his way.

"Oh, that's nice." Doreen sounded almost breathless. "I'm so grateful to hear he's made such a remarkable recovery."

"You should go and visit him at the jailhouse," Kurt said pointedly, doling out his own bit of teasing. "Bring him one of your pies he likes so well."

"You know, I just might do that."

Her words surprised him. "You should. I think he'd like receiving your little kindnesses directly from you, rather than through me all the time."

Her face grew rosy. "You two shouldn't stand out here, and Linda, without a shawl! What are you trying to do, Kurt? Give the poor girl a dose of influenza?"

Instantly remorseful, Kurt addressed Linda. "We should go inside at any rate."

With a few parting words about needing to tend to some matter, Doreen left them. Kurt motioned for Linda to precede him inside. Normally, this late,

Kurt would escort Linda to her room and say good night, then take the room nearby that Doreen had given him. Since he'd put Linda up at the hotel, Kurt had stayed there every night, also.

Kurt touched Linda's elbow to stop her when she turned toward the staircase. She looked at him, her expression curious.

"If you're not feeling too tuckered out, I'd like to resume our conversation."

At first, he thought she might refuse, but she nodded, seeming resigned, and he led the way to the kitchen to talk, which Kurt vaguely noted was becoming a custom for them.

≪

Linda stared at Kurt in confusion. Instead of sitting down across from her, he pulled from a shelf a board with black painted squares and a small box, setting both items in front of her. He pulled the lantern closer. She watched as he dumped the contents of the box on the table. Black and white wooden disks rolled over the planks. Her first day at the jailhouse, she'd seen a similar board on his desk. She looked at the pile, then at Kurt.

He grinned. "Ever play checkers?"

"Checkers?" She shook her head, thinking she must have misunderstood his desire that she tell him of her past. "I thought it was a man's game." She didn't add that she'd rarely had time for such luxuries, and should she have had the time, she didn't wish to play with any of the scoundrels who frequented O'Callahan's saloon. Their modes of entertainment had been drinking, cards, and women, not always in that order. Once she left the saloon, she'd found a measure of peace, but almost every waking moment had been filled with work to get by—usually sewing and cooking that hadn't spoiled her hands. The few calluses she'd gotten at the saloon had softened in the six months she'd lived alone with her mother.

"A man's game?" He chuckled. "Doreen would set you straight on that. I used to play her husband. That was before I became deputy and didn't have as much time for games, though the marshal and I sometimes indulge. If Doreen had finished with her chores here at the hotel, she'd challenge the winner—either her husband or me. Not the marshal. Though that might change in the near future." He chuckled to himself.

Linda felt a smile tease the corner of her lips, also having noticed Doreen's interest perk up when Marshal Wilson's name was mentioned. She hoped that once the marshal discovered Doreen's hankering for him, he would return her affection; Doreen was such a kind woman who would do any man proud. Linda had never found love and wondered if she would be given the opportunity. For one fleeting moment, she pictured herself with the man seated across the table. She watched his long fingers pluck up the disks, setting them in rows on each side of the board. She'd experienced his strength many a time since the morning they'd met, but now she studied the fluid motions of his hands and discovered a quality about them she'd never noticed. He had such large hands, capable and strong, his fingers hard and callused. But his touch could be so gentle. . .

"I've found that a game of checkers makes it easier to relax. Sometimes it helps a person to speak of things that can be uncomfortable to say face-to-face. Gives the hands something to do."

His words startled her into looking up at his eyes, now directed on her, and she hoped he didn't notice the blush that must fill her cheeks. She was glad he couldn't see into her mind and the warm thoughts of being held in his arms, his hands caressing her back in comfort.

Briefly, he instructed her on how to play and told her to go first. She moved her checker; then he moved his.

"Tell me about yourself," he said. "What brought you to Silverton?"

Surprised at his change back to a topic she'd rather avoid, she took a breath and moved her checker. What did it matter what he thought of her? Since he now knew the name by which she was known and the town from which she'd fled, better that the truth come from her. Others could twist things, though her history was twisted enough. But she would prefer he heard it from her first. "A map and a letter—my pa's letter I told you about. I was to meet my half brothers there."

"Oh?" He lifted his brow as he made another move.

"The map was to a silver mine. I was to get a third of it. My pa's legacy."

At her mention of silver, his surprised glance lifted to her, then shot to the door. "If I were you, I'd keep my voice down. You wouldn't want anyone beyond that curtain to overhear. Silver's what brought most of these men to Jasperville." He jumped her checker with his and claimed it. For some reason, his game move brought to mind what Derek had done, though in no way did Kurt's innocent act compare to Derek's corrupt behavior.

"It wouldn't matter if they did hear. One of them—my half brothers— decided my portion of the map belonged to him and helped himself to it my first night there, while he thought I was asleep." Her face went aflame at the memory of Derek's cutting words and rejection of her as his sister. "He didn't think I deserved any part of the mine."

"I'm sorry he treated you badly."

She shrugged as if she didn't care what Derek thought of her, though she cared a great deal and wished she didn't. Whether she liked it or he accepted it, she was kin to Derek and Clay and that would never change.

"Has he always given you trouble?"

His voice came low, comforting, inviting a confidence. She found that moving the pieces around on the board as she revealed to him her dark secrets also helped. "I met both of them last week for the first time." She wasn't sure why, but she found herself offering more than he asked. "I suppose, in thinking on it, that I was a shock sprung on them too sudden-like, what with the way I just arrived at the hotel. I would have thought they'd been told through the letter each of us got that I existed, but apparently not. Once I got there, they acted like that was the first they knew. And they weren't at all happy to hear that they had a sister, especially my older. . .brother." She stumbled over the word. "Derek was downright ornery, and that's the nicest that could be said about him." Not to mention that he was a thief.

"So, the three of you shared the same pa," he said the words half to himself, as he moved another checker.

She brightened as she saw an opportunity to jump him, took it, then glanced up as she laid his disk beside her. He smiled and nodded in approval, and she found herself offering more, words she once thought she would never say to anyone. In this relaxed setting, what before had been impossible rolled off her tongue as if she were discussing a change in climate. "I wouldn't exactly say we shared him. I never knew him. He breezed into town and met my ma, offered her a few weeks' worth of sweet words and empty promises, then breezed on out again before anyone knew I was going to be born. I wasn't sure he ever knew I existed till I got his letter a few weeks ago, telling me to come to Silverton and claim what he'd left me."

She studied the scattered pieces on the board as Kurt made his move. Concentrating on the checkers as she spoke helped to ease the pain some. "My first instinct was to toss the letter in the fire. He ruined both my ma and me from any life of respectability after what he did to her."

Gathering her courage, she glanced up. Kurt looked at her no differently than before, surprising her. Once a man learned that she'd been conceived outside the sacredness of marriage, he presumed she was immoral and treated her as a jezebel. She had never planned to tell Kurt any of her history, but they would contact him soon enough with orders on what to do with her. O'Callahan would make sure he found out the truth of her disgrace, and likely in words much more degrading.

"Sometime after Ma found out about me up till after I was born, she took in laundry to survive. O'Callahan offered her a job that paid much more. At his saloon. He said she could bring me as long as she kept me hidden away, in our room. Ma was always a mite delicate, and tending the laundry and taking care of me was tiring her, or so she told me later. She'd never done hard manual labor. Her father was a wealthy attorney, but he blamed Ma for his wife—her stepmother—dying in an accident. Ma and her stepmother had been arguing at the top of the staircase, when her stepmother fell and died. Ma swore she never pushed her, but her father cut her off. People began to snub her and whisper lies about her. She wanted to start over someplace where no one knew about the accident, so she came west by wagon with a good friend and her family. But her friend's parents snubbed her, too, when they discovered she was with child, and they wouldn't let their daughter see Ma anymore. After that, she had few friends, none of them respectable." Wistfulness saddened Linda's voice. "She was so beautiful and graceful, and she became O'Callahan's dance hall girl and singer. I grew up in the saloon."

She shoved one of her checkers to the next space. "But she didn't want that kind of life for me, and O'Callahan and her fought about it often as I grew older." She winced, remembering one such conversation she had overheard as she'd cowered, unseen, beyond a door. One of the men had grabbed her when she'd been wiping out glasses and tried to kiss her. Her mother's voice vibrated low with malice:

If you or any of your men ever lay one hand on my Lindy, I swear to you, Grady O'Callahan, that'll be the day you draw your last breath. I'll shoot a bullet into your brain so fast you won't have time to blink.

Her mother had retained her beauty and grace, and since she was still of value to him, O'Callahan had reassured her in his smooth, oily manner that he would keep his promise. Then.

"When Ma got sick and started coughing up blood, she was no longer strong enough to dance or entertain his customers, and O'Callahan came to me. He tried to convince me to work for him in Ma's place. When Ma found out, she was livid. She took a pair of shears to all his fancy suit coats and trousers. Before he discovered what she'd done, we left and found us another place to stay. A shack that had been abandoned by some miners. She went back to taking in laundry, but soon O'Callahan put a stop to that. Paying men off not to secure her services, or threatening them. He wanted to make her crawl back to him, to give in to what he wanted. But she refused."

Linda thought back to those days, and what pluck her mother had shown by opposing the powerful tyrant who had strong men shaking in their boots. They might have had to scrape by to live, but when things got really bad and they didn't know where their next meal was coming from, there was always the occasional miner, new to town, who hadn't been warned or bought off and who brought his clothes to be laundered. While her mother toiled at the chore, Linda took care of their meals. Her mother's strength ebbed as the weeks progressed.

"The strange thing is," she said quietly, "I didn't realize she'd stashed away money while living at the saloon, a little here and there through the years. She didn't put it in the bank and didn't tell me about it until right before she died. Said she wanted me to use it to get away and start a new life." Linda chuckled hoarsely. "Much good that it did me."

"It's not too late."

Kurt's quiet words jarred Linda from her melancholy thoughts. "How can you say that? I'm wanted for killing a man, and you're sworn to your duty to take me back there."

"Like I've told you, I'm going to help however I can." His steady words almost had her believing that help could be possible. "I mean it, Linda. Don't give up hope. We'll figure something out."

Her first name on his tongue made her feel warm all over, and she wondered if he realized that he'd taken such a liberty. The second time he'd done so, not that she minded. But it was his inclusion of her as if they were partners that made her stop mid-move and stare.

"I thought. . ." She cleared her throat. "You're not going to turn me over to the sheriff?"

"No, that's not what I meant. Sometimes the mind later remembers things that it earlier forgot. Maybe if we can go back over that day in the banker's office, you might think of something you'd forgotten. Something that can help prove your innocence."

"Let's say I do think of something." She struggled to understand his plan and just what he wanted from her. "No one there will believe me—no one taking orders from O'Callahan, that is." She slammed her checker on a square, wishing for a moment it were the scoundrel's nose. "I suspect that even includes the sheriff, though I can't prove it. But I've seen them talking together privately before."

"Doesn't matter what they think. I believe you. And that's enough for me to do some of my own digging." He jumped three of her checkers before looking up. "Marshal Wilson is back on the job, and he's consented to my devoting my time to this matter. I plan to do whatever it'll take to find the truth to clear you."

For the first time, she smiled, a soft expression of admiration. "You're a remarkable man, Deputy." She longed to say his name but didn't. Though he'd spoken hers, both times likely without even realizing it, she didn't want him to think her ill-mannered by taking liberties to which she had no right. Her beginnings as Michael Burke's illegitimate daughter were enough of a smirch on her life.

Her praise appeared to unsettle him. It did make his face tinge pale red.

The rest of the checker game, he asked her questions about the day that forever altered her life. And she gave him the same answers as always.

"The papers," he said suddenly. "Did you get a look at them? Or the ledger?"

"There was too much blood." She shivered at the memory of setting the gun on the desk to lay her hand on Mr. Townsend's shoulder, preparing to push him backward in the chair, hoping he might somehow still be alive. Her gaze had drifted down to where his hand lay open on the ledger splattered with red droplets. There had been a name written a number of times on the page. She squeezed her eyes closed, trying to recall the image.

"Miss Burke?"

She opened her eyes and her face cleared. "Grady O'Callahan. He had written O'Callahan's name on quite a few lines of the page."

"What kind of book was it? A book of financial accounts? Appointments?"

She shook her head. "I don't know. I only remember seeing his name there."

"All right. Then what?"

"The boy came to the door and started screaming murder. I panicked and ran out."

"Was there another exit?"

"No. I ran past him, shoved him aside." She opened her eyes wider.

"What? What do you remember?"

"A shadow. I saw the shadow of someone against the wall, as if they were standing out of sight, waiting."

He frowned. "Then what?"

"I ran out of the building and down the street. A few people called out to me, but I didn't stop." Her hands trembled at the memory. "I looked around, trying to figure out what to do and saw a horse tied to a post, its owner nowhere in sight. So I borrowed it and—" Her eyes grew wide. "The bank! I remember, I glanced that way, couldn't help myself, and saw O'Callahan walking away from the building. He had his arm at an angle, as if he held something tucked beneath it. Someone called out my name in greeting, and I panicked and rode home quick to get my money. But O'Callahan found me and threatened me, telling me that if I helped him, he would help me and clear my name. I—I hit him over the head with a board and knocked him out cold, but I made sure he was still breathing before I left. I rode to the next town that had a stagecoach station, left the horse tied there, and took the stage out of that town to Silverton. I'd only ever told Mr. Townsend about Silverton when I told him I got a letter from my pa instructing me to go there because of the mine that had been left to us—"

"You told the banker about the silver mine?" His eyes were grave. "Outside of his office?"

"Yes, I told you. He was very kind to me, and that's why I wanted the appointment with him. To talk over the letter. I needed advice on what to do and hoped he might loan me some money. But I'd heard that a ticket on the stage could be expensive and wasn't sure I had enough. I had no idea what I would find when I got to Silverton or if I would need to pay for lodging or meals. The letter was brief in that regard."

He absently nodded.

"You don't believe me?"

"I didn't say that." He gave her a slight smile, hardly reassuring. "I'm just piecing the bits together, or trying to. This is the first I've heard about you knocking O'Callahan out. Seems he does have good reason to come after you, after all."

"I didn't mention it before because I didn't want you to know about the rest. About my life. And I would have had to explain."

"What changed your mind?"

She shrugged and he sighed. "No more holding anything back. Agreed?"

Linda nodded, a bit remorseful. But she hadn't known at first if his considerate treatment of her wouldn't change once he knew all the facts. *Had* she known, she would have trusted him with the sordid details much sooner.

"Did the banker have any family?"

She blinked at the odd question. "Yes, a wife. I think he also had two sons, but one died years ago and the other had gone to California. The Townsends have a big house on the outskirts of town near the creek. The prettiest house in the territory, next to O'Callahan's. Mr. Townsend had the materials transported by locomotive, then hauled by wagon."

"Sounds like Mr. Townsend was a very wealthy man."

"He and O'Callahan were the richest men in town. Of course, everything Mr. Townsend owned goes to his widow." Linda couldn't prevent a yawn from escaping.

"You should get some rest now," Kurt advised.

Though Linda preferred to let this moment in his company linger, she knew he was right.

He escorted her to her room and bid her a respectful good night, tipping his hat to her as he'd so often done. Wistful, she watched him move toward the stairwell before she closed the door and shoved the chair under the knob as he'd instructed. She finished her ablutions in record time, donned the warm gown she'd kept tucked beneath the pillow, and made sure the flame in the lamp was kept low but not extinguished before she slid into bed.

Thoughts of reading the Bible earlier with Doreen and their discussion of how God offers second chances to those without hope mingled with the memory of her serious discussion with Kurt, giving her the strangest dreams. She was running, frantic, from a lynch mob wielding ropes, knives, and guns and toward a bright light hidden in a cave. Inside, a gentle voice promised her new life and peace if she would follow the Light but warned that she mustn't delay. She hesitated a moment too long, and hands like iron manacles suddenly wrapped around her arms while a noose slipped over her head.

She awoke to find her face beaded in a sweat, her damp gown clinging to her, the blanket twisted around her legs. Immediately, her eyes sought out the flame, reassured to find it still burning low. When she'd been a child of eight, a drunken miner had found his way into her dark room and her bed, thinking she was one of the prostitutes the saloon supplied. The moment he lay down beside her and snaked his arm over her chest, she had awakened and let out a piercing scream, startling him. Seeing his mistake, he'd grabbed his boots and run out the door, but the terror of that night never dissolved. She'd slept with the light turned down low ever since.

Linda stared at the small flame, burning so bright and steady, and with it, she felt a small measure of peace. Doreen had once called Jesus the Light of the World. Remembering her dream, Linda put her fingertips as close as she dared to the heated glass globe, near the flame, wishing she could dissolve the light inside her herself and feel warm. Safe. Protected. What she wouldn't give for all those things!

Doreen had also called Jesus a Good Shepherd, searching out the lost sheep in trouble. "I'm like one of those lost sheep in the parable Jesus told," Linda mumbled to herself, drawing her knees up under her chin and clutching her legs. She glanced to the ceiling, remembering how Doreen had also told Linda that she spoke to God as if she was speaking to anyone. Nothing fancy. Just like He was her friend. When Linda seemed shocked and asked if Doreen was sure He wouldn't mind such familiarity, being as how He was the Almighty, as Kurt often called Him, Doreen had chuckled and assured her that a personal companionship with God is exactly what the Lord wanted from each of His children. "That's the way I was taught, and that's how I've done it all my born days, and I've never been more sure of anything in my life," Doreen had said, and Linda felt she must know since she was so smart when it came to the gospel.

"I could use a Good Shepherd," Linda began quietly. "Kurt is a good protector, but one day he'll leave me, he'll have to, and Doreen said You never would. Not even till the end of time—she showed that to me in Your gospel." Her teeth toyed with her lower lip. "So, Lord, if it wouldn't be too much trouble, would You mind accepting me into Your fold like You did my ma? I'd be much obliged if You would. I'm sorry I didn't listen then, when Ma tried to talk to me about You and what she'd learned at those meetings. But I'm listening now. And I do believe in You and all You did."

She wasn't expecting an answer, wasn't sure if she was supposed to feel anything. Nothing spectacular happened. No heavenly voice replied. But she did feel a calm that had been absent when she woke from her nightmare, and she was able to lie back down and close her eyes. Somehow, she believed that He had heard and accepted her prayer.

Before sleep claimed her, an image of Kurt sitting across the checkerboard, smiling at her as if pleased, his dimples flashing, made her own lips lift in a contented smile.

*And if it wouldn't be too much to ask. . .*she thought drowsily, pausing, uncertain exactly what she wanted when it came to the deputy. *Please let me spend some more time with him and don't let us be separated just yet. . . .*

Chapter 10

Dreading the encounter, Kurt stepped into the kitchen. The women hadn't heard him: they were too busy with their chores, both of them chattering and laughing like magpies. Doreen chopped a row of vegetables while Linda whisked the broom at a steady pace and swept the floor.

He stared at the young woman whom he could barely tolerate to think of as his prisoner any longer. In the week and a half since their checker game, they'd grown closer, and she had become to him much more than his charge. Not that he had demonstrated his feelings for her. He'd kept quiet about them, knowing he had no right to act. And soon she would be gone. As the days had elapsed with no word, he had foolishly thought that those in Crater Springs might forget about the existence of Miss Linda Grayson.

Doreen looked sideways. "Kurt! There you are. Dinner will be ready in two shakes of a lamb's tail." Her robust greeting and smile faded as she stared at his face. "Is something wrong? You look as if your horse just died. . ."

He didn't answer, turned his attention to Linda. She'd quit sweeping and looked at him in question. Her face was rosy, her eyes bright, and the shy, sweet smile he'd seen blossom all week edged upward in uncertainty.

"I need to talk with Linda." They had achieved a first name basis in their new companionship, though she still called him Deputy when they were in the presence of others besides Doreen.

"Oh." Doreen set the knife on the table and wiped her hands down the front of her apron. "Of course." She looked at both of them in turn, her face a mask of concern. "I'll just be in the main room if you need me." She hurried away.

Kurt couldn't stand to see the fear sweep through Linda's soft gray eyes, knowing that what he had to tell her wouldn't bring back the sparkle.

"Tell me. Tell me quick."

"I got the telegram. I've been ordered to take you back immediately."

"Oh." The word came very quiet. Both her small hands clenched hard around the broom handle, her knuckles going white, and she used it as if it were a walking stick to give her support to remain standing.

He wanted to go to her, to take her in his arms and hold her, to reassure her that everything would be all right. But he couldn't give such assurances when her fate was out of his hands. If he went to her, he wasn't sure he would be able to prevent himself from declaring his feelings for her or even have any strength of will left to carry out his duty.

"You going to be all right?" His attempt to reach out felt lame and as awkward as the nod she gave in return.

"We both knew it was bound to happen, sooner or later. At least I had more time than I originally thought I would. For a while there I'd hoped maybe they'd forgotten me." Her voice came a little too high, and she attempted a smile he thought she meant to pass for acceptance, but it was too forced, further revealing her terror.

He could no more prevent himself from going to her than he could have stopped a stampede of wild horses. Drawing her close, he held her, feeling her tremble against him. Her heart raced like a spirited filly imprisoned inside. He couldn't stand the thought of her behind bars; she had been his prisoner, but he had given her a parcel of freedom he doubted others would be so merciful to grant. Worse, they might kill her if a judge found her guilty. And he couldn't let that happen.

Pulling away, he cupped her face, looking into her eyes now glassy with tears she hadn't let fall. His thumbs smoothed along her cheeks, soft as satin.

"Don't give up, Linda. There's got to be a way out of this fix, and I'll find it. I have to follow my orders, but the Almighty won't let you down. He's called the 'Almighty' if you'll recall. All-powerful. And I believe like Doreen does, that He made our paths cross for a reason. I promised I'd help you, and that won't end once you leave my guard."

She attempted another smile. This one came a little steadier.

He lowered his hands to her shoulders, giving them a heartening squeeze as he returned her smile with one he didn't feel, either. "I have to take care of some things, but we'll talk more about this tonight."

"I thought your orders were to take me back immediately."

"The stage isn't due for another few days, to my knowledge. Besides, a few more days won't hurt anything."

At her slight nod, he left her with another smile that slipped the moment he left the room. The middle of his chest felt as heavy as his tread as he entered the jailhouse. Marshal Wilson looked up from studying a newspaper. Kurt noticed the cell again stood empty and figured the rowdy Jedadiah Carter must have finally sobered up. Glad to be able to discuss the matter in private, Kurt came straight to the point.

"I got the telegram to take Miss Burke back to Crater Springs. I plan to leave on the next stage."

The marshal folded his paper twice and set it on the desk before giving Kurt his full attention. "You don't sound too sure about that."

"I have no stomach for what I have to do. Hand over a lamb to wolves."

"You think she's innocent of the crime?"

"I'd stake my life on it."

"But it goes a lot deeper than that, doesn't it?"

"What do you mean?" Suddenly wishing to be outdoors, Kurt shifted his stance.

"You're downright besotted with the girl."

At the marshal's grin, Kurt felt even more awkward. "You don't know what you're talking about."

The marshal acted as if Kurt had remained silent, and squinted, as though assessing a perplexing riddle. "I'd go as far as to say that you even love her."

Kurt felt his ears and neck go hot. "I'll just be heading over to Wells Fargo and secure those tickets."

"Wait a minute."

Kurt turned in question.

"Be careful. O'Callahan sounds like a nasty sort of fellow. If she's right about the sheriff there, he could be bad news, as well. You have no idea what you're walking into. You shouldn't go alone."

"If you're offering, I'm not accepting." Kurt shook his head in disbelief. "You just got out of what almost became your deathbed! And I don't aim risking Tillie's wrath by having you come with me."

"I'm not asking. I give the orders, and I'm a lot stronger than I look."

"I'll be fine." Kurt tried to mollify him, knowing the marshal could be as stubborn as a rooster always crowing at the break of dawn.

"I don't seem to be the only former patient here. If you'll recall, you recently got in a fight and busted your ribs."

Kurt thought of the upcoming ride in a stagecoach that would likely jar every bone in his body. He had considered taking Linda to Crater Springs on horseback, but the orders had been for him to get on the next stage. He sighed. "Today is the first I can move without pain. That liniment of Doreen's helped. But Linda is my responsibility, and I'll handle this."

"You mean she's your prisoner."

He couldn't mistake the twinkle in the marshal's eyes, though his mouth remained grim.

"I mean that I aim on doing all I can to help her."

Marshal Wilson sat forward in his chair. "What do you plan on doing, Kurt? Once you turn her over, she's out of your jurisdiction. You won't have any say on what happens to her."

"I know the regulations." Kurt tugged the brim of his hat lower on his forehead. "But I'll think of something."

❧

"I can't tell you what it's meant to me to have you here." Doreen hugged Linda a third time, treating her as a beloved relation going off on a long journey, never to be seen again. Linda surmised that wasn't far off the mark. Once O'Callahan got his hands on her, she doubted that he would let her live.

She hugged Doreen back just as fiercely, the lingering fragment of hope that Kurt had instilled in her days before frayed, now that her time of departure had arrived.

Doreen shoved a pretty lace-rimmed handkerchief into her hands, and Linda dried her eyes, then handed it back.

"Keep it," Doreen insisted. "To remember me by. I wish I had something more to give you than just a piece of cloth."

"You've given me the most important gift I can recall ever getting." Linda's voice trembled with emotion. "You've been so kind to me and you gave me a sense of worth by sharing with me your Savior. *Our* Savior," she corrected with a little laugh.

"Never forget." Doreen held both of Linda's hands, giving them a tight squeeze. "He is just that."

She moved on to Kurt, kissing his cheek. "Take care of her. And yourself."

"You can count on it." He moved his mouth close to Doreen's ear and lowered his voice, though Linda still heard his rich rumble of words. "I don't aim on letting anything bad happen to her. So don't you start fretting once we leave."

"I don't intend to waste my time fretting. I intend to pray. Every time I think of you two. And I imagine that'll be my every waking moment."

He hugged her, then took Linda's elbow, escorting her from the hotel, her first time outside since she'd stood on the boardwalk the night she spoke with him about the Widow Campbell. She withheld a wry chuckle. Such a trivial matter in light of what she now faced, but her jealousy had seemed so monumental at the time.

Kurt accompanied her across the dusty road, her first time on it since the team of horses had tried to run her down. She tensed at the memory, darting a look sideways for any sudden dangers.

Kurt's thumb stroked her sleeve; beneath, her skin tingled at his caress. "It'll be all right. No one's going to hurt you. Not as long as I'm around."

His words of reassurance didn't ease the ache of dread growing inside her chest. What of tomorrow? He wouldn't be with her tomorrow. And she knew she would miss him so much in whatever time she had left. Without a doubt, her enemies would harm her once she was turned over to their possession; O'Callahan would have his revenge against her mother and herself. Her mother had made him look like a fool, and Linda had defied him once too often. Soon she would again be standing in his vile presence.

She briefly shut her eyes as Kurt handed her up into the egg-shaped Concord coach. She took a seat and he swung inside, across from her. The driver shut the door with a harsh slam, making her jump. Kurt seemed to read the question in her eyes, his own eyes gentle.

"Apparently, we're the only people to take the stage today."

She gave a brief nod. On her way to Silverton, she'd shared the coach with a stout man who snored half the time, though Linda never understood how he could sleep while being shaken and bumped about, and the man's companion, an elderly woman who'd said barely a word and had peered over the top of her glasses at Linda for most of the ride. Kurt was welcome company, despite the fact that he represented the law that would soon decide her fate.

As the stage pulled out of town with a sudden start, she drew back the leather curtain and looked out the window opening, watching the buildings, then scenery roll by in a blur of browns and blues and golds. She recalled Doreen's words and how she'd held both of Linda's hands, looking steadily into her eyes as she'd encouraged her to put her faith in the Lord and told her that He would deliver her from her troubles. Linda was so thankful she'd had the chance to meet Doreen. And Kurt.

Her eyes swept his way, and she noted he stared out the same window. She wondered what his thoughts were. Did he think of her and their times together these past weeks? Or would he secretly be relieved to hand her over to the sheriff, considering his duty done? His words of reassurance to her had seemed sincere, but maybe she was reading more into them than she should. It was utter foolishness to lose her heart to this man when she had no future to consider. Even more foolish, considering he was a lawman and she, a wanted criminal. He looked her way, and she saw the same interest there, the same hopeless yearning spurred by feelings that kept her awake at night. She should quench this right now, say something before he might express to her words that, once said, could never be taken back. But she only stared into his remarkable, piercing green eyes, wishing for all the world for dreams that could never be hers to possess.

A distant gunshot exploded behind the stage, the dull thunk of the bullet hitting the back. Kurt sprang into action, shoving Linda down while pulling his gun from his holster. Another shot followed, and the coach jolted as the horses picked up speed.

Chapter 11

S tay down!" Kurt swept back the leather curtain from his side of the window opening and aimed, trying to keep his arm steady despite the shaky ride. He squeezed off two shots, the explosion deafening.

"What's going on?"

"Two riders. Can't see their faces—kerchiefs tied around them."

"You think they're thieves planning to rob the stage?"

"No. Driver has no gold or silver to transport this time. I asked."

Another series of shots came, two more hitting the back of the stagecoach.

"Then wh—" Linda broke off her question as Kurt threw her a weighty glance. She had no need to ask why. Whoever was shooting at them must be after her. A bullet whizzed past, finding its mark on the inside wall near Kurt's head. Linda cried out in shock.

"You hurt?" he asked.

She shook her head in reply, her heart pounding at his near miss with death.

Looking out the window, Kurt frowned. "A third rider came from beyond that hill." He pulled out her derringer from his boot and handed it over to her. "Anyone comes near that window, shoot. Stage horses are trained for this kind of danger—fastest horses around—but you can't be too careful."

She shifted around, falling down onto the seat next to him, so that she also faced the rear of the stage, the window within reach.

"What are you doing?" His expression was incredulous, his tone fierce. "You're making yourself more of a target that way."

"How can you expect me to get a decent shot if I don't have a clear view?" she said just as tersely. "They're coming from both sides now." Another gunshot on her side of the stage made her point clear.

"You can't shoot far with that thing."

"I'm a good shot. I've done a heap of practicing. Ma taught me."

His jaw flexed, as if he were struggling with a decision, then he handed her his other gun. "Can you handle this?"

"I've fired a Colt before." She didn't elaborate.

"Try to aim steady as you can. We don't have a lot of time for reloading."

Linda squashed all fear to a corner of her brain, clenched her teeth, aimed, and fired. The first shot didn't hit its mark, but Kurt obviously had better luck.

"Two left." His voice came grave. "Should be one rider on each side."

Linda concentrated, trying to keep her arms steady as she clutched the gun in both hands and braced her body against the rocking of the stagecoach. She aimed for the rider who again thundered into view, dirt rising like smoke around him. He fired his gun at her. She heard the dull *thunk* of metal hitting metal somewhere outside near her head. Remembering all Ma had taught her on sizing up her target, she pulled the trigger. Her attacker clutched his shoulder and flew backward off his horse.

"Mine's down." She was surprised the husky, wavering sound coming from her throat was her voice. She didn't think she'd killed their attacker and watched him struggle to sit up as his horse bolted far away. She was even more shocked to feel relief that her assumption had been correct, that her attacker was only injured, not dead.

Kurt fired again. "And third rider is in retreat." He pulled back his arm but kept his focus outside the stage, on the lookout for more foes. After a short time, he banged on the roof with his gun.

Linda figured it was a prearranged signal, because she heard the driver call out a command to the horses. The team slowed then came to a full stop.

"You get hit?" Kurt called up to the driver.

"A flesh wound, in the arm," the man called back down, his words raspy in his pain.

Kurt and Linda shared an anxious look. He pushed open the door and disappeared outside. While he was gone, Linda thought about the series of close calls her life had become. How many more attempts would be made to kill her before all her luck ran out? She stared down at Kurt's gun lying in her lap, along with her derringer. Now that the scare was over and she could think more clearly, she felt surprised he had entrusted her with them. She could have held him and the driver up, taken one of the horses, and ridden far away. Two weeks earlier, she might have done just that. But things had changed. She had changed.

Kurt was gone a long time, enough time for her to mull over how even her goals had changed. She still wanted to make a new life for herself, free from the burdens of the past that dogged her every move. And being with Kurt and Doreen had made her realize how much she wanted to be part of a family, never to be alone again. They'd accepted her for who she was, treating her no different than any other woman, Kurt even treating her as a lady might be treated. Linda had never known just what that entailed, but she had a good idea that Kurt's little kindnesses measured up to it.

"I bound up his arm till he can get a doctor to look at it." Kurt jarred her

thoughts as he climbed into the coach, reclaiming the seat next to her and closing the door. "Bullet didn't hit bone, just went through. He's bound and determined to make it to the next way station on time, afraid he'll lose his job if he
doesn't, so we're going on." At her slight nod, he laid his hand over hers.

"I told you I wouldn't let anything happen to you, and I meant it. I don't
know what those men wanted, but I'm pretty sure it had something to do with
you." He glanced at the guns still lying in her lap. "Keep your derringer. Just in
case." He took back his Colt and reloaded it.

"But. . ." She blinked, stunned by his crisp order. "I'll admit, I don't know
the way these things work, but I'm pretty near certain you're not supposed to
give your prisoner a weapon to carry."

He grinned. "Fact is I'm finding it mighty difficult to keep on thinking of
you in those terms. Personal feelings aside, I don't know what we're walking
into. Two attempts were made on your life, and once I turn you over, I won't be
able to do much to help you as far as the law goes."

"As far as the. . ." She shook her head, not understanding.

"The sheriff will take you and more than likely lock you in a cell. I won't
have any say in your treatment, since I'll be out of my jurisdiction, but if anyone
comes near you to try to harm you, at least you'll have your gun handy."

"Won't you get in trouble for doing this?" She still couldn't fathom how the
by-the-book deputy could do such a thing as supply her with a weapon. "I don't
want to get you in trouble, Kurt." As much as he'd helped her, as special as he'd
become, she couldn't tolerate being the reason he might lose his job and likely
get in worse trouble than that.

"I can live with the prospect of losing my badge, but not of losing you."

His words, deep and heartfelt, made her heart strum a few erratic beats. If
he meant what she thought he meant. . .

Lowering his gaze to her mouth, he slowly leaned toward her. She let her
eyes flutter closed, sure he would kiss her. That at any moment she would feel
the welcome brush of his mouth against hers. Her first kiss. Instead, the stage
jolted forward, knocking them both off balance.

Kurt muttered something about timing and grabbed her arms to steady her.
"You all right?"

She quickly managed to regain her emotional equilibrium. "After being shot
at by three armed men, somehow being jolted off my seat hardly seems worth
mentioning."

He chuckled then sobered. "I promise, Linda, I'll find a way out of this fix
for you somehow. You won't spend your life in jail. And the townsfolk aren't
going to witness any hanging, either."

"You're not thinking of breaking me out of jail?" She doubted such a thought would cross his mind; he was much too honorable, and she admired him for his integrity, even if it meant her defeat.

"Nothing like that. But I am going to do some investigating of my own so as to find the real killer."

"Investigating?" She still found it hard to believe he could have faith in her, when no man ever had before. "Then you no longer believe, even the slightest bit, that I could be guilty of Mr. Townsend's death?"

His eyes burned steadily into hers. "I never did."

᷾

Three small words, yet they'd made such a big difference to Linda. Kurt had never seen her eyes so bright with hope as he had when he'd told her he'd never believed her guilty. But as soon as they stepped out of the stagecoach at Crater Springs, that cornered look came into her eyes again, though she kept her head high as he escorted her to the jailhouse.

The town was larger than Jasperville, and he saw a mill and two smokestacks on the outskirts, close to the mountain near the mines. Wooden trestles built for the ore cars zigzagged up the face of the mountain. The town itself boasted the usual buildings of trade lined up in two rows—among them a livery, a dry goods and clothing store, a bank, a place for groceries and provisions, and a tin shop. Many people stopped what they were doing to stare. More women occupied this town than Jasperville, and he noticed they regarded Linda as if she were the mud clogged beneath their shoes. One woman grabbed a boy Kurt assumed was her son and held him close while she glared Linda's way.

"That's the boy who saw me in the banker's office," Linda whispered, following the direction of Kurt's gaze.

He studied the towheaded boy who stood almost as tall as his ma. With his thick arms crossed over his chest, his expression dour, he looked more man than boy. He returned Kurt's stare with what seemed like a challenge.

Kurt firmly held onto Linda's elbow. "No matter what happens once we enter that building," he said low so only she could hear, "just bear in mind this isn't over."

She nodded as they stepped into the dim interior of the jailhouse.

Kurt's first impression of the sheriff wasn't a favorable one. He stood about as tall as Kurt, a bit on the husky side, with an expression of grim determination creasing harsh lines into his face. But it was the look he gave Linda that set Kurt's teeth on edge. The man stared at her as if he would like to wrap his hands around her throat right then and forego a noose or even a judge. His attention switched to Kurt, and a morsel of reason returned as he grabbed his ring of keys off the desk.

"Thank you, Deputy. I'll take over from here. I imagine you'll be wanting to catch the stage back to wherever it is you came from."

The sheriff gave Linda's free arm an unmerciful yank, ripping her other arm out of Kurt's hold, and forced her toward the cell as if she were resisting, though she only tried to keep her balance. Kurt barely kept his temper in check. Linda glanced his way, panic in her eyes, and Kurt pushed down his anger to mouth words of encouragement. "I'll be back."

She gave a little nod as if she understood. Kurt exited the building, scanning the street for the boy. He found him outside the dry goods store, hands tucked around his suspenders, leaning against a post. Kurt came up on him before the boy could notice. By the nervous jump he gave, Kurt had a feeling that if the boy had seen him coming he would have fled.

"I understand you were in the banker's office the day he was shot," Kurt greeted him.

The boy fidgeted but stared up at Kurt as if he would give no ground. "That's right."

"You see anything or anyone that seemed a mite suspicious?" Kurt shifted, making sure the boy got a good look at his badge. His eyes widened, and Kurt grimly smiled, satisfied.

"I already done tol' the sheriff I saw her. She shot him."

"That the statement you gave? That you saw Miss Bur—Miss Grayson shoot Mr. Townsend?"

"Yeah." His Adam's apple bobbed up and down as he swallowed, clearly nervous.

Kurt crossed his arms over his chest. "So you're telling me that, with your own two eyes, you saw the gun go off and the banker shot?"

The boy gripped his suspenders hard, pulling downward until they were in danger of snapping free. "I—I heared it. And I seen her holding the gun. She looked scairt."

"But you didn't see her fire the gun?"

The boy didn't answer, and Kurt switched tactics. "I'd like to pay my respects to the Widow Townsend. Can you tell me where she lives?"

Hesitation written over every part of his face and stunted movements, the boy pointed north. "Big house near the creek."

"And Grady O'Callahan? Where does he live?"

An unmistakable look of fear entered the boy's eyes. "What you want to see him for?"

His edgy behavior further strengthened Kurt's hunch that O'Callahan had something to do with the boy's testimony.

"Let's just say I've got some unfinished business with him."

"You know him?"

Kurt didn't respond; he knew O'Callahan's type. And today he would put an end to the lifetime of terror the black rogue had forced Linda to endure.

Linda sat inside the cell, perched on the edge of the cot, wringing her hands in her skirts. Her random thoughts—that the bedding was filthy compared to the cot in Kurt's jailhouse and that Sheriff Ryder must not have someone like Tillie to wash the linens—seemed foolish when compared to the next indeterminate hours of her life.

The sheriff had yet to speak a civil word to her. She'd kept her gaze fastened to the opposite wall, avoiding his glare that rarely left her from across the room and felt as if it burned holes straight through her.

She closed her eyes, wishing for Kurt's company. He'd done so much to help her, had become important to her in so many ways, and she missed him. Badly.

The outside door opened, brightening the dingy room with sunlight. Hopeful, Linda swung her attention to the entrance. Instead of Kurt, the embodiment of her bleakest nightmares strode inside, standing head and shoulders taller than the sheriff, his manner confident as if he owned the place. Likely, he did. And the sheriff, too.

Linda's assumption became certainty as O'Callahan's dark eyes swept down her once; then he turned his back to her, his attention on the sheriff, and spoke with him in harsh undertones, words Linda couldn't distinguish. From their manner, neither man was happy, which she found peculiar since they finally had her locked in a cell.

"Are we clear on what's to be done?" O'Callahan ended the argument, his voice raised a little louder so that Linda now heard him.

Scowling, the sheriff narrowed his eyes but nodded, handing O'Callahan the ring of keys. Linda watched his approach, feeling like the cornered hare under the merciless, compelling eyes of the snake.

"Hello, my dear," he said, his tone as smooth as bear grease and just as rancid. "So nice of you to join us again. It wasn't very courteous of you to take off as you did and without a word to anyone."

Linda watched in alarm as he fitted the key into the lock, turned it, and swung open her cell door.

Chapter 12

I thank you for your time, ma'am." Kurt sat across from the Widow Townsend, feeling awkward in the fancy furnished home almost the size of Doreen's hotel and using the dainty china teacup that she'd provided him. His fingers were too thick to fit inside the scrolled handle, and he wrapped his large hand around the cup, trying not to exert too much pressure. Surely something so fragile crushed easily, as easily as its owner, his gracious hostess, an elderly woman who looked as if a puff of wind might blow her up and over the mountain. As carefully as he treated the cup, he addressed the widow, not wanting to cause her further grief.

"I do hope I was able to help you. You seem like such a nice young man." She looked sadly toward a daguerreotype of a dignified-looking, bespectacled gentleman. "I'm afraid my dear husband at times could be unwise when it came to his choice of acquaintances, such as that dreadful Mr. O'Callahan. But he did have a kind heart. Hubert made his fair share of mistakes. However, he did his best to rectify them." Her watery blue eyes again met his. "You will do your best to help Miss Grayson, won't you?"

Her gentle inquiry stunned him. "You don't believe she killed your husband?"

"Mercy, no." She looked just as surprised that he would need to ask. "Hubert always spoke well of her, and I know she must have esteemed him to ask his counsel. We had only sons, no daughters. Hubert looked upon her with a fatherly affection. I rarely went into town, but he told me he often greeted her with a smile, wishing he could do more for her, since many in our town treat her as an outcast. Like her mother, she would take no charity, though she did accept the occasional loaf of bread. I often had my cook bake an extra loaf, and when Hubert left for the bank, he would make a stop at her door to leave it there. She seemed so lonesome after her mother died, poor soul." Her tone held no judgment. "I attended the revival and saw the drastic change it made in Mary before she died. During that last week I had Hubert with me, he seemed so pleased that he could finally do something to help Mary's daughter. Though he was quite fretful, too."

"Any idea why?" These were the first significant words she'd spoken since he'd arrived ten minutes ago, and for the first time, Kurt didn't feel as if he'd wasted a trip to her home, with time being so precious.

As if coming out of a daze, she shook her head. "My husband usually shared everything with me, but during that last week, he seemed uncommonly distant and irritable. He did tell me something about Miss Grayson receiving a letter from her father, but he anticipated their meeting. He told me that she'd come to him, seeking advice, and he was delighted. Whatever upset him had nothing to do with Miss Grayson. On the contrary, her faith in Hubert cheered him. It gave him new purpose and made him feel as if he could make a difference in someone's life. I also believe her seeking him out made him question some of his earlier decisions."

"Such as?"

Her expression grew sad, and she hesitated as if uncertain she should speak. "Deputy Michaels, please understand I loved my husband dearly. I accepted him for what he was, both the good and the bad. I told you he was a gentle soul, but he was also easily cowed by those who were nothing more than overgrown schoolyard bullies." She frowned. "I don't know what power Grady O'Callahan had over Hubert, but the few times I saw them together, I supposed an alliance of some nature existed and that my husband felt threatened by O'Callahan. I cannot prove it, but I think O'Callahan is the reason my husband became so distant before his death." She dabbed at the corner of her eye with a lace handkerchief. "I detest speaking ill of my husband in any regard, but for Miss Grayson's sake, I believe my telling you the facts as I know them is a matter of which he would approve."

"I know this must be hard for you, and believe me when I say I appreciate your help."

"Is there any other matter in which I can be of assistance?"

"As a matter of fact. . .I don't want to take up any more of your time, but I'd be beholden to you if you could show me your husband's ledgers."

"His ledgers?"

"His personal effects did go to you?"

"Yes, of course. But I received no ledgers."

Kurt drew his brows together, pondering her words and Linda's recollection. "Maybe they're still at the bank?"

"Perhaps. . ."

"You sound doubtful."

"Forgive me, but I had a trusted servant ride to the bank and personally collect every item on my husband's desk to bring to me. There were no ledgers."

"May I ask why you would do something like that?"

She took in a deep breath and let it out in a rush. "I told you Hubert had associations with people I didn't trust. The fact of the matter is that I didn't want anyone searching his things. A foolish notion, perhaps, in light of what happened, but I couldn't abide the thought."

"Then you think he was hiding something?"

"Deputy, I can only give you my opinion based on the little he shared with me and endured during his last week on earth. I have no proof. But yes, I suspect that someone with evil intent may have wanted to go through his things before I did. After all, my dear Hubert was shot like an animal in cold blood." She lowered her nose and mouth to her handkerchief. "Deputy, if you'll excuse me. . ."

He lowered his gaze to the tapestry rug beneath his dusty boots and cleared his throat, not wishing to ask what he must. "Ma'am, I mean no disrespect, but I need to know. Do you think your husband was involved in anything dishonest?"

She shut her eyes as if to block out the thought but gave a slight nod. "I have often speculated why he should meet up with Mr. O'Callahan as often as he did. He couldn't abide the man, and I suspect that he terrorized my husband in some malicious manner. Poor Hubert didn't have much backbone, though he made up for what he lacked with his gentle, considerate nature. He was rather timid when it came to altercations of any sort."

"Thank you, Mrs. Townsend." He picked up his hat from the sofa where he'd set it. "I appreciate your time. You've been of great help to me."

"I do hope it was enough and that you're able to help poor Miss Grayson."

Kurt again assured her it was and that he intended to do just that. He settled his hat on his head as she saw him to the door. Retracing his trek to the jailhouse, he wished for his horse. The Townsend home had been farther away than he'd realized when he first set out on foot, and he wondered if the livery had any horses for hire. He didn't need to waste time walking when riding was much faster.

Once he entered the jailhouse, he sensed something amiss. The sheriff half-rose from his chair, his mouth parted as if in surprise to see him. "I thought you were headed out on the stage."

"I changed my mind." Kurt's attention went to the barred cell, and his heart dropped to see it empty.

"Where is she?" He barely refrained from shouting the words or punching away the smug expression that suddenly swept over the sheriff's face. Not wanting to invite trouble, Kurt uncurled his fists, keeping his hands down at his sides.

"Well now, Deputy, I can't see that's any of your business."

"I'm making it my business."

"Is that right?" The heavyset man settled back in his chair, regarding Kurt as if he had all the time in the world. "I reckon you'll have to ask elsewhere then, because I don't plan on telling you. But if I was you, I'd tend to my own affairs and head on back to where I came from. We don't take kindly to strangers snooping about town."

Suddenly, Kurt realized he didn't have to ask. He pivoted fast and left the jailhouse, his strides rapid as he located the livery.

∽

Linda paced the ornate bedroom into which she'd been locked. Furnishings of rich mahogany and other lustrous materials of rich brocades, satins, and damasks decorated her surroundings. Once more, she moved toward the turreted window and looked down. It was quite a drop, but if she could somehow pull the hangings from the bed and knot them together. . .

The sound of a key scraping in the lock jolted her from her plan of escape, and she whirled around, hands clenched into fists at her sides. There wasn't time for her to go for her derringer concealed beneath her skirts as the door swung open and O'Callahan strode inside, his smile irksome. He closed the door and locked it, pocketing the key.

"Hello, my dear." He glanced toward a piecrust table and the plate there. "I see you've not touched your food. After such a long journey, I should think you would be famished."

She clenched her teeth. "What do you intend on doing with me? Why did you take me out of jail and bring me to this prison?"

"Prison?" He sank to the edge of the bed and looked up at her, cocking one eyebrow, his manner one of confident amusement. "Such comfortable surroundings could hardly be called punishment. Though that knock in the noggin you gave me deserves a measure of it."

She glared at him. "Why am I here?"

"I didn't wish you to get any foolish notions in your head about leaving my hospitality and trying to find your way back to town. Sunset isn't long in coming. It would be a shame if my bride were to lose her way in the dark and become the nighttime feast of some nocturnal predator."

"Your *bride*?" The word came choked. Facing down a mountain lion was preferable to the thought of marrying this monster.

"Of course. Did I neglect sharing with you my plans for us?" He pretended ignorance. "I've sent for a minister, and he should arrive early tomorrow morning." He rose from the bed. "You had best get your rest. I want my bride ravishing as she stands beside me."

"The only place I'll be standing is over your grave," she spat out. "And dancing a jig on top of it. I would never marry you, Grady O'Callahan!"

Rather than become angered by her outburst, his eyes grew the slightest bit wistful. "You have your mother's spirit, but you'll soon be learning as she did. . ." He covered the distance between them in a few swift steps and grabbed her arm. The anger he had hidden flared as suddenly as a match that had been struck. "I make the rules, and I'll not be crossed."

206

Sudden fear made her icy cold as she stared into his blazing dark eyes. She struggled to shake it off, as she did his arm, and retreated, thrusting her chin up as though affronted. "You despise me as I despise you. Why would you want to marry me? You don't love me, and I certainly don't love you."

"You're such a child at times, Linda. Not all marriages are based on love or even friendship."

She drew her brows together. "Then for what reason could you possibly want this? I have nothing to give you except for my disgust and contempt." Had he merely wanted her body, which she would fight him tooth and nail to protect, she doubted he would demand marriage. Over the years, she'd witnessed how his false charm had wooed any woman he desired to his side as a willing companion. She would never be his victim!

"My dear, how you feel about me is irrelevant. You have something which is of far greater value to me than petty feelings and inconsequential vows from the heart."

"What?" She shook her head in confusion. "What could I possibly have that you would want?" His gaze raked over her, and she pressed her hand to her bosom, thankful she no longer wore her mother's revealing dress. Regardless, she felt as if his eyes burned through the modest shirtwaist.

He laughed, the sound degrading. "Oh, yes, your enticements are many, and I intend to take my fill whenever I wish. Yet that is not why I will marry you. Are you so obtuse as to think that I don't know about the silver mine you inherited? You should know by now nothing escapes my notice."

Her mouth parted as she regarded him in disbelief. She laughed, though she was not at all amused. "It is you who are the fool, O'Callahan! You should have had your lackeys look closer. I no longer have any part of that dratted mine!"

"You have a map." He took another step toward her, and she likewise retreated. "And I want it."

"Only a third. And you'll have to scout all over Nevada to get it, because my darling brother stole it from me!"

"You lie." He calmed. "As you've always done when you've been cornered. Yet being your lawful husband," he said the last word with derision, "I'll be entitled to all of my wife's property. I *will* have that map. Whether you hand it over tomorrow or not, it doesn't matter. We will be wed and the profits of the mine shall belong to me."

She marched over to a chair, plucked up her reticule, marched back, and thrust it at him. "Search my bag if you'd like. Heaven knows everyone else has! But I tell you, it's not there."

He remained immobile, glancing at the offering as if it were of little significance. "Then you've hidden it, and you'll tell me where. Once we are wed,

I'll have the right to exert whatever force I deem necessary to correct a rebellious wife." His grin was malicious. "And I assure you, my dear, it won't be pretty."

"And if I refuse to marry you?" Her voice came hoarse. She knew, no matter what she said, he would never believe she didn't have the map. She had lied to him too many times before.

"Then I'll turn you over to Sheriff Ryder, who will immediately see to your execution for the murder of Hubert Townsend."

"I didn't kill him."

"I know."

Her eyes widened. "You *know*?"

"Of course. I told you, nothing escapes my notice."

She pressed her lips together, narrowing her eyes. "You did it, didn't you? You killed that poor man, just like I thought. I saw you near the bank that day!"

His eyes flashed, and for one moment, Linda thought it might be her last. He visibly corralled his anger and regarded her with disdain. "Whatever you saw or think you saw is of little consequence. My word bears far more weight in this town than the word of a prostitute's daughter."

The loud smack of her slap against his cheek surprised them both. The imprint of her fingers stood out white and blotched against the livid red of his face. She stood her ground even as he raised his hand to return the blow. "You ruined her!" she accused. "She had no choice."

"She came to me of her own free will." He hesitated as if struggling with containing his rage or allowing it free rein, then lowered his hand back to his side. His eyes scorned her. "When I met your mother, her reputation was already ruined—by the man who sired you. I gave her more than she was worth and even allowed her to bring her impertinent little brat to live at my establishment."

Hot tears of revulsion and pain blurred Linda's vision. She wanted to rake her nails across his face, make him bleed as he had made her heart bleed and her mother's, but instead she whirled away from him and crossed her arms over her chest, hugging herself.

"Get out." Her words came low but vibrated in their intensity. "Death is a welcome balm compared to even the mere thought of being married to you."

"Perhaps once we recite our vows and you give me what I desire, I'll grant you that favor." His words mocked her. "But marry we shall. So you had best reconcile yourself to the idea, my dear. I wouldn't want you to display any of your peevishness in front of the minister, or you will sorely regret it. Until tomorrow."

The sound of the door closing and the key turning in the lock filled her with both relief and dread. He had finally left, but she was still his captive.

She grabbed a ceramic figurine, the nearest thing she could find, and hurled it at the door, deriving a grim satisfaction as it shattered and fragments showered to the floor.

Her anger spent, and feeling suddenly weak and unsteady, her knees folded, and she sank to the ground. Somehow she must find a way out of this new prison.

She reached for the bed hanging, which draped to the floor, and gave the heavy material a strong tug, to no avail. Using both hands she pulled harder, using all her weight, until her head swam and her breathing came fast with her exertions. Her palms stung like fire from her tight grip around the ridged material. It was no use. Unless she could find a pair of shears, her plan of escape was hopeless. The comforter and sheet across the bed might get her down several feet from the window, but not three stories.

Tears of frustration rolled down her cheeks as she leaned her head against the side of the mattress and closed her eyes.

Chapter 13

A small, mustachioed Chinaman showed Kurt into a massive study with a marble fireplace that took up a third of one wall. Small, potted trees he didn't recognize decorated the interior, one behind a large antique oak desk, the other near the wall with a window that looked out over the range of snow-topped Ruby Mountains—much closer here than they were to Jasperville. The servant regarded Kurt with suspicion.

"Mr. O'Callahan busy at moment," he said in a halting accent. "You wait here."

"Don't mind if I do." Kurt smiled wide and settled into one of the upholstered chairs as if he planned to make his home there.

The Chinaman regarded him with undisguised disapproval as he left the room and closed the door behind him. The moment Kurt heard the click of the latch, he jumped up and moved toward the desk. As a lawman, he had every right to search for proof that a suspect had committed a crime, especially if an innocent woman's life was in jeopardy.

Quickly he scanned the contents of the desk and the shelves behind it, then opened the desk drawer. Shuffling aside sheaves of papers, his fingers felt along one side of the drawer. He'd heard old desks such as this contained hidden compartments and hoped O'Callahan's did, as well.

Voices outside the room, discernable yet still distant, urged him to hasten his task. He felt along the other side. His fingertips met a groove. Pushing down into the indentation, he heard a spring release. The bottom of the drawer popped up a fraction—a false bottom. He pulled it up. A ledger lay inside, and he made quick work of retrieving it.

Eureka! He'd struck gold. Dried brown spots—unmistakably blood—covered the black leather of a ledger. Opening the cover, he rifled through the pages until he found what he was looking for. A series of dates and transactions for tracts of land sold to various buyers, as well as jotted messages that showed O'Callahan's later purchase of the same land for half a dollar an acre, suggested something seedy. Kurt risked reading further until he found what he needed to know.

The conniving snake. . .

At the sound of approaching footsteps, Kurt closed the ledger and slammed the drawer shut. He took a few steps to the window just as the door swung open. Tall and dark, the owner of the house entered the room and closed the door behind him. The gentleman's expensive clothes and lofty manner assured Kurt that this was O'Callahan.

"Deputy." He gave a brief nod. "My man told me you wished to speak with me?"

"Where is she?" Kurt's demand brooked no rebuff.

"I assume you refer to Miss Grayson?" O'Callahan moved toward a counter and poured himself a snifter of brandy from the decanter. "You need not concern yourself with her welfare. I appreciate your bringing her back to Crater Springs where she belongs, but your duty is done here."

"I'm not going anywhere. Not before you tell me where she is."

"I suggest you keep out of affairs that don't concern you and leave on the next stage while you still can."

Kurt didn't think, only acted. He grabbed the insufferable snob and slammed him against the wall. Gripping the lapels of his waistcoat in tight fists, he pushed his face close. A series of heavy footsteps approached the study, but Kurt didn't release his hold.

"Miss Grayson does concern me," he muttered the threat low, "and if you've done anything to hurt her, you'll be the one rotting in a cell. You may have made it your life's work to harass others, but you don't scare me in the slightest."

"Let me remind you, Deputy, you're out of your jurisdiction."

"But I'm not."

Both men swung their heads to the door in surprise at the gravelly voice, dour with purpose.

Kurt was surprised to see Marshal Wilson standing in the entrance with an elderly man. Despite his snow-white hair and lined face, the stranger looked hale and hearty, ready to tackle a wild boar if need be.

"Who are you?" O'Callahan bit out. "What are you doing in my home?"

"Chief Justice Mackleby is my name," the white-haired gentleman responded. "I'm the law, this side of the territory. And I see I got here just in time."

Remembering his hold on O'Callahan, Kurt released him. O'Callahan brushed off his lapels as if they were caked with a day's worth of grime.

"Jake Fairaday witnessed the ambush on the stagecoach and told me about it," Marshal Wilson explained to Kurt. "I'd sent a telegram to the chief justice days before, who also happens to be an old friend of my father's. As chance would have it, he came into town on the stage that took you and Miss Burke—er, Grayson. You just missed him. We rode hard to get here when we heard of the ambush. It didn't take a lot of finagling to get Mr. O'Callahan's whereabouts from the sheriff."

"Everything you want to know is in that desk drawer," Kurt said, glad to see his friend had come and brought a higher-ranking official. He glanced at the man. "Looks to me like shady land deals were involved, that the banker was somehow in on it, and O'Callahan shot him or had something to do with his death."

"I didn't kill Townsend."

"Then why did you steal the ledger from his desk that same day? My guess is you were hiding something, Townsend knew about it, had second thoughts, and wanted out of the partnership you'd formed. So you shot him."

O'Callahan's eyes snapped black fire, but now that the chief justice was involved, Kurt had more important matters to consider. "Once more, where is Miss Grayson?" When he still didn't speak, Kurt acted. "Doesn't matter if you don't talk. I'll search every room in this house if need be. I *will* find her."

Marshal Wilson nodded for Kurt to go ahead, and he made good on his threat. On the third floor landing he tried a door and found it locked. "Linda?" he called out.

A muffled whimper of indistinguishable words came from the other side, as if she'd been gagged. He didn't bother going back downstairs to demand a key. Giving the wood a hard kick, he broke through as the door crashed inward.

Inside, a young dark-haired woman, bound and gagged, stared up at him with fright. By the simple dress and apron she wore, he knew she must be a servant. He pulled the gag down from her mouth. "Where is Miss Grayson?"

A sputter of words left her lips. "I don't know. She held a gun to me and tied me up. I came to get her dishes."

"She escaped?" Kurt asked grimly as with his knife he sawed through the cording knotted around her wrists. It matched the braided rope that held back the other side of the draperies.

The girl nodded, her eyes anxious. Kurt sighed and kept silent, refraining from taking out his irritation on the timid girl.

Blast it, Linda, where have you run off to now?

⊸⑤

Linda surveyed her surroundings with dread. When she'd fled O'Callahan's house earlier, she thought she'd escaped detection until the sheriff jumped out from behind some rocks and grabbed her. But instead of taking the path into town and back to jail, he forced her to mount his horse, then swung up behind her in the saddle, and headed in the opposite direction.

"What do you want with me?" she tried for the second time. "Where are you taking me?"

"You ask too many questions"—his arm tightened around her midsection—"and also have a nasty habit of meddling where you don't belong. It's high time I put a stop to all that."

Put a stop to what? What did he mean? Linda eyed the blazing sunset that painted the clouds blood red and the mountains great peaks of black. Darkness filled the sky behind, and with a wry thought bordering on hysteria she noted they were traveling west through a valley on the same route she'd taken when she'd escaped to Silverton what seemed a lifetime ago. Why? Why travel west when Crater Springs lay east?

Soon only a glimmer of light remained on the horizon, and it became too dark to travel. He stopped and tied up his horse. She considered trying to jump off the saddle and run, but in the night, with shadowy patches of brush and rock spotting the uneven land, she would likely fall. Sheriff Ryder was quick with a gun, and she doubted he would refrain from using it.

He pulled her off his saddle, tied her hands together with rope, then pushed her toward a large jagged rock. "Sit down!"

She did as he commanded. He took more rope from his saddlebag, wrapping it around both her and the rock so tightly that the hemp dug into her middle while the granite stabbed into her back. Fire lanced a brand of pain around her waist if she moved even a fraction. She tried to appeal to his logic.

"You've tied my hands, and the sky will soon be black as pitch. There's no way I can run. I can barely breathe tied to this rock like you have me. Please. . ."

He scowled at her, and her words dwindled, falling away. Taking a drink from his canteen, he frowned at the sky. "Should have left sooner. Would have if I'd planned it out. Didn't reckon I'd run into you so convenientlike." He chuckled, the sound sinister. It brought chills to her skin that the night air aided. She wore only her shirtwaist, her thin chemise, and her skirt, and the temperature must have dropped ten degrees since they'd ridden from O'Callahan's. Soon the nightly frost would set in. "Yessir, fortune smiled her pretty face on me when I saw you running out that door."

She watched him gather brush and start a fire.

"Why didn't you take me back to jail?" She tried asking again, since he seemed more inclined to talk.

"No reason to. I reckon you're dead either way. Difference is, if you hadn't of interfered and got so nosy, your death might be quicker than it has to be." He shrugged, as if she were the one to blame.

She inhaled sharply; the ropes cut deeper. "You. . .you plan on killing me?" Somehow she hadn't figured on that despite his cruel behavior. He was a lawman sworn to abide by the law, yet she could see he was nothing like Kurt.

"I'll let nature take care of that. Tied up as you are, the bobcats will have their fill, and any other hungry beast that wanders by. If anyone ever does find you, or what's left of you, I doubt you'd be recognized. But I imagine that'll be weeks from now."

His menacing words left her sick to her stomach.

"Why?" Her plea came out in a whimper, and she forced herself to remain calm, putting a stronger note to her voice. "Why do you want to kill me? What have I ever done to you?"

"Always snooping around," he muttered. "Always full of questions. Don't know when to stop."

"Deputy Michaels will find me. Once he does, you'll be the one in jail!"

"Your fine deputy took the stage back home hours ago."

"No." She wouldn't believe it; Kurt was a man of his word, unlike this rogue of a sheriff. "You're lying."

"You better hope I ain't. He comes back and starts snooping, and I'll have to get rid of him, too. I'll get rid of anyone who gets in my way."

Suddenly she understood. "*You* killed Mr. Townsend!"

He sneered at her. "As if you didn't know already."

"But I didn't! How could I?"

"You got the chief justice involved. He and the marshal came from Silverton to question me, so you can thank your deputy for the fix you're in now."

She blinked, trying to piece together his reasoning, surprised to hear Marshal Wilson had arrived. If he'd come to town, she doubted Kurt had left. "But why would you want to kill such a nice man like Mr. Townsend?"

"Don't guess it'd hurt you to know, since you won't be long for this earth anyhow."

Panic almost made her hysterical; her heart beat fast, the ropes digging in each time she drew breath. She squeezed her eyes shut, trying to control her breathing, and waited for him to continue.

"I told O'Callahan not to bring Townsend into our deals, but he wouldn't listen. Just like he wouldn't listen about you. I told him we should get rid of you before you created more problems, but ignoramus that he is, he insisted you had something he wanted."

Linda remembered how upset the sheriff had seemed when O'Callahan had opened her cell door and told her she was coming with him. The sheriff hadn't crossed him or said a word—no one crossed O'Callahan and lived to tell about it—but the sheriff had been so angry his face had turned beet red.

"But why Mr. Townsend?" she insisted. "What did he ever do to you?"

"Townsend was a yellow-bellied coward. Seems he grew a conscience. He wanted out, and I figured he might turn me in, too. So I shot him."

He delivered the words with no feeling, as if he were discussing a tiresome chore. She watched the firelight create flickering light and shadows over the crags of his face, his eyes so intense it terrified her, and for the first time she questioned his sanity. No man who killed another in cold blood could be called sound of mind, but she wondered if maybe he really was insane. How could a man like this have been elected sheriff? O'Callahan. Of course. He pulled the strings that made the town run, and to have a man sworn in like Sheriff Ryder, to look the other way whenever O'Callahan carried out his shady dealings, would have proved beneficial to the scoundrel.

The more she thought about it, and about how O'Callahan and his men used people for their greed, the angrier she got. Gone were her fears of death and how he would execute it. Now her blood boiled, and she couldn't prevent herself from giving him a lashing with her tongue.

"You're the worst excuse for a human being that ever existed, and you have no right to call yourself sheriff. A lowdown, cowardly, deceitful snake is what you are. What you did to that poor woman, in making her a widow, and all because of your greed, is appalling. I hope when they hang you for your crimes they do it twice! And nice and slow so that you suffer long—"

She broke off her irate words as he suddenly stood and withdrew his gun from his holster, aiming it at her forehead. "Maybe I'll just save the bobcats the trouble. . . ."

Linda closed her eyes, waiting for her death.

⁕

His mouth open in horror, Kurt crouched concealed behind some rocks. He had just been about to step forward, his gun raised, when Linda lambasted the sheriff with her scathing words and the beast aimed his gun at her head.

Fool woman! What did she think she was doing?

Two things became clear. One, the man was crazed enough to pull the trigger, and Kurt had been listening long enough to realize that by confessing his crime, the sheriff had no plans to let her remain breathing. And two, if Linda was to die, it might kill him to lose her. He would do what he must to save her, not just because he was a lawman, but also because he loved her. And if they were ever to get out of this alive. . .

Almighty Father, I could sure use Your help and guidance right now.

"Ryder!" he called out. "Let her go!"

The man's head whipped around, but his gun remained fixed on Linda. He peered into the darkness. "That you, Deputy? We were just talking about you." His manner grew mockingly congenial. "Come out into the light where I can see you!"

Kurt first shot a look at the marshal, who stood ready with his gun, before stepping out into the ring of firelight.

"Drop your weapon on the ground," the sheriff demanded. "The other one, too."

Kurt let his gun fall from his hands. As he reached for the handle of the second, the sheriff cocked the trigger of his. "Easy! No fast moves."

Kurt slowly removed his gun, his gaze going to Linda. The fear that had been absent in her eyes, even when the gun was first aimed on her, now shone bright as she stared back at him. And he realized with some surprise that she was worried for him.

He dropped the second gun to the ground and raised his hands slow, stepping forward. "Now that you have me, cut her loose and let her go."

The sheriff laughed. "You must take me for an idiot. I can't let either of you go. I told her that if you were fool enough to come looking for her, I'd just have to get rid of you, too." As he spoke, he slowly swung his gun Kurt's way. "And I aim to do just that."

"No!" Linda screamed. "Please—no!"

The explosion of a gun going off muffled her cry and shattered the silence of the valley.

Chapter 14

Linda's focus stayed on Kurt as she watched in horror, but he remained standing, clearly unharmed. She blinked away tears in confusion. The sheriff dropped to his knees, clutching his chest, and fell.

Before Linda understood what had happened, Kurt rushed to her side and sawed through the ropes with his knife. She saw a blur as another man came from behind the rocks where Kurt had approached and knelt beside the sheriff. The tall, stocky man put his fingers to the sheriff's neck, then took off his own hat, held it to his chest, and bowed his head. Linda looked away. She despised the sheriff for all he'd done, but she equally detested seeing anyone die and felt a thread of pity.

"You okay?" Kurt asked as he cut through her last rope.

She couldn't stop shivering both from the cold and shock, could only manage a jerky nod. Her middle felt as if it was on fire from the pressure of the ropes, and her legs were numb.

Kurt took off his duster coat, wrapping it around her. "You are the most daring, frustrating woman I ever laid eyes on. You near gave me a heart attack when you raged at him like you did and he pulled his gun on you. Don't ever do anything crazy like that again. You hear me?"

"I don't plan on getting myself into that kind of situation a second time."

"Not if I can help it."

Even in her muddled state of mind, she caught on to his grim words. "W–what do you mean?"

He blew out a breath, pulling the lapels of his duster tighter across her chest. The coat was so big she felt swallowed up inside it, his heat lingering in the material. Still, she shivered, and he wrapped his arm around her shoulders. Her teeth had begun to chatter, too.

"I mean I don't ever plan on letting you out of my sight again."

She swallowed hard, almost afraid to hope. "Because I'm your p–prisoner again, you mean? Since the sheriff is dead."

"No. I heard what he said to you, and so did the marshal—you're shaking like a dry leaf in a winter storm." He briskly rubbed her arm with one of his large hands. "You're free, Linda. But I want you to come back to Jasperville. With me."

"Why?" Her heart beat a little faster at his low words and the manner in which he pulled her close, protective, as if he would never let her go. She nestled into his warmth, feeling safe in his strength.

"While I have the courage to do this, I'm going to say something."

"I've never kn–known you to lack courage."

"Not with guns or outlaws or brawls. But when it comes to speaking pretty words, I'm not so brave or so smart. I want you to make your home with me, Linda. I want you to be mine."

"Yours?" She stiffened against him. "You want me to move in with you?"

"I told you I wasn't any good at this sort of thing." He groaned. "I'm offering marriage, nothing less. I want you to be my wife and start a new life. . .with me."

His soft words made even the ache from the cold and ropes dissolve from the joy that suddenly blossomed in the center of her being. To her, his were the prettiest words ever spoken. Despite her lips feeling cracked and stiff, she smiled, and the beam of hope he'd left her with when he first extended his friendship weeks before widened until she felt that brightness heat her insides in a rosy glow.

His eyes searched her face, a hopeful shine in them. She nodded. "I should be most proud to become your wife, Kurt."

He gathered her to him, holding her even closer, and pressed his cheek to hers. She held him just as tightly and thanked the Almighty God for sparing both of their lives.

❧

Three days later, her happiness complete, Linda stood with Kurt in a field of yellow wildflowers near the stream at the edge of Jasperville. The sun covered them in a pool of light, and she liked to think that both God and her mother were giving their approval. The marshal stood beside Kurt, and Doreen stood on the other side of Linda, as bride and groom solemnly repeated their vows before Chief Justice Mackleby. No minister lived within the vicinity, and the chief justice had volunteered to preside over their ceremony. Linda clutched her bouquet of wildflowers Doreen had gathered earlier and stared into Kurt's beautiful green eyes, seeing the unreserved love and admiration she had longed for all her life. He looked so striking in his black suit coat, white shirt, and black string tie. For once, his hat was absent, the sun bringing out both red and gold lights in his collar-length hair and making it glow like chestnuts after a soft rain.

The chief justice pronounced them man and wife, and she lifted her mouth for his kiss, the briefest touch of his lips on hers—all they were allowed before Doreen and the marshal converged upon them with well wishes and congratulations. The marshal kissed her cheek, shook Kurt's hand, and said he had to return to the jailhouse. Linda liked Marshal Wilson, though she still had a problem calling him Sam, as he'd asked. She noticed Doreen no longer had that problem and had sought his company since they had returned from Crater Springs.

She smiled as Doreen bustled away with an excuse of needing to return to the hotel to see to the feast she was preparing for Kurt and Linda. The chief justice shook hands with Kurt, wished them both well, assured them he would come to dinner, then excused himself to talk with the marshal.

"Alone at last." Kurt drew Linda into his arms and held her close, his smile positively wicked. "No one to interrupt us, and the only sound we hear, the quiet trickling of the stream."

She laughed. "We've definitely had our share of excitement these past few weeks."

Dimples creased his cheeks as he grinned. "You could say that."

"First those terrifying days of being a fugitive, then the run-in with O'Callahan—and thank the Lord he finally got caught and is getting what he deserves! Then that nasty business with the sheriff. . ." Her words trailed off. Kurt faced death and men dying often in his job, but she still had trouble talking about what had happened that night in the valley. Shaking off the somber moment, for she wouldn't let anything mar this day, she smiled and continued. "And then having Doreen sweep us both into a whirlwind while she made plans was another sort of excitement all its own. I told her that she needn't bother, that all I cared about were the vows spoken in marrying you and not all the trimmings that come with a wedding, but she wouldn't hear of it."

"She takes pleasure in doing things for others, and let me say right now, that dress looks mighty fine on you." Appreciation shone in his eyes as he studied her form in the blue calico Doreen had made for her. "I can't always promise excitement, Linda." His mock admission was tinged with teasing. "Life could get dull, especially in Jasperville."

"Good. I'll welcome the quiet times. Seems I hardly get enough of them— some upheaval is always brewing. But life with you could never be dull, Kurt. I love you so much. I didn't think it was possible to love somebody as much as I love you."

He cradled her face between his hands and kissed her, the slow and gentle brushing of his warm lips against hers making her heart pound. He had kissed her before, but never like this! She wrapped her arms around his neck, in part to get closer, but also to remain standing. He deepened their kiss, and she thought she might float away.

"The vows said it better than I ever could," he breathed against her hair. "I'll always love you, Linda, until my dying day." He drew back to look into her eyes. "I thank God for the morning He brought me across your path, though that first day I wasn't too keen on thanking Him."

His eyes twinkled, and she laughed. "Whatever happened to poor old Betsy?"

"Never did find the owner. Lance is now its caretaker, and mule and boy seem to get along fine. I imagine you'll be seeing a lot more of the twins." His tone took on a wary quality, as if he awaited her reaction. "They've developed something of a liking toward me, as much as they come by and see me at the jailhouse. I imagine they'll come to like you, too, now that they've accepted it would never have worked out between me and their ma."

"I think they're sweet." Her face flushed as she thought of the day she might give Kurt children and they would raise their own family. His smile broadened, and she knew he had correctly discerned her thoughts.

"Kurt?"

"Hm?" He kissed her temple.

"I want to go back to Silverton."

He froze, then slowly pulled away, his eyes intent on hers. "You sure about that?"

She nodded. "I've been thinking of little else since what happened with the sheriff. Well, except of you and thinking about us marrying, but the sheriff had no family, no kin. You're my family now, but I don't feel right about the way I left things. If Clay is still there, I'd like to try to mend fences with him. He wasn't rude to me, not like Derek was, and well, I'd like to try. Now that the surprise of my existence has had time to settle, maybe Clay will be more hospitable to the idea of sitting down and talking with me. Especially with Derek gone."

"You're sure it's a good idea? I don't want to see you hurt."

"I'll be all right, but only if you come with me. I'm not about to leave you so soon after our wedding. Make that never." She laid her head against his shoulder. "Only thing is, I'm not sure how long Clay plans to stay in Silverton. He might have already left."

"And I told you, I don't plan on ever letting you out of my sight again," he teased. "I'll talk to the marshal about it, but I don't foresee a problem. He's back and fit as ever. And with his friend the chief justice to keep him company, I don't reckon there'll be much trouble in town for a while."

Linda sighed with happiness and stroked her fingers through the back of his hair. She loved the silken feel of it. "Have I told you how grateful I am to have you for my husband?"

"As grateful as I am to have you for my wife." He kissed the tip of her nose. "Wife."

Linda giggled; she had never felt this jubilant. Kurt watched her expression, his own becoming rapt. He lowered his head again, his mouth slanting over hers. His solid arms embraced her, and she melted against his strength. His kisses made her feel so warm and cherished, so breathless and alive. . .

He pulled back, closing his eyes as if he struggled for control, and gave her a boyish grin. "If we stay here alone like this, there's no telling what might happen or who might suddenly come upon us." His tone only half teased.

Linda blinked, still dazed by the fire he'd kindled in her. "I'm ready to go back if you are. Or we could just stay here." She gave him a coquettish smile. She enjoyed being away from everyone like this, alone with Kurt, their first time in days. And if he kissed her on into the evening, she sure wouldn't complain.

He let out a deep breath. "You don't know how tempting that is, sweetheart. But I suppose we should get back before Doreen sends out a search party. Sounds like she made a feast on our behalf, and she'll be expecting us."

Feeling blessed above all women this day, Linda nodded and wrapped her hand around his strong arm as they returned to the hotel. A few men tipped their hats, offering their well wishes, and observed her with respect. If curiosity still shone in a few eyes, regarding her appearance in Jasperville weeks before or the woman she had once been, it didn't matter. Kurt loved her for who she was and accepted her, good and bad.

With Kurt, she had found her fulfillment of hope for a new life.

Epilogue

The moment they stepped off the stagecoach in Silverton, Kurt slipped his hand around Linda's arm in a protective hold. Her eyes lifted to his, full of both love and dread as she reached across her chest and laid her hand over his, squeezing tight. His time with her since they had married three days before had been the best moments Kurt could recall in his life. She had become his life, and he would be hog-tied if he would allow any harm to come her way. He came near to losing her at the hands of a deranged sheriff, and he sure as shootin' wouldn't let any man, blood kin or not, do anything to cause his Linda pain.

As they approached the hotel, he felt her stiffen against him. "It's not too late to change your mind," he reassured. He stared at one of the men nearby who looked at Linda with a little too much familiarity, as if he recognized her. She didn't seem to notice, but the man shifted his gaze to Kurt's glaring eyes, then looked away, having received the message. He shuffled off and didn't look at them again.

Linda stared at the wooden facade that fronted the canvas dwelling as if it might fall on top of her once she walked through the entrance. But she only shook her head, a determined set to her mouth. "I have to do this, Kurt, or I'll never feel right about it. If Clay's not there, or if things don't go as hoped for, at least I'll know I'll have done all I could. And I can live with that knowledge."

Inside the hotel, frustration coiled around Kurt when he noticed all the men look her way, some of them with open recognition, others with interested leers. He slipped his hand from her arm to slide it about her waist, again sending a message. A few miners whispered among themselves. Another disappeared toward the back in a rush as if on a sudden mission.

"Need a place to sleep?" A bewhiskered elderly man came up to Kurt, holding a corncob pipe to his thick lips. He pulled it away. "I'm Hiram Matthis, owner of this here establishment. Ain't no fancy hotel, but we have hides to sleep on, and Jinx here cooks up a fine pot of stew to warm your belly. Ain't that right, Jinx?"

An almost gaunt man missing two fingers raised his hand in salute, his smile wide, revealing a near toothless mouth. "Sure do. Though to look at me you cain't tell it." He chortled, the sound reminding Kurt of a crow's caw.

Kurt smiled in acknowledgment. "As a matter of fact, me and my wife here do need a place to bunk for the night."

At his title for Linda, a few murmurs of shock filled the room.

A tall, powerfully built man came rushing from the back, his expectant gaze finding Linda and remaining on her. A tiny woman with long dark braids followed. On her heels, two little girls came into view, their hair similar to the woman's, the taller child holding a harmonica in her hand.

Kurt heard Linda gasp and felt her body go tense as if she'd turned to stone. He glanced at her in concern. Her face had paled as white as ash.

"It's Derek," she whispered so only Kurt could hear.

Kurt's back went rigid as he sized up Linda's half brother in one cutting glance. He and she looked little alike; his eyes were blue, his hair dark, but they shared the same proud chin and strong jaw, though on Linda it was less pronounced. Kurt's arm tightened around her, and he watched Derek take notice of his protective gesture with curious eyes, before he again focused on Linda.

"I'm glad to see you're all right. We were worried about you."

Linda stared, her eyes widening in disbelief at Derek's words.

He switched his gaze to Kurt and held out his hand. "Derek Burke."

Kurt paused before taking the offered hand and shaking it in one abrupt, civil motion. "Deputy Kurt Michaels. Linda here is my wife."

This time Derek's eyes widened. He stared at Linda. "You didn't tell me you were married."

"I wasn't." Her words came soft and uncertain. Clearly she didn't trust his change in manner and didn't know what to make of it.

Derek raised his brow but said nothing, reaching around behind him to draw the tiny woman to his side. "This is my wife, Penny." Pride and love rang through his words. "And our two daughters, Olivia and Christa."

"Pleased to make your ac–quain–tance," the elder of the two girls said. With thumb and forefinger, she pulled at one side of her skirt and gave an awkward curtsy.

The younger girl put her small hand over her mouth and giggled. "Livvie's learnin' manners."

"You're married?" Linda's soft words to Derek almost couldn't be heard.

"Seems you're not the only one who found unexpected treasure," he affirmed. "Penny and I married last week."

Linda blinked, clearly at a loss. "And Clay? Where is he?"

Derek's easygoing manner dissolved and remorse shadowed his eyes. "He left."

"Left?"

"This morning." Derek glanced around, wary, then looked at Linda and Kurt. "We should talk in private."

He murmured something low near Penny's ear. She nodded and kissed his cheek, smiled at Linda, then disappeared outside with her girls.

Kurt gave Linda's waist a reassuring squeeze as they followed Derek to what Kurt assumed was supposed to pass for a parlor. A worn, dust-streaked piece of muslin covered the entryway to a cramped corner, where a chair and table stood. Hanging from a hook on a post, a kerosene lamp gave off light, and a tattered rug covered the bare-packed dirt. He couldn't hold back a slight grin at the thought of Doreen's shock had she been there and realized this was a hotel. She prided herself on keeping hers as immaculate as possible.

Derek glanced with caution at the muslin before speaking. "Clay took it into his head to ride off and find Pa's mine on his own. I tried talkin' him out of it last night, but might as well talk to a mule. He isn't too fond of me right now." His words held a note of sadness. He reached inside his jacket and pulled out a rectangular packet of papers. His eyes solemn, he handed one to Linda. "This belongs to you. I had no right to it."

Linda stared at the wrinkled and grime-covered slip of folded paper as though it might explode like a stick of dynamite.

"Go on," Derek softly urged. "Take it. It's your rightful share."

"I don't want any part of that mine. It's not the real reason I came to Silverton, then or now."

"Then why'd you come?"

"It's complicated." She gave a sidelong glance to Kurt, and he smiled in encouragement. "I wanted to meet you and Clay. I had no family left and, well, I'd hoped we could be friends if nothing else." She shrugged.

Derek studied her a moment. "When I read about you in Pa's letter, I was furious. But not with you. With our pa."

"Then you knew about me before I came here?"

Kurt couldn't mistake the waver in her voice and wished he could take away her pain. If he didn't know how important this meeting was to her, he'd take her home now.

"I knew." Derek sighed then took a few steps, leaning his backside along the edge of the table and folding his arms across his chest. "Our pa left Clay and me when I wasn't much older than Olivia. After a time, my ma got sick, and I had to find work to earn money for medicine she needed. Trouble was, only work I could find took me far away from her and Clay. When Ma died, well, I hadn't seen her in years and wasn't there when it happened. So from the day our pa left up till just recently, I bore a grudge that would rival the size of them mountains out yonder. Ashamed as I am to admit it, I took my rage at Pa out on you. Years' worth. You have my most sincere apology, Linda. I should have never treated you so cruel."

Kurt watched her reaction. The color had flooded back into her cheeks, and a soft shine lit her silver eyes.

"What made you change your mind about me?" she asked softly. "Was it your wife?"

He chuckled, as if in recollection. "In part. Penny's a fine woman, as you'll soon find out. That is, if you stay."

Linda gave a noncommittal shrug. "What was the other part?"

His smile was mysterious. "Let's just say I had an encounter with God that was a long time in coming."

"Oh." She blinked and stared at him, clearly struggling with a decision, and Kurt wondered if she remembered her own quest. "If you're sure you don't mind having me around, then I would like to stay on awhile, as long as Kurt can manage."

"I don't mind at all." Derek's voice had grown very quiet, and Kurt thought he looked a little sad. Derek moved away from the table, closing the distance. He held out the paper to her. "Won't you take this? I don't feel right in keeping it."

She stared at the paper, then slowly put her fingers to it as if she thought he might change his mind and snatch it away. He stood still, waiting, and she slipped the parchment from his hand. She looked up at Kurt.

"Would you hold onto it? I think it'll be safer with you." Kurt nodded and took the portion of map, tucking it away in his coat.

Shyly, she again shifted her attention to Derek. Both brother and sister seemed at a loss for words. Kurt was stunned to see tears glisten in Derek's eyes.

Derek awkwardly cleared his throat and swiped at his lashes. "I'll be going now. I play the harmonica, and the girls always like a tune before bedtime."

"Derek."

Linda spoke before he could pull aside the muslin covering the entryway. He paused, as if steeling himself for her anger or reproach, then turned in question.

"I wouldn't worry about Clay. God took care of me in some nasty situations. If He did that for me, I'm sure He'll watch out for. . .our brother." Her last two words came hesitant, as if to see how he would react to her including herself in his family.

Derek smiled. "I reckon He will. I'm thankful He took such good care of you. I searched high and low for you when I returned to Silverton with Penny and learned you'd disappeared."

"You did?" Her mouth dropped open in wonder.

"I never had a little sister till now." His tone sounded wistful. "I sure wouldn't wish anything bad to happen to the one I found."

Kurt felt Linda's body relax against him. Tears pooled in her eyes and dripped down her cheeks. He released her, sensing her desire. She moved the few steps toward Derek, paused a moment as she searched his face, then tentatively slid her hands around his shoulders in a hug.

Derek stood unmoving, and Kurt spied a glimmer of wetness on his own cheek before he wrapped his arms tightly around Linda's back. They held each other for a few seconds before Linda pulled away.

"I always wanted an older brother. Seems now I have two."

Derek softly chuckled. "I look forward to getting to know you better."

"I have quite the story to tell." She smiled for the first time, still acting a bit nervous, and glanced Kurt's way. Reaching for his arm, she pulled him to stand beside her. Derek eyed Kurt, his expression one of respectful curiosity. Kurt struggled past his resentment of how this man had once hurt Linda and inclined his head, managing a faint grin. In those few gestures, each man gave his acceptance of the other in her life.

"I'll let you both get some shut-eye," Derek said. "I imagine you're bone weary."

Linda didn't deny it, nor did Kurt. He supposed the emotional strain of this encounter had taxed her as much as the day's travel.

Once Derek left them, Linda held onto Kurt, resting her head against his shoulder, and he wrapped his arms around her back.

"He's right," she said. "All I want right now is to curl up in your warmth and lose myself in your strong arms. I have never felt so safe as I do when I'm with you."

Kissing her hair, Kurt remembered their first night together and how Linda had pleaded to keep the lamp turned low throughout the night, confiding in him the reason she feared the dark when she slept. He'd allowed it then, but on the second night, he'd reassured her that he would always be there for her and no one would ever harm her again. When he extinguished the flame, she practically crawled into him, and he'd held her close, loving her, whispering reassurances until she fell asleep. Only two nights had passed since then, but Linda didn't ask again to keep the lamp lit and awoke with a drowsy smile on her face. A smile that drew him to kiss her again. . .and again. . .

"Thank you."

Linda's soft words scattered his pleasant memories. "For?"

With eyes full of love, she looked up. "For being the dearest, most admirable lawman in all the West. For dropping everything to come with me to Silverton just so I could try and mend things with my brother."

"You're my wife." He kissed her forehead. "I'd do anything for you."

She pressed her cheek against his shoulder, laying one hand over his heart and sliding her other arm around his waist beneath his duster. "I sure didn't expect to find Derek here, but now I'm glad I did. It's too soon to tell if he's sincere or not, but I think this happened as it was meant to. Though I hope Clay is all right, taking off angry like he did. . ." She sighed. "Promise you'll never leave me, Kurt. No matter what. Keep me close always. It seems we Burkes can be a stubborn, quick-tempered bunch."

He realized her soft plea came from years of never knowing where she belonged, having lost so much in her life. His love for her grew stronger with each day that passed, and he intended to make it his lifetime work to show her just how special she was to him.

"You're not telling me anything I don't already know. Your home is with me always, sweetheart." He kissed her hair. "I'll never leave you. No matter what. And with regard to Clay, as Doreen is so fond of saying, let's just see how God works this out. From what I've seen here tonight, the Almighty has had His hand in all the Burkes' lives."

She lifted her face to his, her eyes glowing. "Yes, you're right. He certainly gave me the best thing I've ever known when He sent you to me." Sighing with contentment, she laid her hands on either side of his face. "I love you so much, Deputy Michaels, have I told you?"

He grinned. "Show me."

A mischievous smile lit her eyes. "Gladly."

Her soft, cool lips brushed against his own, setting him afire, and he knew the flame would burn bright the rest of their lives.

A TREASURE
REVEALED

Dedication

With much gratitude to my dear friends who've been there for me in a pinch: Theo, Therese, Paige, Jill, and my mother, always there to help when my deadline lurks ever closer.

Involvement in daily life sometimes shields the treasures right before us, and we tend to look beyond, to try to find what we think will make us happy. So at this time, I want to thank You, Lord, for my many treasures: my two sons, more precious to me than gold or silver; my priceless family and friends; and above all, You, God, and the invaluable love You have always shown me. Thank You for this journey that we've taken together.

Chapter 1

Silverton, Nevada
1869

After all Clayton Burke had endured, the possibility of a scorpion sting or a sidewinder's strike wouldn't be half as painful as working with his scoundrel brother to locate their pa's silver mine. Bad enough Derek should find a treasure like Penny for a wife. Seemed an unjust reward for absconding with Clay's portion of the map and their half sister's in what had been Pa's only legacy to his offspring.

But then, life had never been fair.

Life hadn't been fair to lure their pa away to abandon his family in his lust for wealth. It hadn't been fair to flee from their ma and allow death to steal her before her time. And life sure wasn't fair to force Clay and Derek back together in what must be the biggest mistake ever recorded.

Clay didn't trust Derek's sudden change of heart, didn't trust anything about the man he hadn't seen in over four years—ever since he'd ambled into town to visit their ma's gravesite, boss Clay around and make living arrangements for him, then amble back out the following day.

Frowning, Clay rode southwest through scrub and brush, over high desert and barren valley in what his map portion revealed as the direction to the silver. At least his section contained the *X*. He figured the treasure shouldn't be difficult to find, being as the only river running east to west that he'd heard of in these parts was the Humboldt. Both river and location covered his portion of map, and though he wasn't sure of the distance, he should be able to find the mine without the other two-thirds to guide him. He hadn't resorted to thievery to aid his goal. Unlike his snake of a brother, Derek.

Steam rose off Clay's damp clothes, the cloudburst of earlier chased away by the sun that again blazed its habitual scorching rays. The rain shower—brief though it had been—had surprised Clay. From what little he'd experienced of this part of the West, the land didn't receive its fair portion of cooling water from above. He supposed even nature played unfair. Or maybe it was God who doled out the elements unjustly. Clay winced. Had his ma been alive and able to hear his irreverent thoughts, she might have pulled him by his ear out to the woodshed, regardless that he'd just passed his twentieth year. He turned his attention to the south, then north. Only mile after mile of confounded rock and scrub and bluff. She'd have a hard time finding a tree, let alone a woodshed.

No sooner had the thought crossed his mind than what must have been a mirage materialized in the shimmering heat above the dirt again baked dry.

"What the. . .that's impossible."

Mystified by what he thought he saw, he rubbed bleary eyes, sure his inability to sleep the night before played tricks on his mind, with the intolerable heat as an ally. He brought his horse around and rode closer, but the mirage didn't evaporate into the wavering air.

"Incredible." He kicked his heels into the horse's sides and took off at a pounding gallop toward a young woman staggering in his direction at least fifty feet ahead.

"Miss, are you all right?" he called out as he brought his horse to a swift halt near her and realized she was far from being well. Her straggled hair hung well below her shoulders, her blouse and skirt were torn, and a mix of black soot and dried mud covered her from head to toe. A vacant look swam in her tawny eyes, made even more startling by the smoke black smudges that rimmed them.

His sudden appearance didn't alarm her; she continued staring straight ahead, with no acknowledgment that she noticed him. Prickles raced along his spine at her unnatural behavior, as though he weren't visible, and the most unsettling notion slipped through his mind that *she* was the ghost.

Both to rid himself of the absurd idea and to give her needed support, he dismounted and caught up to where she stumbled. He reached out to grasp her elbow. "Miss. . . ? You don't look well. You should rest."

"W–w–wa–ter. . . ," she whispered, her voice as hoarse as sandpaper.

As though his touch robbed her strength, she folded, her eyes fluttering back in her head as they closed.

"Miss!"

Clay caught her in his arms before she hit dirt and lowered himself to the ground, holding her. Helpless, he looked around, hoping to find an answer in the empty valley. No one or nothing else explained her presence. It was as if she'd appeared out of the shimmering air, though of course that was impossible. Likely she'd emerged from beyond one of the nearby bluffs where he hadn't been looking; they contained enough hollows and jagged edges to conceal a person.

She felt solid and warm, her body trembling against him—nothing ghostlike about her. Clay then noticed her hands, and his stomach clenched in horrified pity.

Black soot covered them, and serious burns had eaten away at her palms and fingers, leaving angry red blisters. He doubted she would ever regain good use of her hands. If she lived at all.

Ripping the knot from the rain-dampened kerchief around his throat, he gently patted her hands with it. She moaned but otherwise didn't stir. He dribbled more water over her hands from the canteen at his hip then put it to her lips. She didn't swallow or choke. The precious water streamed from her slack lips into her hair. She lay as one asleep, a tattered rag doll.

At a loss and desperate for direction, Clay held the pitiful creature, her head in his lap, and begged her to wake up. He stroked the ash-coated hair at her scalp. His fingers came in contact with a nasty lump on the side of her head, and he realized the groan he heard came from his own throat.

He should find her family. Surely they were close. As gently as he could, Clay tied the wet bandanna around her hands then lifted the poor woman onto his saddle and swung up behind her. Holding her slight body tight against him, he urged his horse forward. After scouting the area, he realized that he and the woman were the only two souls in the entire valley—and if he didn't find the help she needed soon, he might be the only one left alive. He gave up looking for her kin and guided his horse in the direction he'd come as fast as he dared go in the heat so as not to kill the horse. His sister-in-law could help with her box of herbs and cure-alls. Silverton lay several hours southeast. With luck on his side, he could get there by nightfall.

The last thing Clay desired was to return to the hotel and face the rogue who called himself brother, but he wouldn't risk a woman's life due to years of ill feeling between himself and Derek.

Halfway to Silverton, he heard her groan and knew relief. She'd been so still and silent he'd been half afraid he was too late. He slowed his horse to a walk, bending close to speak with her.

"Miss?"

Her blackened eyelids didn't flicker, and he wondered if he'd imagined her moan. If not for the slim thread of erratic thumps from her heart against his arm he'd think her already dead. An odd surge of protective emotion rose from his belly, choking his throat, and his eyes misted for the frail, broken stranger who rested against him, so childlike and helpless in his arms.

A prayer rose to his lips, from what source he didn't know but imagined it was owing to his ma, who'd raised him to fear the Almighty. He held little hope of his prayer being answered but muttered it anyhow. "Please, God. Don't let her die."

At fifteen, he'd watched his ma take her final breath, the sight horrifying to behold. A light of peace had entered her eyes before she closed them for the last time, but not before Clay witnessed her misery for days on end, her wasted body writhing, agonized moans ripping through her croaky throat as she cried out for both her sons. Only Clay had been there, and it hadn't been enough. It had never been enough.

He couldn't—wouldn't—be a helpless onlooker to another pointless death, this time to a woman so young she had yet to live.

After what seemed an eternity, Silverton appeared on the horizon, the mountains beyond. The small mining town stood washed in a silver glow as a full moon rose beyond canvas tents of establishments clustered along the town's one street. He heard the warbling of a harmonica before he spotted Livvie sitting on a barrel outside the hotel. Thinking it odd his sister-in-law hadn't ordered her daughter to bed by such a late hour, Clay started to call out, when Livvie spotted him. Her mouth dropped open, the moonlight making the whites of her eyes glow as they grew even bigger.

"Uncle Clay?"

"Go fetch your mama. Tell her to bring her remedy box, then ask Shorty to tend my horse."

As though she'd lost her ability to hear, Penny's girl continued to stare at the woman who lay like one dead against him.

"Hurry, Livvie!"

"Yes, sir!" She shot up from the ground and raced inside, dark braids bouncing against her back.

It was no easy task, dismounting while taking care that the woman didn't plummet to the ground, but Clay managed. He tugged her arm, allowing her to fall into both of his, and turned toward the entrance, the woman held tight against his chest, her head hanging slack over his arm. She appeared so broken, and Clay sensed her body wasn't all that had been wounded.

Penny raced outside with her remedy box. She hesitated in clear shock before continuing his way. "Whatever has happened?"

"I found her wandering in the wilderness as if she hadn't a lick of sense. She keeled over before she could tell me anything."

Penny blinked up at Clay as if her mind was a blank.

"Penny?" he urged.

She shook off whatever ailed her and took charge. "Take her to the cubicle Mr. Matthis gave. 'Tis private. Olivia, tell Linda I'm in need of her help, then go and ready yourself for bed like you should have done. We'll sleep in the wagon tonight."

"Mama!" Livvie complained.

"Now then, I'll be hearin' no more of your impertinence." Her words were both soft and stern as she pressed the back of her hand against the woman's forehead to check for fever. She had yet to see her hands still bound in the bandanna Clay had kept damp throughout their ride.

Livvie kicked at the dirt. "Aw, just when things was gettin' exciting." She disappeared into the hotel at the same time Derek's tall form emerged. Livvie offered him a hug in passing, and he laid his hand against the back of her head. The brief contact made Clay's insides churn. His excuse for a brother didn't deserve a family, least of all a loving one.

Clay clenched his teeth, redirecting his attention to Penny. "Did I hear you say Linda's back?"

"Aye. She arrived a little over an hour ago. Tonight must be a night for homecomings."

Relieved his half sister hadn't become a victim of the harsh land or the miners who'd claimed it, Clay opened his mouth to retort that he had no intention of remaining in Silverton any longer than necessary. Once he felt assured the desert waif he held in his arms would live, he planned to resume his journey in search of the mine. Before he could say so, Penny turned and hurried inside, first whispering to Derek, who nodded and moved away. Clay followed Penny, deciding further conversation should wait.

His sister-in-law guided him to the same room Linda had once used. Penny pulled back the muslin weighted by stones, and Clay walked ahead of her into the small cubicle, noticing Christa asleep on the ground in one corner. With care, he laid the inert woman on the largest of the thick hides. Silverton's hotel hardly deserved so fine a name, but at least it provided shelter from the elements, and Jinx, the cook, often rustled up a good meal to fill a man's belly. Even a hovel like this was preferable for the injured woman; thick canvas walls and roof helped shield from the hot days of unrelenting sun that baked a person dry and kept out the chills at night that were sometimes so cold he felt as if his very bones were shaking inside his skin.

The young woman trembled, and he wondered if it was due to the cold. He reached for another hide to cover her.

"No, Clay." Penny stopped him. "You must leave while I see to her. Would you mind taking Christa?"

"Right." Gently he scooped up his sleeping niece, who nestled her head closer against his shoulder like a contented kitten. She yawned, her downy lashes slitting open. "Uncle Clay." She gave him a drowsy smile and closed her eyes, her small arm sliding around his neck. Before he could beat a hasty retreat and give Penny the privacy needed, he remembered his cursory examination of the woman. "Her hands. Check her hands first."

He pulled aside the muslin covering the door, his attention on Penny, and almost ran smack into Linda coming inside.

"Oh!" The redhead clasped a hand to her heart. "Clay. . ."

"Linda." He hoped his uneasy grin and gentle utterance of her name told her what he didn't have time to say.

She nodded with a smile, as if to assure him she understood his unspoken sentiment—that he'd never meant her harm and felt relieved to see her well. Added to that, the hundred and one other things he wished to discuss with his half sister.

Her eyes drifted down to the bundle Clay held, and a wistful smile touched her lips. "She's precious. So tiny, like a little doll."

Clay would have liked to talk further, but the little doll was beginning to fidget, and Clay didn't think Penny would be too happy if they woke her with their conversation. From his short experience as an uncle, he knew how hard it was getting Christa back to sleep.

"I need to take her out to the wagon."

"Of course."

Clay left the hotel and strode to the spot where Derek kept the conveyance. Being careful not to wake her, he laid Christa on a blanket Penny kept on the floorboards. The tarpaulin remained intact, shielding the child from the elements, though he doubted they would get more rain. He smiled at his sleeping niece, a gentle and unfamiliar tug pulling his heart. Derek didn't deserve this family, but since he'd taken on the responsibilities of two young'uns and had bound himself in holy matrimony to their ma, Clay hoped Derek didn't disappoint them as he had his own kin.

Clay stepped away from the wagon and headed back.

As though thoughts of the man conjured him up like an evil spell, Derek strode from the hotel entrance. Clay changed course but soon felt Derek's staying hand on his shoulder.

"Clay—"

"We haven't anything more to discuss. I just put Christa down in the wagon. Now leave me be."

"We have a good deal to discuss yet." Derek pulled Clay around to face him. Though his action wasn't rough and no one stood nearby to witness it, Clay nevertheless grew livid. Derek treated him as if he were still a boy. "You can't keep up this habit of running off before giving me a chance to set things right."

"You ended any chance of that when you left with our maps to the silver," Clay shot back in a fierce whisper.

Derek darted an anxious glance around the area. "I wish you'd keep quiet about that. Mark my words, one day someone'll overhear, and that'll be the end of Pa's legacy for all of us." He ran a hand through his unkempt hair, a few shades darker than Clay's but just as thick and long. Penny had trimmed their hair before the wedding, but both men kept it touching the base of their necks, and both were now clean-shaven. The similarity in mannerisms rankled.

"You didn't care how it affected us back then, me and Linda," Clay argued. "You wanted the full pot. Wanted to rob us blind and take all of what was coming to us."

"And I told you, I'm sorry. I scarce got a wink of sleep the entire time. I felt so ridden with guilt 'cause of all I'd done." Derek's jaw clenched, a sign of his frustration. "Can't you let the past go? If you can't forgive me for my sake, do it for Ma. She'd be sick at heart to have seen us in strife. You know all she wished for us was to live in harmony."

"How dare you bring up Ma to me," Clay seethed between clenched teeth, though he kept his voice low so as not to rouse interest should anyone exit one of the buildings. "You haven't any place to talk about her or her desires! She begged you to come back in her letter, and you wouldn't budge. The illness took her life, but you broke her heart long before that. She wanted you with her at the end, and you were just too selfish and stubborn to honor her dying wish."

"We've been over all this before." Derek's eyes flashed a warning. "I couldn't just up and leave my job. I was the one earning the money for her medicine and your keep, if you'll recall. By the time I made it home, it was too late."

"All just another passel of excuses. You could've been there had you wanted to. You could've found a way."

Derek grabbed Clay's other arm hard as if he might shake him, then relented and threw both his arms loose from his hold. His action seemed born more from frustration than anger, though in the scant light, it was difficult to read his face. "I've made my fair share of mistakes, Clay. Never said otherwise. Plenty I wish I could take back. But I can't, just like I can't turn back the sun and change what's already been. All I can do is promise I'll do my part to change things for the better. It's what Ma would've wanted."

Clay glared at him. "Don't give me any of your empty oaths. I've had enough to last a lifetime." He turned on his heel, moved away, then whipped around again. "Oh, and just so there's no misunderstanding—once I turned sixteen, I took a job at the mercantile. Old Mr. Dougherty let me bunk in the storeroom there. I never took one red cent of your money, not since I became old enough to get out from under Mrs. Harper's stingy thumb. Anything I needed, I earned myself."

The satisfaction he should feel to see the confused hurt sweep across Derek's face bypassed him. A twinge of remorse tugged his conscience instead.

"Where'd the money go then?"

Derek's low query stiffened Clay's backbone. The money. Of course. Of all Clay had said, Derek's greed would pick up only on that. "I imagine Mrs. Harper hoarded it away. She sure never spent a penny she didn't have to. Maybe if you leave bright and early tomorrow, you can hightail it back to Missouri and reclaim the money by week's end. That's all you're after anyway. Reclaiming fortunes that are 'rightfully yours.' "

Derek sighed wearily. "How long you plannin' on making me pay for what I did, Clay? How long till we can put this behind us?"

"How long till east meets west? Figuratively speaking, that is."

Derek's eyes went dull as he seemed to recall their old lesson. "It doesn't."

"At least you recall some of what Ma taught us. And so, you have your answer."

This time when Clay turned to leave, Derek didn't stop him.

✍

Clay walked for a good hour from one short end of Silverton to the other, then back again. Pacing the boardwalks. Caged like a wildcat, though the mining town had no jailhouse or bars and was about as much in the wilderness as a man could get without baking to death in the dry, barren desert farther west, near Carson's Sink. He should jump on the horse he'd purchased for this trip and ride away beneath the bright light of the moon, leaving his brother far behind. But he knew he wouldn't go. Travel was dangerous at night, and he wouldn't risk his horse breaking a leg in a gopher hole. . .or chance running across a pack of hungry coyotes.

The last thought surfaced as the beasts' mournful howls wavered a dirge beyond the hills west, raising the fine hairs on the back of Clay's neck. Traveling at night was no option. Come morning, he doubted he would leave this last place he wished to stay, either. New bait kept him trapped: news of the woman whose life he'd helped save and news of the woman whose life he'd helped destroy. Or tried to, by omission of his words.

Clay hung his head and stared at the planks beneath his boots, wishing he could slink between their cracks as shame wormed inside him. He hadn't maligned Linda's character with barbs as Derek had, but he'd done nothing to end his brother's cruelty, either. He'd given his half sister his own share of resentful looks, making sure she knew he also detested her existence, so suddenly sprung upon them through their pa's letter. But after thinking on it, he'd realized that wasn't true. What he detested was his pa's lifetime of lies and manipulations.

Once, when Clay had been little more than a tot, his pa had left for a stretch of months. That must have been when he'd first gone west and associated with Linda's ma. Then when Clay was a boy, sitting on the floor by the hearth with a book, his father left again, bestowing no more than one of his usual disgusted glares upon Clay before slamming the door shut behind himself. Clay never laid eyes on the man again. He'd felt closer ties to his gentle mother than to his stern father so hadn't missed his presence. Some of his peers taunted that Clay was too soft and refined for a boy, but once his ma died, all softness and gentleness went with her. His heart hardened to iron, and he reckoned his soul turned to ice.

On that frozen winter morning, four years after his pa and later Derek had left them, Clay cursed the world that robbed him of his entire family. He became the man his pa claimed he would never be. Hardened. Tough. And while he held his ma's frail, lifeless body in his arms, he cried his last tears and turned his back on what she'd always held closest and dearest to her heart—her faith in God.

But since finding the injured young woman in the desert, he'd begun to feel his heart thaw, had begun to *feel* again.

Tinny music from the dance hall jangled Clay into awareness and away from painful memories as the player piano went into its reel. Shouts of appreciation from the men soon followed, and Clay reckoned that Beulah was performing one of her numbers. The bawdy dancing at times embarrassed him, he'd never been skilled at poker, and the drink made him feel awful come sunup. His ma had been justified in warning him to stay away from such places, and he'd soon discovered he preferred his boyhood habit of reading a good book beside a crackling fire to a night of carousing and losing what little money he'd earned. But on the day he discovered Derek had stolen his part of the map, Clay had reverted to old ways. In his anger-filled ramblings, he'd confided in Beulah, who bore a resemblance to Linda to such a degree that Clay, inebriated though he'd been, soon found himself apologizing to the dance-hall girl for every evil under the sun. Beulah patiently listened, telling him that she wasn't Linda while offering kind advice that Clay planned to take when next he met up with his half sister. Incredible that she'd returned to Silverton, though why she would bother after the grief they'd caused her, he couldn't imagine.

He stared at the swinging doors, the area lit up with gaslights beyond. Maybe Beulah could help him make sense of his current situation by letting him talk it through.

He took a step in that direction, then stopped. The burning temptation to lose his discouragement and anger in cards and drink might reemerge should he walk through those doors and seek her out. And he'd invited enough trouble for one day.

"Mr. Burke?"

He turned at the sound of Shorty's voice and eyed the towheaded lad, still too young for whiskers but unusually tall for fourteen years, just a head shorter than Clay's own six feet. Clay was told the misnomer fit the boy when he was a skinny young'un; only these past two years he'd shot up like a thick, burly sprout.

"Mrs. Burke asked me to tell you she's lookin' for you but said no need t' hurry if you was busy."

The title stunned Clay a moment until he associated Penny's name with it.

"Thanks, Shorty. Did you tend my horse?"

"He's at the livery, all brushed down and fed." The boy grinned. "You gonna name him? Or leave him nameless like the other Mr. Burke done his?"

Clay assumed Shorty had witnessed his animosity toward Derek to not address him as his brother.

"Don't know, Shorty. I imagine I will."

"Deputy Michaels says you gotta think long and hard on a name befittin' the horse's personality. He's a right smart man, though I ain't ever heard the deputy call his horse a name, either. I reckon if I ever get me enough money to buy a horse, I'll name him Nugget, though, 'cause that's the day when I'll find me some gold."

Reminded of Shorty's due, Clay pulled a coin from his pocket to give the boy for his help. "Silverton has a lawman?" He was surprised that during the one day he'd been absent, the town had found someone to keep the peace.

"No, sir. He comes from some town east of here with Mrs. Michaels. Ain't for sure how long they be stayin'."

Yet another lady to brave the squalid lodging of Silverton? Clay wished her well. That thought led to the young woman he'd brought to town, and he handed the penny to Shorty, then retraced his steps to the hotel.

He met his sister-in-law coming out of the cubicle. "I'll want to be hearin' all of it," she greeted. "How did she get those burns on her hands?"

"You and I both would like the answer to that." He shook his head, flummoxed. "One minute she wasn't there; the next she was."

"Have you taken to the whiskey?" She peered closely at him.

He held up his hands. "I'm stone sober and plan on staying that way."

"Humph. A good thing, too. You don't need any of that devil's brew to muddle your mind further."

"My mind wasn't muddled. It had just rained. When the sun broke out, there was a mist. The valley was empty. Next thing I know, I'm watching that woman in there stumble toward me. I haven't the vaguest notion where she came from."

"She didn't get those burns while she was with you?"

Clay drew himself up. "Meaning?" That Penny might have so low an opinion of him as to think he would physically harm a woman stung.

"Wipe that wounded look off your face, brother. I meant no slur by my speaking. I only thought you'd been witness to what happened."

Mollified, he calmed. Ever since his quarrel with Derek, he felt about as inept at seeing into the heart of the matter as a blind rooster at dawn. "She was that way when I found her."

"Her burns are bad. I'm not certain my remedies will help, but I did all I could. Poor lass. If she uses her hands again, it'll be a miracle." She smiled. "But then, God's in the business of those, isn't He now?"

"I wouldn't know." Smiling, Clay kept his tone light. "May I see her?"

"She hasn't stirred from sleep."

"Isn't it unusual for her to be out cold for so long?"

"I have no way of knowing. I've no experience with anything of this sort." Clay sighed. "I wish a doctor would arrive on the next stagecoach."

"If you'd not run off as you did and found her, I imagine she'd be dead. You were a godsend."

"Me?" He laughed caustically. "You believe God sent me?"

"Aye. Laugh if you choose, but I believe He wanted her saved. By you."

"Is that what you're trying to do for me, Penny? Save my soul?" He knew she meant the words differently but couldn't resist the question, since for weeks he'd endured similar remarks. "Just as Derek is alleged to have had some sort of divine awakening, though I have my doubts about that, you think I should undergo one, too. Is that what you're aiming for? Let me save you the trouble. I heard a heap of preaching from our ma when I was a boy, and I know about God, but in the end, her faith didn't save her from dying in one of the most agonizing ways I ever saw a body die."

"I lost my mother at an early age, too, Clay." Her tone gentled but remained firm. " 'Tis a grievous choice to let a loved one's death sour your own life. Is that what your ma would have wanted? For you to turn a cold shoulder to the ways she held so dear?" Penny's words made him squirm inside, though outwardly he remained as stiff as the taut canvas. "I only want for you happiness and to know serenity. Derek feels the same."

"Yeah, well, he sure has a peculiar way of showing it." Unnerved that she so accurately identified his torment, his inability to find peace or lasting contentment, Clay moved past her into the cubicle. He didn't wish to argue with his sister-in-law as he had with Derek, and he needed to find solitude before he began a rant.

The woman on the hide lay still as death, her skin almost as gray as pale ash, though most of the smudges had been cleansed from her face. Her lashes, a shade lighter than the soot in her hair, rested in feathery crescents against smooth cheeks. Both hands had been bound in clean, white linen and lay helpless at her sides.

His annoyance toward his family forgotten, pity tugged at his heart, and he lowered himself to the ground beside her. He took the liberty of running his fingertips along her arm, where her blackened sleeve met the bandage. "Who are you?" He whispered his thoughts aloud. "And what calamity put you in such a state as this?" He shook his head sadly.

Her thick lashes flickered. Her eyes rolled to and fro beneath thin lids, restless, and she opened them. Clay felt struck anew as he stared into fever-bright orbs of tawny gold flecked with the palest green.

Chapter 2

W ho. . ." Her throat felt raw, tight. She struggled to swallow, but that made it worse. "Who are you?" Her words came out husky, grating, unlike her usual quiet voice.

She didn't know the handsome face of the man who sat close, striking yet quiet, his deep blue eyes intent on her own, his fingertips on her arm. At the same time, a pinpoint of light pierced her bleary mind. As though realizing he took the liberty, he moved his hand away.

"I know you," she whispered in surprise. "How?" She tried to lift her head and groaned, her curiosity at his presence crumbling away as pain more horrible than anything she'd known wrenched through her limbs and hands. "Oh. . ." A fierce ache throbbed along the back of her scalp, and she dropped back to rest on what felt like fur. Lifting her arms as much as her feeble strength allowed, she stared in horrified confusion at the material wrapped like thick butterfly cocoons around each hand and wrist, halfway up her elbows.

"You're safe in Silverton. In a hotel room, if you can call it that." The man spoke in a quiet voice that somehow soothed. She heard the sound of liquid being stirred. "Here. You need this."

A smooth dipper touched her lips. Something cool and wet dribbled from the ladle and onto her neck. It felt heavenly, and she endured another wave of pain to lift her head and drink what he held. She emptied the dipper of water, and he brought another.

"You have a name?" he asked once she'd taken her fill.

She lay back against the pillow and puckered her brow, trying to think beyond the strange dream to which she'd awakened. A nightmare, in that she lay wounded, yet oddly pleasant because of the handsome and kind stranger who tended her.

"Meagan. I—my name's Meagan. What happened?"

"I had hoped you could tell me."

"What?" She stared in confusion.

He motioned with his hand toward her blanketed body. "How is it you came to be in such a state?"

"I. . .don't know." She grew anxious and more confused once she realized her current situation and that she wore nothing but her chemise beneath the

243

fur coverlet. Surely he hadn't removed her other clothing! Why could she not remember?

"You don't know?"

His disbelieving words pulled Meagan from her own stunned thoughts. He looked at her as if she'd sprouted buffalo horns. She felt as if maybe she had, with the manner in which her skull ached, and realized she must have hit it on something. She groaned as the throbbing increased when she moved her head. The lumpy support beneath her neck smelled of damp animal fur. Not a pillow of feathers, like her own, its soft bristles lightly scratched her nape.

"I can't recall."

"You don't recall wandering alone out in the middle of nowhere?"

"No." She drew her brows together. Even that made her head hurt. She tried to think beyond the pain, to form her words more clearly. "You must be mistaken. Why would I do such a thing?"

"You tell me." He regarded her as if he wasn't sure whether to believe her or not.

"Last I recall I was with. . .Ma and Wayne." She wished to say her words with force, insistent, but they came slow and slurred. "I wanna see her."

A fuzzy memory tickled her mind; she shoved it away, the pain increasing. Her mother would set things to rights once she swept in with her no-nonsense attitude and scattered all of Meagan's qualms to the wind. She had a way of getting to the heart of a problem with her good sense that flustered Meagan's spirited nature at times.

The stranger continued to stare, this time with a blank look Meagan couldn't identify. "Is Wayne your husband?"

"My brother."

"And your pa is. . . ?"

"Stepfather." She struggled to think. "Landon McClinton. He's not here." Odd she should know that, though she had no idea why. Nor could she recollect just where he was.

"So it's your mother, your brother, and yourself?"

His direct questions now seemed invasive.

"You a lawman?"

"No."

"A doctor?"

"No, not one of them either."

"Then why are you so interested in my personal doings?"

The muscle in his jaw jerked, as if she'd taken him by surprise. "I suppose it's because I'm the man who found you."

"Found me?"

"Wandering in a high-desert valley hours west of here. In the hot afternoon sun," he said slowly, as though talking to an invalid. "You were in a bad way." By the careful manner in which his gaze moved along her covered form, she imagined she still was.

"I can't recall. Hurts too much." The effort to try to make sense of what he said made her head pound. Feeling the black mist of blessed unawareness begin to wrap silky nothingness around her again, she fought against succumbing.

"Could you please ask Ma to come?"

He hesitated too long for what shred of comfort she had left.

"She's not here," he said at last.

"She didn't come with you? Then where—?"

"I don't know."

"Don't know? Or won't tell me?" Her whisper bordered on hysteria. His impossible words made no sense. How could this man not know where her ma was? "Is she hurt? And Wayne. Is he hurt, too?"

"I honestly don't know where your family is or what condition they're in."

"But how come? If you found me like you said? They must've been close."

"I'm upsetting you. Don't mean to." He began to push himself up from the ground. "I'll leave you to get some rest."

"No—wait!" She raised her arm, the linen wad making contact with his chest. She winced as pain jarred through her hand, and she lowered it. "Don't go. Please. . .not yet."

The stranger stared, plainly confused by her request, but Meagan felt more anxious about being left helpless and alone in an unfamiliar place than about having her rescuer nearby. He seemed thoughtful enough, considering. The curtain of fog pushed across her mind in its relentless sweep; later she would insist on answers. Right now she only wanted to lose herself again to empty blackness and lessen the pain.

"Just till I sleep," she pleaded, her words barely heard.

"All right." He settled back down. "You rest. I'll stay."

"Promise?"

"Yes."

She parted her lips to thank him, but the effort suddenly seemed too great. His kind eyes, a deep, serene blue, were the last thing she remembered before she closed heavy lids and the coveted mist wrapped around her once more.

ᔥ

"Who you reckon she is?"

"Maybe a princess!" Younger than the first, the second childish voice whispered the words in delighted awe.

"You're such a numskull. A princess? In Silverton?"

"Pa calls Mama his Indian princess sometimes. And don't be callin' me names, Livvie, or I'll tell."

"Not if you want me to teach you to play Grandda's mouth organ, you won't. . .I wonder how she got so much soot on her."

"Maybe it's gunpowder."

"Why would she dump gunpowder in her hair?"

"Dunno."

"Uncle Clay told Mama it looked like she'd been in a fire. That's why her hands got all burnt. He reckoned she used them to put it out."

Meagan did feel as if she'd been set afire, her mind in a smoky haze, but her first worry that Indians captured and tortured her eased as she listened to the children talk. They spoke English, with a gentle, foreign lilt to their words, though at times their speech sounded as western as other emigrants. Her stepfather often told her ma how dangerous native tribes were to white settlers; she'd never met an Indian, though she'd seen some from a distance. But whoever watched her seemed harmless enough. She remembered the stranger with the quiet voice and serene eyes and wondered if that was the girls' uncle Clay.

Bits and pieces of what the children said and what she remembered came clearer, though scattered. She wished to quench all recollections, somehow knowing ignorance remained a far better choice. Relentless, they slithered forward. . .the intolerable heat of fire searing her skin as she pounded at the ever-rising flames. . . a man's gentle hands and anxious voice imploring her to waken. . .distant, frantic screams that rent at her insides. . . .

"What color you think her hair is?" Small, curious fingers snatched up a hank and rubbed it, making a whispery sound near her ear and putting a halt to the beastly memories. A waft of cool air hit where her neck became exposed. "It isn't dark with red like Mama's or real dark like ours. And it isn't red like Aunt Linda's."

"Nobody's hair is as red as that."

"Aunt Linda's is."

A loud sigh escaped. "Never you mind, Christa."

"The dance-hall lady has red hair, too, I saw it. But hers ain't as bright as Aunt Linda's is."

"Don't let Mama hear you talk. She'd tan our hides good if she knew we peeked inside when no one was watchin'."

Meagan felt gentle tugs to her hair, as if it were being twirled around the same curious fingers. "Under all that ash it looks kinda like the flowers that grow by our stream at home."

"It ain't as yellow as them flowers, but with all them glimmers in it and the lamp shinin' on it, it does look like gold dust I've seen some miners pay merchants with. I reckon there's too much soot and dirt to tell."

"I still say she's a princess, Livvie."

"Then why was she out roamin' the valley all alone with no wagon or horse or nothin' with her? Why wasn't she in a grand coach or a castle keep somewhere with servants?"

"I reckon she was out looking for her prince."

The older girl gave a protesting snort. "That was just a tale Grandda told. It wasn't real. You're six years old now, Christa—old enough to know better."

"There are so princes and princesses! Pa said. He read books his ma made him read when he was a young'un that told him so. And Grandda said his homeland is full of castle keeps. So there!"

"Hush up and fetch the water so I can wet this here cloth. Mama won't be happy if she comes in and sees we haven't done what she told us to yet."

Meagan's hair fell back against her neck as the child released it. Light footsteps padded the ground, and Meagan heard water splash.

"Careful with that, or you're gonna spill it all before I get a chance to use any!"

"Aw, the pail is heavy, Livvie. Why can't you carry it?"

"Cause Mama told me *I'm* supposed to wet down her face." Her reply came off sounding haughty. "Your job is collecting water."

"Why do you always make me do all the hard work?" A loud *thump* hit the ground as Meagan assumed what was the pail dropped down close to her head. She jerked a bit in surprise. "Did you see that, Livvie?" The smallest girl's words came in an excited whisper. "You reckon she's finally waking up?"

"Dunno." The dull plunk of droplets being wrung into water met her ears the moment before a cool, damp cloth swathed her burning face. "Her skin's not so hot as before. You reckon the fever finally broke and that's why she moved? Mama'll be pleased."

"Uncle Clay, too. He's always askin' how she is."

As they continued chattering in hushed whispers, the memory of her quandary unfolded inside Meagan's mind. Her uncertainties returned, riding in on a fresh wave of pain. Her eyelids flickered, and she opened them. The midnight dark eyes of one of the girls, inches away and staring into her own, gave her a sudden fright.

She gasped. The child let out a squeal of shock and jumped back.

"Oh! You are awake. Christa, run and get Mama. Hurry!"

Light footsteps shuffled off at a rapid pace.

"What happened?" Meagan forced her voice to work, rusty with disuse.

"You mean you don't remember nothin'? Not the fire? Or your hands getting burnt? Or Uncle Clay findin' you in the desert?"

Meagan closed her eyes against the child's innocent questions, desperate to remain unaware, wishing she could retrieve her query. But the bits and pieces stitched together into a relentless, gruesome pattern, and Meagan could no longer hold them back.

Those men. . .the fire. . .her mama's screams. . .no. . .God, please. . .

"No–o–o!"

The last she rasped in a wail of despair, feeling as if her heart had been cloven in two. She barely noticed the girl back up in slow retreat, her eyes wide with shocked terror.

Chapter 3

At the heart-stopping cry of anguish, Penny fumbled with the pouch onto which she stitched Shoshone symbols and hissed as she jabbed the needle's point in her skin. Alarmed, Clay set down a month-old copy of a newspaper from another town and met her eyes across the table. She popped her bleeding thumb into her mouth as she rose from the bench. He did likewise. Another shriek ripped from the area where Meagan lay hidden.

"Glory be, she don't sound well," the nearly toothless Jinx muttered. His spoon stilled from stirring the stew with his three fingers—a disability acquired when using black powder while blasting in a mine but not escaping fast enough the first time he'd done so, and the source of his nickname.

Christa appeared in the kitchen entrance, her face pale. Sensing trouble, they hurried out before the child could offer an explanation. Penny reached Meagan's bedside a hair's breadth ahead of Clay.

"Olivia, what happened?" Penny darted a glance to her patient, then took hold of her eldest daughter by the shoulders. The girl looked shaken, her back up against the wall of canvas. "What did you do to make her cry out like that?"

"Nothing, Mama. Honest! Me and Christa was just talking. I was wetting down her face like you told me to. That's all."

Clay glanced at the ten-year-old, noting the big tears that trekked down her cheeks, before he turned his attention to Meagan. She lay on her side curled up in a tight ball, her bandaged hands pressed to her mouth, trying to muffle the hollow sobs that tore from her slight body. She trembled beneath the blanket. The pathetic picture confused Clay and ripped his heart asunder. One other time he had felt such keen sympathy, a mounting urge to protect from all evils—with his ma. Then as now, he stood helpless, stunned.

"What's wrong with her?" He directed his question to Penny, who sank to the ground beside Meagan. "Is she going to be all right?"

"How can I possibly know?" Penny pressed a soothing hand against the woman's limp, smoke-blackened hair near the lump he remembered discovering when he found her. "Are you in a great deal of pain?" she softly addressed Meagan. "I can brew a tea to help."

Meagan offered no reply; if anything, she seemed to burrow further within herself.

"Leave me alone with her, Clay."

"I'm not going anywhere."

Penny turned at his staunch declaration, her eyes sympathetic. "I need to examine her burns and make certain they've not gone septic."

"I can help."

"No, it wouldn't be fitting. She has injuries besides those on her hands."

At a loss, he glanced at the back of Meagan's head. It seemed so vulnerable and forlorn against the wool-stuffed hide of elk Penny had stitched up for a pillow. Though he knew he must give Penny the privacy needed, he delayed, not wanting to leave Meagan's side. How could he explain this odd connection he felt for the defenseless woman, when he had little cause to care so strongly? All he knew was her given name, for crying out loud, yet somehow she'd become more to him than a stranger in need.

"Clay," Penny persisted.

"All right. Have one of the girls fetch me if you need me for anything."

"I will."

"I mean *anything*."

"You'll be the first person I seek."

With a nod to Penny, he left the cubicle.

"Clay? Can you spare a moment?"

He tensed at the question issued from his right, but not because he didn't want to talk with his half sister. On the contrary; he'd been wishing to speak with her for days, ever since the night he returned to Silverton with Meagan, and more so since he'd discovered Linda was the new Mrs. Michaels. But where Linda was, Kurt and often Derek lurked nearby. A surprise to Clay, given that over a month ago, Derek had treated their newly discovered half sister as his mortal enemy. Yet he seemed to have attained a good pal in Linda's deputy husband. Clay often noticed the two conversing and laughing together, which didn't say much for Kurt's good judgment. Being a lawman, couldn't he perceive what a black-hearted scoundrel Derek was? Or was Clay the only soul alive who could see past his brother's recent pretense of turning over a new leaf?

He turned, grateful to see Linda stood alone. "You've been quiet these days." He attempted a smile but felt awkward. Guilt still ate away at his conscience. He harbored no doubts that this woman was blood kin. She had their pa's determined jaw and piercing gray eyes. The color reminded him of silver nuggets, while Meagan's shimmered as if they contained flecks of the purest gold.

Where did that come from?

Such a sudden and familiar thought linked to the woman in the next room flabbergasted him. Linda self-consciously patted her flame red locks. "Have I got a cocklebur in my hair or something?"

"Sorry." Clay broke off from staring and glanced at his boot tips. "Actually I'm sorry for a whole lot of things." Sheepish, he raised his eyes to hers. "Can we go somewhere and talk?"

Her smile seemed as clumsy as he felt. "I was hoping you would ask."

Clay scanned the area, wondering where to go for privacy. Jinx was still in the kitchen, cooking up the noontime meal—likely stew of whatever small mammal he could find to fill the pot since he never made anything else—and the hotel, usually empty this time of day, crawled with men talking in huddles, he assumed about the latest news.

"We could go for a walk," Linda suggested.

"Sounds like a good idea." Clay led the way in relief that she'd made the suggestion and opened the door. He hesitated before going through, stepping aside to let her precede him. Her brows lifted in surprise as she walked ahead.

"My ma didn't raise a complete oaf. Besides the daily schooling, she taught me manners. She was a schoolteacher before she married my pa. . .our pa," he corrected.

"I never said—"

"I know," he relented, knowing that his shame was the source of his rapid explanation. He wished this moment of reconciliation had fallen far behind them.

The sun burned overhead, covering everything from ground to tents to their wooden fronts in a bright haze that made him squint. They strolled along the road, facing the range of blue-shadowed mountains looming eastward. Linda swiped at her forehead, which had begun to glisten.

"If it's too hot, we can find shade," Clay offered.

"I'm fine." She sent him another uncertain smile. "I've endured far worse than noonday heat."

"About that." Clay couldn't put off the unavoidable any longer. "I want you to know how sorry I am for the way we treated you when you first arrived. Derek never should have said those things, and I should have done something to stop him."

"It's all right. There wasn't much you could do, I suppose, since he's got a mind of his own." Her voice came soft, almost hard to hear as a wagon burdened down with mining equipment rumbled past. "Like I told Derek when he apologized, I'd just as soon forget it ever happened."

Clay glanced at her in surprise. "Derek apologized? To you?"

"Yes, the moment I returned. He was quite sincere, and I told him the same thing I'm telling you now. Let's let bygones be bygones." She cast a glance at the narrow road and cleared her throat, as if gathering courage. "In thinking on it,

I'd like us to get to know one another and become a true family, work together and help one another. I know I'm only your half sister, but—"

"I'd like that," he hurried to assure, sensing her discomfort over what their pa had done. "I never thought much about having a sister, but it might be nice."

She turned a bright smile his way, her first real smile since they'd ventured on their stroll. "I'm so relieved, Clay. Derek will be, too. He's the one who approached me with the idea."

"What idea?"

"Why, to leave here soon and search for our legacy together, of course."

"No." His reply came swift.

"But. . ." She blinked in confusion. "I thought. . ."

"After all the grief my—our brother caused, I can't risk teaming up with him."

"Then you still plan to search on your own?"

Her words sounded sad, and he winced, hating that once more he was the source of her pain. "Not right away, no. I have business keeping me in Silverton for a while."

"That woman you brought with you?"

He cast a sharp glance her way. "Why would you ask such a question?"

"I just thought. . ." She struggled to find words, her face going redder. "You've shown such an interest in her welfare. I thought you must have known her before."

"I am interested in what happens to her, that much is true. But I never met her before I brought her here." He wished he could get a woman's viewpoint and explain to Linda the strange attachment he felt, almost from the time Meagan fell senseless into his arms, but discussing a virtual stranger with a half sister he had yet to know felt about as uncomfortable as a new wool union suit in July. He returned the subject to smoother territory.

"Once I do search, rest assured, whatever I find, if I find anything, I won't keep to myself. You'll get your fair portion, Linda. I swear it. I won't take what isn't mine. Like Derek did with us."

"Thank you for that."

He nodded, his focus on the distant hills as they walked.

"He's changed, Clay." She laid her hand tentatively against his arm to gain his full attention. "I wouldn't have believed the man I met on first arriving here and the man who returned were the same. Give him a chance to prove it."

Clay's smile was tight. "He seems to have won you over. Your husband, too. But I know him better than the both of you, and I trust him even less."

"I'm sorry you feel that way. I suppose I do understand, given your long association with him." She sighed. "One thing I've learned these short few weeks is that God sometimes works best when situations are at their worst. Good things can come when you least expect them. I'll pray that for you."

He looked at her sharply, never having figured her for being religious. She sounded like Penny. And his ma.

"Kurt and his aunt taught me about God while I was in Jasperville," Linda explained. "Without them helping me along, in so many ways, I wouldn't be here with you now. I'd be an evil lecher's prisoner. Or more than likely, dead."

Clay lifted his brows in surprise.

"It's true. I'll tell you about it sometime. Not now."

He sensed the pain was still too raw for her to talk about it. "If you're expecting a miracle, don't waste your prayers on me, Linda. Not that I believe prayer does any good, but if it ever did work, Meagan could use the assistance instead. She's really suffering."

"I have prayed. Kurt and I both. Derek and Penny have joined us in prayer, too."

Clay changed the subject before she could ask him to join in or introduce more conversation about God. "I'm glad we had this chance to talk. I've wanted to for days, but Derek was always hanging around like a persistent hound dog. He and your husband appear to get along well."

"Yes, they do, and I'm so thankful." She smiled. "When I told Kurt about how Derek first treated me, I was afraid he might punch him in the mouth upon meeting him. He was that upset. But it all worked to the good. We were amazed to discover they both have a friend in common—the marshal of the town Kurt hails from. Derek rode through Jasperville several years back and became friends with him."

"Kurt knew Derek as long ago as that?"

"No. Derek and the marshal became friends. Kurt was still pretty much a boy. He did chores for his aunt at her hotel but didn't recollect Derek's ever being there—not till the two men talked and Kurt remembered an incident Derek brought up, when Marshal Wilson taught Derek tricks with his guns. Kurt remembered looking on from a distance and wishing the marshal would teach him." She chuckled fondly. "He's learned since then, of course. That was near the time he took an interest in becoming a lawman. From what I understand, Derek wasn't yet nineteen, a few years older than Kurt. Marshal Wilson taught Kurt shortly after and, when he was old enough, made him his deputy." She gave a secret sort of smile. "We met while he was doing his duty as a lawman, but I didn't like him much at the time. He soon proved he could be trusted, though. The longer I knew him, the more I began to care."

"He seems like a good man. I'm happy for you, though I'm surprised he isn't with you today. He usually isn't far."

Her skin took on a pretty rose flush. "He's quite protective. We've been through a good deal in the short time we've known each other. But I convinced him to go with Derek to check on Penny's homestead, like Derek asked. Derek also wants to let nearby miners know a man's running the place and he won't tolerate any of the trouble they gave poor Penny. Derek hopes it will further convince those miners to see a lawman involved and that they'll keep shy of the place while it's vacant." She lowered her voice. "Till we figure out what to do about our pa's mine, Derek and Penny can't settle into ranch life."

"Ranch life?" Last he'd heard, Derek was laying tracks for the railroad. Clay ignored an unexpected prickle of offense to learn the two men left without asking Clay to ride along. Not that he would have gone anywhere with his brother, and he had no idea why he should feel insulted the scoundrel hadn't bothered to ask.

"Derek plans to start a ranch when he leaves here. They need the money the mine will bring to buy cattle."

"Good riddance," he muttered under his breath but didn't fail to note her exasperated look, proof she'd heard him.

He was saved any additional comment as a loud hurrah went up nearby. A crowd of men huddled in front of the livery, all of them keyed up, judging from their expressions. Clay's curiosity got the best of him.

"Come along." He took Linda's arm in a protective gesture and approached the men. "What's all the hullabaloo about?" he greeted. "Another strike?"

"No—just as good, I reckon," a man with blackened teeth answered. "Just got the news by telegraph. It's done."

"What's done?"

"Where ya been, young feller?" a bearded gent with hair that grew as thick on his forearms jovially asked, slapping Clay on the back. "The Union Pacific and Central Pacific met up. I heard tell they pounded a golden spike in Promontory Summit in Utah today. Two days later than planned cause o' bad weather, but who's counting?" He laughed. "Long as it's finally done."

A short stick of a man smiled, tears in his watery blue eyes. "I reckon that means my dear old mother will be a-joinin' me. She said if ever they came up with a way to travel that didn't involve months of crossing by wagon train, she'd come out West."

"It certainly is much anticipated, my lads," a usually quiet miner said. The tall Cornishman had been given the nickname Gentleman George due to his mannerly and precise way of speaking. "I look forward to the prospect of sending for my family, as well."

"No more travel by wagon train," Linda said under her breath, though Clay could hear her. "That surely will be an improvement."

"Uncle Clay," Livvie called, "Aunt Linda!"

Both turned to see Penny's oldest girl race across the street.

"Mama wants you. Christa got stung by somethin', and Mama wants you to come quick."

Clay and Linda hurried with their niece to the hotel. He could hear Christa's squalling before he stepped foot inside. He spotted Penny with her arms around Christa, trying to comfort her squirming child. Christa's arm was reddened and puffy.

"Stay with Meagan," Penny told Linda. "I doona want her left to herself. I'm not sure what ails Christa. From the little I could understand, a flying bug stung her. Likely a bee with the way they've been buzzing around. There must be a hive somewhere close."

"You look as if you could use help calming her," Linda countered.

"Go with Penny," Clay inserted. "I'll stay with Meagan."

Linda nodded, and the two women hurried away with the child. Christa's cries grew fainter, and Clay inhaled a steadying breath. He hated to witness any female's pain, be it girl or woman. He thought of Meagan, wishing he knew how to take her heartache away.

Entering the room, he noticed she still lay huddled in a ball, her back to him. The blanket had fallen away in her struggles, her smoke-blackened chemise now apparent. He walked around to face her and hunched down. Her teary eyes were open, but she didn't acknowledge him, only stared straight ahead. Prickles danced along his spine as he recalled her similar behavior when he'd first found her wandering in the valley.

"Miss?" He pulled the edge of the cover over her chemise, trying not to notice how round and soft her bare shoulder appeared. "Can you hear me?"

She didn't respond and flinched when his fingertip brushed her neck as he pulled his hand from the blanket. He released a weary breath, unable to understand the churning inside his heart. He'd never felt this way about anyone and assumed pity caused such intense feeling. Yet when he was with her, pity was only one layer of what he suffered. If he were to believe Jinx, he might think her a wandering gypsy who'd cast a spell on him. But she neither looked like a gypsy—her skin fair beneath the soot, her hair and eyes dark golden—nor did she wear the gaudy clothes of one. Not that he believed such far-fetched tales.

"You're going to be all right," he told the unresponsive woman. Uncertain what to do, he settled into another position, trying to make his long legs comfortable by crossing them. Keeping his touch feather light, he laid his fingertips against the edge of one of her bandages. "I'm not leaving here till you are. I'll help you through whatever it is you're dealing with, however I can. You're not alone—I just wanted you to know that."

She didn't answer, but Clay noticed the tenseness of her jaw slacken and her eyes close, as if in relief. When her breathing grew even and deep, proof that she at last slept, he quietly added, "No, Miss Meagan, there isn't much that'll make me leave Silverton a second time. Not yet. Not the prospect of silver, not being forced to reunite with my black sheep of a brother. I reckon you're stuck with me for a while."

The notion made Clay smile.

✑

Over the next two days, Meagan became more aware of her surroundings each time she woke, but she didn't speak. To do so might break up the dam welling inside, though late at night, when everyone else slept, she allowed hot tears to fall and smothered her sobs in the scratchy pillow. What grieving she did in secret helped, and in sleep, she often escaped memories, but sometimes they slithered into her dreams like vicious serpents, their excruciating bites making her jerk awake with a shock and gasp for breath.

She wavered back and forth between hoping the events must be some horrid, twisted nightmare and knowing it wasn't so. During the latter times, such desolation filled her soul she wished she could again dissolve into the fog that once held her mind captive, with the hope that it would make the anguish disappear, too.

The woman called Penny often tended her wounded hands and fed her, spooning meat broths into her mouth. She bore Indian blood if her physical appearance and moccasins were anything to judge by, though she wore the clothes of a white woman and spoke with a lilting, European burr Meagan had never heard except from the two little girls. She didn't think her accent originated from any tribe in these parts, though she had no way of knowing. Indian or not, Penny was kind, her quiet ways and gentle hands bringing a measure of bodily comfort. Her two daughters often aided her, and their constant magpie chattering helped Meagan to forget her misery for a time. After their first scare while tending her, Livvie and Christa soon recovered and seemed to enjoy their one-sided conversations with Meagan as she lay silent.

When Penny or her girls weren't near, the man she heard Penny address as Clay kept vigil by Meagan's bedside. Whereas the girls were talkative, Clay was silent, often brooding, though Meagan no longer suffered qualms regarding the tall, dark stranger. He'd exhibited toward her a gentleness she hadn't thought a man capable of—especially when she recalled her more lucid moments and the feel of his muscles like iron as he'd held her against him that first day. She realized she had him to thank for what was left of her life.

From beneath her lashes, she stared at him, hoping he would think she still slept. Whether she should thank him or curse him for his act she couldn't decide.

"I thought you might like something to read to ease the boredom." Penny walked into the room, handing Clay a book. "It'll help pass the time."

Clay made a sound of protest after he took the large book in his hands and glanced at the cover. "A Bible? I can't—"

"Now then, there's no use tellin' me you haven't the skill to read." She cut him off before he could finish his sentence. "I know otherwise. You mentioned once that you like to do so of an evening. And your mother was a teacher, Derek told me. Considering what little she taught him in the short time he took lessons, I'm certain she spent years teaching you a good sight more."

Clay grumbled. "Don't you have any other books?"

"I haven't a wide supply at present," she answered wryly. "Most of my da's books I left at the shanty before we took our journey—I had no wish to weigh down the wagon. So you'd best reconcile yourself to what's offered."

"This is the only book you have with you?" he insisted.

She crossed her arms over her chest and raised her brows. "I have two others. A McGuffey's reader that Livvie and Christa use and a book of poetry."

"Fine then. I'll take the poetry."

Meagan thought Penny's exasperated sigh might stir the canvas walls. Had she not felt such misery, she might have cracked a smile at Clay's boyish stubbornness.

"Very well. I'll just fetch it then, shall I?"

"I'd appreciate it."

"Humph." She glanced in Meagan's direction, and Meagan closed her eyes. "Has she come around?"

"No. Hasn't moved from that position ever since I came to guard her."

"Guard her?"

"Need I remind you of where we currently reside?"

Penny let out a breath. "You're wise to be so protective, Clay. All sorts make up a town of this nature. Although Mr. Matthis is kind—and Jinx. They would never cause a lady harm. For most of these men, 'tis been a long while since they've seen a woman. A decent woman. They treat Linda well, to the point of idolatry. And a few give me the same esteem, despite what Shoshone blood I bear, so I imagine Meagan will fare well."

"There are others who think differently."

"Aye. . .there are always others."

At their uneasy manner of speaking, Meagan felt apprehensive. What kind of town had he brought her to?

"I fail to understand why she's not spoken. You said she did so the first night?"

"Not much. She told me her name. That's all that I know about her."

Meagan heard regret in his voice and pondered the cause of it.

"Something dreadful must have happened to the wee lassie to cause her to draw into herself in such a manner." Penny's moccasins made a scuffing sound toward the entrance. "So tragic."

Tragic. Yes. An apt word to describe what remained of her life. Helpless to stop it, Meagan hoped no one could see the tear trickle from beneath her lashes and roll to her temple.

Chapter 4

Clay saw the tear and held his breath.

Had she been awake this entire time and privy to their conversation? Why should she feign sleep? She'd made it obvious she didn't want to speak these past forty-eight hours; nor had anyone forced her since that first evening when he'd fumbled with his questions and almost brought her to panicked tears. He still winced when he thought about his clumsy behavior. Since then, he had tried to think his words over, testing them before he spoke, not wanting to send her over the brink a second time. He'd heard whispers from a few boarders that she must be a mite touched in the head not to recall all that happened. Likewise, he'd never heard of a person losing part of their memory except in their dotage. Nor had anyone else known of such an occurrence. But neither did he think that Meagan lied about her inability to remember. He hoped those men were wrong and she wasn't loco. His gut told him she was as sane as he.

Clay leaned closer to her. "Meag—Miss?" He just prevented himself from addressing her by her Christian name, not wanting to show disrespect, though that's the only name she'd given and that's how he thought of her. "Are you awake?"

Her lids creased, squeezing the barest fraction tighter, and he realized with some amazement she wanted him to go on thinking she slept, much like Christa or Livvie when they played possum. He considered the matter, wondering if he should continue or just let her be.

"Well now, that's a shame. Mind you, the quiet is nice, but hour after hour of it can get trying and creep beneath a man's bones—makes him restless to hear another voice. Enough so that he might start talking to himself for company. . . . I suppose I'll just have to fill the air with my own chatter to pass the time. Like as not, hearing me talk can get somewhat monotonous. So I suppose it's a good sight better that you're sleeping and don't have to suffer the tedium. If you were awake, I don't know how you could stand it."

Her eyelashes flickered, but she didn't open her eyes.

Sure now she must be feigning sleep, he went on, "Still, I was hoping you might wake up soon. You've slept the entire day away. My sister-in-law insists that sleep is good for a body, but too much can't be beneficial. Not when you need nourishment, too. Jinx makes some of the finest badger stew this side of the Rockies, not that I've had badger stew elsewhere. But it puts meat on one's bones—not that I think you need meat on your bones, but it couldn't hurt. To help build your strength. Not that I think you're too lean." He quit, realizing he'd bungled his words and said the wrong thing again, but then he saw the corner of her mouth flicker the tiniest bit. That he might make her smile—something he'd never believed possible when the most he'd hoped for was getting her to open her eyes—made his embarrassment drift away, and he grinned.

"Of course then, there's Penny. My sister-in-law. She could use some meat on her bones, I reckon, though not for strength. Oh no, not Penny. She's got an attitude that's strong as a bull's and thrice as stubborn as a mule's." He moved a little closer to her ear, lowering his voice. "Just don't tell her I said so."

Her chapped lips quivered a bit, as if holding back a sign of mirth.

"But she's a good woman owning a heart pure as snow, though not as cold. Her bones may be little, but there's not a mean one in her body. You can depend on her. She's efficient when it comes to her remedies, wise when it comes to doling out advice. Fact is, plenty of people here care what happens to you, and not just Penny."

"Well now, Clayton. . ."

At the amused lilt of his sister-in-law's voice Clay jumped back a good foot. He tried to cover his loss of composure as she stepped past the curtain. "What are you doing, sneaking up on a person like that?"

"Have a guilty conscience, do you? Huh. If you should wish to see the bearer of an attitude strong as a bull's and thrice as stubborn as a mule's, I'd advise you look in the stream on a clear day and see who be starin' back. Bein' as how my counsel's so wise, I'm assured you'll be takin' it."

This time he didn't mistake the thread of a muffled gasp as Meagan held back a laugh, though she kept her eyes and lips skewed shut. He and Penny shared a quick look. Her smile went wider as she also realized Meagan almost laughed. She looked toward the bed, her brow curious, then to Clay. Before she could open her mouth to query him, he gave a slight shake of his head, still smiling. For some reason he couldn't place, he wanted to let Meagan continue her little game and speak when she was ready. He felt a good deal better knowing they'd given her a dose of happiness, however small, and if her pretense of sleep helped, well then, so be it.

His gaze shifted to Penny's hand. "That the poetry?"

"Aye, it is."

His curiosity piqued at the twinkle in her eyes, he got no further than taking the book, when a multitude of heavy steps from outside drew close.

"Penny, you in there?" Derek's voice came from the other side of the curtain.

She drew it back, her eyes lighting up to see Derek but soon clouding with concern. He hugged her briefly. "Whatever is the matter?"

Derek, Kurt, and another man Clay didn't recognize stood outside. From their tense jaws and sober eyes, Clay knew trouble threatened.

"We need to talk," Kurt said.

They took their conversation to the other side of the curtain.

"On the way from the homestead, we took another route." Derek kept his voice low, but as deep and clear as it was, he may as well have been standing next to Clay. "Wanted to warn any other miners that a man was running the place now. We came upon a shack—what was left of it. Fire burned it."

"Do you suppose it was the same fire Meagan came against?" Penny asked.

Clay shot a glance toward the young woman. Her eyes remained closed, but her wrapped hand moved a fraction.

"Can't say. The shack wasn't empty." Derek's voice sounded grim. "Found two bodies. A woman and a boy. Reckon he was no more than fourteen." He sounded truly regretful about the discovery, which also moved Clay.

"Injuns!" an unfamiliar voice claimed with malice. "They musta done it."

"We haven't had trouble in these parts for some time," Kurt argued. "The tribes that were living here are on reservations now."

"There's always them renegades causing trouble," the stranger staunchly replied. "Can't trust any Injun."

"Just what do you mean by that?" Derek's question weighed heavy with warning.

"Just what I said." By the menacing drawl of the stranger's voice, Clay imagined the man meant Penny.

"Be careful what you say and how you say it," Derek replied, his tone as threatening. "I'd advise you to think on it first, a good long time, before saying anything further."

"You aim on stopping me? I got a right to speak—and I ain't the only one 'round these parts that feels thatta way. So's unless you plan on taking on the whole town, you best think twice before opening your trap in favor of an Injun again."

"Out of respect to my wife, I'll ask you once more to keep your mouth shut."

"Respect?" the stranger sneered. "No one asked you to bring her here."

As the men's words grew more heated with each view aired, Clay hoped Derek had enough sense to take it outside and not start a fight with women present and in danger of getting hurt. He also detested how the scoundrel mistreated Penny.

"Not. . .Indians."

Clay's attention jerked from the argument to Meagan, surprised to hear

261

her small voice amid the growing ruckus. Her eyes were wide open and staring at him.

"Did you say something?" he asked, shocked that she'd actually spoken.

She made a visible effort to swallow. "The men. . .who burned my home. Not Indians."

"That was your home they're talking about?" Dread laced his words. Derek had said they'd found two bodies there.

She nodded, tears glistening in her eyes already red-rimmed from the crying he'd heard each night. Since he'd brought her to Silverton, he bunked outside her cubicle to keep watch. Though his heart had ached to hear her muffled sobs, he'd let her be, figuring she needed time to deal with whatever demons plagued her. Now it appeared as if he would finally learn the cause of her torment.

"Ma," she said. "And Wayne. . .my brother. They. . ." The tears that brimmed in her eyes ran over, and her body began to tremble.

"Shh. It's all right." He gently clasped her shoulder.

The sound of scuffling and grunting rose from outside the cubicle.

"Derek, no!" Penny cried.

Clay shot a glance at the curtain. It billowed as if someone pushed against it.

"You're safe, and I'm here to make sure it stays that way. But you need to tell the others the truth before a skirmish starts out there."

Like a frightened child, Meagan pulled at her lower lip with her teeth but nodded assent. Clay wrenched the curtain aside. Derek clutched handfuls of the stranger's shirt. Kurt tried to hold back one of Derek's muscled arms, Penny the other.

Clay loudly cleared his throat.

Penny looked at him in surprise, as did Kurt.

"If you can stop quarrelling long enough to listen, there's something you should hear." Clay stepped aside to let them enter. As if frozen in place, Derek remained fixed a moment, then released the man's shirt with a little push.

"Don't ever talk that way about my wife again," Derek warned in a low growl before striding into the cubicle. Anxiety plainly written on her face, Penny followed, but the stranger gave them a disgusted scowl and left.

"Who was he?" Penny asked Derek, touching his arm.

"No one." He drew her close to his side. "Don't worry about it. He won't cause further harm."

"Unfortunate as it is, his views are shared by other men here," Kurt reminded grimly.

"Well, we're not leaving." Derek's eyes blazed. "Not till we're ready. And if they try and force us, they'll wish they hadn't."

"Violence isn't the answer," Penny inserted softly. "It just breeds more violence, which in turn breeds more, and it goes on and on, a never-ending circle of fighting and death."

Clay watched his brother's face relax and marveled that Penny had such an effect on him. "I know what you're saying is true. I just wish. . ."

"That we could all get along?" she finished for him. "I agree." She directed her attention to Clay. "It will be a blessed day when we can get along peaceably and put old hurts behind us. It took many years for me to come to that knowledge, but I'm thankful it didn't come too late."

Clay didn't doubt the topic of conversation had altered from the stranger's threats to the clash between himself and Derek. He chose to ignore Penny and looked instead at Meagan, who regarded each of their faces with uncertainty. She had managed to sit up and had turned her eyes his way. Lines of doubt dissolved from her face, and her features relaxed. She looked at him much as Derek had at Penny when her words calmed him, and Clay realized with surprise he had earned Meagan's trust. Though she recalled little, maybe she did remember him finding her in the wilderness.

He gave her a faint smile and nod of encouragement.

Meagan closed her eyes, clearly apprehensive of facing what must be said. Clay knew it couldn't be easy for her.

"Those men weren't Indians," she said. "The men you were talking about. There were two of them. I—I don't know who they were. Strangers I'd never seen."

"Do you remember what they look like?" Kurt assumed a quiet but firm official attitude Clay had begun to associate with the deputy when speaking of matters pertaining to the law.

She shook her head. "No, I. . .they had beards. One stood taller. . .that's all I can recall."

Her description could apply to over half the men in Silverton. Still, Clay had an uneasy feeling she held something back.

"I need you to tell me all that happened," Kurt insisted. "Did they set fire to the shack?"

"I don't remember." She stared at the bandages covering her hands, her breathing more labored.

Kurt blinked, clearly not expecting such an answer. "You remember the men but not what they did?"

"No." Her reply came swift. "I still can barely recall anything. It hurts my head to think."

"If you saw them again, could you identify them?" Kurt persisted.

"I. . .don't know." She pressed her swathed hands to each side of her head. "I saw them for such a short time."

"Did they say anything? Maybe call each other by name? Any information you can give might help."

"I don't know!" She slightly rocked in her agitation. "Please, that's all I can tell you."

Kurt seemed just as upset. Penny shook her head for him to stop when he would have questioned Meagan further. He closed his mouth before he could say whatever he'd planned to and sighed.

"You'll let me know the minute you recall anything? No lawman resides in Silverton. But since I'm staying awhile, I'll look into this and do all I can to help catch these men."

Meagan nodded, her gaze fixed on the blanket. Kurt and the others moved to leave the room. "Wait!" She looked up. "Please, can you tell me. . .the. . .bodies you found. . ."

"We gave them a proper Christian burial." Derek cut off her need to ask the difficult question. "I spoke over their graves, asking the Lord to carry them through to the other side. And the deputy here read a verse or two from the Good Book he carries."

Astounded, Clay listened to his brother show kindness toward a stranger, trying to ease her pain. He spoke about God as if he knew Him. Derek had claimed a newfound relationship with the Lord upon his return to Silverton, but Clay hadn't believed him.

"Were they friends of yours?" Kurt lowered his voice to a respectful level for the dead.

"My family. Thank you. . .for all you both did." On the tail end of her mournful whisper, silent tears dripped down her cheeks.

The sight stirred Clay; the sudden urge to take her in his arms and comfort her nearly overwhelmed him. He looked at the others, who stared at Meagan, clearly stunned and uncomfortable by her admission.

"Sorry to hear that, miss," Derek added, his tone gentle. "We also sang what we know of 'Shall We Gather at the River.' Seemed appropriate, bein' as how the Humboldt runs so close."

"Ma would've liked that." Meagan brushed away the tears with the back of her hand. "She liked to sing."

An uncomfortable silence fell upon the room. No one knew quite what to say.

Recalling his need for solitude after his ma died, Clay took charge, herding the others out of the room with him and assuring Meagan that someone would be in to look after her later. The men walked ahead, deep in discussion. Penny walked alongside Clay.

"That was very astute of you," she whispered, as if surprised.

"I'm not a complete boor," he argued. "I've been in her place."

"Aye. Be thankful you still have your brother."

His defenses charged ahead. "Penny, that subject is dead and buried. I'm not keen on resurrecting it and hashing this out with you again. No good'll come of it."

"At least you have a second chance to do some good," she insisted, turning to face him. "But that poor wee lassie in there will never be talkin' to her brother again. The only thing 'dead and buried' for her is her family."

Clay winced. "Sorry. A poor choice of words on my part, considering the situation."

"Don't be apologizing on my account. But hear my counsel, dear brother, not only with your ears, but with your heart as well." She grasped his forearm, as if concerned he might flee before she spoke, though he hadn't moved a muscle. "My dear da used to say, 'Life is too short to be shouldering a lifetime of grudges. 'Tis a burden that's utterly useless, has no worth, and gives its bearer naught but a great deal of suffering.' A lesson I myself had to learn, and you're far too intelligent a man to carry such a burden on your shoulders."

He managed a wry grin. Even when she chastised him, she had a way of paying him tribute. At one point, before she married his brother, Clay had vied for her affection, never having met anyone like Penny—intrigued by the petite but strong woman who bore a mix of Scots and Shoshone blood. Either his overtures were far too subtle or he'd had no chance to begin with, and on the occasions he glimpsed her alone with Derek, he presumed it was the latter. In the short time since she'd become Derek's wife, Clay had uprooted his newly budded affection for his sister-in-law, thankful it had been given no chance to grow and she'd never suspected his earlier feelings. Instead he showed her the fond respect a brother should. Likewise, she treated him as the little brother she'd never had. But at times, he thought she might drive him to drink, and if he weren't so infuriated with Derek, he could almost pity his brother, as often as she tried to mend the unmendable—neither action a course Clay wished to travel.

"You can't rescue everyone, Penny." He kept his words calm. "Some are lost causes."

"Och, there is no such thing," she scoffed. "I'm a wee bit on the inquisitive side. Ask Derek if you've not yet discovered this fault of mine. But fault or no, I'll do all I can to help my family, which is what you are. 'Tis the way I was raised and the example my parents gave. I can do no less. So you may as well accustom yourself to my involvement."

He gave her an exasperated smile, letting out a harsh laugh mingled with a sigh. "I suppose it'll do me no good to try and ignore you, and you will just have to be my cross to bear?"

"God can take away *all* your burdens, if you'll allow it, Clay. Not just the ones of which I spoke. But those you tell no one about."

Her tone serious again, she spoke as his ma might have. Suddenly Clay wanted to escape. "Could be," he said, not really believing it. "Whatever the case, I just now realized I should go to the livery and check on my horse before it thinks its owner abandoned it." A pathetic excuse, but he moved away before she could tell him so.

"Run if you wish it, but He's not far behind. And when you're weary of running, He'll always be there to turn back to."

"I'm not running from anything or anybody," he muttered under his breath. That she should think he was behaving like a coward made him want to shout out his defense to any and all who would listen. He quickened his stride, giving himself no cause to regret such actions.

∽

Meagan felt warm breath laced with some tangy herb—rosemary, perhaps—brush her face.

"Christa, don't get so close," Livvie chastened. "Mama said we wasn't to touch her. Just watch her till she comes back."

Meagan waited until she heard the soft rustles of the little girl's moccasins and dress scoot against the ground before she opened her eyes. She didn't want to alarm Christa like she'd done with Livvie that first day she'd awakened with the girls in the room.

"Oh—you're awake!" Christa's grin seemed uncertain. Meagan knew the children regarded her with some fear, in part due to the mystery surrounding her—a mystery that she could scarce remember in its entirety. She managed a smile, hoping to reassure the pair she wasn't an evil witch come to harm them.

"Hello." Her voice still sounded husky, and her throat felt raw, likely from the weeping, but after using it the past few days, her words didn't come as feeble as before.

"You *can* talk!" Christa's smile widened, and she clapped her hands together. Had the room not been so small, Meagan supposed the child might have danced about. She knew the youngest of the two to be six, from what Livvie had said, but couldn't help thinking she looked much too tiny and frail. She seemed closer to four.

"Course she can talk," Livvie said with an exasperated big-sister attitude Meagan had often used on her brother. "How else you think Uncle Clay learned her name?"

"Well, she never talked to us," Christa defended.

"She did to me."

"But not me!"

"No, I never have, have I?" Meagan's smile grew sheepish.

Any reserve Christa might have shown evaporated like mist in midmorning. She scooted closer until her knees pressed against Meagan's side. "How come you didn't say nothin' then?"

"I suppose it was owin' to the fact it was too hard. At first."

"Huh?" Christa cocked her head.

" 'Cause of the F-I-R-E," Livvie whispered near her sister.

"Fur?"

Livvie rolled her eyes. "No, dummy." She cupped her hand around Christa's ear and whispered something into it. The small girl's eyes grew bigger.

"Oh."

Uncomfortable with the bend of the conversation and the way the pair acted, Meagan moved to sit up, using her bandaged hands as leverage. They still stung and throbbed dreadfully, though the paste of herbs Penny slathered on them twice a day helped ease the pain. Her hair, matted and stinking of smoke, made her stomach turn, and her damp body and clothing, stinking of sweat, felt just as repulsive.

Looking at the two girls, their faces curious and expectant as if waiting to see what she might do next, Meagan searched for something to say. No words came to mind.

"You like horses?" Livvie asked.

"Horses?" The question took her aback. "I suppose."

"Pa said me and Christa can think up a name for his. He never named her, don't know why. Uncle Clay didn't name his, either. But me and Christa can't agree, so maybe you can help. She wants a name like those from the tales our Grandda told—and I want a name more befittin' a horse in the West."

At the mention of Clay's name, pleasant warmth unfurled inside Meagan, and she remembered the tall man with the clear eyes and soothing voice who'd taken care of her so often during Penny's absences. She tried to cover her interest, hoping the girls were too young to note her reaction, and posed a question to aid them with their quandary. "Will your. . .uncle Clay. . ." She stumbled over the use of his given name. "Will he also need a name for his horse?"

The two girls looked at each other. "I reckon he will," the oldest agreed.

"That would solve your problem then. Each of you could name a horse."

"Why didn't we think of that?" Livvie exclaimed, looking at her sister.

"Let's ask him!" A shine brought Christa's dark eyes to life. They lifted higher just as Meagan heard the curtain draw back. Christa smiled as if it were Christmas. "Uncle Clay! We was just talkin' about you."

"Were you now?"

She jumped up from the ground and covered the short distance to him, wrapping her arms around his middle as if she hadn't seen him in months. He chuckled, his hands going under her arms as he lifted her high. "Lower your voice, sweet potato," he chided, "or the whole town'll hear."

Christa must have barely weighed as much as a small sack of potatoes, but Meagan was sure if she weighed more than a barrel of nails, Clay would have lifted her with the same ease. He may have been on the lean side, but his arms and chest were solid with muscle and strong. She felt her face warm at the fuzzy memory of being held against him.

"How's our patient? She awake?" He directed his gaze Meagan's way; she was certain her cheeks must be blazing berry red after such thoughts of him.

He looked as if he'd come fresh from the barber. His face was clean-shaven, his hair still damp with a slight curl at the ends. A pleasant aroma of wood smoke and sunshine drifted from him, reminding Meagan of her own disgusting condition. Embarrassed, she almost wished she had thought to slip beneath the cover and feign sleep as she'd done before. His smile came open and honest, offering no criticism, and she managed a feeble one, unable to prevent her lips from turning up when looking at him.

"Good afternoon," he said to her as he set Christa back on her feet.

She nodded in turn.

"How are you feeling?"

"Fairly well, all things considering."

His gaze dropped to one of her bound hands. "I imagine they must still give you a good deal of pain."

She felt awkward discussing her wretched condition. "Penny's cures help. But it'll be nice doing things for myself again and not having to depend on others."

She couldn't read his expression as he turned his head away. He acted guarded, as if he suddenly didn't want to discuss the matter. She hoped her comment hadn't come across as unthankful.

"Not that I'm not beholden to every one of you. I'm grateful for all you've done."

"Do you like the flowers I brought?" Christa asked.

At the child's question, Meagan noticed the spray of yellow, blue, and white wildflowers sitting inside a chipped mug on the ground nearby. A few of the stems hung crooked.

"Mama used the same kind of flowers in her wedding bouquet. She said they made her feel like she was holding sunshine. So, bein' as you can't go outside, I brought some to you." Christa ducked her head, acting shy. Before Meagan could thank her, she went on, "Mr. Matthis said I was silly to pick useless plants that was just gonna wither up anyhow, but Mama said it was fine and he just don't know how womenfolk think."

"As if any man does," Meagan heard Clay mumble.

"Sorry some got broke. That's how I got stung. See?" Christa held up her arm. A pink bump swelled near her elbow. "The flowers was growin' near the livery, and a bee stung me. Jinx said it musta been guardin' the flowers and I didn't ask permission from it to take 'em, but Mama thinks Jinx is full of hogwash."

Clay snorted, abruptly stifling a laugh. Meagan didn't know who Jinx was, except that he made the stews Penny spoon-fed her, and assumed he must be quite the colorful character from the little she'd heard.

She smiled. "I'm awful sorry you got stung, Christa, but I thank you for the flowers. They do brighten up the room."

The girl's smile came just as bright.

"Off with you then," Clay said good-naturedly. "Your mama will be looking for you two."

"Can we name your horse?" Livvie blurted.

"What?" Clay's eyebrows lifted in bewilderment.

"Pa gave us permission to come up with a name for his," Livvie went on, "and Christa wants to name it some silly name. But I want to name it something else."

"Princess Rose is not a silly name!" Christa insisted.

"Is so. Anyhow, Miss Meagan said you might like a name for your horse, too. That way I can name one, and Christa can name the other."

Clay looked at Meagan. Embarrassed, she averted her gaze.

"Well, I can't think of a reason why not. With all that's been going on this past month, I haven't had time to give it much thought." He gave a preoccupied nod. "You can name my horse. On the condition I approve your choice. And Princess Rose won't work. It's a stallion."

Christa looked puzzled.

"A boy horse, dummy," Livvie supplied.

"Stop calling me that!"

"Livvie, you know how your mama feels about name-calling. I think it's time the two of you scoot," Clay urged, pulling back the curtain as a sign for them to go. "I'm sure your mama has more chores for you with suppertime approaching."

" 'Bye, Miss Meagan," Livvie said and hurried through. Clay playfully swatted her backside. She shrieked, then giggled, darting away.

" 'Bye, Miss Meagan," Christa chimed in after her big sister and followed, squealing as Clay tried to do the same to her and she blocked his effort with her tiny hands.

"Hard to believe," Clay said once the children left, "but according to Penny, those two were once leery of strangers, and Christa was shy. Since living in Silverton, they've shed their reserve like old skins. Livvie's bolder, not always a good thing, and Christa's vocabulary has grown by leaps and bounds. It's a wonder those two haven't picked up the vulgarities many of the miners use, though their grammar has gotten worse."

"They're sweet. Christa reminds me of someone I know."

"Oh?"

Meagan smiled, unwilling to admit the child reminded her of herself, especially at that age. Her ma always said she walked with her head in the clouds with all her daydreaming. Thoughts of her ma increased the ache in her heart, and she changed the subject to one more manageable.

"I'm sorry I interfered. I had no right speaking to them about naming your horse, not without talking it over with you. I only hoped to end their quarrel."

"No harm done." Clay chuckled wryly, as if his mind lay elsewhere. "It's a crying shame, but Livvie grows less tolerant of Christa with each day that passes. I imagine all siblings struggle with problems. Especially as they grow older."

Meagan sensed his last words weren't about the girls. They also made her think of Wayne. She couldn't avoid the issue forever but wondered if the pain of loss and burden of guilt would ever ease.

"Mr.—I'm sorry. I don't know how to call you."

"Oversight on my part. Full name's Clayton Thomas Burke. Folks call me Clay. And you're Meagan. . .?"

"Foster. Middle name's Elizabeth." It seemed odd exchanging official introductions; she felt as if she'd known this man her entire lifetime when in reality it must be nearing a week. Ever since she'd opened her eyes and looked into his, she'd felt a keen regard toward him. "You can call me Meagan, bein' that's how everyone knows me."

"Meagan it is." He smiled, his eyes lighting up, and she had the oddest sensation of her insides doing a somersault.

"Thing is. . ." She noted the small croak in her voice that had nothing to do with disuse and cleared her throat. "You've done so much already—finding me, takin' care of me. I know I have no right to ask for anything more, bein' as how I'm nothin' but a stranger. . . ." She hesitated, wondering if he would think she asked too much.

"Go ahead, Meagan. Tell me what's on your mind."

The way he spoke her name—quiet and deep—gave her delicious chills, and she could drown in those eyes of his and be grateful for the experience. "I have a favor I'd like to ask of you. . .Clay. . .that is, if you wouldn't mind."

His ready smile gave her all the encouragement she needed.

Chapter 5

Clay exited the hotel, his mind so caught up in the last few minutes that he walked right past where Kurt and Derek sat in two chairs in the shade and had to retrace his steps. Most of Silverton's storefronts had no boards laid out for walking, though a few did. Clay surmised the hotel would have done far better to replace their scratchy hides for comfortable beds with feather mattresses than to waste time and expense nailing boards together underfoot, when a man's boots got just as dusty after stepping off them.

Kurt's aunt ran a hotel in Jasperville, and he told Clay that Silverton's public mode of lodging maintained some of the meanest standards he'd come across. The town had sprung up after a recent silver strike and, with more merchants and miners arriving each day, hadn't been in existence long enough for improvements. "A few months," Jinx had said, which by the cook's standards of recording time could mean anywhere from two to twelve months. Clay felt it must be the former, as shabby as the town appeared. All except for the fine boardwalk of smoothed-down planks, of course.

"Clay," Kurt greeted. "Something on your mind?"

"Or someone?" Derek added.

His amused words sparked the memory of his brother ribbing him in the days they got along before Derek left home. He grinned at Clay, and for a fraction of time, Clay wished things could go back to the way they once were. No need telling either man that he pondered the inane use of outside flooring; they might think him as crazy as many assumed Meagan was, and he winced when he recalled the nickname "Mad Meagan" that some of the miners now called her.

"As a matter of fact, I do have something I'd like to discuss." Clay addressed Kurt, planting one boot in the street and propping the other on the edge of the boardwalk. He casually rested his arm against his leg and leaned forward. "Meagan wants to visit the site where her family's buried. As I don't know where that is, I'd like you to come along."

"Be happy to," Kurt replied. "It would also give me the opportunity to take a look around the area, get more of an idea what happened, maybe rustle up some clues."

"I can help there," Derek added. "Don't plan on making a second trip to visit the homestead for a while, and until we can all sit down peaceably and discuss what we aim to do about Pa's legacy, I have too much time on my hands." He cracked a smile. "As Ma used to say, 'Idle hands make the devil's tools.'"

And some not so idle. The irritated recollection of Derek's recent thievery of the map rushed through Clay's mind. Regardless, the black fury that once roiled inside had tempered to weary bitterness. A week ago, Clay might have strongly objected to his brother including himself in the events, unasked. He didn't anticipate spending more time than necessary in Derek's company, but strength grew in numbers. And Clay had no idea what they might find or if they might run across the outlaws responsible if those men returned to Meagan's former home for whatever reason. Illogical, but such men couldn't be called rational. Still, he couldn't deny Meagan her one request on the weakness of his speculation.

"So you have little doubt that the fire was no accident?" Clay directed his question to Kurt, ignoring Derek's not-so-subtle introduction of the mine, a subject he often brought up and Clay just as often avoided.

"The boy had been shot. Found him outside. I doubt his own ma shot him. Also, bein' as how she was trapped inside—barred in from the look of things— she would've never had a chance."

"Who would do such a despicable act?" Clay shook his head, disgusted.

"I have a hunch," Kurt admitted, "but don't want to say anything till I have more to go on."

Clay narrowed his eyes in disbelief. "Surely you don't think—"

"Meagan?" He finished Clay's question. "No. She's mighty peculiar, all right, claiming no recollection of what happened. But I doubt she's a cold-blooded killer with a heart so black she'd murder her own kin. She's much too distraught over what happened—what she can recall of it at any rate."

"Poor little gal." Derek's tone was sympathetic. "Left alone in the world and so young. Come to think of it, she must have kin elsewhere—didn't she mention a stepfather?" He directed his question to Clay.

Clay doubted a man like Landon McClinton cared about the family he'd left to struggle on their own and was surprised his brother would ask, owing to the personal history they shared. Unable to curb his mounting irritation, for the first time Clay addressed him. "She did, but I doubt he'd be concerned. You're right about one thing, though—it is hard being left alone in the world without a soul to turn to or to care what happens. At least Meagan has us to help her through this. And I reckon a group of concerned strangers makes far better company than an estranged family member who puts his own desires first and lets his family suffer." As soon as the words left his mouth, Clay felt petty, wishing he could retrieve them, though he did nothing to make allowances for his jab.

From the wounded look in Derek's eyes, he got the message. He rose from his chair. "Well, I reckon I've wasted enough time in the shade. I'd best see if Penny needs me. She has her hands full these days, and the girls have been a thorn in her side. This mining town is no place for them." He looked at Clay. "Once we find what we came for, I can take them home where they belong."

Clay refused to rise to the bait. "No one's stopping you."

"And I told you, I'm not searching unless you and Linda ride with me. That's the way Pa wanted it, and that's the way it's gonna stand."

Clay was surprised to hear Derek defend their excuse for a father. When they'd first reunited in Silverton, he'd been as disgusted with Pa as Clay had been. Now Derek spoke as if he'd forgotten all the old man had done to them. Before Clay could think of how to answer, Derek stepped off the boardwalk and strode toward his wagon.

"I know I haven't any right speaking on matters that don't concern me," Kurt said, watching Derek's back, "but I'm going to say my piece anyhow, since Linda's my wife and it concerns her. And I don't like seeing her unhappy." He shifted his attention to Clay. "I've known Derek going on a week, besides what little I saw of him when he came through Jasperville. He's a good man. Marshal Wilson wouldn't have befriended him had he not seen something admirable in his character. Sure, he's made his share of mistakes. He'd be the first to admit it and has told Linda and me what a selfish cuss he was, staying away while your ma was ill—"

Clay raised his hand for the deputy to stop. "I've heard all this—"

"What he hasn't told you," Kurt went on, deaf to Clay's words, "is that when he returned to Missouri after your ma died, he wanted to stay. But he didn't feel he had the right to ask or that you'd want him near. He did the best he knew how, and if you ask me, that's what counts when all is said and done."

Kurt moved to his feet, tugging the brim of his hat down to shade his eyes. "Truth is. . ." He looked at Derek, who Clay noticed had stopped in the street to greet a miner. The deputy shifted his gaze back to Clay. "I'd trust that man with my very life. And Linda's."

Lost in thought, Clay watched Kurt stride off after Derek. His brother seemed to have acquired an ability for easily gaining loyalty and friendships. Too bad he couldn't have shown the same respect and consideration toward his family.

Such sour thoughts once made Clay feel righteous in his resentment. Now they only made him feel. . .sour.

∽

Penny bustled through the curtain, a cheery smile spreading across her face when she saw Meagan awake and alert. "How are you this fine morning?"

Meagan didn't even try to smile. "My hands still ache something fierce."

"That's to be expected." Penny set down the clay bowl she carried. "Let's have a look then, shall we?"

Meagan held her breath as Penny unknotted and unwound the bandage from one of her hands. She had glimpsed them before when Penny tended her, but it had been enough to turn her stomach, and she'd averted her gaze every time after that. On this occasion, she forced herself to look. Now, as then, she grimaced at the shiny, rose-colored skin, save for sickly white blisters that had at least diminished in size and number. But the improvement amazed her. New skin had even started to grow in places.

"Praise the Lord for His mercy and goodness," Penny exclaimed, clearly pleased with the results. "Mind, you'll likely have scars, but you're mending nicely. Can you move your fingers?"

Meagan did so and winced. "They feel tight. Like the skin is stretched over bone."

"Don't look so sullen. 'Tis also a good sign of healing." Penny unwound the bandage of the other hand, then picked up the bowl, which contained the sticky paste she used for her poultices.

"And they itch something awful," Meagan added.

Penny laughed. "Another good sign."

"Just what is that?"

Penny seemed surprised by the question, since she'd used a concoction like it twice each day. But whereas Meagan never wanted details before, now her interest was piqued.

"A wee bit of herbs and extracts of plants my mother taught were good for such purposes. I don't know them by name, only by sight. Her mother taught her to use them—my grandmother Kimama. She was of the Eastern Shoshone tribe. . . ." Penny continued to speak of her family as she spread the meal-like paste on a clean cloth and wrapped it around Meagan's hand. The warm poultice soothed her skin, and the itching eased. Meagan watched as Penny did the same to her other hand.

"There now," she exclaimed softly with a smile when she finished. "You'll be up and about in no time. How's your head feeling?" She leaned forward and applied gentle pressure to the lump, no longer as big as an egg. "It seems to be improving, as well."

"You're so good to me." Meagan's voice came quiet. "Why? I don't deserve such kindnesses."

Penny regarded her in surprise. "Whyever not? What have you done that's so terrible?"

Meagan shifted her gaze to the blanket.

"God doesn't want any of His children to suffer."

"You don't know what I've done."

"No matter. No sin lies beyond forgiveness."

Meagan only shook her head.

"Is this about what happened to you?"

She didn't answer. The memory may no longer exist, but her guilt lingered. How could she have left Ma and Wayne like that? After her talk with the deputy, a fleeting recollection had returned of walking through the wilds in her need to find help. Wayne had been sleeping, and she'd been unable to rouse him. . . . Something prickled in the back of her mind, something that urged her to remember. She shook her head, hoping the feeling would leave.

"There now," Penny soothed. "I think I know what you need to lift your spirits." With a mysterious smile, she retrieved the bowl and rose to her feet. "I'll be back shortly."

Alone, Meagan pondered her bleak situation, then thought of these people who'd done so much for her. Strangers—but they treated her like a cherished family member, spending time with her, taking care of her needs, even trying to make her smile. Something Meagan never thought possible until she spent time with Clay. He rarely spoke, but when he did, his words, whether trivial or significant, made Meagan feel good inside. Especially when he tried to be funny. After their first awkward moments, she enjoyed his company, as well as the children's. And their mother, Penny, was the kindest woman Meagan had ever met. It was only because of her Meagan had broken her silence. She couldn't abide listening to Penny suffer the brunt of blame the cruel man had tried to place on her for the fire, and only because her blood was part Indian.

Thoughts of the fire again took Meagan to that dreadful day. . . .

"No, stop it," she whispered, pressing her bandaged hands to her head. She couldn't let herself remember. . .so much lay in a haze she hoped never would resurface, because she didn't think she could bear the agony of knowing.

A razor-edged sliver of truth festered beneath her goose down layer of forgetfulness and hinted at something so terrible, she was certain it would make these good people despise her and want nothing more to do with her should they also learn the facts. She'd borne so much grief and didn't think she could endure Penny's disgust. Or Clay's rejection. Dwelling on tragic events would only bring her final ruination; she was sure of it. In disregarding what little she knew and trying to never recall those forgotten, shadowed areas lay her best course, and she feared returning to the site of her former home for that very reason. But her desire to bid her loved ones farewell and pay her last respects loomed more powerful than her fears. She owed them that much since she hadn't been there when they met their deaths. Or had she? No, she couldn't have been; she never would have walked away had she been in her right mind. Though after hearing two men talk outside the curtain's partition, she knew some in this hotel thought her crazy.

A persistent irritation jabbed at the forefront of her mind.

What if being there brings the memories back?

Meagan closed her eyes. She couldn't stay away; she just couldn't. If and when the time came, she would have to muster up strength to deal with the situation then.

Penny returned, Linda behind her, breaking Meagan from her relentless brooding. Both women bore bowls, containers, and cloths that made Meagan lift her brows in curious wonder.

The women smiled, and Meagan's heart gave a little jump of expectation.

Chapter 6

"Clay, would you look in on Meagan?" Penny gave a sideways nod to the cubicle, her arms full of dirty linens. "I need to see to these."

Clay watched her swift retreat in surprise. Not that he minded spending time with Meagan; he often devised excuses for that very thing. But he thought it odd Penny would ask, odder still she would leave without awaiting his answer.

Meagan had long passed the critical stage and was slowly on the mend in body. As for her emotions, Clay suspected they were still in tatters and would remain that way for a while. Only time could heal deep wounds involved in the loss of loved ones and under such dreadful circumstances. He wished he could do something more for the plucky little sparrow, a term he'd begun to apply to her in his thoughts. Dirty, forlorn, and bedraggled, like a weak and helpless but brave little bird who'd flown through a bad storm. . . .

He stepped past the curtain and gaped, coming to a swift halt. His eyes soon stung from holding them wide in incredulity. Unblinking. Uncomprehending. . .

"Unbelievable."

He whispered the last to himself as he looked at the golden-haired angel in the blue-sprigged frock. Shyly, she regarded him. The black cinders and dirt washed from her hair, it shone dark golden, thick, and lush over her shoulders; the flame of an oil lamp caught glimmers of a lighter hue, like sprinklings of gold dust touching the strands. Her face scrubbed clean, the soft rose of her creamy skin heightened as he stared. But he couldn't help himself.

She broke eye contact and looked down at the blanket. Only then did Clay manage to force his gaze to something else. The flowers Christa brought. He wondered how they would look in Meagan's hair. The thought brought his wondering gaze back to her shining tresses.

Silence grew thick, and he knew he should speak. To gawk at her wasn't polite.

"You look better." He could have slapped himself at his gross understatement and lack of tact. His ma had taught him deportment and how to conduct himself in a lady's presence. "I mean, as if you're feeling better," he amended.

That didn't sound much improved—could he not have managed to pick and utter one of the many compliments revolving like a windmill through his head? He could have kissed her hand in homage to the princess, as Christa called her, when she offered him an understanding though still timid smile.

At the thought of giving her any kind of kiss, his face warmed.

"I, uh. . ." He scanned the confined room. Never before had it felt so small, and he scrambled in his mind for something to save him from the invisible noose that pulled tight around his neck. His eyes lit on the books sitting where he'd left them. He grabbed the top one of poetry. "Have you had a chance to thumb through this yet?" As soon as he asked, he remembered her condition and glanced at her bandaged hands.

Stupid, stupid. Of all the asinine remarks to make, that would range in the top few. . . .

"I was never taught how." She shrugged and smiled again.

Clay silently thanked her for disregarding his thoughtless question.

"Would you like me to read it? To you?" He tugged at his collar, realizing he sounded like a callow youth who lacked the ability.

"Please." Her eyes sparkled with anticipation. At least she showed confidence in his skill, even if he felt as though his tongue might stick to the roof of his mouth if he tried. Why was it suddenly so dry?

The poppy blue in her dress brought out the golden flecks in her eyes. Her dark lashes made them glow even brighter.

He decided he needed a dipper of water first and felt grateful Penny had left a container behind.

"That's remarkable that you know your letters," Meagan said as he drank. "I never met a man who could read. Except you. And your friends."

"Uh, yeah." He didn't sound as if he could string two decent words together, let alone read them. "My ma was a schoolmarm back East. When she lived there." *Of course when she lived there—when else?* Now if he could just get other things to work right, like his brain.

Clay took a seat on the ground, wondering if he sat too close. She leaned forward in anticipation. "I never had anyone read to me before. Ma didn't know her letters well, even if we'd had books to read. She tried to teach me what she did know, but there wasn't time. Always too much work to do." A waft of her fresh scent rushed over him, reminding him of a sweet meadow of spring flowers.

Much too close.

He scooted back as far as the canvas wall allowed and noted the curious tilt of her head. He'd sensed her attractive features beneath the layers of soot, but he'd never taken her for a beauty. The most beautiful woman he'd ever seen. . . He swallowed over the fast-growing lump in his throat and flipped the book open at random.

Read, he commanded himself.

He cleared his throat and began, " 'So far as our story approaches the end, which do you pity the most of us three? My friend, or the mistress of my friend with her wanton eyes, or me. . . ?' "

The heat building inside burned through his face and over his ears. "Uh, let's try another one. That poem sounds like it began earlier in the book, though I started with the first line, but I'm sure I can find something more suited to the occasion." He flipped pages, figuring the second title that caught his eye—"The Englishman in Italy"—would give no further embarrassment.

" '*Piano di Sor–rento*,' " he stumbled over the foreign words, " '*For–tù, Fortù*, my beloved one, sit here by my side. . .on my knees. . .put up both little feet—' " His last words came out a bare rasp.

He flipped the pages again, in danger of tearing them as he pushed them aside, as if the printed words might somehow take a mind of their own and rise from the pages, blaring out their unseemly messages. The heat crawled to the back of his neck. "Time's Revenge" sounded far safer and much more distant. He heaved a calming breath and again cleared his throat. " 'I've a Friend, over the sea; I like him, but he loves me. . . .' "

He slammed the book shut, noting the author, Robert Browning, and promising himself that Penny would pay for her little joke on him. *Dramatic Lyrics* was the misleading title the book had been given. A "book of poems," his sweetly conniving sister-in-law had said—more like a book of love sonnets! He'd read poetry—before he went to live in Mr. Dougherty's storeroom. Old Lady Harper had a shelf of books he'd "borrowed" when he was sure he could take one without her knowledge in between the many chores she allotted him—but that book of poetry that had appealed to his boyish senses and told of a horseman's ghostly ride held nothing like what this book contained.

Clay didn't dare look at Meagan. The words he'd read lingered in the air, taking on an uncomfortable association with the woman who sat so vulnerable and trusting at his side. They wove a closeness that made him all too conscious of the scant distance separating them. Every whisper of movement she made, her sweet scent enticing, her long fall of silken hair tempting his touch. . .

Afraid his hands might actually betray his thoughts, he clasped the book tighter. If it were made of glass, it might have cracked in his desperate grip.

Silence crept on uneasy toes between them but seemed to snicker behind its shielded mouth at Clay.

"That was Penny's book," he said in apology. "I'd never read it before now and had no idea. . . ." His words trailed off.

"What about the other book?" Her voice also sounded hoarse. "Would you read that one to me?"

"Uh, I suppose." Clay withheld a groan, wondering if Penny had left behind the first book she'd offered as part of a plan, knowing this might happen. At least that book wouldn't make his insides crawl or shock his listener with prose that felt far too familiar, as if the intimate words applied to Meagan and himself and not two fictional characters the writer had fabricated. He'd heard the message of the other book before, so he knew there would be no undesirable surprises. That was the most he could say for reading it.

With a sigh, he picked up the huge volume Penny had wrapped in cloth, unwound it, and laid it on his lap. He opened to the first page.

" 'In the beginning God created the heaven and the earth. And the earth was without form, and void; and darkness was upon the face of the deep. And the Spirit of God moved upon the face of the waters. . . .' "

Feeling calmer, Clay settled into a more comfortable position and continued to read aloud.

∽

"How are you feeling? You sure you're ready for this?"

Meagan smiled at the almost constant consideration Clay showed her.

"I'm much better," she assured for what seemed the hundredth time that morning. "I'll sit inside and won't do any walking till we get there."

He rested his hand at her elbow even before they reached the wagon and sent her insides all topsy-turvy again. But this new sensation that came with frequency the past week and a half had nothing to do with the fast-diminishing lump on her head. She had recovered to the point that she'd left the bed and had taken to joining the Burke family at their meals. This was her first outing.

"Something paining you?" Clay asked in concern. He looked down at her hands, wound in bandages, though not so thickly as before.

She hadn't realized he watched her every expression and had seen her wince. "I was thinking how last time I took a journey it was months by wagon with Ma and Pa."

"You never did mention what happened to him."

Meagan smiled sadly. "His health was always poor. We hoped moving west would change that, but he died on the journey. That was near two years back. . . and now settlers will be coming all the way from the East by locomotive, their journey taking less than a week. It just doesn't seem possible, does it?"

Meagan looked past the small, bustling town and snow-topped mountains eastward, as if she could already see the column of smoke from a distant locomotive. What would it be like to travel by such means? Would she ever get the opportunity? She couldn't imagine riding through wide barren plains without feeling the scorching rays from the sun, or traveling so high in the pine-laden mountains, without freezing from sudden snowstorms or getting dizzy. How wonderful to ride through the West by railroad and suffer no ill effects, only to sit and look at the beauty of the land laid out all around her. . . .

"Any time you're ready, I think they're waiting on us," Clay urged, his voice quiet. Tenderness misted his eyes, making her heart beat a little faster. Their color was the clear blue of a mountain lake, and the manner in which he looked at her made her feel light-headed—despite their low altitude or the lack of a lump on her noggin.

Her mouth too dry to speak, she nodded, and they walked to the wagon. The two couples and children smiled at their approach.

Penny had insisted she come along, since some of the seeds and plants she used, both for remedies and her beautiful pouches, grew near the river. At supper the previous night, she'd assured her husband, who opposed the idea because of "possible danger," that she could handle a firearm as well as any man—and hadn't she proven so when they first met? At her claim, Derek had grinned, and they shared a private look Meagan had since wondered about.

Whereas Derek would prefer his wife remain behind, Kurt wouldn't hear of such a notion with regard to Linda. The spirited redhead offered to stay in the hotel with the children, but Kurt refused, and Meagan assumed he feared for her security. She knew something of their past through supper conversation, including Linda's recent abduction by a crooked sheriff from her hometown. Two outlaw brothers, wanted dead or alive, had worked for him and his cohort. Kurt wanted to take no chances with Linda's safety should the pair of outlaws arrive in Silverton.

Meagan had asked Clay to come, wanting his support more than all the others, so it turned out all of the Burke clan, their spouses, and the children would accompany Meagan. Penny and Linda had even packed a picnic for the occasion, thanks to Jiny's generosity in giving them supplies from his kitchen.

Still unable to use her wrapped hands without difficulty—Penny insisted the bandages stay on, her condition for this trip—Meagan pondered how to climb into the wagon bed. She stood alone at the rear, the others having congregated to the front and sides, talking in groups. She heard the scuff of shoes in the dirt as someone approached from behind. "Need some help?" Clay's deep voice came to her, and before she knew what was happening, he swept her up into his strong arms.

Her heart beating as fast as the chirps of a nearby bird, she blinked up into his shuttered eyes, only inches from her own, and held her breath. His heart raced just as fast beneath her arm trapped against his chest. Yet before she could wonder if he might actually kiss her—and, oh how her head swam at the sweet thought—he gently deposited her in the back of the wagon.

She could barely think, much less frame words to thank him. He tipped his hat and grinned before striding away, sending her heart, much battered from all its rapid drumming, straight into her stomach. Or so it felt. What was wrong with her?

She'd seen Clay every day for more than a week. Going on two. When she was laid up, he'd visited and they'd talked. He'd read to her from the Good Book, which so intrigued Meagan, she had asked him to read from it whenever they were together. But here she sat, acting as if she'd never seen the man. No, that wasn't exactly right. . .more to the point, acting as if she'd like to see much more of him. Alone. To sit by his side and put her little feet upon his knees, as in the poem he'd read. . . .

Livvie and Christa appeared, breaking into Meagan's wistful thinking. They climbed in the back, chattering about their upcoming adventure. Face warm, Meagan forced her mind to abandon the dangerous territory of Clayton Burke and focus instead on the girls. Christa held a doll with a cloth face and black seeds sewn for eyes and nose, red ones for a mouth.

"Is that your doll?" Meagan asked, smiling at the child.

Christa nodded. "I had another, but it got ruint, so Mama made this one for my birthday." She hugged the rag doll close, and Meagan noticed its dress matched Christa's red calico. She thought of her own doll, "ruint" when Wayne, as a tot, used to gnaw on it and bit off one of its button eyes. She, at five years old, had slugged him when she saw Jane dangling from his mouth, but not hard enough to hurt, though he'd squalled as if she did. The recollection brought a bittersweet jab to her heart. She and Wayne fought, like all brothers and sisters, but they had their good times, too. Now she only had memories.

"Dolls are for babies," Livvie staunchly remarked.

Meagan noted Christa's downcast eyes as she hugged her doll closer.

"I know how special they are," she told Christa. "I had a doll once. Had her till I was nine years old, if I remember right." She chuckled. "Truth is, I can't remember when I stopped carrying her with me."

Her words brought back Christa's radiant smile. Livvie only grunted.

Linda climbed inside, and Kurt followed, resting a rifle over his legs. Meagan hoped his defensive act was ingrained, that of a lawman's routine, and not a sign that he expected trouble. He caught her glance at the weapon and gave a reassuring smile.

With everyone packed inside, the space grew cramped. Penny sat beside her husband, who drove the wagon, and Clay rode behind on horseback. As they traveled, from time to time, Meagan glimpsed his fine form through the gap in the canvas tarpaulin that covered the wagon bed. The creaks and rattles of the wagon soon became natural, and the dreaming of which her ma so often accused her once more took wing in Meagan's heart.

What would it be like to sit beside him in the shade, away from all eyes, with his arm around her shoulders? Or perhaps near a glowing hearth as he read to her from that poetry book, those words becoming theirs. . .to run her fingers along his strong jaw and feel his lips brush against hers? Cool as refreshing water or warm as the morning sun? She pondered what it might feel like to kiss Clay, to belong to him completely, as Penny belonged to Derek and Linda to Kurt. She would pass her eighteenth year come July, already past the conventional age of marrying, according to her ma, who'd wed Meagan's pa at sixteen. . . .

"So, tell us, Meagan, how did you come to live in the wilds?"

The abrupt question probed into her pleasant daydream.

Linda's eyes regarded her with friendship, nothing cruel or superior about them. Meagan was sure by now these good people were rife with curiosity regarding her history and couldn't begrudge their interest. But she was extremely grateful Linda couldn't read her mind! She might think she *was* a woman from the wilds, or more to the point, a wild woman with little sense.

"When we left the wagon train, Ma met Landon McClinton. He was panning for gold. She didn't have enough provisions to feed us and couldn't continue to Oregon, so she married him and settled here. He made his home where he searched and found enough gold dust to scrape out a living. Last month he left for Carson City when he got wind that a former partner who'd robbed him was staying there. . . . Landon left us behind to guard the land from claim jumpers." Her last words came slow as the reason why her stepfather left resurfaced without trouble, when before it had been lost beyond the dark curtains that clouded her memory.

"Claim jumpers?" Linda and Kurt shared an alarmed glance, which made Meagan wonder, but she felt more anxious with her own predicament than curious over theirs.

Were those bleak moments lost to her coming back? If so, she might remember all that happened, and she wasn't certain she could bear it. The dread that she might somehow have been responsible for her family's demise ate away at her newly acquired calm. If outsiders had done it, why had they spared her? Why were her hands so badly burned, but, save for the lump on her head, the rest of her body suffered only minor injuries?

"I think Whisper would be a nice name, bein' as how Princess Rose won't work." Christa's voice broke the quiet.

"Whisper's a stupid name." Livvie rolled her eyes. "Whoever heard of a horse called Whisper?"

"Uncle Clay's horse makes a whispery sound when it whickers."

"All horses do that."

"Uncle Clay's horse does it even more," Christa argued with a pout.

"I think what you girls need is some fresh air and sunshine," Linda broke in, likely an effort to bring peace before yet another skirmish arose between sisters.

"Aye," Christa said, acting more grown up than her years and hugging her doll close. "Ruby and I want to pick flowers."

"Ruby is your doll's name?" Meagan asked, grateful for her mind's reprieve. "That's pretty. Rubies are rare jewels. I've never seen one, but I hear they're dark red in color like your dresses."

Christa beamed at her.

"I wanna go outside. My legs are all cramped up stiff from sitting like this." Livvie approved Linda's suggestion, though her words came out as a complaint.

"Derek," Linda called up. "The girls want to walk."

The wagon rolled to a stop, and the two crawled out, eager to explore the land as they followed along. If Meagan felt able, she would have joined them. She'd always preferred the wide outdoors to a stuffy room, and trapped behind the tarpaulin, she could see little of the broad sagebrush plain.

"Are you feeling all right?" Linda's mouth drew down in concern.

Meagan didn't feel well at all but assured Linda she was. What ailed her couldn't be treated with rest in bed and poultices.

Chapter 7

Y ou two get restless already?" Clay greeted the girls as they scampered through the scrub and short grass toward him. "It hasn't even been an hour."

"Can I ride?" Christa greeted, her dark eyes shining as she tilted her head all the way up to see his face.

"I thought you wanted to pick flowers," Livvie said.

"Right now I want to ride with Uncle Clay." Christa raised her arms high to be picked up.

Sensing the friction between the two, Clay wrapped his reins around the pommel.

"All right, sweet potato, get on up here." While holding the saddle with one hand, he leaned down, wrapped an arm under both of Christa's as she clung to his shoulder the best she could while holding her doll, and hoisted her up in front of him. She weighed so little, and he recalled Penny's concern when she and Derek first arrived in Silverton. Christa had been sickly but with rest had soon recovered, though she still looked young for her scant years and weighed little more than his bedroll.

"Now then, what's wrong?" he asked once they were underway and following the wagon.

"I don't like Livvie," Christa complained. "She's mean. She never used to be thatta way, not before we moved to Silverton and she started spending time with Jinx and Tucker. I like them, but it seems she's always in their company. And she's always bossin' me around and tellin' me what to do like Tucker does Jinx."

Clay recalled Penny's qualms that her girls might pick up the poor habits of the miners they lived among and watched every day. Too bad they didn't spend more time in Gentleman George's company. Not only would their speech come out proper, they might learn a manner or two.

"I imagine you'll be friends again soon," he soothed, though he had no idea how to counsel his niece. Mrs. Harper and Mr. Dougherty both had small children, but Clay had never been accepted as a member of either family, treated more as a servant without a logical thought of his own. Not that he minded Mr. Dougherty's gruff instructions, since he considered himself as making his own living there, but in Old Lady Harper's household, her frequent condescension and slights against "that dreadful orphan boy" had stung more than he'd let on.

He'd never had much of a true family and desired to say and do the right thing by his niece, aside from the fact that should he fail in his duties as an uncle and lead Christa astray, he might expose himself to a dose of Penny's motherly wrath. And lately, she'd been acting more than a little strange.

"Livvie doesn't wanna be my friend no more," Christa insisted. "Not ever. She doesn't like nothin' about me."

"That can hurt," Clay commiserated. "But you mustn't let her hateful words get the best of you, 'cause they can squeeze all the happiness clean out your middle—and then where would you be?" He tightened his arm around her midsection in a squeeze of mock admonishment, and she giggled. "All tight and hard and cross, that's where. You've gotta learn to rise above others' taunts, Christa, be satisfied with who you are. If Livvie doesn't like you, I reckon that's her problem, not yours. Just ignore her. Eventually she'll get to wondering why you're not bothered any longer and might even want to make peace when she sees her taunts don't affect you as they once did."

Christa craned her head around as far as it would go to look at him. "Is that what you and Pa did when you were young?" Her earnest eyes shone up at him.

He grinned at the idea that she considered twenty old, but her innocent question brought to mind his boyhood squabbles with Derek, usually rectified by sundown. A nostalgic pang stung him, and he wished things could go back to what they once were, then felt surprised at his change of heart. The situation as it stood wasn't Clay's fault, despite Penny's and Linda's gentle rebukes to make him feel otherwise. Derek had created the breach by stealing the maps. Clay had every right to be cross and not trust his brother.

Christa returned her gaze to the wagon, sparing Clay the need to reply.

"I don't care if she likes Ruby or not. Miss Meagan likes her. And Miss Meagan's nice. Pretty, too, like a princess in one of Grandda's tales. You think she's pretty, Uncle Clay?"

His awkwardness advanced to a loftier height. "Uh, sure."

"I asked Mama if she could come live with us and be my sister, bein' as how she hasn't got family no more. But Mama said she'll likely wanna start her own, since she's a woman and not a child." She craned her head to look up at him again. "I think you should marry her, Uncle Clay. Then we can keep her with us forever."

Her earnest remark so staggered Clay he nearly let go of the reins. He tightened his grip as the leather strips burned through his fingers, adjusting his hold before he lost all control and his horse took the bit and galloped off. Much as their innocent conversation about sibling rivalry had done.

With a keen sort of desperation, he hoped Christa would drift to another subject, as she was apt to do, or run out of steam for the current one and grow silent.

"Please? Say you will. I don't want her going away when her hands get better and she doesn't need us to wait on her no more." She blinked up at him, clearly expecting an answer.

"Christa, I can't marry her." He scrambled for a suitable reply. When she didn't look satisfied he added, "Such matters aren't even discussed till after the courting is done."

"What's courtin'?"

Beneath his hat, his ears burned in his discomfort. "I never courted a woman, but I hear it's when two people take a liking to each other and spend time in one another's company."

"You've been spending time with her and reading to her," she said with childish wisdom so lacking in adult sense.

"Well. . .yes." His face grew uncomfortably hot, having little to do with the great ball of sun blazing overhead. Her innocent remark brought to mind the not-so-innocent book of poetry.

"Don't you like her enough to marry her?"

"Sure I do. I mean, no, I can't." He felt as flustered as a boy who knew nothing of love, not that he claimed to know much at all.

"She likes you. I can tell."

He managed to swallow over the lump in his throat. "A person can like another person without wanting to marry them, Christa."

"So you don't wanna marry her?"

How did the conversation lose all semblance of control and speed downhill so fast? He looked ahead to the wagon, hoping Penny might call for her girls, that the wagon might stop for a rest break, that Livvie might backtrack with a question—anything to save him from this current predicament. But no such luck. The wagon plodded on, its occupants not calling out any orders, while Livvie kicked something aside with her foot and bent to collect what Clay assumed was ammunition for her slingshot—not running back with any questions.

He had dug himself into this pit, handing Christa the shovel with which to bury him. Now he had to find a way out before he choked. The neckline of his shirt came low, but his throat was tight; he couldn't seem to draw enough air into his lungs.

"Matters of marriage should be discussed between the two who plan on doing the marrying. Not among outsiders, especially not small children."

His serious explanation triggered the opposite reaction than what he'd desired.

"Then you *do* like Miss Meagan and wanna marry her!" she exclaimed with a smile as big as Christmas.

"No, I didn't say that," he hastily amended. "Only that when and if the time ever comes to talk over the matter, it should be done in private, and only between me and the woman I'm courting." Just saying the words made him uneasy. His hands felt clammy. "But I've got far too much to take care of before I look into finding a wife and settling down."

"You mean the silver mine," she said matter-of-factly, and he sent a sharp glance her way.

"You know about that?"

"Me and Livvie heard Mama and Pa talk when they was alone."

"Seems to me you two eavesdrop a lot more than you should." He spoke with a sense of relief that the conversation had veered to another course. Upon hearing his words, he worried she might get the wrong impression and tried again. "You shouldn't eavesdrop at all. It isn't polite."

"I just did it 'cause Livvie did."

"Like you followed her to the dance hall the other day?"

Christa looked stricken with worry. "You know about that?" she whispered.

"Beulah told me. A woman who works there. I saw her in the tin shop," he hurriedly added. He didn't want his niece to think he'd visited an old pastime and taken to the drink again. She might tell Penny, and, misconception or not, he'd never hear the end of it. In fact, the old temptation hadn't revisited once since he'd found Meagan.

"Mama would take a switch to our backsides if she knew. I just went 'cause Livvie called me 'a lily-livered baby coward' when I said Mama wouldn't like it. We didn't go inside, just looked through the slats in the doors." She sucked in her lower lip. "You won't tell?"

Clay considered her plea. "Only if you promise never to go there again. It's not a place for little girls. Especially good little girls, like your mama is raising you to be."

She nodded in an exaggerated motion. "I won't be bad no more."

"That's good to know. But if you break your word, I'll tell. Promises work both ways."

After solemnly swearing she would stay far from the dance hall, she grew quiet. Clay felt thankful for the stretch of peace and especially that she'd forgotten her childish matchmaking ploys. The last thing he needed was a wife. He had no income, no homestead—certainly no way to provide. Regardless, Christa's words pecked at him like a hen's sharp beak. No matter how he tried, he couldn't erase their association to Meagan from his mind.

Soon Christa wanted down, and Clay brought his horse to a halt. Her glossy dark braids bounced near her waist as she sprinted through small clumps of sagebrush to catch up to Livvie, her animosity toward her sister evidently forgotten. As Clay watched the two walk together, he pondered what a child of Meagan's might look like. Bright yellow hair, golden green eyes, and a smile as potent as sunshine after a long rain. . .

He caught himself and shook his head to clear it. Riding in the hot sun all morning had muddled his thinking. His thoughts sure didn't need to inhabit such trails.

At noon they stopped to eat half of what the women had packed. Clay felt grateful for the strips of meat between slabs of mesquite bread. After a daily diet of Jinx's stews, the women's labors in the kitchen came as a treat, and they'd made enough to feed a small army. In retrospect, he figured that's what they were.

He sat apart from the others, knowing he wouldn't make good company at the moment, but when Meagan came near, he didn't suggest she join the women. Nor did he offer much by way of conversation. Christa's promptings of marriage whined inside his head, and he couldn't help but notice Meagan's confused glances in his direction.

Once they were underway again, Clay relaxed, then grew alert as they approached the area where he'd first found Meagan. Any moment they should arrive at the gravesite, since Kurt mentioned he hadn't buried her family far from their home.

The wagon continued plodding forward. At each minute that elapsed, Clay's amazement increased. He realized how full of pluck Meagan was to have covered such an expanse of ground on foot and in her condition. She was a remarkable girl in every sense of the word, and if Clay had something more than himself to offer, he would take Christa's words to heart. Once he found Pa's mine, maybe then he could consider the prospect—at least tell Meagan how he felt. And he did feel something for her, deep and true and dear, but he certainly wouldn't admit that to his six-year-old niece.

The wagon rolled to a stop after about an hour. Clay looked around him. Nothing but flat scrubland and low hills. Then he noticed it far up ahead. What remained of a small shack stood before a hill. Much of the roof had caved in, and what rocks formed the walls had blackened. A gap stood where a door had been. The entire place looked in danger of collapsing. He wondered what marvel of gravity kept it upright.

Slowly they piled from the wagon, and Clay watched for Meagan. Once she emerged with Kurt's help, he dismounted, his gaze never leaving her slight form. She remained silent as Kurt pointed toward two mounds of dirt. Rocks in the shape of a cross were piled over each one. With hesitant steps, she approached and stood at the site where her loved ones lay buried. Her shoulders bowed, and her head hung low.

Clay wanted nothing more than to go to her but felt she needed time alone. Not once, though, did he take his eyes off her small form.

❧

"Ma, I'm so sorry," Meagan whispered, the guilt overwhelming and pressing in as she dropped to her knees. "If I'd been where I should have, maybe none of this would've ever happened." The details were still sketchy, but since arriving at what remained of her home, bits and pieces grew clearer.

She'd been foolish to come but couldn't pass up the opportunity of being close to her family one last time, to pay her respects. Her gaze shifted to the second mound of dirt, shorter than the first, and her fingertips pressed gently into the fine grains. "Wayne, I'm sorry I yelled at you for cracking the eggs. You couldn't help being clumsy. Seems we fought every day, but I still loved you. I loved you both."

Shadows moved across the land, and she glanced at the sky. Gray-rimmed clouds swept over the sun. . . . She wrinkled her brow as a memory tried to surface.

"I just wanted you to know that," she whispered quickly and stood, brushing the soil from her skirt. She felt Clay's presence behind her, giving much-needed support.

He laid his hand against her upper arm. "The others have gathered at the river."

His words reminded her of the song Derek had told her they'd sung here, giving her some comfort. She nodded that she was ready, and Clay helped her walk the short distance, his arm supporting her shoulders as though afraid she might stumble or fall. The sky had darkened a shade, close to the color of ashes, and a picture of another day flashed across her mind. She abruptly stopped walking.

"Meagan?" Clay asked in concern.

She closed her eyes, and the picture faded. "I'm all right." Her voice came hoarse, proving her words a lie.

"If you'd rather go back to the wagon. . ."

"No." She straightened her back. "I want to join the others." If she concentrated on other things when the pictures flashed through her mind, she could do this. She'd sat inside the stuffy wagon half the day and could scarce tolerate the thought of returning to its confines.

Once they came to the river near the rocks where she and Wayne had scouted in their own childlike quest for precious ores, Meagan noticed that Penny and Linda sat there with the girls, quietly talking.

Upon seeing her approach, Christa slowly rose and just as slowly walked toward her. "I'm sorry 'bout your mama," she whispered, uncertain. She held out her doll. "Would you like to hold Ruby? It made me feel better to hold my doll after my first papa died from a snake bite."

Touched by the sweet gesture, Meagan offered the child the best smile she could muster under the circumstances and took the rag doll. It did help to hold on to something. She stood at the river and stared into the water. Another glimpse of that awful day rushed through her head, a moment she'd forgotten. Flashes of light and shadow. The dour laughter of men.

She shut her eyes.

"Meagan?" Clay asked in alarm. "You've gone white as a ghost! What's wrong?" He took hold of her arm as though worried she might fall. "You're remembering, aren't you?"

She didn't respond, only looked westward along the river's course. The clouds overhead blocked out the sun and resembled the way the region had looked that day. As though a force greater than her strong will propelled her, she moved trancelike along the riverbank, slowly breaking from Clay's hold while she clutched the doll to her bosom. Flashes brought further images to mind. Once more, she halted her steps and shut her eyes tight, willing the images away. . . .

This time they didn't fade.

✧

Ma would be angry. Nothing but a dreamer, she called Meagan, and Meagan supposed Ma was right to feel that way. She should have been home ages ago, but the way the sunlight danced along the surface of the river made Meagan forget her chore of collecting the water. Instead she watched it glisten and move as though it were a living thing. The beads of golden light jumped along the slow-moving river, entrancing her, and she wondered about life beneath its sparkling surface, about the fish that swam there. What would the light look like from beneath? Just as bright and dazzling or mysterious and ghostly? She wished she could find out.

The golden nuggets of light disappeared from the ribbon of brown water, and she looked up, puzzled. A thick veil of storm clouds had pushed across the glowing face of the sun. Regardless, she doubted it would rain; the land seldom received any.

"Well, now, what have we here?" a man's drawl from behind sent a bevy of instant chills popping along her arms.

She jumped up in shock, upsetting the empty wooden bucket and knocking it into the river. The current tugged it toward the middle. Before she could grab the container, the man closest to her clamped his huge hand around her arm.

"My brother and I are thirsty. Fetch us a drink, girl."

"M—my bucket." Woefully, she stared at the bucket, now yards away in the deeper water, then at him. "It's too far out."

"Then you best go get it!" He gave her a push that sent her falling on her hands and knees. Water splashed into her mouth and nose, making her cough and choke. The men's evil laughter churned her stomach in knots of fear.

"Please. . ." She tried to rise, but her knees shook so badly, she fell down again. The current pulled at her dress, increasing her panic. "I can't swim!"

The man grabbed her by the arm again, pulling her from the water and to him like a spineless rag doll. Holding her tight and dripping against him, his chest and arms were as solid as the nearby rocks, his manner as ruthless. Tears burned down her cheeks. "Let me go! What do you want with me?"

"Well now," he leered, studying her sodden form. "I can think of a good many things. What do you say, Amos? Shall we have some fun?"

She struggled to escape, but his grip was too strong, her wet skirts too heavy. Suddenly he sent her sailing from him with a push. The other man caught her from behind, his arms wrapping like steel rods around her middle. His fetid breath made her feel she might heave as he whispered near her ear, "She's a beauty, all right. And we got nothin' else to do till we find them maps." He nipped her lobe hard, chuckling when she yelped in pained revulsion, then tossed her back into his brother's arms. The first man held her the same as before, his hand taking liberties that shocked her virginal mind and summoned her fighting spirit from hibernation.

"No! You won't touch me, you lechers!" She fought and kicked and scratched, making it difficult for him to keep his hold on her. The other man tried to grab her legs, but she kicked him hard in the face with the heel of her shoe. He groaned, backing up and holding his nose. Blood poured from both nostrils. The sight gave her added courage that she *could* escape, and she twisted her upper body, bringing back her elbow fast, and knocked her evil captor hard in the jaw. He lessened his hold on her with an oath, and she scratched at his eyes.

That won her complete freedom. She darted away, bending down to pick up a fist-sized rock while facing them off. "Either of you come one step nearer, and I'll bash your brains in, so help me." She tried to appear brave and strong, though salty tears fell without control, leaking into her mouth. Backing up, she raised the rock high in continued threat, then spun around.

Hampered by her sodden skirts, she fled as fast as she could in the opposite direction from home, finding refuge in a shallow cave she and Wayne had discovered weeks before. There, she hid within its dark recesses, her arms tight around her knees as she shivered, the dank air chilling, while she kept her ears attuned to the least little sound. Some time passed before she gathered enough courage to leave. Slow and careful, she trekked home, keeping watch for the men, the rock ready in her hand. She had never let it go.

The pungent odor of smoke alarmed her as she took the bend of the hill leading home. In horror she saw what had been their shack, flames from the inside shooting from the sod and stone, up toward the darkened sky. Wayne lay facedown on the ground near one wall, the fire not yet reaching him.

"Wayne!" She raced to him, stumbling on legs that felt like jelly, and pulled at his shoulders to rouse him. "Wake up! Hurry! The house is on fire!"

Terrified and confused, she noticed the door, barred from the outside. Fire licked through its planks. She gave up trying to rouse her brother and tried to lift the bar, pounding at the flames with her bare hands, to no avail. Her palms throbbed in agony as the flames seared her flesh; the foul black smoke made her choke. Nevertheless, she persisted, screaming for her ma, screaming for help from heaven above until her throat felt as raw as her hands and her pleas became ragged croaks. Something from above—likely a rock—broke from the wall and hit her skull.

Next thing she remembered, she woke up with a throbbing headache, coughing as her throat tickled and burned. She turned part of her face out of the mud and blinked up at the sky from where she lay on the ground, as sodden as she. The fire had petered out, the sound of rainwater an almost comforting splash as it poured from what remained of the roof to puddle on the ground. In places, small patches of fire still burned low, but all was too wet to give the flames added fuel.

"Ma?"

No answering sound came from inside the cabin. Worse, Meagan could recall nothing of what happened or how she'd ended up flat on the ground in a seldom-received rainstorm. It had all seemed like a strange nightmare with no beginning. . . .

❦

Meagan kept her eyes shut as slow tears dripped down her cheeks to run off her jaw. Clay's hand on her shoulder gave her the strength needed to recall the rest of that day. She had remembered the worst; she must recall the rest.

She had managed to rise from the mud, her hands throbbing with fierce pain, her sole aim to find help from somewhere, all the while wondering where her ma had gone, her mind blocking out the truth. She kept calling for her ma as her brother lay still. In her shock, she'd been sure he only slept or figured he'd been conked on the head, too. She recalled Landon's talk of miners with a claim to the west. Trancelike, she'd staggered from the remnants of her home without a second glance at Wayne, hoping her ma would soon return from wherever she'd gone and rouse him.

The sky had still loomed overcast from the sudden squall. With no sun to guide her and her mind so muddled that the hills crowding the area all looked alike, she had walked east instead of west until Clay found her. Looking back on it now, she felt surprised she'd gotten so far. Penny once told her the Almighty led her to Clay, and Clay to her. But why should someone as powerful and great as the Almighty God whom Clay had read about save such a wicked girl as herself? The truth she had dreaded became clear—she had been partially to blame for her family's deaths.

Once she'd awakened in Silverton, even the memory of her need to find help had abandoned her, along with the other bleak and frightening recollections that the curtain of blankness concealed. But now she remembered all she'd forgotten.

Contrary to the breakdown she'd expected, a strength she never anticipated gave Meagan new resolve. She turned eyes still wet with tears to Clay, her mouth fixed in a grim line. She would not cry, not again.

Linda approached, cautious, and Meagan looked from Clay to his sister. "Tell your husband I recall all of what happened and have the information he needs to catch those men. They killed my family. I want them brought to justice."

Linda wrapped her arm around Meagan's shoulders. "I'll come with you."

"I'll come, too," Clay said as Linda moved with Meagan in the direction of the wagon. He took only a few steps before Linda turned.

"Best stay with Penny, Clay. I think she has something she'd like to discuss with you." Her words sounded almost apologetic.

"She's right, I do need to speak with you," his sister-in-law said from behind.

He didn't bother hiding his impatience. "It can't wait?"

"No. It cannot." Penny looked just as determined.

Chapter 8

Clay sighed, watching Meagan walk away, then turned to Penny. "If this is another method of yours to get me alone to harp on me about Derek. . ." Her mouth pulled into a thin line. "No, but it does concern him."

"Penny," he warned.

"He and I discussed the matter on the ride here, and we think it would be a grand idea to stay overnight. Linda's agreeable; I spoke with her earlier. She wants to talk to Kurt, but I can't see that he would refuse."

Clay regarded her with some surprise. "Don't you think staying in this area where her loved ones were murdered might be difficult for Meagan after all she's been through?"

She drew her brows together in concern. "Aye, it would. I'd never dream of causing her such grief. I intend to speak with Derek about moving upriver. There's enough daylight remaining to put some distance behind us."

Clay blew out a frustrated breath. "And just why is this so important?"

"It will give us opportunity to discuss the mine freely without fear of being overheard."

"What about Meagan?"

"Neither Derek nor myself nor Linda think she's a concern. Do you?"

He didn't but wouldn't give in that easily. "Like I told Derek, I'm not interested in discussing the mine."

"Well now, you're not the only Burke alive!" Her eyes flashed, but her voice remained calm. "Whatever you decide, whether you'll be joining us or not, is entirely up to you. The rest of us wish to discuss the matter before the days become too hot to search." She turned with a whirl of her skirts.

"Penny—wait!"

She stopped her swift retreat and looked over her shoulder.

"A question." He kept his voice moderate. "Were you really wanting my vote or hoping for my compliance?"

"Both, of course."

He snorted. "Fair enough. I can give you one—I don't mind staying the night. But not the other. I have no intention of discussing the mine." He only spoke the truth of his feelings; so why did he feel like such an ingrate? She had a way of doing that to him, and he hated it. It made him feel much younger to her than the seven or so years that separated them.

"About what I expected. Now if you'll be excusing me, I need to see to dinner."

"One more moment of your time?"

"Aye?" The word seethed with frustration. She halted but didn't turn to him, offering only a partial view of her face.

"About that book of poetry. . ."

He thought he saw her mouth flicker in a smile.

"That was a cruel move, Penny. I'm sure it embarrassed Meagan as much as it did myself."

"You read it to her, then?"

"Till I couldn't stand to read any more."

"Well now, Clay." This time she pivoted all the way around to face him. "It was your choice to read it. I dinnae twist your arm. I offered another book first, a much better one, but you refused. So doona be parceling out blame where blame's not due. I'm not a walking library."

Pulling his mouth in a scowl, as upset as she, Clay looked away and stared at the slow-moving water.

∽

Penny offered Meagan a sandwich, but she shook her head. She didn't think her stomach could tolerate food.

Sitting at the edge of the wagon, their legs and skirts dangling nearly to the ground, both women stared toward the sun, almost a memory now as twilight closed in and the clouds cresting the hills turned violet.

"You must eat," Penny urged. "You cannot starve yourself in punishment that you don't even deserve."

"If I hadn't hidden in that cave and instead had warned them, Ma and Wayne might be alive," Meagan argued, her words full of self-recrimination. "I never acted that way before. I was always the first to take up a challenge." She had related to Penny all that happened, risking rejection in her need to seek guidance from this woman she'd come to admire so greatly.

"Any woman who'd suffered under the hands of those despicable snakes would have been just as frightened and fled. And hidden, if they were able. When people live through terrifying experiences, some react in ways from which they cannot refrain and never expected, contrary to their nature. I did. Some weeks ago, I encountered two such scoundrels, the likes of what happened to you. Had Derek not arrived in time and scared them off, I might have suffered the same fate as your mother. The girls and I both."

Meagan eyed Penny in shock, wondering if she referred to one of the miners Meagan had glimpsed once she left her room. Most men at the hotel steered clear of her, though they did a lot of curious staring, likely because they thought her demented. A few had been kind, while still others leered at her much as those men at the river had done. She shivered, grateful for Clay, who she'd learned had slept outside her cubicle as her guard.

"Was this at the hotel?" she asked Penny.

"No. Before Silverton. I thought I might travel farther west to Carson City. Derek acted as our guide. One morning, the girls and I were at the campsite. I made breakfast while Derek visited a hot spring." Her voice was hollow as she recalled that time, and a furrow formed between her brows. "Two horsemen rode up to me and the girls, taunting us. One tried to have his way with me, and Derek shot at them from where he'd kept hidden." A wistful smile tilted her mouth. "My husband is clever with a gun and warned the two away quite successfully."

"I just wish I'd warned Ma." Meagan's gaze fell to her lap. It helped to know that she'd not accidentally started the fire. Nonetheless, her burden of guilt weighed almost as heavy as before.

"Meagan, you cannot be blamin' yourself. 'Tis a crying shame what happened, and we're all aggrieved for your loss, but you cannot be shoulderin' the blame."

"I disobeyed her."

Penny shook her head in confusion. "What?"

"Ma told me to fetch water and be quick about it." Meagan bowed her head. "But I got caught up in daydreams. It wasn't the first time. And this"—she lifted her bandaged hands from her lap—"is my punishment."

"Punishment?" Penny's tone was incredulous. "From whom?"

Meagan blinked her way. "The Almighty God, of course. Clay read to me how He punished the children of disobedience. He allowed them to be stolen from their homes, and all manner of destruction came against them."

"Clay read that to you, did he?" Penny again shook her head, slowly this time, her expression amazed and exasperated. "I suppose I should have urged him to start with the New Testament—an accounting of Jesus and the covenant God gave through Him, His Son. A new covenant." She laid her hand on Meagan's forearm. "God is not desiring to destroy you, Meagan. On the contrary—He wants to save you from destruction. He wants you to know Him."

Meagan felt confused. "But I disobeyed Ma. That's why she and Wayne are dead. If I'd only done as I ought, they could have at least been prepared to fight off those men."

"What else could you have done? Run the other way and let those hooligans chase you home? It might have gone worse if you had—you might also be in the grave." Her eyes shone intently. "Mind you, I don't condone disobedience. At times, lately, it's been a trial getting my own girls to behave—and not only at fetching water. 'Tis a fault many children tend to share."

Her tone came light, wry, and Meagan sensed she tried to ease her remorse. "Truth be told, if God decided to punish or do away with the children who defied their parents at one time or another, I strongly doubt the earth would be inhabited." She chuckled. "But I love my girls dearly and would never cause them harm. As much as I love them, God loves His children with a love far greater. Enough to sacrifice His life to save a sinful mankind—those who would repent of their evil ways and follow Him and His teachings."

"But it said in that book that the people who disobeyed were punished," Meagan insisted.

"Aye, but if you take notice, those were the ones who chose to worship foreign images and idols rather than their true Creator. Their sin was great because they turned from God to worship His creations instead of Himself and His teachings. And we both know what happens to those here in the West who defy the law."

Meagan nodded, a ray of understanding beginning to dawn in her mind.

"God did warn His children of the dire consequences, many times. But their hearts were hard, and they turned away. That's why they suffered. Their disobedience was continual and without remorse. Yet even then, God loved them so that each time they repented He answered their cries and delivered them from their persecutions."

Meagan brooded over Penny's words. She'd known that God existed but always thought of Him as somewhere high in the clouds, distant, with too much to do above to pay much attention to the people below. Yet the words Clay had read and Penny now uttered described a God who involved Himself in His children's lives and cared about their choices.

It was an unsettling thought.

"Do you remember when you first came to us, I told you the good Lord can—and will—forgive you of any wrongdoing?" Penny broke the silence that had arisen.

Meagan gave a distracted nod.

"Well, then." She squeezed her arm again. "All you have to do is ask Him." Penny slid to the ground and wrapped her half-eaten sandwich in its brown paper. "I advise taking up your next reading in the Gospel of Matthew."

"I don't know how to read."

Penny looked at her. "Is that a fact? Often I forget how blessed I am that my da knew and taught me." She smiled. "If you're wantin', I can teach you."

As wide as she opened her eyes, Meagan felt them burn. "You'd do that? Despite all I've done?"

"All you've done?" Penny looked confused again.

Meagan glanced down. "I was sure you'd come to despise me once you knew the truth. And Cl—the others, too." She just prevented herself from blurting out Clay's name, but with the manner in which Penny's eyes lit up, Meagan guessed she hadn't been fooled. "It was one of the reasons I was afraid to recall all that happened. I didn't want you throwing me out. When we were at the hotel."

"Throwing you out? Goodness, no! And the 'others' have no cause to look spitefully at you, not that they would. The good Lord said to a mob ready to stone a woman that he who was without sin should cast the first stone. Needless to say, those men dropped their stones without further ado." Penny's smile was infectious, making Meagan grin. "I cannot think of a soul in our party able to wield a rock had they been there. One young man in particular. Stubbornness can be as much a sin as disobedience, and he has it without measure." Penny frowned.

Meagan doubted she spoke of her husband or Kurt. Twice she'd glimpsed Penny speaking with Clay; neither time had Penny looked happy when she left his company. Meagan wondered what sin of stubbornness Clay must have committed.

Penny's brow smoothed again. "If you're of a mind to do so, I could read to you and teach you letters. I brought the Holy Book with me. Never would I think of leaving it behind."

"I'd appreciate that. But I wouldn't want to keep you from the others."

"I offered," she reminded with a gentle smile. "Besides. . ." She climbed back in the wagon with a little grunt. "That is one meeting I've no wish to attend!"

At her curious words bordering on grim exasperation, Meagan lifted her brows but didn't ask Penny to explain.

※

Clay stood, hands on his hips, and stared at the crackling fire. Derek, Kurt, and Linda sat around its warmth, discussing the mine, as they'd been doing for a good fifteen minutes. Nearby, Livvie pitched stones in the river with her slingshot while Christa watched. Penny and Meagan sat inside the wagon where they'd been for the past hour, doing who knew what, and Clay didn't wish to interfere. Though his sister-in-law could be a trial, she could also be a blessing, and Meagan needed comfort. Comfort Clay wished he had the right to give.

He kicked at a clump of undergrowth. He couldn't very well go for a walk to remove himself from the small gathering—the sun would make its full disappearance soon and it would be too dark to see. His little nieces seemed withdrawn when he'd tried to get them to speak—likely tired from the day's travel. And so he was stuck with the others by the fire and privy to their conversation.

"Claim jumpers?" Derek asked in response to information Kurt just revealed.

"I hadn't thought of that. The clerk in Silverton didn't give me reason to believe we had anything to worry about—didn't say much at all, as a matter of fact."

"I just thought I'd bring it up after what Meagan said earlier. That's why her stepfather left their family behind. To protect his claim from such vagrants, much good that it did."

A melancholy lull passed, and Derek wondered if claim jumpers had killed Meagan's kin. Still, it didn't make much sense that they would burn down the house and leave the area if they'd stolen the claim.

"I'll check with the clerk once we get back to Silverton," Derek said. "Or maybe I won't have to. . . . We could continue west in search of the mine, bein' as how we're this far along. Plenty of game to keep us well fed, and Penny brought along extra blankets. I have my bedroll, and Clay has his."

"I'm fine with the arrangement," Kurt agreed. "I have Linda's part of the map on my person. Never go anywhere without it."

"And I have mine. Not sure about Clay, though."

Clay didn't want to join their conversation; neither did he like being a third party and discussed as if he weren't there. He spoke up.

"Sorry, plans won't work. I need to return to Silverton and attempt getting a message to Meagan's stepfather in Carson City. She has no one else in this world, and the man has to be told what happened someday soon."

"But I thought. . . ," Linda began as if confused.

"What? What did you think?" Clay struggled to keep his frustration in check.

"Nothing." She looked into the fire.

Kurt frowned but didn't say a word, except to whisper something near Linda's ear. She nodded, and the two rose. "Whatever you decide is fine with us," Kurt said to Derek and nodded to him in parting, ignoring Clay. The couple left, Kurt's arm around Linda's waist, their heads together as they talked.

Clay supposed he could follow them to the wagon, despite Kurt's irritation, and see what Meagan and Penny were up to. . .though he still burned from his earlier conversation with his opinionated sister-in-law and had no real desire to speak with her. Best to just turn in early.

Ignoring Derek, he retrieved his bedroll from his horse and threw the parcel to the ground near the fire. Derek hadn't moved from his spot. At least he remained quiet, and Clay felt thankful for small favors.

Clay worked the knots loose from the twine and spread out the thick canvas but felt too alert to sleep. He needed something to occupy his mind, to get his thoughts off Meagan and her troubles and away from the silent, dark figure staring at him from across the fire. With nothing more to do and wanting to seem occupied, he fished out his map portion from his jacket, unfolded it, and stared out over the river to the hills farther west. Perusing the snaky line he assumed was supposed to symbolize the river, he followed it to the point of the *X*. Too bad there wasn't much else to go on for his third of the map.

"No use searching in these parts," Derek said, breaking over the peaceful sound of the crackling fire. "You have to pass Three Leaning Rocks, and we've yet to reach it. Penny and I found the place on our journey. It's about another eight days' west."

His mouth tight, Clay folded his map. Not that he believed Derek farther than he could throw him, but all interest waned at his brother's interference.

Derek released a weary breath. "Given any thought as to what you might do once we find the mine?"

Clay shrugged.

"I'd like to offer a suggestion." Derek's words came slow, hesitant, as if testing the waters of Clay's cooperation to listen. When Clay didn't respond, Derek went on. "As you know, Penny and I plan on starting a ranch. Raise some cattle. Our homestead is in a pretty little valley, with a stream running near the shanty. Once we locate the silver, I plan to build a bigger place, hire some hands to help run it. If you haven't made plans for the future, you might consider taking up with us."

Derek wanted him to be a ranch hand? To *work* for him and *serve* him? Of all the low, twisted, and cruel. . .

Watching his face, Derek quickly added, "I want us to be partners, Clay. Even thought of a name for the place, if you're agreeable—the B & B Ranch, for Burke Brothers. I'd like us to live and work side by side, carve out a good life for our families." Derek smiled, clearly taken with the notion. "I reckon you plan on starting one soon, what with the way I've seen you look at Meagan. I know you spend a good amount of time in her company."

Clay felt the heat brand his face. Were his feelings so transparent that everyone thought the two of them should be hitched, from the youngest Burke to the oldest?

"I regret the years we lost, and I want to make a fresh start. You're the only brother I have, and I don't want to lose you, like we lost our ma. And Pa, too."

It was the wrong thing to say. Like a flame to dry tinder, all the bad memories blazed to life and burned inside Clay's mind. "I haven't taken handouts from you since the day I was old enough to manage on my own, not a single one, and I don't intend starting now, *brother*." He said the last in a cutting way.

Derek flinched as though struck. "At least take some time to think about it."

"I've had *four years*." Clay stressed the last two words, making his message clear. "I've done all the thinking necessary."

"Then I reckon there's nothing more to say." Derek's voice came low.

"You're right about that."

Clay noticed his brother moved slower than usual as he gave a slight nod and rose to his feet like an old man whose bones had withered with age. Any smattering of triumph evaded him, and Clay felt hateful, petty. The time spent in his brother's company these past weeks hadn't eliminated his animosity, but it had been enough to shave off the rough edges and wasn't wholly intolerable.

Clay thought back. With his own eyes, he observed some of the changes Derek had admitted to. His tender affections toward Penny, his devotion toward their girls, his ability to sit and listen to an old, homesick miner pour out his problems—whereas the old Derek in his restlessness wouldn't have noticed the old man, much less offered helpful advice. Clay despised the envy that tightened his chest when he witnessed the consideration Derek so often gave others, where before he'd had little of the same kindness to grant his own kin. Clay's state of mind had led him to speak sharper than he might have done if he hadn't been so annoyed, to the point he was almost willing to call his brother back and apologize.

Almost.

He had little time to dwell on his own shortcomings as, without warning, a shower of ice-cold water streamed over his head in a blinding torrent.

"What the. . . !" Blinking hard and wiping the stinging water from his eyes, he noted Christa and Livvie had turned from the river and stared up behind him, their mouths hanging wide open, and he managed to stifle the rest of his oath. He jumped to his feet, swinging around to face the culprit.

Penny's eyes blazed as she held the rim of the empty water bucket in one hand. "Linda may fear a rift between the two of you should she speak, what with your differences so newly mended, and my dear husband may continue playin' the martyr, feeling he's deservin' of your ill will—but I've had enough of your balderdash, Clayton Burke. I have a great deal to say, and you'll stand there and listen to every word!"

Clay gaped at his normally sane sister-in-law, still too befuddled to form a retort. His mind felt numb and senseless, frozen by the chill—from both her dour expression and the river water.

"Show me a man who never makes mistakes, and I'll show you a man stone cold in his grave," Penny sputtered, her brogue strong. "Your pigheadedness is causing this family a good deal of strife and heartache, and 'tis high time you put a stop to it. Your brother has done his utmost to make amends, but I do believe you get a perverse joy out of seeing him suffer." She threw down the bucket with a sideways thrust, keeping her snapping eyes fixed on him. "There'll be an end to that, as well. I love you as if you were blood kin, but no longer will I tolerate such nonsense. If you're wantin' to be sharin' with others your harsh behavior, you may as well make your home in these parts, among other creatures of the wild—but if it's human companionship you're after, then I advise you to start behaving like one!"

With a whirl of her skirts, she swept off toward the wagon.

Kurt stood nearby, as transfixed as Clay. Derek approached from some distance, his expression stunned as he took in Clay's appearance. Clearly he struggled over what to say or do. "I, uh, apologize. She's in the family way, and her moods have taken on a mind of their own. One minute she's singing like a mockingbird; the next, spitting like a wildcat. I best go check on her." With an uneasy nod, he strode to where his wife had disappeared.

The girls gaped at Clay, then took off running after their parents. Kurt shook his head and also turned to the wagon, just as Linda came hurrying from the back.

"Here." She thrust one of the blankets at Clay. "It's not much, but it'll help you dry off before the cold sets in."

If that was all she was worried about, she was too late. He had already started to shiver as twilight chilled the air that the sun's warmth had abandoned. "Thanks." He took the blanket.

She seemed nervous as she watched him towel off with half of the long length of wool. He was thankful to note his bedroll had received almost none of the downpour.

"I've never seen her act so upset," Linda said after a moment.

Clay thought the matter over and sighed. "She had good reason, I suppose."

"You two don't get along?"

"We have our moments." Clay tossed the damp blanket by the fire. "Usually when she brings up one of two subjects: God or the silver mine, and what I need to do about both."

Linda studied him, then looked toward the river.

Recalling Penny's accusations, he sighed. "You have something you want to say? You needn't be afraid to come out and say whatever's on your mind, Linda. It sure can't be any worse than Penny's methods." He kept his tone light and inviting. The last thing he wanted was for any woman to fear him, especially his own kin.

"It's just that. . ." She hesitated. "It's odd how we didn't meet till recently, but both of us suffered the same misfortune: we both had only our mothers to rely on as children, and our mothers were taken away too soon by disease. But each of us reacted so differently to the loss. Losing my mother made me yearn to draw close to what she believed in and find God, while you did the exact opposite when your ma died and refused to have anything to do with Him."

"I don't know if I'd go that far. . . ." Her words rang dead true, making him ill at ease. Memory of the recent scripture he'd read to Meagan only aggravated the problem. God punished those Old Testament people who'd turned from Him and His precepts and in a manner that made Clay cringe inside. Bondage, starvation, even death. . .

"Well, I don't know what else you'd call it," she insisted, her tone and eyes anxious, not argumentative.

"Don't worry about me, Linda." He smiled with forced confidence and bluster. "I've taken care of myself a good many years, and I'll go on doing just fine."

"Will you?" she insisted. "I'm not so sure. It's just that. . ." She drew her shawl closer around her shoulders. "We're family. Now that we've found each other, there's no reason for you to live life alone. I want you to be happy, too, Clay, and I sense you're far from it. I want to share with you what I've found. . . ." Her brow wrinkled.

His heart softened at her hesitant words. "That means more to me than I can say."

"Does it?" She looked unconvinced. She moved toward the river and stared into the dark water. "May I speak frankly?" she asked, turning to face him.

He tensed but nodded.

"You can't see them well now, but ever notice how the rocks beneath the water are smooth, their sharp edges worn down? But the rocks outside the current. . ." She looked to the rocks scattered near her feet. Picking one up, she held it out. "They're hard and stony, sharp. Some dry as dust and easily crumbled."

"Guess that's why they call them rocks," Clay joked, and she smiled.

"Did you know in the Good Book the Lord said He's like streams of living water and in Him you'll never thirst? If I had my choice, I'd rather be immersed in His living water, letting His love shape me and soften the coarse edges, than just lying within reach, but on the outside—the heat and sun baking me hard and dry." She looked at him, awaiting his response.

"If I had my choice, I'd rather not be a rock—though Pa often said my head was full of them." His little joke came out feeble, her words affecting him more than he let on.

Her lips smiled, but her eyes remained sad. "Well, that's all I wanted to share. It's something that came to me as we were sitting here earlier and I was looking at the river. I should go help Penny."

"Linda," he said before she could leave.

She regarded him in question.

"Thanks for sharing that with me. Having a sister is as nice as I hoped it might be."

Her eyes lit up at his compliment, and she smiled and nodded before moving away. Clay watched her go, then turned to gaze into the river and what little he could see of the stones beneath.

Deep in thought, he didn't move until he heard a step directly behind him. He quickly turned, leery after Penny's recent dousing.

Meagan came to a swift halt, her eyes as clouded as the earlier sky.

Chapter 9

C lay regarded Meagan, his manner cautious. She felt bad about startling him. "Sorry, I should've spoken—"

"No harm done," he reassured. "Feeling better?"

"All things considering. I just wanted to warm myself by the fire. . . ." Meagan's words trailed off as she noticed his wet shirt and dripping hair. Surely he hadn't taken a swim in the river with his clothes on, and with the cold night approaching! Had he fallen in?

With a wry grin, he grabbed a hank of his hair and squeezed water from the long strands. "A gift from my sister-in-law. Guess she thought I needed cooling down."

"Penny did that to you?" Meagan could scarcely believe the gentle friend who'd been so gracious to her only minutes before could do such a shocking thing. Upon leaving the wagon, Penny had grabbed the pail off a hook, expressing the need for water. Meagan had been so absorbed with her exciting new undertaking of learning to read she hadn't paid attention to the group at the river.

"Something I said." Clay shrugged. "Or didn't say. One can never tell with her."

Meagan searched for a suitable reply. "I hope you work out your differences."

"I doubt that'll happen." At her curious stare, he released a weary breath. "She's angry because I won't see things her way with regard to my brother." He looked toward the river, clearly uncomfortable.

"It's all right," she reassured him. "You can talk about your brother in my company. I'm not made of glass. I won't break."

His eyes gentled as he turned her way. "No, you're not, are you? Fact is, you're one of the strongest women I've run across. You exhibited courage going back there today. Even to pay last respects, I'm not sure many women would have done the same if they thought there could be danger."

"You think there still is?"

"No. Our fears were groundless. But I can't help but wonder what you'll do once those bandages come off your hands."

He seemed uneasy, and she put into words what he didn't say. "You mean if I'm crippled, if I don't regain good use of my hands."

"Penny thinks you will, and she's a better authority than I am with all her cures," he was quick to offer.

Meagan nodded, lifting her hands to look at them. "Yet I would gladly give both if I could have my family back. Even Wayne, trial that he was. It seems we fought every day, but I still miss him." She looked at Clay. "I suppose I didn't appreciate what I had till it was taken from me. Now it's gone and I have nothing left."

Clay winced. "What about your stepfather?"

"I don't imagine he'll care much one way or the other. He'll mind that his shack is gone and the things he'd left behind. But he didn't care much for me or Wayne, and I doubt he had fond feelings for Ma."

"I'm sorry."

"Don't be." Meagan attempted a careless shrug. "I'm just grateful I had my parents' love. Some people don't. Pa—my true pa—was often ill, but he made me feel special."

"You are."

"What?" Meagan looked at him in surprise.

"Special." His face flushed a shade darker.

Tongue-tied, she could only stare.

Clay moved a few steps toward the river. "What will you do now?"

With so much to endure, Meagan hadn't given the future much thought. "I don't know. I never learned a trade befitting a woman—never was good at sewing, but I don't suppose Silverton has much use for a seamstress, even if I am able to hold a needle again. The little I saw, your town was teeming with men and very few women."

"It's not my town."

"Pardon?"

"I'm only traveling through. I don't plan on staying."

"Oh." That he would one day leave had never occurred to Meagan. She wondered why he would want to go and when, felt upset that he planned to, but masked her feelings. "Penny is teaching me my letters and how to read. I'm not sure what good that'll do me—it's nice to learn, but really, I don't know what I'll do."

For the first time, Meagan realized she wasn't much use at all. Clay was wrong; she wasn't special. In a mining town, she didn't know how she would manage, especially without Clay to go to for advice or company. She had come to expect his presence, his friendship. However would she even survive in such a place? She could never give herself to men like the saloon and dance-hall prostitutes did. She pondered the idea of traveling farther west to a big city like Carson

City. She imagined that, no matter the size of the locale, she would face similar problems.

"Do you have family back East?"

"No. It's just me."

The sudden knowledge of what that meant terrified her, though she tried to remain strong. Clay must have heard the catch in her voice; he turned to look, then walked her way again. Whatever unease had sprung up between them dissolved as she moved into his open arms. His shirt was cold and damp, causing her to shiver, but his hands were warm at her back, his embrace comforting as she melted against him. Held close against his strength, her fears began to ebb.

"Meagan, it'll be all right," he soothed. "We're not going to leave you floundering, I promise. Never would I do that to you. You're not alone in this world, no matter how you feel at the moment." His strong arms tightened around her as if he were afraid she might try to move away.

She had no intention of moving a muscle. His fingers spread slightly and stroked her hair, and the memory of being carried in his arms drifted to her. She smiled against his shirt, never feeling so safe as when she was near him, so close she could feel his breaths and the beating of his heart. But unlike the first time, she suffered no fatigue, and her senses remained alert. Her heart stirred, and she held her breath, hoping by doing so she could force time to still. That he might hold her like this forever. . .

He retreated a fraction, and she wanted to protest; his eyes met hers, and she forgot all else. She immersed herself in their deep blue, darker now with night approaching. Lost in their depths, she did not want to struggle to save herself from drowning, wishing only to sink further as the seconds froze into eternity.

His gaze lowered to her mouth the moment before his cool lips brushed hers, his kiss so gentle it might have been no more than the touch of a feather, the effect so forceful she felt as if a feather could knock her to her knees. She closed her eyes and gripped his damp sleeves. Sweet warmth coursed through her in rivulets, the chill of his wet clothing forgotten. His arms tightened around her. His mouth, now warm, pressed more firmly against hers, making her heart pound so loud she heard it in her ears, when suddenly he moved away.

Where seconds before his gaze had been intent, now he seemed incapable of looking at her except for the briefest of glances.

Meagan sensed his nervous state was the forerunner to an apology. Though she also felt awkward, she couldn't bear for him to sum up a long-anticipated moment into a thoughtless mistake. Her first kiss, her only kiss, but if it must be their last, she would not have it sullied by hurtful memories of his remorse.

"Meagan, I. . ."

"The night has a chill, more so than I thought," she interrupted, "and the fire isn't as warm as it looks. I should retire and leave you to your drying out." Foolish words, but Meagan barely knew what she said, only that she must speak so he would not.

She turned to go, but his hand on her arm stopped her. A little shiver went through her when she recalled how only moments before that same hand had pressed against her spine and his gentle fingers had woven through her hair.

"Meagan, please don't go away angry."

"I'm not." She shouldn't look at him but couldn't help herself. The pain and regret swimming in his eyes lanced an arrow through her heart. She must go before he completely ruined whatever happiness remained.

"Honest, I'm all right. Please, Clay. Let me go."

"I never meant to hurt you. That's the last thing I wanted to do."

Then don't say another word. She attempted a smile to mask the cry that begged to peal from her throat. "I'm just tired. It's been a long day, and tomorrow will be another."

"Of course." He released her arm. "I apologize. I didn't mean to keep you."

"You didn't. Good night."

Meagan hurriedly walked away. She wanted to race to the dark solitude offered in the wagon bed but feared doing so would alert the others that something was wrong. And something was definitely wrong.

She should have known better than to kiss him, to let his kiss linger, should have pushed him aside. But her foolish heart had yearned for this for days.

If only she could turn back the sun, erase those last moments. But time flew ever onward, and she wondered what difficult cost of suffering the future days might exact from her for her mistake in thinking Clay returned her love.

৵

In the darkness settling around their camp, Clay could barely see the rocks Linda had pointed out earlier. Maybe Pa had been right, and his head was full of them.

Had he frightened Meagan, upset her, or both? He'd had no right to kiss her, and she'd made it pretty clear she wished he hadn't. He'd never planned or intended to follow through with what had been revolving inside his head since she joined him. He'd thought her soft lips had answered his gentle quest and she wanted him to continue, but he must have imagined it. What an unfeeling rogue she must think him! After all she'd suffered—then to crown her nightmarish day by shocking her with his unwelcome affections. . . .

Sighing, he picked up the blanket, using the drier half to rub at his damp clothes. The fire wasn't doing the trick, not working as fast as he would like. And he didn't relish the idea of sleeping in this condition.

Footsteps crunched through the scrub, and he darted a wary glance over his shoulder.

"Looks like you got a heap of women troubles," Kurt said in greeting.

Clay eyed him with reservation, wondering if he addressed Clay as friend or foe. The deputy made no mystery that he sided with Derek in the quarrel between brothers.

Kurt lifted his hands in the air. "I come in peace. Between Penny's dousing and what I just saw, you looked like you could use a friend."

"What you saw. . ." Clay left the words hanging, fishing for exactly what Kurt had seen.

The deputy put his hands down. "You kissing Meagan. The both of you sharing words. Her rushing off upset."

Clay's face blazed as he continued toweling dry with the blanket. He'd thought the others too immersed in their own nighttime tasks to take any notice of him or Meagan. He should have known better.

"I saw Linda giving you a peace of her mind earlier, too," Kurt continued when Clay didn't respond.

"At least she was kind about it."

"Really?"

Clay looked at his brother-in-law. "I imagine my sister is one of the meekest and most gentle women I've met."

Kurt snorted. "Meek? Linda?"

"That's the impression I got."

"That's because she's trying so hard to be cautious around you. Give it time." Kurt chuckled. "Don't misunderstand. I love my wife, but she can be as much of a wildcat as Penny. Fact is, the day I met Linda, she pulled a derringer on me. When I wrestled it from her, she clawed and kicked to escape—even knocked me in the jaw." He grinned and settled his hands on his hips. "Of course, she had just discovered I was the law and only doing my duty. She didn't take too kindly to me at first, especially when I took her as my prisoner and locked her up in the jailhouse. At the time, I thought she was a young hellion with a weakness for breaking the law."

Clay raised his brows in amazement. Linda had neglected to fill him in on a good deal of what happened after she disappeared from Silverton.

The deputy shook his head. "Just goes to show we can't always judge by first encounters. She was none of those things. Well, except spirited—she still is that—and at times impossible. She definitely has a will of her own."

"Yeah, she does," Clay agreed. "It's that stubborn Burke blood."

Kurt chuckled. "I imagine I was wrong about you, too. In watching you with Meagan since you brought her to Silverton, I've noticed something good and noble about you that I hadn't thought existed."

"Not after talking to Derek, you mean?" Clay asked wryly.

"I form my own judgments. I don't need others telling me how I should feel."

Clay gave a short nod. "Good to know."

"The first night we met," Kurt drawled, "I saw two sides of the same man. The side who would sacrifice everything for a woman in need, and the side who would sacrifice his brother to meet his own needs."

Clay snorted. "Not that ornery, I trust. I may have been fuming, but I wouldn't wish Derek dead."

"Glad to hear it. I'm not always sure when I hear you talk. Thing is—"

Clay's gaze flicked beyond Kurt a moment, the rustle of skirts warning of someone's approach. Kurt's attention returned to Clay. "A man can't satisfy both sides and be at peace. Either he's got a good heart, or he doesn't, and a man with a good heart can't live in any sort of true peace and despise his brother. There's a time to put an end to bitterness, Clay. For your sake. And to ask yourself which man you want to be."

Resigned to his entire family trying to interfere in his quarrel with Derek, Clay gave a tired nod. Each day that passed, his defenses wore down a little more. "I'll keep that in mind."

"Do that. The man I saw taking such devoted care of a lady in distress these past weeks is a man I'd like to call friend."

Penny came into view, and Kurt nodded a farewell to both Clay and his sister-in-law. "Evenin'." He walked away, and Penny advanced.

Before Kurt was out of earshot, Penny began, her eyes snapping. "I had full well intended to come to you with an apology—"

"I accept."

"That is, till I put the children to bed and saw that poor girl in tears, hiding in the wagon."

"Meagan?" His heart plummeted to hear she'd been that upset.

"Who else? I tried talking with her, but she won't speak of what ails her. What did you say to make her cry?"

His tattered defenses rose to the fore. "Must you always assume the worst when it comes to me?"

"You were the last one with her. I've heard the sting of your words to your own brother this night, so don't give me that righteous attitude, Clayton Burke. Bitterness has a way of spreading to those not deserving of it. And you were as bitter as a dill pickle."

Her comparison amused him, puncturing a hole in his temper. "I didn't say anything to hurt her." He wanted to suggest that Meagan might still be upset over the day's events and mourning her family or, better yet, not say a word, but his tongue played traitor and admitted the truth before he could think twice. "I kissed her, if you must know." Again his face burned flame hot.

Penny gaped at him in disbelief. "Kissed her?" she repeated below her breath. "And you no more than an hour ago telling us you doona intend on courting her? You would trifle with such a sweet girl's affections like that?"

He wondered if he should just jump in the river and save Penny the trouble of fetching the bucket.

"First," he said ruefully, "I would never do a thing to harm her. Second, I never intended it to happen."

"And that's supposed to excuse such behavior, is it?"

He grimaced and crossed his arms over his chest. "I tried apologizing, but she wouldn't let me."

"Perhaps you didn't try hard enough."

Letting out a sigh, Clay closed his eyes. Maybe he hadn't. Fact was, he wasn't one bit sorry he'd kissed Meagan—only that she'd been offended. And yes, he'd told the others that he didn't intend on courting her, but in that moment, even before the kiss, he'd questioned such a decision.

"I know you care for Meagan and would never willfully hurt her—anyone with two eyes can see that." Penny's tone gentled. "But if you've made up your mind there's no future for the two of you to share, then you must do what is in her best interests. Especially now. She's so fragile after all that's happened."

"What do you recommend?"

Penny shook her head in dismay. "As much as I hate to say it, you shouldn't keep company with her any longer, not as you've done. When a man kisses a woman, a decent woman, 'tis a sign he wants to extend their friendship. To spend time with her after tonight will only confuse and injure her further when you do pull away."

Clay didn't want to admit it, but she made sense. Nor did he want to think of the day when he must leave Meagan, but Penny was right about that, too. He had no desire to put down roots in Silverton; once he knew Meagan would be safe and prosper in her new life, he had every intention of searching for the mine.

Yet thoughts of leaving her rankled him. He didn't see how she could survive with her scarred hands that may never regain full use, with no family to care for her, in a mining town of gruff men, the only womenfolk for company being ladies of the evening. He winced, then thought of Beulah. Despite her chosen profession, she had a gentle heart. Perhaps he should introduce her to Meagan, then wondered how. He didn't intend to step foot inside a saloon or dance hall again, and Beulah rarely left the one where she worked. On second thought,

Beulah might influence Meagan unfavorably, and he couldn't stand the thought of her resorting to an immoral life. Silverton was no place for Meagan, either.

Clearly expecting a reply, Penny continued staring. "And you don't think it will hurt her to put distance between us?" he asked.

"It will hurt her a good deal more if you don't."

Something occurred to Clay. "That is, assuming she has feelings for me. Like as not, she doesn't, in which case this conversation is moot, though I do owe her an apology."

She studied him as if he spoke a foreign language. "You're smarter than that, Clay. You're not ignorant even if you do have a few ignorant ideas. Surely you're not blind to the fact that she lights up like a sunbeam whenever you walk into a room."

"I assumed she was happy to see a new face."

"She never responded in such a manner whenever Linda or I entered."

Penny's words both delighted and distressed him. To learn Meagan might conceal the same depth of affection for Clay gave him hope they could share a future together, but the truth of his bleak situation immediately scattered it. He had nothing to offer her: no home, no money, no material goods. Once he found the mine, those circumstances could change, but Derek had questioned the silver's existence more than once. Much as Clay hated to admit it, his brother could be right. Their pa had been a liar and at times played cruel jokes. Maybe this was all an elaborate prank, and they only wasted their time.

He expelled his frustration somewhere between a sigh and a groan. "Agreed. I'll stay away."

"It wouldn't be a problem if you felt differently, but as you don't. . ." She shrugged, her manner sympathetic. "And before I'll be forgetting, I'll be giving you that apology now. I never should have let my temper get the better of me."

Clay attempted a smile. "I probably deserved it."

"Aye, but at least I might have waited for the sun to warm the sky again." Her eyes twinkled in mischief, and she squeezed him in a half hug. "Linda is putting some coffee on. That will help warm you."

He nodded, his mind already elsewhere. . .somewhere he didn't want to go. Penny left him and walked back to the wagon. Clay looked past the fire, catching sight of Derek on the other side.

Chapter 10

The reprieve Meagan hoped for got cut short as Livvie and Christa climbed into the back of the wagon, chattering as if they were again the best of friends. Meagan swiped at her wet cheeks, and the girls quieted. They looked at one another, then at Meagan. She worked to get her mouth to smile, then started as a coyote howled.

"You ain't afraid of them coyotes, are you, Miss Meagan?" Livvie's question preceded another distant howl. " 'Cause there ain't no reason to fear. Uncle Kurt and Pa are good shots; don't know about Uncle Clay. And I can hit anything dead on from more'n a distance of five wagons end to end," she boasted, patting her slingshot that she'd tucked in some twine knotted around her waist.

"Livvie helped get me away from a pack of coyotes," Christa said, her big eyes shining in all seriousness. "When we was on the trail."

"Sure did," Livvie boasted. "Hit one smack on the nose. It went yipping off, and we never saw hide nor hair of it again."

"Really," Meagan said, trying to sound as if she hadn't been crying. "It sounds like you're quite handy with that slingshot, Livvie."

"And I been practicin' every day to get better. One day I'm gonna be as good as David. He was a shepherd boy before he became king, and he killed him a lion and then a giant all the men feared. But I ain't afraid of anything—just like David."

"A giant?" Meagan inquired.

"A man so tall, I reckon he's as tall as the hills."

"It's in the Holy Book Mama reads to us," Christa whispered in reverence.

"Oh." Meagan glanced at the book, where Penny had left it in the corner of the wagon. Both Penny and Clay had told her what the Bible contained weren't made-up tales but accounts of actual occurrences. Penny had read to her from the New Testament earlier, which told of the Lord Jesus in such an appealing manner that Meagan was no longer certain of God's punishment toward her; instead she wanted to know more about the Son of Man—also the Son of God—whose humble beginnings in a stable brought kings to kneel before Him. He walked among the people, teaching them day and night, never too weary to heal their bodies, always giving of Himself and His love. She could use a good dose of all three of His gifts. She imagined He wouldn't fear a giant either, though she'd never want to run up against a man so tall!

"I'm not afraid, Livvie. Not of coyotes at any rate."

"If you're not afraid, what are you?"

"Pardon?"

"Why are you hiding in here and not outside with Mama and Linda?"

"And Uncle Clay," Christa added. "Don't you like him no more?"

"Sure I do. I mean. . ." Her face grew warm. "I suppose I'm just sad after all that's happened. And going back to where I once lived made it worse."

Christa pulled her doll from a nearby blanket where it had been tucked in up to its cloth neck. "Would you like to hold Ruby again?"

Meagan stared at the curious, shining faces of the two little girls she'd come to care for as family. "You know what I'd really like?"

Christa shook her head.

"A big hug." She tentatively held her arms out to the girls in invitation.

They rushed toward her and wrapped their arms around her. The momentum sent them flying backward, and Meagan's head and shoulders hit the canvas cover. As she slid down, she heard the wooden rib nearest her creak in protest and hoped it wouldn't splinter. The girls' giggles were infectious, and Meagan joined in as she lay there with them sprawled on top of her.

"Well, and just what mischief have I come upon?" Penny's cheery voice broke through the giggling. "What are the two of you doing to poor Miss Meagan?"

The girls let go and sat up. "We weren't doing nothin' wrong, Mama," Livvie hurried to say. "Honest!"

"I'm to blame," Meagan explained, not wanting the girls in trouble.

"Never you mind. It's good to see you smile." She looked from Meagan to her girls. "Now then, go tell your pa good night."

"Are we in trouble?" Christa asked.

"You will be if you don't mind." Penny gave her youngest a gentle tap on the nose. "Your pa said he might play the harmonica, but only if you hurry and do as you're told."

With excited squeals, the children scrambled from the wagon.

"I brought coffee." Penny offered Meagan a tin cup she held. "I thought it would help take the chill off."

"Thank you." Grateful, Meagan scooted to the rear of the wagon, took the steaming cup, and sipped the strong, black brew. A wash of heat rushed through her veins, and she sighed in contentment.

"Have you given any thought to your future?" Penny climbed inside.

"Not much."

"I have something I'd like to discuss. Something I talked over with Derek. He'll be leaving soon with Linda and Kurt on a trip farther west, and we've decided I should return to the homestead with the girls. The journey might be too harsh for Christa—of late I've had reservations about taking her more than a day's journey—and, well. . ." Her cheeks flushed. "I'm expecting a wee babe come mid-winter—all the more reason Derek and I wish to move to our homestead soon."

Meagan smiled. "I'm happy for you both."

"God has indeed blessed us, but I had a reason for speaking so. If you've a mind to consider it, I want you to come and stay with us."

Meagan's mouth dropped open in shock as fresh tears wet her eyes at so generous an invitation. "I don't know what to say. I wouldn't want to impose."

"There now, don't cry." Penny's voice shook, and she dabbed at her own eyes. "You'll get me started. It's bad enough my emotions are all in a tizzy these days." She laughed. "Truly, it would be no imposition to have you stay. No one lives for miles around except miners, and though Derek has made his position clear to them and I don't foresee any more problems, I would feel better having another woman nearby."

"I don't know how much help I can be." Meagan ruefully stared at her ban-daged hands. She could now manage a cup, though it was a trial holding a fork, and she still needed assistance at the most mundane of tasks.

"Even if you do nothing but keep me company, I would consider it a bless-ing. The days are getting longer and can be lonely without adult companionship. And the girls have taken a liking to you, as well."

"When you put it like that, I don't see how I can refuse."

"Wonderful!" Penny brightened. "I'll continue with teaching you to read, perhaps even to write."

"How long do the others plan on being away?" Meagan hoped Penny wouldn't think her rude but needed an idea of how long her stay might last. She felt foolish for fretting over what she might do once she left the Burke home but couldn't keep from it.

Penny averted her gaze, seeming a mite distracted. "There's no way of tell-ing. It could be a matter of weeks, even months."

"Then they're going in search of the mine?"

Penny looked at her sharply, and Meagan knew she'd said something wrong. "Where did you hear of that?"

"I overheard the girls talk. I'm sorry."

"They know?"

Meagan nodded. "They told me in Silverton. When I was laid up, they were talking to each other about it. I just hope your husband and family have better success than Landon did."

"They shouldn't have said a word." Penny's brow wrinkled in concern. "It's supposed to be kept secret."

"I'd never tell anyone."

Penny patted her arm, but Meagan could tell she was still upset. "It's not you I don't trust. If Christa or Olivia mentioned it in the wrong company. . ." She slid forward and dropped to the ground. "I must speak with Derek. Will you be all right?"

"Yes." Meagan lifted her coffee between her hands. "I have this to keep me warm."

"Ah, that reminds me. A word of caution. . ." Penny's brow relaxed. "Olivia is a restless one, even in sleep—she kicks. I often woke with bruises during our journey. And Christa is a snuggler—you may find you cannot breathe of a morning because she's found a spot atop you—but at least there's little chance you'll be cold."

"I won't mind." Meagan laughed. "When I was their age, I wished for sisters to share stories with at night. It'll be fun."

"Just don't keep them up long. I don't want them dragging their feet tomorrow."

"I won't," Meagan promised.

She watched Penny leave, sensing a small hole in her heart filled by this generous family, once more feeling as if she belonged, as if she were wanted. Her sole regret was that Clay had no desire to be included in the group who wanted her.

⁓

Clay passed the night with the recent admonitions of his family battering his dreams as he searched for Meagan within them. When he found her inside a mine, she sadly acknowledged him without a word, then turned and walked away, disappearing into the thick inner darkness. He hurried to catch her, never able to, but soon realized she was only part of what he searched for—both aspirations as vital to him as air. He felt suffocated in the dank cave as he ran within its bowels, which echoed his hollow cries. Alone. Uncertain. Unable to find the exit into light and air as the blackness swallowed him into its big belly and he could no longer breathe. . . .

He woke with a start, the canvas covering his mouth and nose. Irritated, he wrenched at the top of his bedroll and straightened from his curled position, noticing no light yet filled the sky. Hearing a boot shuffle near the fire, he looked in that direction.

Derek squatted before the low flames. He grabbed the coffeepot handle, using one of Penny's cloth napkins, and poured himself a cup. His eyes flicked to Clay, and he lifted the pot, brow raised in question. Clay nodded and sat up, throwing aside his bedroll. He tipped his boots upside down and pounded the soles in case one of the high desert's occupants had decided to make its home there for the night. Finding both boots empty of snakes, lizards, or scorpions, he pulled them on, his mind wrapped up in the next few minutes. He could well imagine his ma smiling down from above, pleased that her two sons still shared the lifetime habit of waking before dawn, before anyone else in the household stirred—which now led him to this moment.

Alone with his brother, and no one else able to hear.

He tied up his bedroll, then shoved it aside and approached Derek. His brother handed him a tin of steaming black coffee. Clay took it but remained standing.

"I watched our ma die, crying out your name over and over, almost to her last breath, and I hated you for not being there."

In the firelight, Clay took note of the sudden surprise and hope that sparked within Derek's eyes. Never in all the time since their mother's passing had Clay spoken to Derek in so deep a manner, letting his brother know his personal feelings about that awful period. Feelings he'd told no one else. He'd lambasted him for not being there but never told how it affected him.

"I used to cry when I was a boy, when I was sure no one could see or hear, wishing you'd come home and things could be like they once were. When Ma kept getting sicker, I blamed you. Since the money you sent for her medicine wasn't working to make her well, I blamed you for that, too. I figured you were just like pa and didn't care about your family. You were so rude when we met in Silverton, after having not seen each other for four years solid. Then you robbed me and Linda of our maps. I was sure you were the same sort of irascible heel our pa had been."

"Irascible?"

Clay smiled slightly. "Short-tempered. Irritable. Petulant."

"At least one of us got something out of Ma's books." Derek shook his head. "If I could live life over and undo what's been done—"

"I know. You would. Watching you with Penny and the girls these last weeks and seeing you accept Linda, acting as her big brother, opened my eyes. You are a changed man. And Penny's right—every man makes his fair share of mistakes. But not every man is sorry for them."

"Penny spoke up for me?"

"Every day. As a matter of fact, she wouldn't let up." Clay studied the coffee in his tin. He had yet to take his first sip. "Then I couldn't stand it. Now I'm glad your wife is as persistent as she is."

"Meaning?" Derek's eyes were hopeful.

"Meaning I don't know what the future holds. I'm still not sure I can trust you enough to search for the mine together. Let's just take this a day at a time and see where the road leads." Clay sighed and took a sip of the strong brew.

"Fact is, I'm tired of being your sworn enemy, like I promised you when I was nearly sixteen and you rode off, leaving me behind again, so as to take up your nomadic life."

Derek grunted in amusement. "That's what Penny called me—a nomadic drifter."

"Where do you think I got the name?" Clay asked with a smirk, taking a seat on the ground.

Derek grew serious again. "I didn't suppose you'd want to go with me, even if I'd asked. Didn't think you wanted me near you."

"Deep down, I wanted you to offer, but I never would have broken down and told you so even if you'd have threatened me with a hot branding iron. The Burke pride had its grip hard on me then. I still grapple with it."

"We're quite a pair, aren't we?" Derek shook his head and sipped his coffee. "A reformed rogue and a stubborn mule." He smiled to show he only teased.

Clay snorted. "Better than our pa, not as saintly as our ma, striving for someplace good in between."

"And Linda is the best of us three."

Clay nodded his agreement.

"At least we're striving to be better men."

"Yeah, we are at that."

No more words passed between them. Though they'd reached no real understanding, something significant had changed in their relationship. Penny noticed it when she awoke and raised her brows to see Clay sitting beside Derek. Kurt and Linda noticed it when they smiled at each other after Clay responded in a civil tone to something Derek said.

Something significant had altered between him and Meagan, too, but not for the better. When she emerged from the wagon, she barely glanced in Clay's direction and avoided him all morning.

As Derek hitched up the team, Linda packed the few items while Penny rounded up the girls, who'd wandered, thrilled for the chance to play in wide-open spaces. Alone, Clay found an opportunity to speak with Meagan. But words evaded him when she turned her tawny gold eyes his way.

He searched his mind for a greeting. "Did you pass the night well?"

"Fair enough."

"That's good." Uneasy, he pulled the brim of his hat down though the morning sun shone behind. "It can get mighty cold of a night."

"We had plenty of blankets, and the girls kept me warm."

The unexpected thought of himself in their position with Meagan made his mouth go dry and tied up his tongue. Catching sight of Penny's admonishing look from afar, he again glanced at Meagan, who now eyed him strangely.

He nodded in farewell and moved to his horse, both grateful for his sister-in-law's watchful eye and perturbed by her nosy attitude. What was the harm of passing a few minutes alone with Meagan, speaking of routine affairs? Surely Penny didn't expect him to avoid her completely.

Without a doubt, staying away would not be a simple matter.

Chapter 11

Meagan sat outside the hotel and watched Livvie take aim on an empty tin with her slingshot. Christa sat on the boardwalk nearby, taking no interest in the chair Penny had recently vacated.

Silverton appeared much as Meagan had expected a mining town to look; she'd taken only brief notice the day of the outing, and she studied the area now, hoping to see a particular face.

The area crawled with men from all walks of life, all with one shared hope of finding gold or silver and striking it rich. Canvas tents with wood fronts lined the dusty street, some belonging to tradesmen, with crude signs offering their wares, though a few all-wood buildings were in the process of being built. Near what resembled a factory, the ring of pickaxes and sledgehammers sang through the air as miners slammed their tools on a hill where a vein of silver had been found months before. And there were those adventurers who struck out to distant parts unknown, hopeful to claim a parcel of ore-filled land and become millionaires overnight, though few men had.

Meagan wondered what category Clay fit into. According to what she understood, he wished to search for their pa's mine alone. With his absence all morning, she wondered if he'd taken it into his head to leave without even a good-bye. But if he'd gone to search, surely the girls would know and be full of such news, and they hadn't spoken of their uncle at all.

Almost since the time he'd brought her to Silverton, she had witnessed Clay's animosity toward his brother but kept silent, feeling it wasn't her place to speak or offer unsolicited help. Lately, however, she'd noticed a change. The charged feeling when Clay and Derek were near one another, once as tense as a lit fuse leading to a charge of black powder, had all but disappeared.

Clay had made himself scarce since two nights before, when he'd kissed her, but when he hadn't shown up for breakfast, she worried that he'd actually left Silverton.

"Why do you keep looking up and down the street?" Christa wanted to know.

"Was I?" Meagan hedged, embarrassed to be caught. "I, um, noticed your Uncle Clay hasn't been around this morning." Meagan kept her voice detached, hoping Christa wouldn't notice her interest. "Did he leave town?"

"Why? Do you miss him?" The child's eyes danced with mysterious delight.

"I, uh, have something I want to discuss with him. In private."

"Oo–o–h–h." Christa's eyes grew rounder, as if she'd been presented with a coveted gift. "Things only the two of you should talk about that aren't fit for a small child like me to hear?"

What an odd question. But she presumed any news of Landon McClinton, which Clay might have learned by now, would be unsuitable for young ears, and nodded.

Christa squealed and clapped her hands, further confusing Meagan.

"He's probably talking to Miss Beulah," Livvie offered and loped forward to set the tin upright in the dirt, then ran the distance back and took careful aim again.

"Who?" Alerted to the name she'd never before heard, Meagan stared at Christa, who glared at Livvie.

"A dance-hall lady. But Uncle Clay doesn't like her, Livvie. Not really."

"Shows what you know. I saw them talking in the street earlier."

Meagan absorbed the information. Clay was involved with a dance-hall girl? A twinge of jealousy made her frown. Was she pretty? Is that what kept him from keeping company with her and reading to her—a woman named Beulah?

Eyes downcast, Meagan studied her hands. That morning, Penny had taken the bandages off for good. No longer a pretty ivory, the skin was blotched pink in places and shiny in others. She wondered if the dance-hall girl—Beulah—had pretty ivory hands. . . .

"Here he comes now!"

At Livvie's announcement, Meagan's head shot up, and Christa jumped to her feet. Meagan hid her hands between her knees, in the folds of her skirts. Their eyes met, and he slowed his steps, placing one boot atop the boardwalk but not coming any farther.

"Hi, Uncle Clay!" Christa threw her arms around him. "Where you been?"

"Just taking care of some business. Your ma said to tell you she needs you and Livvie both. She's at the dry-goods store, trading her pouches for supplies."

Livvie abandoned the battered tin, and she and Christa took off running down the street.

Clay seemed ill at ease. He looked Meagan's way, and she wondered if it was only business that occupied him all this time. "Good morning." His thumb and finger on the brim, he tipped his hat.

"Morning." She nodded, partly fuming, partly overjoyed to see him. She hoped he might stay and share her company.

He hesitated, then moved to the chair Penny had scooted close to Meagan's and lifted the Holy Book left there before taking a seat. The closest Meagan had been to him in days. No part of her touched him, but this near, she felt his warmth and smelled his pleasant musky scent. Her heart rate took up a faster pace with strong, unsteady beats.

"Penny been reading to you?"

"Till I learn how."

"That's good to know." Slumped over with his elbows on his thighs, he held the large book in his hands. His mind seemed elsewhere.

She took a chance.

"I've missed your reading to me. You have such a strong voice, so easy to hear when there's a lot of ruckus going on. And with the way you say some of those long words—you sound like a well-learned teacher."

He turned his head to look at her and grinned. "Is that right?"

She chided her breathing to remain steady. "There's so much about you that sets you apart from other men. You and your brother both have deep voices, but you. . ." She paused, wondering if she'd revealed too much.

"Go on. You've got me interested to hear what comes next."

She would *not* tell him how the sudden sound of his voice gave her delightful chills and set her blood stirring. She struggled for how to finish. "At times you talk like any other man of the West, using slang so common hereabouts. But you also sound well educated, sometimes using words beyond my grasp. So unlike your brother."

He nodded thoughtfully, shifting his focus back to the book he held. "I had the experience of my mother's training far longer than Derek. After our pa left us, my brother had to do most of the chores and didn't have time for books. But I tended to enjoy them far more than Derek ever did." He paused, his lips turning up at the corners, as if reliving those times. She admired his features, all the more attractive when he smiled. "Even when Ma got worse, she still found enough strength to see to my education. She stressed it was just as important to train the mind as it was the hands. She wanted more for me than what had become Derek's lot."

"You still miss her, don't you?"

"Every day."

"I understand."

A quiet moment elapsed as he looked at her, and a sympathetic understanding passed between them.

"The ache never really goes away, though it eases a good deal," he reassured.

"I'm glad to hear that."

He shifted in his chair. "Meagan, there's something I need to tell you."

She waited for him to go on.

"It's about Landon McClinton. He's dead."

~∽

Clay watched in concern as the rosy wash of color faded from her cheeks. He'd spoken quietly, but perhaps he should have broached the subject less quickly.

Meagan pulled one hand from between her knees and pressed her palm against her bosom. "My stepfather's dead?"

"I got the telegram from Carson City this morning. Details are sketchy, but he appeared to die of heart failure during a barroom fight with his rival."

"He must have found his old partner. He went there to try to get back what the man stole from him years ago." She looked away and shook her head, dropping her hand to her skirts. "We never did get along, but I never suspected. . ."

Clay gave in to the temptation to lay his hand over hers in comfort. She jerked a bit in surprise but didn't remove it from beneath his.

Since they'd returned to Silverton, he'd taken Penny's advice and avoided Meagan—physically. Her presence in his heart and mind, however, remained constant. After confiding to Beulah his feelings for Meagan, which had become more intense than the infatuation he'd first felt for Penny, he'd learned a portion of Beulah's history; now he further questioned his resolve to avoid Meagan. Beulah had run away, going west, after she learned the young man she loved had been killed in one of the final battles during the War Between the States. They had agreed to wait, months before the war started, since he'd had no more to give her than his heart, and a bayonet's deadly point had robbed him of even that.

Beulah urged Clay not to make the same mistake—that if he loved Meagan and knew their being together was right, to act on that love and ask her to be his wife. "Life is too fragile," she'd said. "None of us knows how much time we have left. If Will had not been so pigheaded, I would have insisted we marry no matter how poor he was. His heart was all I wanted, and if Meagan loves you like you've come to love her, I have a feeling she'll tell you the same."

Clay knew if he would yield and not cling to the Burke pride, he did have a home to offer her at Derek's up-and-coming ranch, though he doubted he could ever consider it his own or become his brother's business partner. He thought of Meagan's stepfather, so full of hatred that he'd tracked down his thieving former associate, and to what end? His own. Clay had moved past loathing his brother but still felt unable to trust Derek and questioned if he ever would be ready to take that step of good faith.

"What will you do now?" He removed his hand from Meagan's and placed it around the edge of the book.

Her hand went to join the other between her knees. "Penny's asked me to stay with her while. . ." She hesitated, clearly uncomfortable.

"While my brother and sister search for the legacy," he finished, glad his sister-in-law had offered her home. That eliminated one concern.

"Penny said I shouldn't speak of it," she explained with a rueful smile.

"You can always talk to me." Clay tried again, realizing how intimate those words sounded. "But she's correct. In mixed company, we need to keep quiet."

"Like I told her, I'd never tell a soul. I'd never do anything that might cause any of you the least amount of remorse for taking me in and being so kind."

"I didn't think you would." Clay smiled. "So, are you planning to take her up on her offer?"

"I imagine I will. I haven't anywhere else to go, and I do get along with Penny and her family, though I don't know her husband—your brother—that well."

"Don't feel bad. Neither do I." Clay's chuckle came wryly.

"But I thought you two were getting along so much better." He looked at her sharply and she shrugged. "It wasn't difficult to tell there's been trouble between you."

Clay had made no mystery of his bitterness but felt ashamed she had witnessed his failings. "It's been a long time since we've seen one another. Coming to Silverton was an unwanted reunion my pa planned for us. Matters are still shaky, but Derek and I have reached an understanding."

"I'm glad. Family can be difficult at times, but it's nice to have them around."

Clay's heart went out to her as he recalled her reason for being there.

"Tell me about your family. What was it like growing up for you?"

Clay considered her question. "As boys, Derek and I were good pals, despite the age difference. We fought hard but stayed loyal. Then one rainy morning, our pa left, having heard about a silver strike in the West. . . ."

He told her everything, sparing himself no excuse for his ill behavior toward his brother these eight years past. When he finished, she looked at him with eyes glistening in sympathy and understanding, surprising him.

"It must have been hard, you being so young and feeling all alone like that. The woman who took care of you sounds more like a jailer."

"She did treat me as her slave," Clay agreed. "But I didn't stay long."

"I'm so grateful I had you and your family to turn to after. . .what happened. I think Penny is right and God must have had a hand in us meeting."

"Now that's just what I like to see and hear," a man suddenly exclaimed from the street.

Shocked at the intrusion, Clay and Meagan turned their attention his way. A silver-haired stranger wearing a week's worth of whiskers and dusty, sweat-stained clothing approached with a toothy grin, leading his mule by a rope. He came to a halt before the hitching post. "A man holding the Lord's Book in his hands and a woman giving the Almighty the glory for her life."

"And you are?" Clay inquired.

"Preacher Dan is what the folks 'round these parts call me." He removed his battered hat, nodding to Meagan, then held out his hand to Clay. Clay reached across the hitching post and shook it. The stranger looked at Meagan. "Excuse my sorry condition, ma'am. I just returned from weeks' worth of visiting miners on their claims and haven't had opportunity to visit the bathhouse yet. Was told by the agent at the claims office that someone at the hotel needed to discuss something with me, so I wandered here first. You wouldn't by chance know Derek Burke?"

"He's my brother," Clay said with some surprise and peered more closely at the preacher's face. "Aren't you the same man who married Derek to my sister-in-law, Penny?"

"Hard to recognize under all this filth, aren't I?" Preacher Dan chuckled. "I thought you looked familiar. I had to leave in a rapid-fire hurry last time and wasn't able to talk after the wedding. I've been sworn to secrecy, a matter I've since questioned and never felt comfortable with. Giving me reason to believe I should have stayed, at least long enough to put your minds at ease."

"Pardon?" Clay tried to follow the odd man's ramblings.

Preacher Dan looked around to make sure no one stood nearby, then glanced at Meagan and back to Clay, the question apparent in his eyes.

"It's all right to speak with Miss Foster present."

"A little matter about a claim," the preacher said in a much lower tone. "And a legacy left to you and your siblings."

Clay opened his eyes wide in shock. "You know about that?"

"Sure do. I was with your pa when he drew up the map, and I gave him what little aid and guidance I could near the end, may the good Lord rest his soul."

"You knew my pa?" Clay reaffirmed, not sure he'd heard right, still stunned.

"I met him a year back when he was strong and able and as stubborn as a mule in full harness. He wanted nothing to do with me then." The preacher chuckled as if in recollection then grew sober. "After the disease struck his body, I visited him often. His mind wandered near the end; I was with him then, too. He didn't die alone."

Clay wasn't sure why he should care one whit about anything having to do with his pa, but the preacher's words oddly brought comfort.

"My brother is out at the moment," he said. "Would you mind returning later? We can talk then."

"That'll give me plenty of time to make myself presentable," Preacher Dan agreed. "Good day to you both." He pulled his mule around, heading in the direction of the bathhouse.

Clay watched the preacher amble down the road, sensing that, with the arrival of the lone newcomer, something significant was about to occur that would change all their lives.

᙭

Meagan excused herself from the kitchen, where the Burke clan gathered around the outgoing preacher, choosing instead to be with the girls. She preferred to dwell in the fresh air and sunshine, having been cooped up amid canvas walls far too long during her convalescence. Nor did she feel comfortable being party to what clearly was a family issue.

Outside, Meagan breathed in deeply of the warm breeze. It felt good to feel her hair stir and experience the wind upon her face.

"Miss Meagan?"

She directed her attention to Christa and smiled in question.

"What do you think of the name Thunder for Uncle Clay's horse?"

"And Lightning for Pa's?" Livvie added. "Bein' as the two go together—and Pa and Uncle Clay are brothers. And bein' as they can be loud and fight—and lightning and thunder do that, too."

"Do lightning and thunder fight, Livvie?" Christa wanted to know.

"Well, they sound like it," Livvie defended. "Lightning strikes out, and thunder bellows back. And both names are strong—like Pa and Uncle Clay. They're not sissified names, like Princess Rose or Whisper."

Christa pouted. "Names aren't sissified!"

"Shows what you know." Livvie rolled her eyes skyward.

"You're mean, Livvie."

"Well, you're stupid."

"You two shouldn't always bicker," Meagan admonished softly, recalling how she and Wayne had done the same. "Be glad for these times together. They don't always last."

The two didn't respond but didn't continue squabbling, either.

Christa looked toward the street, her eyes suddenly going big. "There's Tricks!" she exclaimed, pointing to a big yellow dog.

"Tricks?" Meagan asked.

"Jinx's dog that went missing a few weeks back. I gotta tell Jinx!"

"He ain't inside the hotel." Livvie stopped Christa in her tracks. "I saw him go inside the gambling house, and you know we can't step foot near there. Besides, Mama said to stay near the hotel."

"But Tricks might run away again! And this sure wouldn't be the first time you didn't mind, Livvie."

As if the dog heard its name and didn't want to be caught, he scampered off down the road.

327

"Oh, no!"

Before Meagan could stop her, Christa took off running after the hound. An oath unfit for a child shot from Livvie's mouth, and she raced after her sister.

Shocked and exasperated, Meagan stared after their retreating forms, growing smaller every second, then at the hotel doorway. Should she tell Penny the girls had run off, and with night approaching yet? She didn't want to disrupt an important meeting when she felt sure she could handle such a small matter.

Stepping off the boardwalk, she hurried after the girls.

⊷

Clay sat forward on the bench, elbows on the table, and eyed the preacher, who sat directly across from him. "Claim squatting?"

Preacher Dan chuckled. "A little joke on my part. Only want to reassure you folks that there's no chance of claim jumpers taking over your mine." He kept his voice down as they all did, though the preacher and the Burkes were the sole occupants of the kitchen. Most of the guests staying at the hotel were out visiting the gaming houses, dance halls, or saloons. "The claim squatters are my two nephews. Both boys have done some hard-rock mining and jumped at the chance to settle down awhile, since Bart's wife is expecting soon. I couldn't protect the area like your pa asked. My vocation won't allow it what with all the traveling I do. But you couldn't ask for better men guarding the place. Jake and Bart aren't the type to steal your claim, either—both are God-fearing, honest men."

"So there really is a mine," Derek wondered aloud, echoing Clay's thoughts.

"Almost. You'll have to bring in the machinery and man power needed to drill."

Clay stared. "How are we supposed to gain enough capital for that? I barely have two cents to rub together and have no experience in mining."

"Neither do I," Derek agreed.

"I suggest you unearth as much ore as you can load in a wagon, enough to bring a substantial price and assure you a bank loan for the needed equipment. My nephews will help and show what needs doing. They'd jump at the chance to enter a profitable venture like this one. And both have mouths tight as beaver traps. They can keep a secret till you're ready to go public with the discovery."

"You're sure it's so profitable?" Derek asked. "I've heard stories from miners of what they hoped would be a strike that turned into little or nothing."

"Seen it with my own two eyes. High on a hill, a pretty vein of silver three feet wide, going straight down. No telling how far. If Michael had dug a little to the north or south, he'd have missed it. He's had it tested by an assayer. It's galena—a mixture of silver and lead—and worth a small fortune by the ton. That's a cube no more'n two and a half feet on a side. And who's to say there might not be other veins? Since your pa discovered the strike, per the regulations for ownin' claims, he gets another three hundred feet. That means he owns six hundred feet of that hill—now all yours."

They all stared at him in shock, and he grinned.

"Where'd you think I visited your pa? At a church meeting? I often ride over the land to visit with miners on their claims and see to their needs, spiritual and otherwise."

"Can you take us there?" Linda asked.

"I wish I could, little lady, but that'd go against your pa's wishes."

Kurt placed his hand on her back in comfort. Derek grunted in frustration at the man's staunch declaration, and Clay knew just how he felt.

"I may have broken my vow of silence and admitted my involvement in the matter," Preacher Dan explained, "but I didn't feel it right he should leave you to do so much worrying."

"Yeah, well, you didn't know our pa like we did," Clay grumbled. "He derived pleasure out of seeing others suffer."

"Is that a fact?" The preacher's drawl came thoughtfully, his eyes seeming to look through Clay, making him want to squirm. "Well now, I just wanted to set your minds at ease."

"I have a question," Linda said.

The preacher nodded for her to go ahead.

"Why didn't he want us to know of your involvement? We thought the clerk was the only man to know of our legacy. Whyever would our pa swear you to such secrecy?"

Preacher Dan sighed. "Sorry, ma'am, but as much as Michael revealed to me, I couldn't begin to understand the workings of his mind. He had his reasons, though. Now if you'll excuse me, I need some sleep. We can talk more in the morning if you'd like." He halted. "Oh—almost forgot. Comes with age." He grinned, pulling something from his pocket, and handed it to Derek. "Your pa did tell me to give you this."

Derek took the chain, from which a brass key dangled. "What's it for?"

"All part of the mystery." Preacher Dan winked. "You'll know soon enough."

Once he left, they stared at the key and questioned what it led to. Hearing a step outside, they quieted, and Derek pocketed the key.

Shorty rushed past the curtain. His excited gaze latched onto Kurt.

"Amos and Jonesy Greer are in town!"

Kurt jumped up from the bench, reaching for his rifle. "Where?"

"Dunno. Just heard from Tucker and came to tell you. They told him to spread the news they're looking for Derek Burke." Shorty glanced at Derek with something akin to awe that the outlaws would ask for him by name.

Penny clutched her husband's arm, shock written on her face. Derek remained dead calm, though his eyes snapped with disgust and anger.

"Those are the boys who shot Marshal Wilson and robbed the gold shipment a few months back," Kurt said. "They probably think they're safe from getting caught with no lawman in town. They've got another thing coming." He kissed his wife's cheek, warning her to stay in the hotel with the others and keep her derringer close.

"I'll take you to Tucker." Shorty hurried after Kurt.

Penny suddenly jumped up from the table. "Wait—the girls! Were they sitting on the hotel boardwalk like I told them to?"

"No, ma'am. Didn't see no one outside." Shorty moved away from the curtain.

Derek grabbed his wife's arm before she could follow. "Let me handle this. You have the baby to consider."

"I canna just stay and do nothing! The girls could be in trouble."

"I'll see to it." His firm tone brooked no refusal. "Stay here. I mean it, Penny. I don't want you anywhere near those scoundrels again."

Clay rose, his grave stare meeting Derek's. "I'll help." His heart beat hard against his ribs in dread when he remembered Meagan had gone with the girls.

His brother hesitated. "You got a gun?"

"Pa's old shotgun."

Derek winced and handed him one of his pistols. "Know how to fire one of these?"

Clay nodded and took the weapon.

Linda slipped her arm around Penny's shoulders. "It'll be all right. We'll pray and ask God to keep the girls safe. Likely they only took off wandering as they often do and are just fine."

Before he left with Derek, Clay heard the tremor in his sister's voice and realized she didn't believe a word she said.

Chapter 12

Meagan lost sight of the girls and went on intuition alone. Without her forming it, a prayer drifted to her mind. *Please God, help me find them before they get in more trouble.*

She ignored the outright stares she received from a number of men, most of them near the saloons, and hurried through the street, peering between buildings. Hearing a dog bark up ahead, then give a sharp yelp, she picked up her skirts and raced toward the sound. She turned the corner near the livery and stopped dead in her tracks. The yellow dog ran past her.

Christa stood, trapped by a burly man who stealthily approached. Her eyes wide with fright, she backed up until her backside hit the wall.

"Well, if it ain't the little Injun gal," the stranger said, his tone chillingly familiar. "Your pa wouldn't be Derek Burke, now, would he?"

Christa began to cry.

"Shut up. I know who you are and what your pa has. And I want it."

Meagan stepped forward, ready to attack and beat the rogue with her fists. He moved to snatch up Christa, and she glimpsed his profile. She froze in stunned terror, then slipped back around the corner of the building, pressing her shoulders to the wall. Her heart pounded so hard and painful, she thought she might die as unwanted memories gripped her: held in his ruthless grasp; the reviling way he took liberties; his taunts as he almost drowned her, tried to have his way with her—he and his brother murdering her family.

Now he had Christa.

The reminder that there were two made her scan the area, panicked, but she didn't see his brother or anyone else for that matter. She must help Christa—didn't dare run off out of fear or to secure help. She'd done that once. She would not fail a second time.

"Get your hands off my sister!"

Meagan's blood froze when she heard Livvie's order. She peeked around the corner. The girl must have been hidden before.

"Livvie!" Christa cried before the man's huge hand covered her mouth.

"You want her back?" he asked Livvie, facing Meagan's direction. "You tell your pa to meet me and my brother here in a quarter of an hour. Or your little sister is as good as dead."

Christa's frightened cry came like a weak kitten's mew behind his hand.

Livvie glared at him, her legs apart, arms akimbo as if she might run up and punch him in the stomach or kick his shins.

No, Meagan silently pleaded. *Livvie, you don't know who you're dealing with. God, please help them escape. Help me do what I can.*

The evil stranger turned and walked away with Christa. Before Meagan could act, Livvie raced after him.

"I know what you want! And I know where it is, too."

In the falling twilight, Meagan's gaze fell on a pitchfork leaning against the opposite building. To get to it, she would have to step out where he could see her, which could endanger Christa further. Or the scoundrel might let the child loose and grab Meagan to finish what he and his brother started weeks ago.

The horrific thought made her insides churn, but she couldn't let him further harm the children. She must be patient and strong, must wait for an opportune moment. *God help me. I'm terrified. Give me the courage I need so badly.*

The outlaw turned to face Livvie. "What does a little Injun runt like you know?"

"I know there's a mine—Pa's mine. And you're wanting the map that leads to it." He started in surprise, and she nodded. "I know where Pa hid it. Let my sister go, and I'll take you there."

"How about you take me there this second, or I break her scrawny neck like a twig?"

Christa squealed in panicked fear as he jerked her head sideways with his hand. Tears ran down her cheeks.

"Okay!" Livvie yelled. "Just don't hurt her."

"Take me there now."

"Okay," Livvie said, subdued. "It's over there."

He looked to where she pointed. "Behind the livery? You expect me to believe your pa hid the map in a public place?" He did something to make Christa squeal beneath his palm. "Think again."

"He did! Honest! He hid it in the eaves. Didn't want to keep it on him for fear someone might take it when he was sleeping." She tentatively walked his way and moved ahead. "I'll show you."

The two moved out of sight, and Meagan darted across the area, grabbing the pitchfork. Her fingers ached holding the iron handle, hot from being in the sun all day. But she didn't release her grip. Silently, she followed until they came into view and halted, waiting for the right moment to attack.

"Aye." Livvie pointed up. "More to the left, near them yellow flowers."

He stopped and looked at her in suspicion. "You get it."

"I would, but I can't reach."

While he stared at the eaves, Livvie made eye contact with Christa. A signal seemed to pass between them. Livvie slowly backed up, pulled her slingshot from the twine at her waist, and bent to retrieve a small rock. She positioned it in the sling, her hands down in the folds of her dress, and slowly lifted the weapon to eye level.

"Now, Christa!"

"Ah!" The rogue released Christa and shook his hand in pain. "You little brat, you bit me!" She fell to the dirt, jumped up, and sped toward Livvie, who let her missile fly. It made a dull *thwunk* in the eaves above the outlaw's head. Meagan stepped into sight, motioning to Christa, as a dark buzzing cloud descended on the villain.

"Oww!" he yelped in pain. Foul curses flew from his mouth as he slapped at the cloud of bees, then dunked his head and shoulders in a nearby trough of stagnant water, drowning most of the poor winged bugs.

"Run back to the hotel, Christa. Don't stop for anyone," Meagan whispered when the child raced to her and threw her trembling arms around her skirts. Meagan patted her hair. "Hurry now. Tell your pa and uncles what happened. You, too, Livvie—run!"

The girls nodded and sped away. Realizing his prey was escaping, the outlaw went in pursuit and might have caught up, but Meagan stepped into sight, blocking his path, the tines of the pitchfork aimed at the vile creature's belly. Several of the bees still buzzed around, but they seemed intent on his flesh and not her own.

"We meet again," she seethed between her teeth, glaring at him. "Only this time I'm not running away."

❧

"Pa!"

Clay and Derek swung around upon hearing Christa scream. Derek opened his arms to his youngest, who flew into them, wrapping her arms tightly around his neck.

"The bad men on the trail are in town," Livvie said breathlessly. "One of 'em got Christa."

Horror swept across Derek's face as he gently unearthed Christa's face from where she'd buried it in his shoulder. "You all right, sweetheart?"

She nodded, tears shining in her big dark eyes. Clay noticed the fingerlike bruises at Christa's jaw at the same time Derek did. His mouth firmed into a line, white around the edges. Clay also felt like punching whoever had done this to his little niece.

"Livvie, where's Meagan?" His blood chilled when he realized she hadn't run up behind the girls.

"She cornered the bad man with a pitchfork so we could get away. Pa—it was the same man who tried to hurt Mama."

"Where, Livvie?"

"In back of the livery. He wanted the map."

"Just one man?" Derek tried to set Christa down, but she held on tighter. "Run on back to the hotel to your mama, sweetheart."

"No, please, Pa! Don't let me go," Christa begged, terrified from the ordeal she'd suffered. She held Derek's neck in a death grip, wrapping her legs more tightly around his waist and pressing herself close, as if she might crawl into him. Clearly, she needed her father.

"You take the girls back to Penny," Clay said. "I'll take care of this."

"Clay! Wait!"

He raced off before Derek could do more than call out his name.

⌇

The villain glared back at Meagan from eyes that had begun to swell from the stings. She kept her grip firm on the pitchfork, though her hands felt as if they were again touching fire and ached something fierce.

"A snake like you deserves all the torment you get—and more besides," she hissed.

His eyes sparked, and she realized he now remembered her. "The girl by the river. Gave my brother a broken nose and me a passel of bruises."

"Say the word, and I'll gladly do it again."

His smile came sinister. "Got you a lot of pluck, gal. But I wonder if you'd act so high and mighty if you knew that your brother got down on his knees and begged me not to shoot him—right before I pulled the trigger."

His admission made her want to retch. Her body began to tremble. "Stop it."

"And your ma begged Jonesy to tell where you was, worried some calamity had befallen you. We assured her it had." He chuckled and slapped a bee buzzing near his arm, killing it with the palm of his meaty hand. "Yep, I reckon that took the smug look off your face."

"No more," she whispered. Her grip on the pitchfork loosened, and she felt as if she might collapse from the shock of hearing the horrifying details.

"She begged him not to barricade her in the shack right before I told him to set fire to it. If she'd been more hospitable, we might have let them be. But she wouldn't give us grub when we asked, and you wouldn't get us water. Your brother had the nerve to wave around a shotgun and demand we leave. So we backtracked and took him by surprise."

"You are the most evil, despicable vermin ever to walk the earth—"

From behind, someone wrenched the pitchfork from her hands at the same time a man's strong arm wound painfully around her ribs and pulled her against him. She struggled for breath.

"Hold her tight, Jonesy. She ain't getting away from us this time."

⚮

Near the livery, Clay saw no one. Twilight had deepened, the shadows making the darkness thicker. A light flickered behind the livery, and he followed it.

"I'm not getting on your horse. You can't make me." Meagan's voice came clear, and Clay's heart jumped in both panic and relief.

"We could kill you," a man suggested.

"Go ahead. You've taken everything else of mine."

"Not everything. . ."

At the man's evil gibe, Clay's skin crawled. He peered around the corner.

Meagan stood with her back against a man who held her trapped. Her face shone like an angel's in the light of a lamp. Resolute. Unafraid. Calm—stunning Clay. Another man faced her.

"What do you say, Amos? Reckon we ought to tie her up and throw her over the saddle?"

"Reckon we should. We'll come back later for the map." He turned to get some rope, and Clay made his move. A few steps, and he cocked the trigger, aiming the muzzle at her captor's head.

"Let her go, or you're a dead man."

"Amos?" the man questioned, as if he didn't possess a mind of his own.

"Do it," the other man grunted.

Jonesy released her. She hurried to Clay, who grabbed her arm and pulled her close. He took a moment to glance at her, keeping the gun at the outlaw's head. "You all right?"

She nodded.

"Put your guns on the ground," Clay ordered Jonesy, "and kick them over here." He took the brace of pistols from Jonesy's gun belt, handing them to Meagan, then picked up Amos's guns, tucking them in his pants.

"Let's get you out of here," he whispered, his hand going to her waist.

They'd only taken a few steps when a shot rang through the air and one of the men yowled in pain. Clay turned in surprise. Jonesy held his bleeding arm. A knife lay at his feet. Amos was nowhere in sight.

He looked back to the street and noticed Derek standing there, a smoking gun in his hand. "You almost had a knife in your back," he explained to Clay. "I'll take care of him till Kurt arrives. You take her back to the hotel."

Clay nodded. "Thanks."

"No need to thank me. I'll always take care of you, little brother."

Anxious to get Meagan back to safety, Clay said nothing more.

Chapter 13

Meagan stood outside in the cool of the evening. The only noise came from the tinny player piano inside a nearby dance hall and cheers from the men inside. Kurt had returned five minutes earlier to grimly report he had shot Amos, who'd found another gun during his attempted escape and fired at Kurt. One of the Greer brothers lay stone dead in a wagon outside; the other sat wounded in the livery, since no jailhouse existed, with a guard posted outside until Kurt returned.

Meagan wasn't sure what she felt. Relief, certainly. Unease. Sorrow.

Kurt told them Jonesy had been blubbering for his dead brother. A simple-minded man, Jonas Greer offered no resistance and needed to be told what to do at every turn. Linda wanted to despise him for setting fire to their shack at his brother's orders but couldn't help feeling a twinge of sympathy. What chance did a man like that have with a brother like Amos? And to learn that those same two had tried to attack Penny. . .

A step on the boards behind made her whirl around, still tense from her encounter with the outlaws.

Clay looked at her in apology. "Sorry to have startled you."

She smiled to see his handsome face. "I'm just glad it's over. I talked with Preacher Dan, and he helped put my mind at ease." She had told of how she appealed to God when Christa was in danger, and the preacher taught her more about Him. How the Lord had been born to a virgin, died blameless on a cross, and was resurrected. Amazed, she had listened to the most fascinating story she'd ever heard, a tale that was true, and at her agreement, he'd led her in prayer, asking Jesus to be her Savior and Lord.

"I talked to Preacher Dan, too. He helped me see areas where I've thought wrong, especially about Ma's death. For everyone, there's an appointed time to die, and sometimes, no matter how we pray, it's inevitable." Clay stepped closer to Meagan, his manner seeming both vulnerable and determined. "When I knew the Greer brothers had you, I prayed hard, harder than I've ever prayed. This time, God answered—it wasn't your appointed time—and I'm indebted to Him for life."

Something about his expression made her catch her breath. His eyes were intent, glistening with unshed tears. He took her hands in his own, looking down at them. Remembering their appearance, she pulled them away.

"Did I hurt you?" he asked in concern, looking up again.

"No, it's just. . ."

"You don't want me touching you." His words came dull, making her sorry she'd reacted.

"It's not that at all." She averted her gaze again, feeling her face warm.

"Then what?"

She shook her head, feeling petty to give in to vanity after all that had happened. "They're ugly."

At her whisper, he again took hold of her hands. His thumbs caressed hers. "No, angel."

Her heart melted at his endearment.

"They're badges of honor—the hands of a woman of strong will and courage. A woman who'd sacrifice herself for those she loves. A woman I would love to call wife." As he spoke, he lifted both her hands and kissed each in turn. His soft hair brushed her mottled skin, and she stared at his lowered head in surprise. She felt she might swoon at his sweet words and touch.

He lifted his gaze. "Surely you must know how I feel about you, Meagan?"

"But you've been so distant. . . ." She felt breathless with the manner in which he stared, his eyes shining deep blue in the lantern light.

"I had plenty of things to sort out—I didn't want to confuse you when I didn't know my own mind. I've decided to accompany my brother to search for our legacy and to become his partner at the ranch. He saved my life tonight; I can trust him. And I want you to be part of that life, too, Meagan. Before Preacher Dan leaves Silverton tomorrow, I want him to marry us if you'll have me. Say you will."

Her breath caught. "What about Beulah?"

"Beulah?" His brow creased. "How do you know about Beulah?"

"Livvie told me you were interested in her—"

"Livvie needs to learn to keep quiet when she doesn't know what she's talking about." His warm hands cupped her face. "Beulah is a friend who helped me through some rough times. It's you I love, Meagan, you I want to spend my life with."

Before she could say yes, his cool lips found hers, soon growing warm, his touch making her head spin. Happier than she could remember, she wound her fingers through his hair and, with her kiss, silently gave him her answer.

⁓

In the breaking dawn, Meagan stood beside Clay, their family near, and recited her vows. Joy as golden as sunshine brimmed over inside her heart. It didn't matter that their wedding took place in a dusty street, with many of the townsmen stopping work to watch. Or that, instead of wedding bells, the sound of pickaxes rang through the air. She would become Mrs. Clayton Burke and would now share a lifetime with the man she loved.

That was all that mattered.

Holding tightly to the pretty bouquet of wildflowers Christa had picked, Meagan smiled.

Preacher Dan pronounced them man and wife, and Clay kissed her amid Christa's squeals and Livvie's handclaps—and a few good-natured jests from Derek and Kurt. Penny and Linda gently admonished their husbands while Livvie began playing a sweet lilting tune on her harmonica and Christa skipped and danced around them.

Meagan looked into Clay's eyes, finding herself there.

"I love you so," she said quietly, so only he could hear. "I knew it for certain when you tried to read that poetry book and got so nervous. Will you read it to me, now that we're wed?"

"Whatever you desire, angel. But I plan on us making our own poetry."

He smiled in a way that made her heart race and kissed her again.

❧

Clay, Linda, and Derek searched for more than a week—and finally found the short canyon with their hill of silver, meeting the preacher's nephews who guarded it. They supped together and talked for hours, at the end of which both Jake and Bart agreed to team up with Derek and Clay to unearth the ore. It would take some time before they had enough to commence with the plan Preacher Dan suggested, and Clay was grateful to God for their successes so far, but he only wanted to get back to his new wife.

Three days and nights with Meagan had been like granting a dying man a dipperful of water, then sending him back to the desert. The memory of the feel of her in his embrace made him want to speed up the process so he could return to the haven of her soft arms. At least she was safe and comfortable with Penny and the girls in their home in the valley.

Kurt had been unable to join the search, needing to return Jonas Greer to Jasperville, where he would be tried and hanged. Though his life on the earth would soon end in punishment for his crimes, his life in the Great Beyond would just begin with a Savior who'd forgiven all of them. Preacher Dan had visited the simple man, ministering to him, and the former outlaw had tearfully repented of his multitude of sins and given his heart over to God. After Kurt told the family, Clay had held Meagan close that night, seeing her upset, but she'd told him her tears were ones of relief.

"I've seen enough death," she'd whispered against his chest. "I thought I'd be pleased to hear Amos was dead, but I don't feel the satisfaction I'd hoped for. He must have gone to an eternity of hellfire, and I can't be happy about that for any man. Jonesy will receive his just punishment—yet at least his suffering will be brief, not eternal." She moved to look at him, pressing her hand against his jaw. "But I don't want to think about any of that right now. I just want to think about us and the wonderful life we'll have together."

Clay had stared at her, amazed. "You're incredible," he'd whispered, then kissed her soft, warm lips. "So beautiful. . ." His mouth had traveled to her slender neck and along the perfect slope of her shoulder. . . .

"We were told to give you this," Jake's gruff voice broke into Clay's pleasant memory. Grudgingly, he brought his attention back to the present and the barren land on which they now camped.

The preacher's nephews looked young, but their strapping builds would certainly deter claim jumpers. Jake set a small chest in front of the Burkes. "It was partly hidden in the scrub at the foot of the hill."

His wife, Edna, moved silently, filling their tins with coffee; then the three new members of the team disappeared inside a tent, giving the Burkes privacy.

Brothers and sister looked at one another before Derek took the chain with the key that Preacher Dan had given him from around his neck. He fitted it into the lock and turned it with ease.

"What's inside?" Linda asked.

"A Bible," Derek said in shock, lifting it and thumbing through the pages. A piece of paper fell out, and Clay grabbed it.

"Well?" Derek asked once Clay unfolded it.

"It's from our pa."

"Don't keep us in the dark," Linda urged.

" 'To my own: Derek, Clayton, Linda,' " Clay read aloud. " 'You must be wondering why I drew up a map, with orders each of you was to get a piece, then led you on this long hunt. Well, if you're reading this, you must not have killed each other by now, so I'm assuming you quit being so stubborn, boys, and learned to work together. And that you all spent a fair amount of time getting to know one another. Good. 'Cause that was my intent all along. . . .' "

Clay stopped reading, and the three stared at each other, stunned.

"Go on," Linda urged. "What else does it say?"

" 'I did wrong by each of you, and your mothers, and I'm powerful sorry. I was an ornery, selfish old cuss. My dying wish is that you won't let what heartache I sowed ruin your becoming a family. That and this book are the best treasures I could wish for you, something I learned too late for one but not the other. Oh, you get the silver, too, and I want Preacher Dan to have a share for all he's done and for writing this here letter since I never learned how (side note from Preacher Dan: The share isn't necessary).' "

Derek chuckled and Clay smiled. "Sounds like something he would say."

"But he will have his share," Linda affirmed.

"Absolutely," both brothers responded at once.

Clay went on reading. " 'Derek—you've been a good boy, helping your ma when I wasn't around, becoming man of the family before you were old enough for whiskers. I'm proud of you, son. But don't let your yearning for adventure and riches cloud your judgment like I did. You're more like me than you realize; I want better for you than that.' "

Clearly moved, Derek ducked his head, pulling his hat low.

" 'Clayton—I hope you're still reading them books, son. I gave you a hard time about it when you should have been doing chores, but truth is, I admired you for your brains and wished I'd learned how. Maybe then I could have written my own blasted letter.' " Clay whisked his fingers over his damp lashes so he could see to read the rest.

" 'Linda—I wish we'd met. I heard about your ma's recent passing and wish I could have helped somehow, but I hear you're as beautiful and strong-willed as ever she was, so you'll do all right. Boys—I'm picturing the look on your saintly mother's face and have to chuckle, hoping she won't flat keel over when she sees me approach the pearly gates. To think a wandering preacher finally got through my thick skull; if it weren't for this disease, I might have never listened. So I both curse and bless what's become my lot.' "

They stared at each other in shock, not knowing what to say.

"Pa found God?" Derek shook his head in wonder. "I would have never believed it possible."

Neither would Clay. He read on: " 'You children might not understand, but I did love both your mothers after my own fashion, as well as I knew how. Soon I'll join them, that is, if they don't kick me out once they see me. I imagine I'll get quite an earful from both. I only wanted to strike it rich for all of us, take your ma back East, and find her a good doctor, boys—and Linda, I don't regret one hour of knowing your ma since the day I stumbled through her town, dyin' of thirst, and she fetched me water from the well—but it was in her best interest I left. If I'd known what troubles she would face afterward with them snobs she came west with, if I'd known you existed, little Linda, I would have done what I could to help. I learned too late. My greed and wrong ways of thinking and doing cost me my family and my health, something I deeply regret. I looked for silver and found it but won't live to enjoy the reward of my labors. You do that for me, but don't let the stubborn Burke blood that also runs through your veins come between you and God or family, you hear?' "

"We won't, Pa," Linda whispered.

"There's more," Clay said. " 'Linda, find a good, trustworthy man for a husband, one who'll stay by your side and you can depend on.' "

"I have." She laughed through her tears.

" 'Derek, Clayton—a good woman is more precious than rubies, at least that's what this Good Book Preacher Dan read to me says. I reckon she's more precious than silver, too.' " Clay thought about Meagan and smiled wistfully. " 'Find a wife who's honest and true and will stick with you through bad times. Enjoy the wealth, enjoy each other, but remember, the three of you: what this chest contains is the most satisfying treasure you could ever own. Sincerely, and with much remorse and regret, I am your erstwhile pa, Michael Aloysius Burke,' " Clay finished and laid the letter down.

Silence thickened the air as each of them stared at the paper, then at each other.

"He may not have given us much when he was alive," Derek said at last. "But he did bring us together."

"To be a family," Linda added, holding her hand out to Derek, who took it. "Never again in want." She held her other hand out to Clay. He took it, then reached for Derek's hand. The three sat, hands clasped, and grinned at one another.

"And for all that, Pa, we're eternally grateful," Clay finished for all of them.

Epilogue

Three years later

Meagan nursed her tiny daughter, Eloise, as she sat with Linda and Penny on the veranda of their sprawling ranch house. The women kept a watchful eye on the children who frolicked near the stream. Yellow and blue butterflies flitted around, the spring evening pleasantly warm as the women lazed in the shade.

Livvie piggybacked her little sister, Kimama, whom they called Kim for short. Christa helped her brother, Angus Aloysius, named for both Penny's Scots grandda and Derek's pa, to take small steps. Holding his chubby hands, she jumped up and down after each accomplishment made, almost knocking the tot over.

"Careful, Christa," Penny admonished. "And do watch out for Wayne! You don't want to knock your cousin into the water."

Meagan shook her head and smiled, noting her two-year-old digging his fingers into the moist streambed—likely to find worms. "Christa," she called. "Make sure Wayne isn't eating what he finds."

"I will, Aunt Meagan," the girl promised. Her frightful experience with the outlaws hadn't altered her sweet nature; the most visible change she'd undergone, the height to her slender frame. Now she stood mere inches shorter than Livvie.

Since their ordeal in Silverton, Livvie had grown far more tolerant of Christa and, at fourteen, was blossoming into a young woman. Meagan noticed her attention often drifted to a tall, strapping ranch hand who'd just turned sixteen. Still, Meagan wondered if the day would really ever arrive when Livvie would trade in her long braids and slingshot for pinned-up hair and longer skirts.

Eloise pulled away and cooed. Meagan adjusted her blouse, smiling down into her daughter's beautiful blue eyes.

"She has Clay's eyes, too," Penny murmured.

"I know, and I love that. Though Clay told me he'd like it if our next child has golden eyes and hair like mine." He often complimented both in words as lovely as any poet's, making her blush.

Penny laughed. "Did he now?"

"I miss him. They've been gone for weeks."

"I know. I miss Derek, too. At least we women have each other while our men are away on business."

Meagan covered Penny's hand with her own. "And I'm so grateful for that."

Clay kept accounts for the ranch and mine but often rode with Derek on visits to oversee the mine's production and on cattle drives, like now. They'd hired managers and workers for each, but the Burke brothers preferred getting their own hands dirty. They ran their ranch because they enjoyed hard work, not because they needed income. Owning tens of millions may have altered their circumstances, but it hadn't jaded their characters. Meagan rejoiced to see how unaffected they were by their wealth and how their bond of brotherhood and friendship had prospered.

But oh, how she missed her husband!

After three full years of marriage and two children, their love had only grown deeper. Sometimes he cradled her in his arms and read to her from Browning, and they softly laughed about the first time he'd tried to read from the same book. She loved to hear his rich voice recite the beautiful words, though she could now read. And write. Her hands were scarred, but she'd regained full use of them. And she'd written her daydreams into collections of short stories he'd urged her to publish. But they were private, the wanderings of her heart. Maybe someday in the future she would gain courage and share them with the world. . . .

"The men should be returning soon," Linda said, breaking into Meagan's thoughts. "They're never gone longer than three weeks at a time." She cradled her five-month-old little girl, Faith, an answer to her fervent prayers. After two years of marriage, Linda feared she might be barren when month after month brought no child inside her belly. Faith proved it wasn't so, and the slight bulge beneath Linda's skirts attested that Faith might have a brother or sister come autumn.

"As much as you're with us, you really should have built your home closer than just outside Silverton," Meagan teased.

Linda laughed. "We would have, but Kurt has to watch over things there, though he enjoys going on these drives when he gets the chance. Shorty has done well as deputy, and Kurt feels confident leaving him in charge." With his success in ending the notorious Greer brothers' reign of terror, the people of Silverton begged Kurt to stay on as sheriff, even building a jailhouse. An encouraging telegram from his mentor aided his decision.

"And Beulah? How is she?"

"I'm still trying to encourage her to leave her life at the dance hall." Linda deeply sympathized with Beulah's situation since hers had once been similar. "She's expressed a desire to go back East to her family, so I'm hopeful. They never approved of the boy she loved, and when he was killed at Appomattox, she was hurt and angered by their indifference and came west. Since Preacher Dan spoke with her, I think she's ready to put that bitterness behind her now. I told her I'd do all I can to help, of course—buy her a train ticket, suitable clothes, whatever she needs. But you know how she is." Linda shook her head. "Please continue praying for her."

"I will," Meagan reassured. "Clay and I do every morning." Beulah possessed a compassionate heart and had wished Meagan well after her marriage to Clay, sincerely happy for them both. It didn't take Meagan long to see why Clay considered her a friend. In their concern for her, Clay and Linda had each offered the vivacious redhead money to start a new life, but Beulah wouldn't take it.

Profits from the mine had made the Burkes and their associates wealthy overnight. For himself, the preacher took only a small portion of his share, which the Burkes had needed to force upon him, and gave the rest to charities. Kurt and Linda sent a tidy sum to his aunt Doreen in Jasperville, to help fulfill her dreams of funding a charity for poor miners and their families and for building a church. The Burkes also gave, and eight months earlier, they hit the mother lode, a bonanza that had all the state buzzing and brought mine workers out in droves. A mining town had sprung up—Prosperity—and Clay and Derek had built a home there, too. But all the Burkes preferred the peaceful, open spaces of their beautiful B & B Ranch.

Meagan had never owned so many gowns, all of them fine, or seen so many jewels as Clay gifted her with, the last a ruby pendant. Each time he presented her with a necklace or earbobs or a bracelet, she quietly protested, telling him all she needed was his love, and each time he smiled and told her she would always have that, but it pleased him to give her the world if he could since she was so precious to him. Soon she hoped to give him a gift, one she'd toiled over for days. . . .

"They're here!" Livvie shouted, running down the wildflower-laden hill where she'd wandered. "I just saw them over the rise."

Her heart drumming madly with anticipation, Meagan laid Eloise in her carved cradle and glanced at the east wing of their sprawling ranch house, where she and Clay resided. Tonight he would be there with her, his strong arms holding her. She missed his loving and their long, intimate talks late into the night. Even with their two children and nurse sharing the same wing, Meagan felt lonely without her husband near.

"With dinnertime upon us, I suppose I should be lettin' François know,"

Penny muttered, though her eyes were alight with excitement. "If I hurry, I c
return before they ride over the hill." She winked at Meagan, who laughed. Thoug
they had servants, Penny often preferred to do her own cooking, to the chef's
displeasure—a Frenchman Clay hired two years before who, much to everyone's
amusement, crossed opinions with Penny whenever she entered his kitchen.

"There they are!" Christa squealed, grabbing up her little brother. She ran
with Livvie to meet the men approaching on horseback. The children's nurses
came outdoors to collect their small charges, and Penny abandoned her errand.

The three women rushed to greet their returning husbands.

Clay dismounted and swung Meagan around, then kissed her hard. She
held onto him as if she might never let go.

"I missed you, angel," he murmured against her hair. "You're all I thought of."

"I'm so thankful to God that you're home and safe."

After another kiss, this one long and gentle, they walked arm in arm to
the ranch house behind Derek and Penny, and Kurt and Linda. A stable hand
rushed to take the horses.

"How are the children?" Clay asked, handing over the reins.

"Eloise can lift her head now."

"Can she?" He chuckled.

"And Wayne still enjoys his daily mud baths."

He let out a deep belly laugh, squeezing her close to his side. "That's my
boy!"

Meagan smiled. "Lightning foaled. Christa named the colt Little Cloud."

"Interesting name."

"And I have a surprise for you."

He abruptly stopped walking and swung around to look in her eyes, then
below her waist.

She laughed. "No, not news of another child. At least not yet."

"What else would cause you such excitement?"

"First, you need a good meal to fill your belly—and a hot bath to relax. Then
I'll tell you."

"Mmm. After weeks of riding in dust and wind to find good pasture, with
only cattle and irritable kin missing their wives for company, that sounds like
music to my ears."

She hugged him close. He did look weary but happy.

After they'd eaten and said their good nights to the family, once she'd tucked
the children in bed, she dismissed the maid and personally drew Clay a steaming
bath in their claw-footed tub, waiting hand and foot on him like a loving slave
to her king. Afterward, he drew her close in their huge bed, which no longer felt
so empty, and looked deeply into her eyes.

"Tell me your surprise."

She smiled but, now that the moment had arrived, felt nervous. "I wrote a poem. For you." Leaning over to reach the table beside their bed, she picked up a paper scroll wrapped with a red satin ribbon and handed it to him.

As he read, she softly spoke the same words that were a part of her soul:

> *"In your absence, the stars shine less brightly,*
> *My heart grows heavy, laden with storms;*
> *I yearn to pull you to me so tightly,*
> *Our lips pressed together, so warm.*
> *In your arms I am whole and complete,*
> *My universe achieves balance when*
> *Your presence so needed, so sweet,*
> *Makes me whole and alive once again.*
> *I pray you return to me, never to part,*
> *You are all I require, you are my very heart."*

Clay looked up from the paper, his eyes glistening.

"It's not as good as Browning," she apologized. "But it's how I feel."

"It's better than Browning." He laid the poem aside and drew her close. "It's how I feel about you, too, angel. You're my real treasure. Not the silver. Not the ranch. I've missed you so, and each time gets worse. It's been so long. . . ." His voice came hoarse. He kissed her passionately, and she melted against his strength.

"Much too long," she breathed near his mouth, "but oh, the homecomings are so sweet. . . ."

Clay showed her without further words just how much he agreed.

A Letter to Our Readers

Dear Readers:

In order that we might better contribute to your reading enjoyment, we would appreciate you taking a few minutes to respond to the following questions. When completed, please return to the following: Fiction Editor, Barbour Publishing, Inc., P.O. Box 719, Uhrichsville, OH 44683.

1. Did you enjoy reading *Silver Mountains* by Pamela Griffin?
   ❑ Very much. I would like to see more books like this.
   ❑ Moderately—I would have enjoyed it more if _____
   _____
   _____

2. What influenced your decision to purchase this book?
   (Check those that apply.)
   ❑ Cover   ❑ Back cover copy   ❑ Title   ❑ Price
   ❑ Friends   ❑ Publicity   ❑ Other

3. Which story was your favorite?
   ❑ *A Treasure Reborn*   ❑ *A Treasure Revealed*
   ❑ *A Treasure Regained*

4. Please check your age range:
   ❑ Under 18   ❑ 18–24   ❑ 25–34
   ❑ 35–45   ❑ 46–55   ❑ Over 55

5. How many hours per week do you read? _____

Name _____

Occupation _____

Address _____

City_____ State_____ Zip_____

E-mail _____

FREEDOM'S CROSSROAD

THREE-IN-ONE-COLLECTION

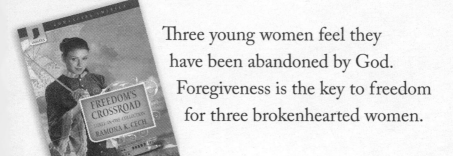

Three young women feel they
have been abandoned by God.
Foregiveness is the key to freedom
for three brokenhearted women.

Historical, paperback, 368 pages, 5¾₁₆" x 8"

Please send me _____ copies of *Freedom's Crossroad*. I am enclosing $7.99 for each.
(Please add $4.00 to cover postage and handling per order. OH add 7% tax.
If outside the U.S. please call 740-922-7280 for shipping charges.)

Name _____

Address _____

City, State, Zip _____

To place a credit card order, call 1-740-922-7280.
Send to: Heartsong Presents Readers' Service, PO Box 721, Uhrichsville, OH 44683

HEARTLAND HEROES

THREE-IN-ONE-COLLECTION

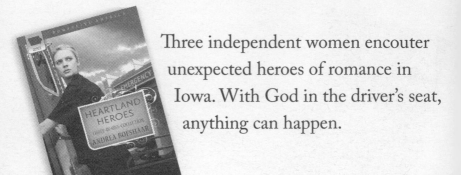

Three independent women encouter unexpected heroes of romance in Iowa. With God in the driver's seat, anything can happen.

Contemporary, paperback, 384 pages, 5⁷⁄₁₆" x 8 "

OZARK WEDDINGS

THREE-IN-ONE-COLLECTION

Love disrupts the lives of three
women in the Ozark Mountains.
Will these women dare to take a
chance at romance?

Contemporary, paperback, 352 pages, 5¾" x 8"

Please send me _____ copies of *Ozark Weddings*. I am enclosing $7.99 for each.
(Please add $4.00 to cover postage and handling per order. OH add 7% tax.
If outside the U.S. please call 740-922-7280 for shipping charges.)

Name _____

Address _____

City, State, Zip_____

To place a credit card order, call 1-740-922-7280.
Send to: Heartsong Presents Readers' Service, PO Box 721, Uhrichsville, OH 44683